THE TAO DECEPTION

The Tao says:

Breathe in, Breathe out
Forget this + forget any chance
of attaining Enlightenment

I hope you enjoy Tori Swyft's
new story.

John M Green

E16

PanteraPress

From

nurturing

the **NEXT** GENERATION

of best-loved **authors**

➤➤ ⓣⓞ CHAMPIONING

LITERACY

AND THE *joys* OF **READING**

we're ⓐⓛⓛ ⓐⓑⓞⓤⓣ great storytelling !

 SCAN HERE for more on our **GOOD BOOKS DOING GOOD THINGS** programs.

And drop in to **our website: PanteraPress.com** for news about **John M. Green** and our **other talented authors,** as well as sample chapters, author interviews and much, **much more.**

THE
TAO
DECEPTION

A TORI SWYFT THRILLER

JOHN M. GREEN

PanteraPress
great storytelling

great storytelling

First published in 2016 by Pantera Press Pty Limited
www.PanteraPress.com

Please send all permission queries to:
Pantera Press, P.O. Box 1989 Neutral Bay, NSW 2089 Australia or info@PanteraPress.com

A Cataloguing-in-Publication entry for this book is available from the National Library of Australia.

ISBN 978-1-921997-46-4 (Paperback)
ISBN 978-1-921997-47-1 (Ebook)

Cover and Internal Design: Luke Causby, Blue Cork
Cover Images: © Adobe Stock
Editor: Lucy Bell
Proofreader: Desanka Vukelich
Author Photo: Erica Murray
Typesetting: Kirby Jones
Printed in Australia: McPherson's Printing Group

Pantera Press policy is to use papers that are natural, renewable and recyclable products made from wood grown in sustainable forests. The logging and manufacturing processes are expected to conform to the environmental regulations of the country of origin.

In memory of Sylvia Green,
whose magic fingers conjured dresses out of sacks,
whose presence charmed sunshine out of gloom.

More novels by John M. Green

Nowhere Man
Born to Run
The Trusted

TORI SWYFT NOVELS
The Trusted

ISABEL DIAZ NOVELS
Born to Run
The Trusted

Tao (道): the Universe's natural order, its essence

'To get rich is glorious!'
—**Deng Xiaoping, China's paramount leader, 1978-92**

'The march of the mujahidin will continue to Rome,
by Allah's permission.'
—**Abu Bakr al-Baghdadi, Caliph, Islamic State, 2014**

'A nuclear EMP attack would kill two-thirds of America's
population, 200 million dead in one year from starvation, disease and
societal collapse.'
—**Task Force on National and Homeland Security, 2016**

PROLOGUE

Three years earlier – Tehran, Iran

'D-D-DID WE JUST HAVE SEX?' THE husband of two sputtered from under his black shoe-brush of a moustache.

Tori Swyft shuddered at the mere notion, yearning to shout *As if!* Instead, she forced out a slow wink, lowered her shoulder strap and sidled back to the bed.

In truth, the man revolted her. His arrogant swagger, his shameless ogling, even his hair; it was like it had dropped off the top of his head and stuck to him everywhere else. Tori had made out *on* a couple of rugs but never *with* one. And not even a crucial catch like Dr Masoud Mahdi Akhtar, head of Iran's atomic energy organisation, would make her change that.

To reel him in, all it had taken was a slinky black dress, an airy whiff of her gardenia fragrance and a few husky whispers.

1

After that, the redheaded CIA officer had flown the living Persian carpet to her hotel room where she'd plied him with his first dose of dazzle—the street name for midazolam—quickly laying him to rest so she could get on with her mission.

Carving her mouth into what she hoped was a seductive smile, she leant over the bed and flashed her cold green eyes at him. 'You were magnificent, Masoud … a lion,' she said in the steamiest Persian she could muster from her recent training.

For the second time, she twisted the tip of the vintage urn on her charm bracelet and tipped four more drops into the tumbler on the night table. She stirred it with one finger then pressed the glass to his lips. 'Drink this to give you energy, then let me feel you roar inside me once more.' She cringed. *As if.*

Then she smiled, genuinely this time. *I christen thee Asif,* she decided. *Well, not so much 'christen', but definitely Asif.*

With the exception of the mullahs themselves, Asif was as powerful an official as they came, palpably close to Iran's political heartbeat and one of a handful with unfettered access to the nation's nuclear secrets.

With his head nestling into his pillow, Tori went back to the desk where she'd piggybacked her tablet onto his smartphone and continued trying to crack into Iran's nuclear control and operating systems. Her mission: to reconfigure and supercharge Stuxnet, a computer worm that had first spun Iran's nuclear centrifuges out of control in 2009.

Every minute increased her risk of being gatecrashed by VEVAK, Iran's infamous secret police and, glancing at the timer on her tablet, she'd already been at this for 125 of them. Asif was snoring but VEVAK wouldn't be.

The drug top-up would give her another two hours but tiptoeing inside Iran's network for that much longer was too great a gamble, with their digital trip-wires everywhere.

Besides, the battery level on her satellite phone, with its aerial poking out the window to secure a signal, only gave her thirty minutes more at best.

To work faster, she needed to think faster so she reached for her most sure-fire accelerant: classic surf rock. Popping in an earbud, she picked out a track on her tablet and began streaming it from her ear into her fingers. The opening tremolo twang and the urgent, dangerous drums crashed over her like waves pounding a sea wall. As she resumed her tapping and typing, she imagined herself standing precariously on the wet, stone blocks, breathing in the briny smell, the spray cooling her skin, the salt prickling her tongue. And as she worked through six repeats—fifteen pounding minutes of The Break's *Groyne*—a sparkling Aladdin's cave of the country's most precious digital treasures started opening up before her.

Lifting every binary rock, poking into every crevice, she unearthed the perfect hidey-hole for the 25,000 lines of code that a CIA tech team had spent eighteen months creating, refining and squashing into ten tiny digital packets.

With the music's work done, she turned it off. Then her fingers froze and her ears cocked. Out in the corridor ... a scuffle? Something ... someone dragging?

VEVAK?

She twiddled her left pearl earring, ready to snap it open and swallow the kill pill inside it if she had to. Her eyes spun around the room, landing on the cold plate of kebabs on the nightstand. Grabbing one, she pushed the meat cubes off the metal spike and crept to the door. Standing to the side to avoid casting a shadow, she held the skewer point up as she put an ear to the wood. Holding her breath, she stretched over to look out the peephole.

A man, his face in darkness, was tottering on a stepladder and fiddling with a dead light bulb, one Tori was sure had been burning brightly when she'd used her card key to enter the room. Her jaw clenched and she twisted the spike downward.

She pulled back to the side, her breath quickening, sweat beading on her forehead. A ribbon of light wavered across the crack under the door and she leant back to the peephole. The back of the man's head was now bathed in light. He boxed the dead globe and dropped it onto the tool bag on the carpet below him. As he turned his face toward her door, her body tensed and she raised her fist, gripping the skewer. Then she blinked and smiled, her arm falling beside her, muscles at ease.

Jaman from her extraction team, also realising her time was running out, had come to stand watch. She dropped her eyes to his bag, which she knew concealed the respectable black chador he'd brought for her escape and the Heckler & Koch UMP submachine gun intended for anyone who tried to stop her.

Relieved, she darted back to the desk to finish her assignment. Within minutes it was apparent how good Asif and his nuclear minions were. Brilliant in fact. But for the noise it would make, she would've been whistling at their technical wizardry; one expert's awe at another's work.

Then her mouth suddenly dropped, her admiration boiling into loathing. At first tens, then hundreds of lines of code started scrolling up in front of her, lines so recognisable she was mentally reciting the next one before it appeared on the screen. The filthy, thieving bastard lying on the bed had filched *her* model, the protocol she'd earned her nuclear engineering PhD for.

She squinted at one line, then six, then sixty … new lines of code. Tweaks. Enhancements. *Improvements*. The bastards hadn't just pilfered the intellectual sweat of her brow, they'd made revisions she now knew she should have thought of herself. With reworks like these, she realised, Asif would have squeezed so much extra juice out of Iran's nuclear cores their program would have been fast-tracked by years, far beyond what the CIA's intel had revealed.

The new virus wasn't just important, it might prove crucial. Her fingers worked even faster than before and she'd just hidden it in place when Asif groaned. She grabbed the skewer and spun around, but judging by the lewd smile drooling from beneath his moustache he was still in the land of nod.

Her mission was complete. This was officially go time. But unknown to her superiors she was going to push her luck, implanting another tiny block of code. This one she'd written herself.

Tori worked for the US government, but that didn't mean she trusted them to control Iran's nuclear ambitions. And now, with her own code hibernating alongside theirs, she didn't have to.

1

Present day – the Vatican

T FIRST GLANCE, AUGUSTINE APPEARED MORE like an affable grandfather than a pope. In reality, his silky tousle of white hair, feeble pink eyes and soft translucent skin camouflaged a stiffness of backbone and a moral rigidity that only the brave or foolish dared challenge.

Strangely for a cleric, he'd struggled with the notion of miracles until a hundred days ago, the day God gave him one. His fellow cardinals had elected him Bishop of Rome and Vicar of Christ, entrusting him to grip the papal wheel and lurch the Church back onto its true path, to restore the wreckage the populist Latino had left in his dust.

Showing only a trace of his trademark fervour, Augustine's frail eyes fluttered open at the first sparks of a new dawn. His bedchamber was aglow as the sun's rays began bouncing off all the gold: the rococo furniture, the Renaissance picture frames, the glittering gilt thread woven into the brocade tapestry, the urns banded in shiny saffron-yellow ribbons. Even the light switches were plated with the lavish metal.

Augustine saw the light and though it was harsh and bright, it was good. Except unknown to him, the real dawn was three cold, grim hours away.

His bedroom blushed with an eerie holiness, a twinkling in the air like golden sunbursts fading into mist. Whatever this was it prickled against his skin, more numb than cool. He sniffed at the odour, which oddly had none of the astringency of the bare-leafed winter morning outside. It was sweeter … a little like milk.

His ears pulsed with a crinkly thrumming, as if papery wings were fluttering just out of his reach. A dragonfly or a bee, perhaps.

An angel?

Curiously, he couldn't shift his head even an inch to see what caused the rustling. He blinked as a laser-sharp beam of golden light shot through the open window, slicing through the veil of mist then circling around and around his head like a sculptor's knife carving a target out of clay.

A second spray of the sweetness—this time more luscious—burst out along the beam and puffed its creaminess, cool and fresh, over the bullseye of his delicate face. He tried to lick the flavour off his lips but his tongue stayed stuck in his mouth. He went to rub his eyes but his hand wouldn't budge from his side. He tried his other hand but it wouldn't lift either. He couldn't move his legs, not even his toes. All he could control were his eyes; his insipid, pathetic eyes. His genetic weakness had become his only strength.

The mist encased his head like a plastic bag. He panicked, tried to scream out to his valet who, at 5 am, should have been outside his door awaiting the call to enter. But Augustine's mouth wouldn't open, not even a crack, and he couldn't raise his voice beyond a rasp.

His eyes engorged with terror and his suffocating breaths became shallower and shorter. As the mist around him dissipated, the bag muffling his head dissolved and relief began to wash over him.

He saw. He understood. He knew.

An angel. It hovered a sceptre's length inside his window, above his water jug. This too was a miracle, and God, on this day and at this moment, was blessing his papacy.

This angel bore no resemblance to the classic depictions in Bible stories, but that didn't perturb Augustine, it thrilled him. With no face, no eyes, no arms, no legs, not even a single wing, his angel was far more miraculous. The dull, unpolished sphere the size of a football was perfection itself, its meshed surface matte gunmetal grey. A revelation.

A bizarre thought struck him. If his valet hadn't insisted on opening the window last night when the central heating got stuck on high, would this angel still have come? His windows were bulletproof. What if they were angel-proof?

The mist finally cleared and the golden light paled and sputtered out.

Augustine's ears no longer heard and his lungs no longer breathed. The light left his pink eyes and they grew peaceful, but they no longer saw.

Adieu, adieu, adieu. Remember me.

THE DRONE FLEW forward, hovering directly above Augustine. When its operator, 5,063 miles away according to the

GPS, was satisfied the job was done, the metallic orb glided out the window as unnoticed as when it had entered.

The video feeding back over SATCOM was so sharp, so real, that the assassin could almost inhale the sweet unction His Holiness liked to dab on his forehead before sleeping.

The pope's killer replayed the video frame by frame, by the end confident the autopsy would bring in a verdict of death by natural causes. Only then, after the toxin had passed its first independent trial, would the clip be released and RUA, Rome Under Allah, would proclaim itself to the world.

Allah is truly in the details, the assassin laughed. This was a great moment. A triumph. Step one in the immaculate deception.

2.

White House, Washington, DC

ISABEL DIAZ FLUFFED UP HER PRESIDENTIAL pillow, slid it back and wriggled her shoulder blades into it.

For her, waking at 5 am was ingrained, a habit she'd developed working the breakfast and every other shift in the family restaurant she'd built into a nationwide chain and then sold before entering politics. But today the twinge in her stomach woke her early, her bedside clock clicking over at only 4.07 am. Was it the meat patties she'd rustled up for herself in the kitchen last night? She hoped not. She'd hate to think the old Burger Queen—her first nickname when she'd entered politics—had lost her magic touch.

The glow from the clock lit up her fountain pen as it too lay awake, stretched across the top of her draft State of the Union address. The speech was weeks off but she'd started work on it early. She was struggling more with the tone than the words, so crucial when her utterly unpredicted and unprecedented rise to office was still raw in the nation's throat. Yes, she was the most popular president in recent history, but flung into office by a constitutional earthquake, not swept in on a voters' landslide, meant her every nuance would be scrutinised far more than usual.

She ran her fingers through her hair, which these days she kept in a manageable, shoulder-length black bob. She'd been in office eleven months. Eleven months since her predecessor's first and only State of the Union, the chill February evening only weeks after his own Inauguration when he left Isabel, America and the world gasping by resigning on the floor of Congress and handing her the keys to the Oval Office.

Her thinking for her own State of the Union address was to stand in the same spot, explicitly acknowledge the crisis that pitched her into office and seek closure for it. Her advisers disagreed, arguing her approach could rip open the nation's wounds after a year of healing, and offer her opponents a fresh chance to scratch at her naivety, to point anew to the red flags she'd missed, the bloodiest being the man who used to sleep in her bed. And the beds of others as it turned out.

His son, Davey, squirmed and rolled toward Isabel under the pastel blue sheet, his golden hair softly curling across the pillow. His free hand poked out from the bed covers and patted around until it found his fluffy penguin, Pip. He dragged the soft toy back under the sheet and nestled it to his chest, nuzzling it with his chin, the musty smell reminding Isabel that Pip hadn't seen water for far too long.

Every day, she negotiated with people speaking at her in Russian, Chinese, Hebrew, French, German, Arabic and, in the case of her Australian chief of staff, what passed as English.

But all those exchanges were picnics compared to a ten-year-old's tantrum over Isabel wanting to 'drown' his penguin, all conducted in American Sign Language.

God, how she loved her stepson. In these early morning moments she often felt like cradling him in her arms and gobbling him up, his pale complexion stark against her natural olive skin. She'd fret over whether it had truly sunk in for him that he'd been the one to expose his father's treachery, terrified he might be blaming himself for her husband's—his dad's—suicide.

But today there'd be no time for cuddling with the red night-light above her door starting to flash. The circus had begun. She placed a hand on the phone waiting for it to ring, not to stop it waking Davey since he wouldn't hear it, but because she didn't like to keep her people waiting.

'Madam President, I'm sorry to wake you.'

'I had to answer the phone anyway,' she laughed, even though it was a quip Narthex Carter, her national security adviser, had heard her make at least twenty times. 'Aren't you supposed to be surfing in Hawaii?' She glanced at Davey, thinking she might add a beach vacation to their own list.

'Flying out later this morning, ma'am, but I've had the Vatican on the line. Augustine died in his sleep. Natural causes.'

'Good,' she said, spite pinching her mouth before she could stop it.

'But with you as—'

She sighed. 'As the world's highest ranked Catholic *political* leader, they want me to kick off the news cycle with some uplifting words—'

'Exactly.'

'—about a man who on his tenth day as Bishop of Rome let it be known that he saw me as an apostate?'

'You're not going to say anything, are you?'

Silence.

'Ma'am?'

'Did you hear my lips moving?'

'Surely you could say—'

'What? That Augustine's death proves that God really does exist?'

'Er, I guess not.'

'Then it's *aloha* from me.'

'Pardon, ma'am?'

'Go pack your wetsuit.'

3

Oahu, Hawaii

COMING TO THE BANZAI PIPELINE ON Oahu's North Shore was a pilgrimage for Tori. While this time the break was courtesy of her eccentric boss, Axel Schönberg III, her original visit here fifteen years ago was with her first inspiration: her dad, her mentor, her coach. And her best friend. Swyfty had brought his twelve-year-old wunderkind here for surf training, to terrify her with the fury of the seething, thundering walls of water that jacked up, hurtling and crashing over the coral reefs, to get her to conquer her fears. Only later did she realise it had also been life training.

That day, with her quaking on the beach, deafened by the roar, eyes screaming and mouth agape, Swyfty had grabbed his board, scratched some wax on top and dashed into the water where the current was flowing parallel to the beach at six or seven knots. It dragged him and the sand it was ripping off the beach to the little gap between Gums and Ehukai where it turned, pushing out at an angle. He paddled until he reached the shoulder to sit with maybe twenty other board riders, the surges welling beneath them, all of them keyed up waiting for the perfect wave.

She couldn't have been more focused, mechanically chewing on gum that had lost its flavour, wired as she watched him reading the direction, sensing which way a lip might curl, waiting for his tell—the face flicker—that fleeting moment of commitment when a surfer forced back fear to tip over a lip and take a line.

This was it.

Tori had leant forward as her father dropped down the liquid curtain, a sheer twenty-foot drop, hundreds of tonnes of water surging behind and above him. Halfway down the face as the Pipe started rolling and crashing beside him, he turned to the side, crouching, grabbing onto his rail with his left hand and pressing his heels down to drive the right edge of his board into the wave. The tube kept coming at him, overtaking and finally enveloping him—Tori fearing the worst—until seconds later it spat him out with a whoosh of spindrift and spray, his arms punching the sky. Hot tears welled in her eyes.

When Swyfty got back to shore, the smile on his face was almost as wide as the beach. But, he'd reminded her, that trip wasn't for him, it was to prepare his daughter for the upcoming world title where she'd be competing against girls five, six years older. Taking no time to bathe in his glory or gather his strength, he took her straight out for step two of the most intimidating, exhilarating lesson of her young life.

Yes, she'd flipped the surfing world on its head and won the junior women's crown, but it was a hollow, short-lived triumph when not long after, on her thirteenth birthday, her dad fell forward into a wipe out and didn't come back up ... the instant she decided to quit competitive surfing.

She hadn't returned here, to Sunset Beach, for ten years after that. But since then, she'd been back three times, trying but never conquering Swyfty's mastery. Not in her eyes.

That said, the fifteen-foot colossus she'd just caught was possibly her best ride anywhere, not that anyone else would care. Heading back in to shore exhausted but euphoric from her conquest, she passed a blond guy heading out. He gave her the briefest nod as if he'd been watching her ride. Was it, she wondered, a mark of respect?

Back on the sand, her legs crossed, she watched him go out, her eyes straining until his board licked the lip of his wave and she saw it ... his moment of commitment. Without thinking, she scrambled to her own feet as if his were controlling them.

Her mouth fell open as she watched him plunge from the lip, down inside the raw, unbridled power of the churning, barrelling whorl. Apart from him being a goofy-footer, it was like seeing Swyfty again but somehow better, breezier, more languid, his moves almost belying the muscle of the water, drifting like the clouds that shadowed him from above.

He was breathtaking, the guy and his board at one with the Pipe, on it yet in it, the monster wave driving him yet, at the same time, he was driving it. Tori was possessed by it, bewitched by it ... by him.

Sunset Beach was sinuously long, two miles point to point, but when Tori's wave wizard, his board under one arm, rocked out of the water at a spot directly below her, it was hardly surprising since she'd repositioned her towel on the sand in line with where she'd seen him heading. Given her lousy history with men, the move was risky. This one could surf, but could he think? Could he talk? If he could, he was one magician she wouldn't let escape like smoke through her fingers.

She feigned interest in her novel as he approached, her eyes sneaking a peak at the dripping Adonis through her fringe, the sun searing it redder than normal, almost scarlet. With his turned-up nose and optimistic blue eyes that managed both warmth and scrutiny, he was even more strangely magnetic.

And yes, he could talk, but much more than that, he could think. The more time they spent together that day, surfing, running back onto the sand, shaking the water out of their hair, flopping down onto their towels, chatting, laughing and touching, initially to spread sunscreen over each other, the more she knew he was special. Maybe not the *one*, but closer to it than she'd ever got before.

His one negative was his name, Tex, the same as that redneck she'd been forced to share a desk with on a six-month assignment in China. Though Surfer Tex was nothing like Beijing Tex, the fleeting twist of her mouth or the stiffening of her shoulders must have revealed that his name bugged her. Almost immediately, leaning over to offer her his sunscreen, he casually threw out how he hailed from Arizona, that 'Tex' came courtesy of his archaeologist parents.

'It's from the myth where Prometheus stole fire from the gods,' he said, pointing the tube of cream to the sky, 'so he could bestow it on mankind. He carried the fire to Earth inside a giant fennel stalk, a narthex. That's my actual name, Narthex. Actually, it's worse than that.' He leapt to his feet and bowed, and Tori had to stop herself staring. 'Let me formally introduce myself, ma'am, Narthex Prometheus Carter.' He flopped back onto his towel. 'Can you imagine a kid going through school with that mouthful?' He sighed and leant back on his elbows, the sun glimmering on his chest. 'To my parents, I'm always

Narthex. But with the constant explaining and spelling, I cut it back to Tex. Except at work. My boss,' he added, 'sticks with the formality, like my folks.'

'Why?'

He shrugged. 'I guess she wants to give my relative youth more gravitas around the place.'

The place. As he sprawled next to her, long and lean and tanned, like a dribble of honey on the golden sand, his deliberate vagueness had Tori's neck hairs twitching on alert. 'And what *place* might that be?' she said, deliberately focusing on rubbing sunscreen onto her legs.

'It's ... I'm in, you know ... in government.' He said it hazily, scooping up a handful of grains and letting them spill back between his fingers.

Tori's alarm bells were clanging like crazy. If this Tex, or Narthex, was CIA then this thing she was feeling, if it was a thing, it was over, done, *finis.*

She bit her lip. Would she ask him or not? Damn it, she had to. She capped the tube of sunscreen and handed it to him. 'If you told me *where* you worked in government, would you have to kill me?' She did her best to make it sound light, almost nonchalant. But to Tori, it was deadly serious.

4

TEX'S EYES DARTED AROUND, LIKE HE was checking no one was close enough to hear. Then his face flushed and he shrugged, a thin cake of sand falling from his shoulder, the foreshock ahead of the quake. 'It's nothing clandestine, not the CIA or the NSA, nothing like that. I, ah, where I work … Tori, it's the White House.'

A shadow floated over them and Tori looked up to see a red-tailed tropicbird, silky white, unhurried, its coral red streamers trailing behind it. An omen, she hoped, if it didn't spray them with crap. 'The White House?' she asked, relieved, imagining him as a backroom guy, a speechwriter maybe. 'Do you ever get to meet with the president?'

His wince, though brief, was unmistakable. 'Sure, but I kinda avoid talking about work in, you know, social situations.'

'Because people ooze all over you and want you to fix them up with a ride in Air Force One or a visit to the Oval Office?'

'Mostly they cringe like I've got Ebola.'

'Hmm, you are a little infectious,' she laughed, pushing a strand of hair behind her ear. 'But relax, I'm not the oozy type and I don't need you to pimp me an audience with the president. I got to shake hands with her a few weeks ago, not that I'm boasting, but since you work there and all.'

'What?' he said, startled. He perched on one elbow and pushed his sunglasses up to his forehead, his eyes searching hers.

Hoping the reflections of the sun and the green of the sea were glistening in her irises, Tori went on, 'She was presenting me with—'

'A Presidential Medal. You're *that* Swyft?'

'Guilty as charged.' She laughed again, then worried it came out like a giggle. But even so, she threw her head back, exposing her long throat and hoping her red hair might also catch some of the sun's fire.

'So you're not just Tori Swyft, amazing Australian surfer, obsessive sunscreener—'

'Hey, beneath this perfect tan I'm as pure as the driven snow,' she said, before quickly adding, 'you know, red hair, green eyes, fair skin.'

'Sure,' he said, either not hearing the double entendre or ignoring it, 'but you're also *Victoria* Swyft ... *Dr* Victoria Swyft ... ex-CIA ... who stopped the cyber-terrorists single-hande—'

'Not by myself, but yes, that's me. And about your Ebola, I'm not that kind of doctor. Just so you know.'

'Hence the paranoia when you thought I was with one of the security services! After how those bastards treated you, I don't blame you.'

How they'd treated her. What an understatement when her former CIA bosses had effectively accused her of treason. If it hadn't been for the backup from her new boss, Axel Schönberg, and her work colleague Frank Chaudry, right now she'd be decked out in an orange jumpsuit, shackled and shoved down a hole in some off-the-books black site. Instead, here she was lazing under the sun in a skimpy turquoise bikini next to Mr Dreamy.

Tex—she could cheerfully think of him as that now—let out a long breath full of ... what? Reverence? Too much. Deference? Maybe, but Tori didn't want either. Not from him.

He shook his head, pulled his sunglasses down over his eyes and lay back against the sand. 'Dr Victoria Swyft. Well, blow me.'

She'd known him less than a day, but frankly the notion kind of appealed to her, even if he hadn't meant it that way. She kept her eyes on him for several silent seconds, possibly in a swoon, though having never experienced one before she wasn't sure. Just this once, maybe she could park her despondency over men and try being spontaneous, perhaps enjoy the strange electric sensations that were suddenly tingling all through her.

Tex pulled a tablet out of his duffel bag. Almost unconsciously, he started scrawling his fingertip over the screen as he questioned her about her life in the most charmingly inoffensive way, like a pleasant ramble through a maze getting closer and closer to the prize. More than asking, he listened.

She had no clue what he was doodling until later, when with a slight flush of pink in his cheeks, he passed over his tablet and showed her a screen full of brushstrokes, a woman crouching on her board halfway up to standing, her hair flying behind her, redder and more fiery than she ever saw it herself. Disarmingly, he'd added more fabric to her postage stamps of a bikini, seeing a modesty in her almost ingenuous brashness that she found, well, charming. He'd made her nose less ski-jumpy, more Scarlett Johansson than the one that bugged her every day in the mirror. How did he pick up on that? Her eyes. He'd noticed them too. A lustrous, flecked jade leapt out of the screen, shimmering like gold dust sprinkled over a sea of liquid emeralds.

And, almost like an afterthought, jags of lightning shot out of her pinkie ring as if it were enchanted. The vibe of a woman who could conquer the world. Or perhaps him.

Not knowing what to say, she smiled and turned over onto her chest, unsure if she was trying to muffle her thumping heart or mask the sudden, awkward zing in her nipples.

Tori hadn't met a man like Tex for a long time, maybe never, apart from Frank Chaudry, but as Frank's boss that relationship was doomed to stay professional.

Good men were out there but until Frank, and now Tex, she'd kept missing them, landing the guys who saw questions as ruses, her answers as opportunities to interrupt. Those who weren't grandiose narcissists play-acted as sponges, pretending to thoughtfully soak up whatever she said, all the while waiting for a pause, a chance to jump her, simply viewing her and every other woman in their compass as little more than life support systems for their vaginas.

Tex … Narthex … he wasn't like that even though all she knew about him so far was that his folks were a Mr and Mrs Indiana Jones who had taken him on some very exotic digs, that he was an academic China expert now working in the White House, and that he was a fine artist, a dazzling surfer … and an eyeful.

At the beach, although Tori dressed loosely, she kept her history and her thoughts wrapped up tighter than a cocoon, so opening up to Tex was an unfamiliar sensation. And despite her initial reservations, it felt natural, cosy, like pulling an old baggy sweater down over her head, its familiar musty smells of last year's winter, sleeves stretched too long by the years, warm on her fingers.

'As an Australian,' he asked, 'how'd you get into the CIA? Isn't there a—'

'I've got dual citizenship, so they gave me special consideration. My mother was American and—'

'Was?'

Tori sat up. The sun was high and its rays strong but she folded her arms as if suddenly freezing. She turned her head away.

What mother deserts a two-year-old? she asked herself, the old shame stinging her, that it was her fault her mother abandoned her and her dad. The chronic, paralysing pall of black hung over her, the blame for breaking up the family, for forcing her father's one true love to run away, ruining Swyfty's life. Tori was still plagued with guilt that his death too had been her fault, that once he'd helped her win the world title, he felt free to go. It was nuts, she knew that, but she'd lived her life to prove him wrong, that a surfing crown wasn't going to be the pinnacle of her, or Swyfty's, achievements.

Tex didn't press his question and he knew not to reach a comforting hand out to her. 'That brick in there,' he said, tapping a finger on her beach bag, 'kind of big to be lugging to the beach?'

Relieved he'd changed the subject, she broke through her cloud and slid out her copy of *À la Recherche du Temps Perdu* so he could see its battered cover and curled, yellowed pages. 'Proust only comes supersized,' she said. 'The plan's to devour the whole thing. Eventually.'

'And in French! I hit a wall struggling through it in English.'
His expression turned serious and he pointed at her shoulder and
stomach. 'Looks like you hit a few walls, too. CIA mementos?'

He leant over and hovered his finger close to the tiny scar
on her stomach, so dangerously close she wanted him to touch
it … to touch her. He must have felt it was too soon, that he was
intruding on her personal space, and pulled his hand back. She
closed her eyes. He put her on edge. Not an edge like teetering
on the brink of an abyss, but more like the anxious schoolgirl
she never was, praying this boy would ask her to the dance.

EIGHT DAYS LATER, on the roof terrace of Tex's rented condo,
the roar of the waves below had calmed to a gentle rumble. The
rustling whispers of the surrounding coconut palms afforded the
sleeping, naked couple a handy seclusion.

Tori blinked her eyes open, running them down the scratch
on Tex's shoulder from their last bout of lovemaking, his chest
rising and falling rhythmically, his stomach flat like a drum she
suddenly wanted to tap on.

For anyone else this would've been idyllic, but with Tex
flying back to work the next morning, Tori was torn. He'd asked
her to come stay with him for the last two weeks of her own
vacation. If he'd been the nerdy researcher or lowly policy wonk
she'd imagined at first, it might have been easier to say yes. But
it turned out he didn't just 'work in the White House', he was
a heavy hitter, the president's go-to on foreign policy, so she
was less sure. Besides, would it be too much too soon? She was
terrified she'd risk destroying what they had started by rushing it.

Was he asleep? A waft of wind blew over them, a palm frond
lightly brushing over the balcony safety rail near their feet. She

raised herself onto her side and synchronised her breathing with his. Then she reached over to him. Instead of drumming on his stomach, she let her fingertips float over his chest until she could feel the wisps of hair, before lightly running her nails downward, lingering at his navel. She began making circles, tiny at first then bigger and bigger, meticulous in her teasing.

Her nipples hardened as he groaned and his mouth curved into a smile, his eyes still closed. As she circled lower, she discovered he wasn't the only one now awake. She noisily licked her lips. He beamed.

And then she slapped it.

'Hey!' he squealed, springing up and staring at her in outrage. She burst out laughing and he grabbed her, pulling her back down to the bed where they lay, her head resting on his shoulder. He held her close. 'So tell me. Are you coming?'

'Let's find out,' she said, one hand caressing between his legs and the other moving between her own.

5

Sydney, Australia

THE SUN WAS YAWNING BEHIND THE Norfolk pines. Tori watched as it stretched its shadowy fingers across the sand to the churning, creamy froth. 'Here, miss,' said the barman, passing her a light beer, the same burnt umber as the tangles of kelp that were flopping around in the surf below.

She and Tex had agreed to take time out, give it all a chance to sink in, see if what they had tasted together was as good when they were apart. It had only been a day so far. Half an hour ago, he'd texted her a copy of the 'portrait' he'd sketched of her on their first day together, but this time he'd added himself and his board into the frame, or at least a caricature, his spindly arms splayed out, his body gawky and off balance, about to sprawl backwards.

It was 4 am his time when he'd sent it, and he was still stuck in the White House. Of course he was. But instead of Tori twiddling her thumbs waiting for him to come home every night in his freezer of an apartment or staying in Hawaii where his absence would've sliced a hole in her heart, she'd flown back to her home town.

She popped a couple of macadamia nuts from the bowl into her mouth, savouring the smooth oily crunch. She looked around, the bar swarming with surfers and, annoyingly, blowflies.

Yet, despite the cheery clinks of glasses and hollers and whoops over stories of wave domination that grew louder as the evening drew on, Tori felt alone. In the last glow of sunset, with the salt dusting her skin like icing sugar on caramels, she slid her mound of coins forward to leave as a tip.

Grabbing her beer, she pushed through the huddles of bodies to catch the final wink of the sun. But when she got to where the crowd thinned out at the back, her phone buzzed under the side strap of her bikini bottoms. Her breath caught in her chest. Tex calling on his way home?

Damn! *Glocked Number* flashed up on her screen, Frank Chaudry's idea of a joke. A fairly sick one, she'd told him the first time when their brush with a bullet from a Glock sub-compact was still pretty raw.

She hadn't spoken to Frank since they'd both left for vacation, his in Whistler. She pictured him calling from the top of some ski slope, wearing that awful tweed jacket he seemed to live in.

As she stepped away from the bustle to take the call, the skip in her step took her by surprise. 'Hey,' she said, unable to stop the smile creeping across her lips. 'How's the skiing? ... You're back in Boston?' Odd since, like her, he had two more weeks' vacation. 'Me? ... Noisy, yeah. It's a bar and no, I can't sit down ... Axel's what?'

The beer glass slipped from her hand.

China

TO GET INTO THE MINDSET FOR editing the video, the pope's assassin slipped the SWAT-style disguise back on and stared into the mirror, getting a kick out of the icy blue eyes that peered back.

The masked figure moved to the computer. Topping and tailing the kill scene with the head-to-camera clips where RUA would soon reveal itself and its demands to the world. Distorting the audio so no one could make out the intimidating speaker's accent, sex or age ... applying a second, then a third round of encrypted voice masking. Frame by frame, dissecting the entire video, cutting any shot that even hinted at the existence of the drone or gave a clue to the RUA spokesperson's real identity.

The killer smiled, the grin unseen beneath the mask. In a few days, the pope's autopsy would prove that the toxin was medically undetectable and Rome Under Allah would instantly become a name on everyone's quivering lips. Finally, the headshot closed in on the unnaturally cold blue eyes glaring out of the blackness. The assassin switched off the computer and removed the balaclava, putting it beside the lens case to idle there until the next kill and the next video that would rattle China and shake the world.

7.

Boston, Massachusetts

HOSPITALS USUALLY REEKED OF DISINFECTANT AND misery to Tori, but here at Massachusetts General the private elevator taking her up to the new wing smelled more like a brand new car, with its rich notes of leather and walnut. By floor three, something less agreeable, like gym socks, intruded. Tori raised her arm and sniffed. She hadn't noticed it in the cab, but with her driver seemingly on the reserve bench for the stink Olympics, how would she? She fumbled in her backpack for some deodorant, reached under her sweater and shirt and rolled it on. That taken care of, by floor ten she was zipping her bag closed and wondering if flying west to Sydney one day and east two days later cancelled out jet lag. If it didn't, maybe she could lean on one of Axel's nurses to swing her some glucocorticoids. She counted, not the floors but the hours.

Taking account of her time in the surf, Tori had spent more time in the air the past three days than she'd spent on land. Anything to stop her thinking about hospitals. She hated hospitals, having been in too many of them, mostly as a concerned colleague but multiple times as a patient. The only time she'd wished for a hospital visit was after her father had been pulled out of the water. But he'd been pronounced dead on the spot.

Twenty-fourth floor. She squeezed her eyes closed and held her breath as the doors slid open, rubbing her fingers into her sweater just above one of the points where the knife had gouged her in Mosul, Iraq, two years ago. She shuddered as she recalled the faceless woman in the next bed to hers, who'd stunk so much from a gastrointestinal bleed and necrotic bowel Tori had worried that sharing the same air might infect her own wounds.

She sniffed. Not a hint of bleach up here, nor urine. Pine and menthol, the pristine tang of a Swedish sauna. She opened her eyes and stepped out onto a plush purple and black carpet, matching the tones of the petunia painting hanging on the wall. Axel had one like it in his office, by Georgia somebody. She checked out the plaque. O'Keeffe. It *was* Axel's. Lucille, his exacting personal assistant, must've had it brought in for when he woke up.

There was no grime here, no clatter or commotion, just Axel Schönberg III lying comatose beyond the observation window. An instrumental version of *Nowhere Man* was piping through the speakers, soothing but tastelessly ill timed, she thought, given Axel's condition.

She stepped up to the observation window. A knot of plastic tubes slithered around her boss pumping a pharmacopeia of clear, yellow, crimson and disgustingly brown fluids in and out of his lifeless lump of a body. On the other side of the thick glass there'd be beeps, whirrs and clicks, but on her side there was only the drone of the air conditioning. And that song.

Seeing his trademark gold *begleri* worry beads looped over the lamp on his bedside table, ready for a twirl should he wake, almost made her smile. For a man so utterly well connected, Axel was disarmingly eccentric. His only serious flaw was his bewildering fealty to Ron Mada, his second-in-command, a man whose finest hour would've lasted thirty seconds at best.

Short and pencil-thin, Mada was as insubstantial as a stunted stalk of wheat, congenitally unencumbered by any of Axel's charm or wit. After Tori's first meeting with Mada, she had nicknamed him 'Zell', short for 'mad-as-hell', reflecting his explosive temper as much as her anger at how he treated her.

In the cab here, she'd checked her voicemails, two from Frank and Tex which she'd returned immediately, and one from Mada which she'd deleted without listening to it. Just thinking about dealing with that man gave her the shivers. He was so irritating she was sure even the Mormons avoided him.

Up to now, Zell's influence on her had been as trifling as his genius, but that was because she'd had Axel as a buffer. Without his protection, without his flair at the helm, the firm had no pull on her, and with Zell in the top job the pull was becoming a push.

She hadn't deleted his message because of his grating, sneering voice. She'd scrubbed it because she didn't want to hear the words, 'You're fired'. If she was going to leave, she'd be the initiator, not him.

If only it were that simple, she reminded herself. Leaving Zell in charge with no one to challenge him would betray the debt she owed Axel—a considerable one—and, digging her fingernails into her palms, she forced Zell out of her mind.

Axel. Gone was the perpetual motion dynamism that used to quiver through his pufferfish of a body, gravity flattening out his adorable chins and jowls, spreading them onto his chest like a lumpy dollop of pancake batter. The slope of his supine stomach was so steep that the white cotton bed sheet wasn't quite tuckable, revealing a hint of a floral gown in so many tints of powder blues and pale pinks that her boss would be aghast if he knew. To a stranger, his skin would look translucent against the pastels, sickly, verging on angelic. But Tori knew that was his normal complexion.

She owed this man big-time. Barely a month after the CIA had spat her out, he almost literally plucked her off a Sydney beach and, having never met her before, offered her the job of a lifetime, a jaw-dropping salary and a full directorship at SIS.

Initially his company's name 'SIS' confused her, since his accent was Bostonian and the only SIS she'd heard of was Britain's Secret Intelligence Service, also known as MI6. Axel, it turned out, had contrived the confusion when he shortened the name from his grandfather's Schönberg International Services.

With Axel's penchant to employ former spies who were as numerate as they were canny, his SIS wasn't so much an MI6 as an MI6-meets-Morgan Stanley, a firm of moles-turned-sharks or, as he explained it, 'Part investment bank, part security agency'. It was why Tori was a perfect fit, he told her. With six years at the CIA she had the security part and her PhD in nuclear engineering and half a Harvard MBA had given her the other part.

As she took a step back from the isolation window to stop her breath fogging up her view of his body, a familiar cologne mingled with the menthol. A moment later Frank's reflection sidled up beside hers.

Was it the haze on the glass or were his eyes cloudy and distant? The pools of crème de cacao that, pre-Tex, had sometimes kept her awake looked stagnant, grey, empty. Normally their heads rose to the same five foot ten but this morning, as she waited for him to speak, he was slumped, coiled, a few grey hairs struggling for air prickling out of his chin and an unfamiliar cut chiselled into his forehead.

She lowered her gaze and the barest crack of a grin forced itself onto her face. If fashion was what came in one year and went out the other, Frank was tone deaf. What was it about that tatty, scratchy tweed jacket of his?

He cleared his throat. 'Your break?' he asked, still looking ahead.

'Wet and warm,' she said without thinking. She rushed on, tilting her head toward his. 'Your cut?'

He touched his forehead. 'Nothing really … snowboard … mogul … tree.' The full story, Tori expected, was undoubtedly more dramatic, like he'd been hurtling precipitously close to a ravine when he was flung through the air, his head glancing a low-hanging branch before … whatever. He'd never tell her. When it came to talking about himself, Frank was the epitome of understatement, the son of immigrants who out-Britished the British.

Axel, he said, had phoned him in Whistler three days ago, asking him to cut his vacation short and come back to Boston for the 'deal of the decade'. When he'd rushed back he'd found Lucille fretting over their boss's whereabouts.

Half an hour before, she explained, Axel had got some troubling news on one of his private lines. He'd edged past her desk to chew on it over a cigar in the yard, under a heater. No, he didn't tell her who or what it was, he merely muttered something about Ron Mada, which, as Lucille had said 'wasn't unusual since everyone mutters about him.'

When Lucille had checked the yard a little later she found it empty, not even a smudge of cigar ash anywhere. Axel wasn't out front either, or in the street. She'd tried his cell phone several times then called around the office and by the time Frank arrived all they could do was wait by the phone.

After ten minutes' foot tapping, shrugging and throat clearing, Frank was pressing Lucille to call Ron Mada, whom he'd seen jumping into a cab when his own had pulled up from the airport.

'Mr Mada's been dealing with a lot lately, poor thing,' she'd said.

'*Poor thing*?' Tori interjected. 'Zell's birth certificate is an apology letter from a condom factory.'

'Tori!' said Frank. 'You're not helping.' He went on, telling her that when Lucille tried Axel's cell one more time they'd both expected the call to go to voicemail, again, but a woman answered.

'Who is this?' she'd said.

'Who's *that*?' said Lucille, frantic. 'That's my boss's phone you're answering and we've been trying—'

'He's unconscious. Maybe he slipped on the snow, I don't know.' The woman gave her name. 'I'm out walking my dog and … I was already dialling 911 on my phone when I heard the cell ringing in his pocket … with your call. He's breathing, but only just.'

Lucille called 911 on her other line while she got the woman's exact location. And once Frank heard they were only half a block away, he shot out the door.

'The police,' Tori said, keeping her eyes fixed on Axel through the glass as if staring at his recumbent body might pump enough energy into him to bring him back, 'what do they say?'

Frank's eyebrows leapt to attention. 'We didn't ... couldn't ...' His honey timbre was deeper than usual, and slower, like molasses off a spoon. 'Tori, he collapsed, pure and simple. Involving the police ... Goodness gracious! We'd have them *and* the media tromping all over SIS, and you know what Axel would say about that.'

'Two words,' she said, nodding. *'Avoid* and *plague*, with emphasis on *plague*.'* In the near century of the firm's existence, the three Axel Schönbergs, senior, junior and Axel III, had kept a profile so low the public and the media barely knew they existed.

'Besides,' said Frank, 'I got to Axel in seconds and, fortunately, a light snow cover had cushioned his fall so I could see that the only footprints around him, apart from his own, were the woman's and her dog's. No evidence of a scuffle, nothing. Just the smell of cigars, a hint of milk on his breath, no wounds, no cuts or bruises—'

'Milk?'

'A cappuccino before he'd left the office apparently.'

'Anything else?'

'Not really ... Oh, yes, a balloon, one of those metallic ones. It was stuck up in the branches of a tree overhead, probably escaped from a birthday party.'

Just like she expected from a man who'd worked at the 'real' SIS—MI6—for nine years, Frank was over every detail like calamine lotion on an itch. But still there was something Tori couldn't put her finger on.

'When Axel got here,' said Frank, 'the doctors did a full once-over, a thrice-over really. Turns out he's their biggest donor. Their verdict isn't pretty but it does have a ring of truth about it. His body simply shut down due to a lifetime of overindulgence.'

'Did they find anything unusual in his bloodwork or stomach, bodily fluids—'

'Unusual for a stomach that isn't Axel's.' He counted them off on his fingers, 'Champagne, oysters, Patagonian toothfish.'

'No toxins?'

'Plenty of cholesterol and plaque, but you asked for unusual. Even after his triple bypass two years ago, they say it's a miracle he hasn't had a heart attack.'

'The cappuccino?'

'Apologies, yes they got that.'

Her phone started to ring and when she saw the caller ID her eyes rolled back in contempt. 'It's Zell!' she huffed, showing Frank the screen. Then she remembered something. 'You said Axel was muttering about Zell, and that he'd left the office just before you found Axel. Could those things be connected?'

'Tori, I know you two don't get on but ...' He let the sentence hang and placed a palm on the glass, she assumed to help the heat drain out of him.

She answered her phone and after three crisp words, 'Yes ... When? ... Okay,' she hung up. 'He wants to see me ... now. Should I let him fire me or should I resign and deny him the satisfaction?'

'If staying is an option,' he said, a blush deepening his cheeks, 'I'd much prefer that.'

8

TORI WOULDN'T EMPLOY RON MADA TO run a bath. Yet here she was as *his* employee, at least for now. From behind his usual illegal and offensive haze of smoke, he lifted a finger and beckoned her in, then crammed his cigarette into his ashtray.

Even with him in it, Mada's office was soulless, empty, the walls unpunctuated walnut veneer, not a single painting nor even a graduation certificate gracing their surfaces. With no shelving either, the room was devoid of books, knick-knacks, family photos, virtually anything except his desk, two visitor chairs and over by the window a three-piece lounge centred around a bare glass coffee table. What always hit her in here was the sour cigarette stink and the even more fetid malevolence.

The intriguing oddity was Mada's sole personal effect, a red and gold lacquered box by the windowsill, and even though Tori had been dying to know what was in it ever since she'd started working here, she would never risk prolonging a visit to ask.

Mada was so short Tori couldn't tell if he was standing until he walked around his desk. The tendril passing for his mouth mimicked a smile. 'It's my job to sort out SIS without Axel.' He gestured for her to sit.

'He's not dead.' Her whisper begged to be a scream, but she held it in. As she sat, she focused on the ridiculous tufts of white that sprouted off his chin, more like cotton candy than a goatee. 'About Axel,' she said, 'what's the latest?'

He retreated to his chair. 'What's to say? After years of gorging himself on caviar, *foie gras* and all that other gourmandising crap, his body gave up. They say it's a diabetic hyperosmolar coma.'

'Could he die from it?'

He smirked. 'We all die. Look Tori, I'm not happy—'

'Then which dwarf are you?' she snapped at him, instantly wishing she hadn't.

Mada sighed, like this wasn't the first time he'd heard the taunt. 'Swyft, right now nothing would please me more than to hear you say goodbye for the last time, but the needs of SIS take precedence over my preferences.'

'And those needs are?'

'Project Chant. A deal Axel put together. A giant deal. He was close to wrapping it up with Henry Harvey's help, but when Henry took ill he asked Frank to wing it back here to help him tie the bows around it and—'

'Now Axel's out of the picture, you want me to take over the lead?' The notion that Zell would entrust Axel's deal of the decade to the firm's newest and youngest director, one he utterly despised, only made sense if was manoeuvring for her to fail, to give him proof of her incompetence when—if—Axel revived. 'You want me to step into Axel's shoes?'

'Correct,' he said, lifting himself out of his chair again, this time padding across the room in his socks—black silk—to latch the door closed before returning to sit. He picked up his heavy-rimmed glasses, placed them on his nose and steepled his fingers. 'What did Frank tell you about the deal?'

Was the question a trap, she wondered, to check if Frank had breached confidentiality? 'Just that it was big. Nothing else.'

He nodded. 'If we ... you ... get it over the line, it'll be the biggest merger in history. The shitterverse, or whatever you call that mindless swamp of social media, will go ballistic over it.'

Blah, blah, she thought. 'Who's merging with who?'

'How about Mingmai for starters?'

Tori flinched. Mingmai was enormous, a ... no, *the* Chinese telecommunications, media and IT colossus. On her way back to Boston, she'd read a puff piece on the CEO in the airline magazine. Surprisingly unsung in the West, Jin Yu was a folk hero in China, a rags-to-riches entrepreneur and philanthropist whose story made Bill Gates seem like a scrooge.

Most of it she'd taken with more than a grain of her cynical salt, but what moved her was Jin Yu's profile as a father. Despite an unremitting schedule—meetings, functions, travel—he didn't let his work isolate him from his son. If a destination was tolerable, six-year-old Mingli travelled too, with tutors in tow. As a result, Jin and the boy packed in a lot of time together. Their joint passion was reading, with Mingli's Chinese favourite the classic *Dream of the Red Chamber* and, in English, everything by Tolkien. 'It's become a hobbit,' she recalled Jin joking in the article.

'Who are they merging with?' she asked. 'Alibaba? Huawei? Lenovo … IBM?'

'Ólympos,' Mada said with a smirk, 'the empire of your good friend Soti Skylakakis.'

The air quotes he'd put around *good friend* flustered Tori. Her impulsive, wrong and frankly dumber-than-dumb one-night tryst on the Greek tech titan's yacht had indeed made her more friendly with him than she cared to admit or wanted to remember. But Zell couldn't possibly know about that. Could he?

'Skylakakis says he wants you—'

She felt ill.

'—but if I give you to him, you can't fuck this up like you fucked up his last deal.'

Don't bite … Stick to Project Chant, she told herself.

The in-flight magazine had quoted Jin Yu's company, Mingmai Inc, as worth $600 billion, which was three times the value she and Axel had placed on Skylakakis's company last time round. This deal was bigger than anything, ever. Axel might be able to do it, but could she? She felt like she was dropping off the lip at the Pipe for the first time, her entire self shaking with the terror it would overrun her, drown her. The numbers were mind-boggling, the multi-jurisdictions, the nuances, 800 billion of them.

And what about the politics? 'The defence and security issues will kill this stone dead,' she said. 'You can't seriously expect the administration in Washing—'

'Axel told me,' said Zell, straightening his tie, though not pulling it tightly enough for Tori, 'that Washington would be no problem because—'

'They've blocked far less significant China deals … like that crappy wind farm some Chinese company wanted to buy.'

'Which was situated way too close to a weapons training facil—'

'Ólympos isn't *close* to facilities like that, its technology is their *foundation*. The defence industry is Skylakakis's biggest segment. Shit, Ron, the president's not going to hand China the passwords—the keys, damn it—to the world's most sensitive installat—'

'You're over dramat—'

'What about Congress ... and the Europeans?'

'Swyft,' he said, checking his watch, 'it's like Axel said, with the shit state *all* these governments' budgets are in and China being the cornerstone owner of US debt, let alone the world's biggest buyer and seller of virtually everything that moves and half of what doesn't, the last thing DC or Brussels or London or Bonn will risk is a trade war over a successful, respected Chinese company merging with a Greek one. Beggars ... choosers ... get it?'

'Jin Yu's a gazillionaire Mr Nice Guy, I get that. But that won't make this deal fly, especially if it's true he's got connections into the People's Liberation Army,' said Tori remembering something else she'd read. 'Besides, why would Soti want to surrender control of Ólympos when he's spent his whole life building it?'

'Hmm,' said Mada, twisting his chin hairs into a point. 'How about the pots and pots of money that Jin Yu wants to shower him with?'

Tori shook her head. 'Ron, this is nuts.' She looked at his ashtray. 'What have you and Axel been smoking?'

'Is it nuts if Axel got Mingmai to pay Ólympos a 100-million-dollar go or no-go deposit just to get Soti to sit at their table? Half of that, by the way, Soti's already paid over to us as an advance on our fee. And then there's our success fee on top of that. If you do get this thing to fly, here's what we'll get paid on top of the fifty mill we've already banked.' He scrawled an eye-watering number on a sheet of paper and held it up to her.

Zell hadn't been offering her a hospital pass. He didn't want her to fail. He might be willing to give up some money if it meant discrediting her, but not a fee like that. She leant back in her seat. 'But surely Soti would only agree to a fee of that magnitude if he was getting Axel's personal attention.'

Mada swivelled his chair to face the window. 'Do you think Axel was sitting on his hands before the coma? He was all over this deal. He virtually engineered it. And he's taken it to the point where it's as good as done, so actually there's not much you can fuck up. For some reason, Skylakakis thinks you're a fucking genius and he wants you, and if we can't give him Axel *or* Swyft, Project Chant happens *without* SIS. I'd have to refund the fifty bars, our success fee would be history and that Hermès elephant-design scarf I put a deposit on to buy you for next Christmas, forget that too.'

Tori smiled, despite herself. Mada making light of anything, particularly money, was a novel experience. 'Hermès, huh? I guess that means I'm in.'

'Your first meeting's in New York at three o'clock tomorrow.'

Her head exploded with an image of a leaning tower of paper being wheeled into her office.

Mada continued. 'It's a page-turn of the draft deal documents so you better brief up quick or the Chinese will seize the upper hand.'

'What about the due diligence?' A transaction like this would involve enormous investigation, checking through all the underlying business contracts, the leases, title deeds, intellectual property, litigation, physically kicking the tyres on the factories, and more.

'I won't say relax,' said Mada, 'but most of it's been taken care of. As soon as Axel got the two principals to shake hands on the key terms, he got them to assign half the northern hemisphere's accountants and lawyers onto all that diligence shit and, lucky for you, all that's left is a few site visits.' He checked his screen. 'If you get through tomorrow's page-turn without screwing up, you and Chaudry will be putting your feet up on Axel's Gulfstream on your way to China the day after. And once that's out of the way, all that's left is steering *MV Chant* safely through the shoals of the politicians and bureaucrats. Like I said, Swyft, there's fuck all left for you to fuck up.'

She dug her thumbs into her palms. *Why did cancer kill good people when shits like this got to live?*

9

A HINT OF BEESWAX AND TURPENTINE was in the air as Tori brushed her fingers over her own desk. The oak was soft to the touch but not tacky, so she guessed the repolishing must've been done as soon as she'd gone on vacation.

On her computer screen were nearly 200 tightly-packed pages of financial spreadsheets, a merger structure diagram that looked like someone had tossed a plate of spaghetti over the page and a forest of legalese that, if she printed the documents and spread them out, would probably cover every square inch of Boston Common. She cast her eyes out her bow window and over the street to the ghostly woodland of grey, spindly branches lightly dusted with snow. This was a far cry from lazing under the sun in Hawaii, or Sydney.

She returned to the documents, flipping them page by page, getting slower and slower, like she was wading into quicksand. The work she had to cover would normally take days, days she didn't have. Fortunately, Frank was thirty-plus hours ahead of her. He'd thrown himself into Project Chant straight after the paramedics hoisted Axel into the ambulance, working his way through the same piles she was now churning through, scouring the public databases and brokers' reports. Whenever he hit something he couldn't follow—which was often, he'd told her—he'd apologetically phone Henry Harvey, who was heaving his guts out at home, as well as push as much as he could onto the 'cast of thousands' that SIS's co-advisers at EuropaNational had thrown at the deal.

As Tori scanned the reams of valuations, schedules, multiples, net present values, ramp ups, flip outs, clawbacks and all the other deal jargon whatchamacallits, the image of Axel lying on his back kept coming back to her.

She pressed her hands down onto her desk to help her think. His body might well have shut down due to some form of diabetes, but how could she be sure the hospital's bloodwork hadn't overlooked something? Taking a deep breath she closed her eyes, counting her heartbeats and holding for three minutes, not long for a surfer but long enough to clear her head and bring the question that had been nagging her back to the surface.

Mada. Zell. Where had he been rushing to when Frank saw him leaving the office just before Axel was found? She picked up the phone to ask him straight out.

'A private matter,' he snarled, and hung up on her.

✝

THE SIS BUILDING was virtually deserted. After hours at her desk, Tori needed to stretch her legs and reoxygenate her blood. After running up and down the fire stairs three times, she was on her way back to her office when she passed Mada's. She slowly came to a stop, then turned to face his door.

Instinctively, her eyes scanned for a CCTV camera despite knowing that Axel's house policy strictly banned them from the work and meeting floors. Checking the corridor was deserted, she pushed open his door and stepped inside expecting the reek of cigarettes, instead getting a sharp slap from the cleaners' lime-scented air freshener.

Apart from his now empty ashtray and the other bare essentials, Mada's desk was barren, not even a scrap of paper or a pen cluttering it. His computer was off, damn it, and when she switched it on she was asked for a password. She turned it back off and tried his drawers, but they were locked. While locks weren't barriers, only challenges to Tori, now wasn't the time to parade those skills.

Maybe it was her fatigue, but the lacquered box by the window suddenly captivated her. A man like Mada would have accumulated scores of curios and trinkets over the years, so why had he left this one alone out on display? She flipped open the lid and lifted out a parchment-coloured card. It was signed by the governor of Liaoning during a trade mission Mada had made to the Chinese province back in the 1980s. Beneath the card was a white marble block with two Chinese characters carved into its base, a Chinese signature seal, she guessed. It had to be expensive since she couldn't imagine Mada ascribing sentimental value to anything.

A phone rang down the hall, startling her. She quickly placed the card back inside the box and closed it as Frank called out, 'Tori, phone! Where are you?'

†

'IT'S OUR CLIENT,' he told her, pointing to his phone as she entered his office, not as neat-freak as Zell's but displaying a sense of order that came from four of his nine MI6 years being stationed in dicey overseas posts that ran the daily risk of being overrun.

Apart from the four Project Chant tree stumps of paperwork on his desk, and the pizza box, the only discordant note was the grungy tweed jacket hanging off the back of his chair, though she still wondered about a grown man giving pride of place to a cricket ball. Pressed into a green velvet cushion on his credenza like a priceless antiquity in a museum display case, she guessed it made sense since it was autographed by some childhood hero of his, a famous Pakistani she couldn't name if her life depended on it.

'He's calling us from *Fun Cool*,' Frank said, referring to the 400-foot super yacht which operated as Skylakakis's home, office, resort as well as his mobile tax haven. And the locale of an evening with him Tori remembered too well but would rather forget.

They'd planned on calling Skylakakis the next morning, after she'd had a chance to get up to speed, working through the key documents and getting her own flavour of the transaction. Right now, it would be up to Frank to fill in whatever blanks he could.

She glanced at the phone, at Frank, then shrugged and punched the speakerphone button. 'Mr Skylakakis, is it good morning, evening or afternoon for you?'

'It's *good* nothing. Whenever I speak to you, it is always the *best* part of my day.' He paused, then spoke in Greek.

Tori knew some Greek but Frank's education in the Classics gave him more, his grin almost cracking his face apart. He tapped the phone back onto mute, enjoying her squirms as he explained how their client missed the smile of his princess's green eyes.

'The flames in my heart have not subsided—' Skylakakis tried to continue but Frank, to protect Tori as much as himself from further embarrassment, coughed and said, 'Mr Skylakakis, it's getting quite late here and—'

'Of course. It's what … midnight in Boston? What of our beloved Axel? My dearest friend, my trusted confidant. Tori, Frank … such a shock. A tragedy. A heartbreak. But look, despite Axel's terrible situation, let me say how good it is we're on the same team again, especially,' he sighed, 'now I don't have to waste another minute talking to that *maláka* Mada. What Axel sees in—'

'Mada's our boss, Soti.' She glanced at Frank.

'Of course, I'm sorry. Tori, you've only been back a few hours so I want to give you my perspective on the deal.' Tori and Frank listened as he explained that Mingmai's offer was double what he thought his own company was worth. He ran them through a top-level overview of the financials: what parts of his business were going into the deal and what parts he was keeping; how much of the deal was in cash and how much in stock; and what the combined board's composition would be, with Jin Yu as CEO and Soti as chairman. 'So all that's left,' he said, 'is to fine-tune the paperwork and the final pieces of due diligence in China, checking on their supply chain and quality control. All of which, Mada says, the two of you will be my eyes and ears for over there. Does my summary meet your understanding?'

'Apart from you underestimating the risk,' said Tori, 'that politics and the bureaucracy in the US and Europe will block it.'

'Tori, if they say *no*, they'll unleash an economic typhoon. Think about it … if China even threatens to turn up at the Fed's teller window to withdraw the trillions of dollars it's got in US Treasury bills, it'll send the global economy into a tailspin. So governments won't block this deal. They might massage it, force us to take out this bit and that bit, but if they do, that's Jin Yu's problem, not mine.'

'Soti, I really—'

'Enough. Before I go, we released the Beta version of FrensLens 2 for live testing today. You'll be getting a pair tomorrow. Take them to China with you and let me know how they work over there. Now, no more chitchat, delightful as it's been. You two need to finish your work then get some sleep, or vice versa. And Giselle here needs to finish pounding my back. Say *au revoir* to the nice people, Giselle.' He hung up as a woman giggled in the background.

'Heavens,' said Frank, his hand on his chest. 'Did we have that entire conversation while he was lying on a massage table?'

'And naked, probably.'

'What did Marx say about the rich? *They'll do anything for the poor, except get off their backs.*'

10

TWO HOURS LATER, TORI WANDERED INTO Frank's office. He was slumped over his desk, head nestled in his folded arms, an elbow pressing against his keyboard silently typing lines and lines of question marks down his screen. She coughed. He didn't stir. She prodded his arm and he slowly lifted his head, blinked and then sat bolt upright. 'Sorry, Tori, I—'

'I'm surprised you stayed awake as long as you did.' After he'd been dropped into Project Chant, Frank hadn't been home once, not even to change. 'There's a shower upstairs that's quite keen to say hello to both of us. Separately that is,' she added. 'But first you need to see something.' She moved round to his side of the desk. 'I'll drive, okay?' He rolled his chair sideways and she edged in, bent over in front of his screen. She minimised the page of question marks and began tapping on his keyboard.

'Here,' she said, popping up one of Mingmai's financial spreadsheets: the summary page for the group's expenses for the past fourteen years. She highlighted a row about halfway down, labelled *M&A*. The little rectangular cells spread across the page showed Mingmai's total spend on mergers and acquisitions each year had totalled 650 billion yuan.

'That's a hundred billion, give or take, in US dollars,' Frank said, 'but so what? Their takeover activity's been regarded as part of their magic formul—'

'Magic is one word for it. Trick is another. Pick a year, any year.'

Frank took a few sips from the half-drunk Coke on his desk and chose 2011, a year the sheet told them Mingmai had outlaid US$6 billion to buy up other companies. When Tori clicked on the 2011 cell, it opened a sub-sheet listing all Mingmai's takeovers for that year.

'Now pick a deal, any deal,' she said.

Frank chose that year's largest deal, a company called Pingyuan, which had cost close to $3 billion. When Tori clicked on that cell, the screen opened up a separate thirty-two-page workbook, the top sheet outlining Pingyuan's core activities as well as the key acquisition parameters. Frank skimmed it. 'Hmm. Why would a company like Mingmai buy a drone-maker?'

'Ask Google or Alphabet or whatever they're called this week,' said Tori. 'If *they* bought one, why shouldn't Mingmai?' But then she put a finger to her nose and with her other hand clicked through to a page setting out the drone-maker's profit history. 'I've got no problem with the concept but if you average out Pingyuan's profits before Mingmai bought it, they're—'

'SFA,' said Frank, getting as close to profanity as he felt comfortable.

'Or more precisely, three *million* dollars a year. That's a lot to you and me but—'

'They paid a thousand times that to buy it?' He whistled. From the summary sheet, it was clear that Pingyuan wasn't remotely like an Uber, an Airbnb or a Facebook, the kinds of high-growth businesses that early-stage investors habitually paid eye-popping multiples for. More relevantly, after Mingmai bought Pingyuan, the drone-maker's earnings hadn't soared, they'd crashed.

'Here,' Tori said, pointing at the screen, 'if that's not crazy enough, Mingmai paid out almost half a bill of that three billion for "advisory fees" meaning they spent two and a half bill for a company with net assets of jack shit and a profit stream, like you said, of sweet fuck all. And on top of *that* they paid their advisers a whopping twenty-per-cent success fee for negotiating the worst deal in history.' Advisers' fees could vary enormously, but both of them knew that for a deal this size even one per cent was generous.

Tori tabbed back to the summary sheet. 'Now pick another deal, another year.' Frank chose 2008 this time, with the acquisition of Laji, a paperless office business. It was an even bigger deal with Mingmai shelling out $8 billion, yet again a paltry earnings stream and a meagre balance sheet.

'A fair price might have been eight *million*, not billion,' said Frank, and he noted what Tori already knew, that this time the advisers' fees were even higher, at $600 million. 'I suspect Axel got us hired by the wrong client,' he said. 'Either that or it's fraud.'

'Precisely,' said Tori. She continued to work the screen, clicking on the advisory fees for both deals showing him the names of the lucky advisers who'd pocketed these extraordinary sums. Not only were neither of them from the usual list of Wall Street gougers, googling them showed they cast an even shorter shadow than SIS, so short that Tori doubted they existed, suggesting Mingmai—or someone high up inside Mingmai— was using these deals to funnel funds out of the company. 'Frank, I've worked through ten of their thirty M&A deals so far and only three look legit. As far as I can tell, Mingmai looks like another Olympus scandal waiting to happen.'

'When was *our* client in a scandal?'

'Not Ólympos ... *Olympus*, the Japanese optical and audio technology company.'

Frank gave her a blank look and she sighed. 'A few years back, after Olympus appointed its first non-Japanese as CEO, he uncovered a history of massive overpayments for both acquisitions and advisers. It turned out the old guard had been window-dressing the financial accounts, making them appear way more profitable than they really were.'

'You're saying Mingmai's entire fourteen-year profit history is phony?'

'As real as your Rolex,' said Tori, tapping Frank's watch.

His dark cheeks flushed and he leant back in his chair, arms folded. 'A giant Ponzi scheme.'

'Like Hamlet said, there's something very, very rotten in the state of—'

'Actually, it wasn't Hamlet,' said Frank. 'It was in *Hamlet*, but it was Marcellus speaking.' His Rolex might have been outed as a backstreet fake, but Frank clearly wanted to remind her that his Eton schooling was the real deal. 'Tori, we need to tell Skylakakis about this.'

'Marcellus, you say?' The green sparkle in her eyes dimmed as she mentally turned the pages of Shakespeare's Folios to check. She nodded. 'Yes, Marcellus. But no, we won't call Soti, not yet.' Her eyes lit up again. 'Touching this dreaded sight, twice, we will watch the minutes of this night.'

In a Shakespeare contest, Eton College and Manly High School drew a tie.

11

New York City

KONG FENG RUBBED HIS EYES. 'IT'S three o'clock
in the morning, Dr Swyft, what could possibly justify
this call?' Mingmai's chief financial officer sighed and
turned the glare of his bedside clock away from him.

'We want to give you a heads up ... before we meet this
afternoon,' said the woman.

'A heads up?' Kong said warily, and sat up.

'Advance warnin—'

'I know what a heads up is, Dr Swyft. What is your
point?'

'I've just emailed you a screenshot of some data we've been
looking at,' she said.

He dragged his laptop over from his bedside table. 'Wait ...
Yes, I've got it. So what is this I'm looking at?'

'A summary of the advisory fees Mingmai's paid on its past few years' acquisitions.'

Kong Feng shot bolt upright, alert as a deer hearing a twig snap.

'Some of the fees,' Swyft continued, 'they look, well, only Mount Everest is higher. We calculated the percentages ... See, there in the fourth column? Look, Mr Kong, I know this is all ancient history to you, but I've only just come onto Project Chant so I apologise if this got covered in the negotiations before—'

'Covered? What the hell are you talking about?'

'Mr Kong, we need to know what Mingmai intends to pay its advisers on this merg—'

Kong fumed. 'You have no right—'

'Normally I'd agree that you could pay whoever you want whatever you want, but Project Chant isn't a buyout like your past deals. It's a merger where you end up owning two-thirds of the combination. That means our client will wear a third of those advisory fees. If they're in the typical range, fine. If not, we'll need you to shrink your slice of the pie to compensate him for them.'

Kong wasn't the slightest bit worried about Project Chant's actual fees. Not even about the slice of the merger pie. With the intense scrutiny Mingmai's first big deal in the West would get when it went public, these fees had to be within normal bounds, not that anything on Wall Street was normal.

What spooked Kong was this Swyft woman poking her nose into Mingmai's *old* deals, sniffing out the billions in diverted funds that, until now, had been kept hidden.

12

Kinshasa, Democratic Republic of the Congo

KINSHASA WAS A SPRAWLING CONGOLESE SHANTY town where too many of its ten million inhabitants spent their days clawing for survival and their nights slapping at malarial mosquitoes. Almost nothing worked, the squalid streets reeked of piss and murders were commonplace.

As his plane landed, Jin Yu swatted away Kinshasa's filth as casually as the bug buzzing round the cockpit. This was his seventeenth flight into N'djili Airport, a crisscross from Beijing via New York, then via Bihar in India to pick up supplies from one of his pharma labs. These labs pumped out generic drugs at prices the developing world could afford. Often, he got them out onto the streets before the original, patented version had won regulatory approval. Despite his own wealth, Jin despised how Big Pharma gouged excessive profits out of global misery.

Tuoma was Jin's aerial workhorse, a Russian-built supersonic Tupolev-160. Luxury had its place but for this trip, speed and carrying capacity took priority, even if that—and the local health risks—meant the devoted father had to leave his son in Beijing.

On this flight, after more flooding in Kinshasa and with dysentery at plague proportions, *Tuoma* was carrying fifteen tonnes of mosquito nets and twenty of a generic auranofin he'd picked up in Bihar. Technically, the drug was an arthritis medicine but he wasn't going to wait for FDA and WHO sign-offs before it could be used to combat amoebic dysentery. And nor would the DRC hierarchy. They didn't give a hoot about foreign approvals. Especially when they got first crack at black marketing the incoming cargo.

Jin expected nothing in return for his charity. He didn't need to since the Congolese had already given him what he'd wanted. The licence for his local pharmaceutical factory had come through three months ago and the green light for Bolamu, his second diamond mine, had been granted five minutes before *Tuoma* took off from Bihar. Not that he ever linked his philanthropy to favours.

Antoine Youlou Bomboko, Jin's main man on the ground here, came up the airstairs. Bomboko's day job was *Son Excellence Monsieur le Ministre de la Santé Publique*, the beleaguered country's minister of what passed as public health. His usually cheery round face was long, his step lumbering and, for a strapping thirty-eight-year-old, his clothes were soaked in more sweat than the heat and humidity outside justified.

With the risk that Bomboko himself was suffering from dysentery, Jin decided there'd be no handshakes. Remaining seated, he looked at the sweaty hand Bomboko thrust at him, letting it hang in the air unclasped, then turned away awkwardly. 'Antoine, you seem unwell.'

'It is not my health, Monsieur Jin,' said Bomboko. He withdrew his hand and took the refresher towel the steward offered him, wiped the sweat off his face and neck, handed back the cloth, then accepted a glass of iced water and slugged it down.

The African eyed the seat next to his benefactor, clearly waiting for Jin's invitation to sit. Shuffling his feet he continued. 'Not five minutes ago, when I was watching your touchdown, my car radio reported that *le Pape* ... may God rest his soul ...' His voice caught and he paused, took the towel back, dabbed it to both eyes and crossed himself. Bomboko, like half the populace, was a devout Roman Catholic.

'I saw the reports of the autopsy just before we landed,' said Jin. 'They confirmed he died of natural causes, that the rumours of foul play were wrong. Why are you upset?'

'Oh, Monsieur Jin, a band of terrorists ... they claim the autopsy was flawed. They have released a video claiming they assassinated *le Saint-Père* ... the Holy Father. And there is more ...' Fresh beads of sweat dotted his forehead and upper lip. 'There is no other way to say it, Monsieur. These people, this *détritus de l'humanité*, they are ... your compatriots.' His body tensed, eyes wide as he waited for a reaction. When it didn't come he added, 'Monsieur Jin, I did not know China had any Muslims.'

Now that Jin knew it wasn't disease that was bugging the devoted Catholic, he patted the seat beside him. Pointing his remote control at the TV fixed to the panelling of his aerial office, he set the channel to China's international English-language TV station.

—minutes ago, a group of Chinese Islamist terrorists calling themselves RUA, or Rome Under Allah, released a video claiming they assassinated Pope Augustine and declaring independence from China for their so-called Islamic Caliphate of Uyghurstan, a part of Xinjiang autonomous region.

'*Another* Caliphate?' said Bomboko.

'Shh!'

RUA's claim directly contradicts the official Vatican autopsy which, after almost two weeks of rumour and controversy, was released only an hour before and stated that His Holiness died of natural causes.

As proof of RUA's claim, the video contains explicit footage taken inside the Apostolic Palace with an unnamed substance being sprayed over His Holiness. At this stage, it is unknown how RUA entered or exited the palace.

They give two reasons for killing the pope: to herald their independent Islamic Caliphate, and to fulfil an ancient prophecy that Islam will conquer Rome.

The video also contains a chilling warning: 'Let other leaders of the crusader coalition know that from today, with Allah's permission, there will be no safety for them in their own lands.'

Bomboko fidgeted, obviously itching to speak, but not daring to as Jin leant forward to concentrate on the commentary:

Xinjiang, China's largest region, is home to ten million Turkic-speaking Uyghurs, a bigger Muslim population than Jordan and Palestine combined.

Xinjiang is economically important to China with forty per cent of the country's coal reserves and one-fifth of its natural gas and identified oil, in addition to salt and gold deposits.

A Uyghur spokesman in Urumqi, Xinjiang's capital, told reporters, 'Uyghurs deplore all violence. If RUA exists, we openly condemn its barbaric act. But we have never heard of RUA. We suspect it is a fiction, contrived by the enemies of the Uyghur people, to incite hate and hostility against us.'

'A *fiction*?' cried Bomboko, outraged. '*Le Pape* is dead. Is *that* a fiction? Show us the video,' he shouted at the screen.

'Give it time, my friend.'

—spokesman for China's Hui Muslims, who are ethnically distinct from the Uyghurs, said, 'The Hui utterly reject RUA's act and its aims. They are a complete perversion of peace-loving Islam and a grave insult to Allah.'

We will now broadcast the video, though we warn that many viewers may find it disturbing …

Piercing blue eyes filled the screen and, as the camera pulled back to reveal a face clad in a black balaclava, Jin turned off the TV. Bomboko jerked forward in his seat. 'But the video! You don't want to see the video?'

'My friend, I cannot watch it … My own countrymen … It is unimaginable.' Frowning, Jin reached for the phone on the armrest bracket. 'I'm sorry,' he said, 'but I have urgent business to attend to. *Au revoir*, Antoine.'

Bomboko stood, his eyes darting back and forth between the phone and the grim countenance on Jin's face. Then he bowed and left. As Bomboko's feet hit the exit stairs, Jin pulled out the phone and speed-dialled one of Beijing's most private numbers.

A smile came to Jin's face, as it always did when speaking to his son, his one peace in a world that was a torrent of pieces. 'My beautiful Mingli ...'

13

Washington, DC

HARDLY A PEOPLE CITY, WASHINGTON CLINKED and clattered over infinite power breakfasts, liquid lunches and working dinners. Acquaintances, allies and even adversaries breathlessly air-kissed, elbowing genuine relationships aside for what they were all really here for: power, one-upmanship or, if they couldn't get either, frequent flyer air miles.

Singles were seventy per cent of the population, yet hardly any came here expecting love. Most wanted to make a difference, to create change, to sway opinion. If that was too much of a stretch, they'd settle for a nod of recognition from a cabinet secretary or a hack, or try to become starfuckers, brown nosers or whatever catty tag best described people who velcroed themselves to whoever was on the up and up, basking in their glory as if it were their own.

With all that adrenaline coursing through Washington's arteries, sex was in overdrive, though it was loveless sex. What Tex Carter called an occupational haggard.

In his ten months' burning DC's midnight oil, Tex Carter—Narthex here—had kindled more flames than he had ever thought likely, or decent. But after Hawaii—after Tori—it hadn't happened once, despite his assistant Loucineh's sultry attempts at persuasion.

He'd pleaded exhaustion to her, after working through the nights so the president didn't have to. With the latest crises in Iran, Libya and, of all places, Albania it was an excuse with the virtue of truth, though his real reason was Tori.

From the moment he buckled in on his flight back to DC, her accomplishments, cheeky smile, sassy wit, grace and, okay, yes, her looks, all kept flashing *The One* at him. But now, at 4 am, standing outside the president's bedroom, this was no time to fantasise about surfing into the sunset, about marriage, about children, about ... He shook the notions out of his head.

After buttoning his jacket and nodding at tonight's Secret Service agent, he'd hardly knocked on the president's door when she cracked it open like she'd been standing behind it. She was tying a silk belt around her robe, a flowing crimson. Red was a colour he'd never seen her in, despite Rosa being her middle name. Her hair was the perfect black bob it always was—how did she do that?—shoulder length, pushed back behind her ears, glossy like a shampoo advertisement, yet somehow giving her the casual, reassuring look of a soccer mom rather than the leader of the free world.

'Ah, Narthex.' She stepped out into the hall and smiled, as if finding a nervous young man at her door at such an early hour was perfectly natural. She flicked back her hair, her robe singeing it with reddish highlights. 'What global panic possibly needs me today at … what, is it? … 9 am in London … 5 pm in Beijing … What place on my globe will you be spinning us to?'

'Ma'am, the late Pope Augustine—'

'Again with the dead pope?' Her eyes narrowed. 'A sanctimonious—'

'The Vatican, ma'am, they've—'

'Narthex, I'm Catholic but I won't drop to my knees whenever the Vatic—'

'Ma'am, please. A new—'

'With them, it's always something new. Augustine was a—'

'Yes, ma'am, but hold that thought, er, please, until you watch this video.' He raised a tablet in front of him, feeling suddenly like he was using it to shield himself. 'A new Islamist terror group, *Chinese* Islamists—'

She sucked in a breath and stepped back. 'China has—'

'They have two Muslim minorities, ma'am, the Uyghurs and the Huis.'

'Ah, yes.' She rubbed her forehead then steadied her hand on the doorjamb, glimpsing back into her room to check that her stepson was still curled up and the light from the hallway hadn't woken him. 'Davey's been coughing half the night. I only just got him to sleep.'

Narthex blushed, wondering if he was the cause. Since he'd been back he'd been taking the boy outside into the gardens to help him prep for his school pageant. Maybe he should've insisted Davey keep his parka and gloves on when he kept wrapping his arms round the trees to 'feel their souls'.

'Narthex?' said the president.

'Sorry, ma'am. It's a new Uyghur group … they're claiming they assassinated Pope Augustine.'

'That's not possible. The Vatican sent me an embargoed copy of the autopsy last night. It said he died from natural causes … Or more likely, in my opinion, from God's will.'

'The video's explicit, ma'am. It shows Augustine's last moments alive, in his bedchamber, and this group—'

'They have a name?'

'RUA … Rome Under Allah.'

Isabel closed her eyes.

'They say it's an attack on—'

Her eyes snapped open. 'On what? The infidel West? Christendom? The damn Crusaders? Any other shibboleth they've lifted out of *Webster's Medieval Terrorist Phrasebook*?'

'All of those, ma'am.'

She tucked a loose strand of hair behind her ear and nodded to the agent posted by her door. 'Would you mind using your wrist thingy to rustle up some coffee for Narthex and me … maybe some donuts? And Narthex, we'll need to convene an urgent meeting of the National Security Council—'

'Already on it, ma'am,' said Narthex. 'Calling together the NSC, I mean, not the donuts.'

WITH LIGHTNING SPEED after RUA released their video, Beijing launched a comprehensive and brutal crackdown across the country, especially in the Uyghur's home territory of Xinjiang. Taking to the nation's living rooms by TV, radio and the internet, President Hou Tao declared an immediate ban on all unlicensed public association in the region, and asked all citizens to inform police immediately if they suspected anyone of being a RUA member, donor or sympathiser.

As the night wore on, hundreds of Uyghurs were snatched from their homes, as well as scores of other dissidents and, unusually, these operations were covered live on national media. Reports in the first three hours revealed that police and security forces had uncovered over a hundred secret caches of semi-automatic weapons, rocket launchers, suicide vests and jihadist videos, and were already boarding up eighty-two Uyghur schools after receiving new evidence they were 'seething hotbeds of Sunni Islamist and separatist propaganda'.

The sun wasn't even a glimmer in the eastern US and Latin America when RUA had released the video. In Europe and Africa where it had been mid-morning, spontaneous and often bloody anti-Muslim demonstrations began breaking out, the police and, in many places, the military doing their best to secure mosques and protect Muslim schools and citizens.

By lunchtime in Greece, Hungary, Austria and Serbia, wild mobs were baying for blood outside refugee camps, in some cases pushing over the chain-link fences, despite armed police, dogs and horses resisting them. In those countries alone, 300 protesters had been arrested after clubbing fifty refugees to death, including five children, and injuring thousands more.

Across the globe, political leaders called for calm. Very few people were listening.

14

Boston

FRANK PLONKED A TRAY BESIDE TORI'S laptop after finding her in the boardroom. He'd been gone an hour, he realised after checking his watch. 'Apologies. I nodded off in the kitchen waiting for the water to boil.'

She pushed her computer away and reached for a muffin. She tapped a finger on it then took a small bite. 'Mmph. Apple and almond. Stale, but otherwise the best I've ever had.'

He watched her wolf it down then brush the crumbs that had fallen onto the table into her hand before spilling them onto the tray, her pinkie ring catching the light. Somehow the ring, modest and simple as it was, emphasised her beautiful, elegant hands, hands his mental meanders often embarrassed him about what they could do to him.

He plopped into the chair opposite her and they both sipped from their mugs. He waited. Almost from her first day here they'd been as close to a workplace Yin and Yang as he'd imagined possible. Often when he didn't know something, Tori did, and vice versa. And if neither of them had a clue, one of the array of contacts they'd collected between them could usually help out.

They were a great work fit, which was how they'd probably stay, how he knew they should stay. Sadly, there'd never be anything more between them than that. Nothing personal anyway. For sure.

Probably.

Maybe.

He watched Tori suppress a belch and wipe the back of her hand across her lips, ignoring the white napkins he'd placed on the tray. *Yin and Yang*, he thought again, stifling a smile.

'I needed that,' she said, patting the chair next to her.

He moved around to her side of the table as she drew her laptop closer again.

'That screenshot we sent to Kong,' she began, then stopped, screwing up her nose. She looked sideways at him. 'Frank, do I smell as bad as you?'

She wasn't as fresh as usual, that was true, but he hadn't noticed until she mentioned it. He lifted an arm and sniffed. 'We'd better take that shower before anyone rolls in. Showers, I mean ... like you said before,' he added quickly.

She laughed and poked her tongue out. 'Anyway,' she continued, 'as I was saying, I attached a Trojan—'

He jumped out of his seat so suddenly it rolled back and flipped over. 'Are you *mad*? You never said—'

'You never would've agreed.'

He was shouting, something he'd never done with her. 'That's *illegal*, Tori. Not parking-fine illegal ... go-to-prison illegal! Even ignoring that,' he said, slapping his forehead then wincing because he'd hit his ski wound, 'and I can't see why you would, you're toying with one of the most sophisticated telcos on the planet. You don't think Mingmai would have cyber-security strong enough to follow your Trojan's tracks back here, to you … to us … to SIS?' He bent forward glaring at her, his hands gripping the edge of the table.

'Are you finished? I trust you didn't slip into my coffee whatever you tipped into yours,' she said. 'You're mostly right but the teeny bit where you're wrong … Here, see for yourself.' Her eyes were smiling and she wiggled a finger at him to come closer.

Frank raised his hands and looked to the ceiling, as if to say *Why me?* then picked up his chair and moved it back. As he sat, she split her screen into two windows, one a darkened outline of a world map with a riot of fluorescent green lines darting over it, and the other an image of a vault branded *Caribanco* with six golden arrows jabbing at it like they were trying to pierce it.

'My Trojan borrowed Kong's personal passcodes to the internal—'

'*Stole* them!' Frank said. With his last job pre-SIS as MI6's chief 'hacker-whacker', where he ran a team countering cyber-crime and cyber-terror, condoning Tori's actions hardly came naturally.

'Borrowed, stole. Whatever. The thing is that after Kong opened my screenshot, my little worm started digging itself into Mingmai's accounts payable systems where it found—' He went to speak and she touched his arm, continuing on, 'I know what you're going to say. Yes, it did set off a spontaneous back-attack but it never found us … me. Look.'

On the map screen, the green lines were arcing everywhere except Boston. 'They'll never locate us,' she said, with way more confidence than his experience told him was wise. 'This laptop's not connected to SIS's system, I'm using a prepaid network card and I routed to Mingmai and back via two dynamic proxy servers, then through three ...'

He had to admit her precautions were impressive. As she went on, he blinked a few times, trying to think where her Achilles' heel might be. 'The screenshot,' he said. 'They'll detect the code behind it so they'll know it came from you.'

'Nope,' she said, winking. 'When the Trojan heard their cyber attack dogs barking a few nanoseconds away it severed the feed and committed *harakiri*. Trojan? What Trojan? It was never there. At best, the event gets logged as a false alarm and, at worst, a botched hack from God-knows-who but one they successfully repelled.'

'Not so fast. What about the timing of Kong opening your screenshot? The attack started straight after so they'll hone straight in on—'

Tori brushed a strand of hair off her forehead. 'Unless someone fiddled with their server's timestamp to make it look like the alarms went off three seconds *before* Kong received my screenshot. They can hone in as much as they like, Frank, but an email that arrived *after* the attack started won't incite one shred of interest.'

Her self-assuredness still worried him, but she'd done it now so he asked her the obvious.

'The accounts,' she answered, 'recorded eight separate amounts over the years, each one paid to a different firm. And six, totalling well over two billion US dollars, got wired to ...' Tori performed a drum roll on the table, 'one account in one bank. Why, I ask you, would six separate investment banks—if that's what they are—share a single account tucked away in the Cayman Islands inside a bank that—'

'—that no one's ever heard of called Caribanco,' Frank finished for her, pointing to the second window on Tori's screen. He sat mesmerised as the golden arrows bounced off the bank vault image. 'I'm guessing the back-attack started before your Trojan found out if Kong had the access codes to the account?'

She nodded and picked up her mug, swilling the contents around before deciding not to drink the dregs. 'Any ideas?'

Frank stood and walked to the bay window, peering through the thin venetian slats. Tori's discovery could be explained innocently. Caribanco could be no more than a clearing bank to centralise and disburse Mingmai's international payments. What he and Tori needed to know was where the funds went *after* Caribanco. If it was a legitimate destination, fine, however improbable that was. If it was a swindle, the more likely outcome, the kind of swindle mattered. At worst, they'd be kissing goodbye to Project Chant—and its fees—altogether, advising their client to extricate himself from the deal as fast as possible. On the other hand, Frank knew Soti Skylakakis was no innocent himself when it came to accounting 'finesses', so there was also the option of feigning shock at catching Mingmai out, then using it to lever himself into a far better deal. His and Tori's job, he knew, was first to find the facts. After that, they'd lay out the options to their client so he could decide which course to follow.

As Frank twiddled with the venetians' tilt rod, the interior lights of a black SUV came on in the street below, a few doors up from the SIS building. The driver's door opened and a woman stepped out. Frank pulled a few of the slats down and squinted into the darkness. Was that Lucille coming in early? Before he could decide, she got back into her car.

He frowned, checking his watch, then turned around. 'With or without my Rolex, this British sleeve has a few useful tricks up it. But tracing the money after Caribanco will take hours, time we don't have with what we still have to do before we fly to New York this afternoon and—'

'We need to shower, change, eat.'

'Right, and you need some sleep,' he said, covering his mouth as a yawn escaped. Perhaps he needed more than the hour he'd just had himself.

'So what do you suggest we do?' she asked.

'Not *we*.' He reached over to the middle of the boardroom table and hit the green button on the speakerphone.

15

A FLOCK OF VIOLINS AND RECORDERS screeched at them from down the phone line. 'Thatcher,' Frank shouted over the music, 'what about a tune I haven't heard a billion times and which was composed later than 1721?'

Tori rolled her eyes. These two and their obsessions, Thatcher with his Bach and Frank with his Wagner. Surf instrumentals clearly topped both.

'Dear Chowders,' Thatcher yelled over the strings, using the nickname he'd bestowed on Francis Xavier Chaudry when as boys they'd first collided into each other in the dining hall at Eton. 'Thatcher will play the Bwandenburg evewy single time you wake him up at such a fucking widiculous hour!'

Tori tried, as usual, to ignore Thatcher's idiosyncratic R-to-W habit, one Frank had told her his friend had only 'acquired' after slavishly mimicking a young Royal in their Latin class.

She heard the telltale *pshht* of a cork and Frank gave her a look. As if she needed reminding that Thatcher fashioned his entire existence so a chilled bottle of champagne was never more than a finger snap away.

The sparkles splashed into a glass as Thatcher continued, 'Just listen to it burbling ... so lofty, so unearthly, Chowders, just like your heavenly Dr Swyf—'

'I'm on the call, too,' Tori cut in as Frank began laughing.

'Dear, dear girl,' said Thatcher without missing a beat. 'What's it been ... a month ... two perhaps? How Thatcher has missed that quaint antipodean lilt of yours, his nasal hairs twitching as it evokes the pungent, kelpy tang of your wild windswept beaches, your—'

'Thatcher,' said Frank, 'there isn't a single follicle inside your bulbous nose that has ever been remotely close to Australia.'

'And this isn't a social call,' Tori added, nudging Frank to get on with it.

'Are you suggesting that 5.15 am isn't a *normal* time for spur-of-the-moment chitchat?'

For such a notorious hacker-for-hire and purveyor of illicit electronic whizzbangery, Tori thought 5.15 am would be entirely normal, but she didn't want to inflame him so kept her mouth shut. Frank's friend was temperamental at the best of times. 'We need your help, Thatcher. Again.'

Bach's *Brandenburg Concerto No. 4* ceased abruptly and Thatcher's exaggerated upper-class voice carried on, 'A damsel in distress is music enough for Thatcher's subtle, delicate and incredibly refined ears. Is Thatcher to assume, dear Victoria, that you're following up on the same question that perturbed Dr Schönberg but two weeks ago? Is the good Axel also with you?'

Tori and Frank exchanged glances. 'Axel called you?' she asked.

'About what?' said Frank.

In Thatcher's dark profession, revealing confidences was taboo but when they told him about the coma, both his voice and his wall of silence cracked. 'Axel ... he charged Thatcher to make a sweep of the Dark Web ...' He paused as if getting himself together. 'That's the internet's seedy back alleys—'

'We know what the—'

'—to dig up the dirt on a group called *Shi Xiongdi*.'

'Chinese,' said Tori, looking hard at Frank. 'Could it be connected?'

'*Connected*?' asked Thatcher. 'To what?'

'We're working on a project involving a Chinese company that seems to have washed some colossal payments through a Cayman Islands bank. We need to know where the money went after that.'

'Ah! Money trails ... right up Thatcher's alley. The company's name, dates and amounts?'

Tori told him.

'Mingmai? Forget it. They're impregnable, unassailable, an oriental Fort Knox, the very reason why there's a bounty in Thatcher's world for the first person who hacks the CEO's emails and posts them.'

Frank gave Tori an admiring nudge but she ignored it. 'Thatcher, can you chase the money for us or not?'

'If anyone can, Thatcher can.'

'Good. Now, about what you were doing for Axel?'

'Thatcher neither reads nor, for that matter, eats Chinese, so

he had to cut the job short. All he found was that *Shi Xiongdi*
was a family of superheroes from an ancient Chinese myth.'

'Does the name translate into English?' asked Frank.

Tori, who had passable Mandarin, and Thatcher, who didn't,
answered together: 'The Ten Brothers.' As soon as the words
left her mouth Tori continued, 'Thatcher, Frank, that can't be,
can it? Ten Brothers ... Nine Sisters?'

The trio had only recently engaged with the so-called Nine
Sisters, brilliant but extremist environmentalists mutually
pledged to destroy the global economic system. For over a
decade, they'd secretly insinuated themselves into positions of
power and influence to advance their goal. If not for Tori, with
Frank and Thatcher's support, they would've succeeded.

'Axel asked the same question but to find an answer he
needed a hacker fluent in Mandarin so Thatcher had no choice
except to find him one,' he said, his tone begrudging. He added
the hacker's name before Tori could ask.

'Red Scorpion?' Frank let out a low whistle and muted the
phone. The hacker, he told her, was not only Thatcher's fiercest
competitor but for years had been Frank's own *bête noire*, a virtuoso
of the virtual world responsible for some of the most notorious
cyber-attacks on Britain's intelligence and law enforcement
services. He unmuted. 'Can you ask Red if he found anything, if
he gave Axel any information ... and what information?'

Thatcher gave an odd laugh. 'Consider it done. Chowders,
one last thing before you go. Thatcher shares the devastation you
must be feeling over the tragedy that has befallen your people.'

Tori had no idea what Thatcher meant and looked at Frank
questioningly but he shrugged.

'My people? Something's happened in Pakistan?'

'Not those people,' said Thatcher. 'Your pope. He was
assassinated.'

16

RON MADA LET THE RINGING OF his phone ricochet off the hard surfaces in his kitchen as he slid the last of his thirteen pills and capsules down his throat. The ringing was incessant as he placed his glass in the dishwasher and returned the bottles, boxes and blister packs to the drawer, laying them out left to right, large to small. Only then did he pick up the phone, crooking it between his cheek and shoulder as he pushed the drawer closed.

'I'm constipated—' said a voice.

'Excuse me? Is that you Mr Kong?'

'—with your firm. Mr Jin and Mr Skylakakis are trying to conclude their transaction, but your people at SIS insist on getting in our way.'

'Mr Kong, really, I—'

'First it's Schönberg and now it's this new Superwoman of yours who is poking her nose into places—'

'Be assured,' said Mada, pulling the drawer open again and fingering the large red box containing what his doctor called a wonder drug, 'I'll look into it right away.'

'Don't just look, Mada, fix it.'

17

New York City

THE ELEVATOR DOORS SWISHED OPEN ON the cavernous lobby. It was 11.03 pm and Tori and Frank had bolted out of the eighty-seventh floor conference room as soon as the last comma had been debated, the last T carefully crossed and the last page turned. They'd left Kong Feng as well as his Ólympos counterpart and the twenty-five accountants, bankers, lawyers and other corporate executives behind to say their inane goodbyes.

'Eight mind-numbing hours, Frank. How did we stay awake in there?'

He placed a hand on her shoulder as they stepped into the lobby. 'By you commandeering the meeting. Maybe you found your true vocation up there.'

She turned to him. 'With no thanks to your punctuation

fetish. At one stage, I felt like you were giving the room a semi-colonoscopy.'

He chuckled. 'So it's a good thing we dashed off.'

She groaned. As the doors slid closed behind them, Frank's cell phone beeped. 'Please, let it be Thatcher,' she said, glad for the interruption to what Frank apparently saw as amusing banter.

They'd both been waiting since dawn for Frank's hacker friend to dig up information on the Mingmai-Caribanco money trail and find out what Red Scorpion had given Axel.

But Frank huffed when he looked at the screen and passed her the phone. 'No, it's from Peter.' He was the driver who'd picked them up at the airport, checked them in at their hotel and brought them to Wall Street.

'In *this* weather?' she said, reading the text message. 'It's ten below outside … damn him!' She handed back the phone. 'He could have waited for us on the driveway like he was supposed to, but no, we've got to freeze to death walking round the corner to him.'

As they continued toward the exit doors, Tori swung her satchel under her arm and started buttoning her coat, a navy faux fur that looked swankier than its sale price at Macy's would suggest. To an observer, her tan kid leather satchel might have been chichi once, but now its stitching was frayed, its flap patched and its surface pocked with all manner of stains, gouges and scrapes. It would've looked more at home against Frank's scrappy tweed jacket, had he been wearing it. Amazingly, he'd turned up at the airport in an actual suit—until then she hadn't known he owned one—an elegant Italian creation in charcoal wool. True to form, though, he'd ruined the effect with the shabby, red and white ski jacket he'd insisted on zipping over it, making him look more like a candy cane than a fashion plate.

Why, she asked herself for the hundredth time, did a guy with such a deep velvet voice and athletic body—more untouchable than ever now she had Tex—insist on dressing like chaff?

He tailgated her into the revolving doors. 'Still nothing from Thatcher,' she said, shaking her head. She pulled on her hat and gloves.

As if on cue, Frank's phone rang. Staying within the doors, they shuffled back round inside while he answered, spilling out when they returned to the lobby. Frank hung up and pointed to the ceiling. 'A paralegal upstairs. We left without our Chinese visas for tomorrow's flight.'

Despite the crackdowns across China, the three sub-groups of advisers were still flying there. To allay anyone's fears, Kong had videoconferenced Mingmai's global risk consultants into the meeting. According to them, Dandong—the city where Frank and Tori's group was heading—was 'minimal risk' after China cleaned it up a few years back when police killed three Uyghur terrorists in a counter-terrorism raid. Tianjin and Harbin, the other two destinations, were 'low risk'.

'You go back for the visas,' Tori said. 'I'll brave the elements and see if I can get Peter to bring the car round and pick you up.' She stepped back into the revolving doors. As the glass panels began to swing around, she noticed the driveway had plenty of free space, enough for two or three more cars. *Damn you, Peter.* She hiked up her satchel again, thrust her hands in her pockets and strode into the street, squinting against the icy wind.

Three freezing minutes later she rounded the corner, her body bent and shivering, her steps shorter to avoid slipping on the glassy pavement. A pair of headlights flashed at her from the first of two cars further along the street. Shoulders hunched and head down, she rushed to the car as carefully as she could. Just as she was about to snap open the rear door and fling herself inside, Peter jumped out, his arms wide, face smiling. He threw open her door apologising profusely for making her walk. Tori climbed in, waving off his excuses.

Once he'd closed her door, she fiddled with the vents, swivelling them to pump warm air directly at her ice-block of a face. When her teeth stopped chattering and her blood started flowing again, she slipped off her hat, shaking her hair free, took off her gloves and shimmied off her coat. She heaped them all on the seat beside her and put her satchel and phone on top.

She looked up and Peter gave her a reassuring nod via his rear-view mirror before busying himself typing into his GPS, presumably plugging in the address for the hotel.

'Frank will be out shortly,' she said, settling back into her seat. 'Can we zip round to pick him up at the entrance? The driveway's pretty clear now, so we could wait for him there.'

Peter gave her a thumbs up. Then, just as she clicked in her seatbelt the engine of the vehicle behind them revved and roared, its wheels spun and it slammed into the back of them. Amid the shriek of crunching and splitting plastic and metal, Tori jolted forward, her head whipping back against the headrest and the belt cutting across her chest, forcing the air from her lungs.

Like her, Peter was shouting and swearing. He opened his door about to leap out when the other car backed up and rammed them a second time, harder. His door flew out of his hand, bouncing back to slam shut. Clearly deciding against a confrontation, his own engine roared and, wheels spinning, he tore off. Tori was thrust back into her seat again, the other vehicle following close behind, whacking and thumping its front bumper into their rear.

As Peter spun the car around the corner, the wheels screeching and the rear fishtailing on the icy surface, Tori caught the bright red and white of Frank's ski jacket as they hurtled past. She tried to wind down her window to scream to him, but it wouldn't drop. At the last second she saw him look up and judging by his look of horror, he must've seen Tori's face and hands pressed against her window. She fumbled for her phone to call him but the other car rammed into them again. Her phone flew out of her hand onto the floor, her satchel and coat following fast.

Peter took a right into a tight alleyway, knocking trashcans and shopping carts aside, at one point narrowly missing the feet of a terrified homeless person by little more than the word 'Fragile' stamped on the flap of his cardboard shelter.

Looming ahead was a glass storefront. The alley seemed like a dead end but Peter kept barrelling forward at full bore. Tori braced herself and just before they careened into the massive window he yanked on the handbrake, spinning the car left into another laneway until Tori saw, a few car lengths ahead, five hip-high stainless steel vehicle barriers spaced across the width of the road.

Her driver gripped his steering wheel and planted his foot down. From where she was sitting, the Lincoln badge sticking up from the hood lined up with the centre-most pillar, like crosshairs centred on a target.

Peering back through the rear window, Tori saw the second vehicle, a black SUV, take the turn badly, its tail smashing into the store window, raining glass down on the street. But it recovered quickly and began making ground.

Peter's bumper hit the central pole, apparently with such force it snapped, and Tori was catapulted forward, her belt lashing her chest, the jagged stump of steel screaming as the car's undercarriage ripped across it.

Peter's hands were locked onto the wheel as he took a squealing right. Tori saw her phone on the floor light up, barely

hearing the ring. It was Frank and this time his *Glocked Number* 87
joke didn't seem at all funny. She stretched down to pick it up
but Peter took the corner so sharply they were running almost
entirely on the passenger-side wheels, and the phone slid away
from her. Suddenly the car veered sideways. Up ahead a wide-
load truck was pulling a crane onto its trailer. Peter corrected
just in time, cutting in front of the truck and swinging a left to
go the wrong way into a one-way street, swerving between the
oncoming cars and forcing one of them up onto the pavement
to crash into a bus stand.

By now, Tori's phone was completely out of her reach under
the front seat. Hanging another left, with the SUV still tailing
them, Peter slammed his fist on his horn when a young couple,
arm in arm, stepped out. The woman saw him first and yanked
her partner back but not far enough as a loose chunk of Peter's
rear bumper swung out and sliced into her boyfriend's leg. By
the time the man screamed, Peter had sped too far ahead for
Tori to hear him. She sat as square in her seat as she could,
trying to calm herself. The car stank of gasoline and she
guessed, terrified, that the traffic barrier must've punctured the
fuel tank when Peter drove over it.

Suddenly, he slowed as the traffic lights ahead went red. She
turned back to see their pursuers fly past the sobbing couple,
bearing down hard. 'Floor it, floor it,' she shouted, banging on
the back of Peter's headrest. He hit the pedal, ignoring the red
light but aiming the car off the street, toward a warehouse on
the other side of the intersection, its roller door halfway up and
rising. She looked behind again. The SUV was closing in on
them. 'Not in there,' she shrieked. 'Keep going.'

But it was too late. Peter ran the red, missing a Kombi van
coming from his left by a micron, hit the gutter, crunched
his chassis on the pavement ramp, bounced up and into the

warehouse loading dock and squealed to a stop inches from the brick wall ahead of them, a hand's width between the side wall and the driver-side doors. He cut the engine and lights.

This might actually work, Tori thought. She looked over her shoulder and the SUV was only half a block away. She pulled on her door handle but it was locked. 'Peter, unlock my door,' she yelled, but he stayed silent. He was leaning forward … Was he hurt? Had he hit his head on the wheel? 'Are you oka—' she started to say just as the SUV flew into the warehouse beside them and jammed on its brakes, positioned so close she couldn't have opened her right-side door more than an inch even if Peter had managed to unlock it. 'Start her up again and reverse. Peter, reverse!' she yelled. He sat there motionless, in a daze, shocked, unable to move. Sandwiched between the wall and the SUV, there was no escape.

A sliver of moonlight spilled down from a skylight casting a faint glow in the narrow space between the two cars. The SUV cut its engine, and all she could hear was metal creaking as it cooled, her driver's heavy breathing, or maybe it was her own, and what sounded like a trickle of water. A pungent smell … gasoline. The fuel tank was definitely leaking.

'A gun?' she said. 'Peter, have you got a gun?'

He swivelled around and pointed one at her.

18

THATCHER WINCED. MAYBE THERE HAD BEEN too much garlic on the snails he'd cooked, or maybe the *Brandenburg* had finally lost its oomph for him. Whatever the reason, Caribanco's electronic vault doors exasperated him. How could this tropical tiddler of a bank keep him at bay when the doors of a colossus like JPMorgan Chase were open to him at all hours, even when the bank counted on them being closed?

He needed to think, to really think. He turned off the Bach, switching to *Turandot*. But whose *Nessun Dorma* this time ... Plácido's or Luciano's? He flipped a coin, then with Pavarotti's silky tenor lifting him from his funk, he returned to his kitchen. In time with the music, he folded the hand-churned butter into the pastry, his mind conjuring up the sweet, scrumptious aroma when he'd be dolloping his trademark jam over croissants pulled fresh from his oven. He'd been making and eating fig jam for so long that he used it as his hacker handle, the alias he went by in his dark cyber world. Some of his rivals liked to quip that it was an acronym for *fuck I'm good, just ask me*, an entirely boorish notion to Thatcher since, after his genius, humility was his greatest virtue.

As a glob of butter squished out to the side, the tenor soared into *Dilegua, o notte! Tramontate, stelle!* and the eureka moment hit him. Instead of wasting more time trying to bust into the bank, he would simply loiter outside and wait for the garage door to roll up on the armoured trucks as they headed off to deliver Mingmai's cash to its ultimate destination. At that point, he'd lick his fingers, hail a virtual cab and follow.

Pressing his thumb into the pastry, it sunk in with perfect resistance. *Vincerò! Vincerò!* indeed, he smiled, until he saw the flaw in his brainwave. Mingmai had made the payments years ago. The 'trucks' were long gone and, despite his brilliance, his electronic kitbag didn't include a time machine.

Fortunately, he knew where to find the closest thing to one, an organisation which had spent decades recording everyone doing everything everywhere: the National Security Agency. Unknown to the NSA hierarchy, his inside man, known to him as Storm King, guaranteed that their archives were Thatcher's archives.

He knew he should cover the pastry but thinking it wouldn't take long, he slipped into his ops centre to leave instructions for Stormy. He also checked his various drop-boxes. While there was nothing that couldn't wait, one thing was odd: Red Scorpion still hadn't replied to his message about the job for Axel.

19

TORI'S DRIVER SWITCHED ON THE VEHICLE'S interior lights. 'So we can get better acquainted,' he said, the gun apparently giving him the confidence to smile at her. His black eyes were blinking. She assumed he was trying to flush away the sting from the gasoline fumes. Trained to know details were important, she took them in almost automatically. He was a left-hander, judging by how comfortably he was pointing the pistol through the gap between the two front seats. Tori knew Glocks and this was a baby G26, normally perfect for keeping snug in an ankle holster except the magazine jutted down below his pinkie, so it was a fifteen- or seventeen-rounder, quite an arsenal. Mid-twenties, with a thick, broad New Jersey accent, Peter was a redhead like her, but his eyebrows were shaved, a silver stud in the top of his right ear. In the rear-view mirror she could see the back of his head and, behind his ear, a tattoo: +

What was it? A cross? Crosshairs? It was bluish-green ... no, more purplish. The colour stopped mattering when he pulled back the slide to chamber a round.

'Hey, Pete,' Tori said, pasting a grin on her terrified face, forcing herself to stay calm. As she tried to keep him in conversation, her right hand began slowly patting around on the floor for her satchel. 'Are you an Uber driver? A cab driver friend reckons Uber's unsafe. What do you think?'

'Perhaps Uber X ... where X marks the spot, ma'am.' He laughed as he waved the gun.

Tori's fingers found her satchel's handle. 'Do I still owe you a tip from—'

'Lady,' he said. That she wasn't *ma'am* any more might be a bad sign. 'If you don't shut the fuck up,' he continued, 'I'll give you a tip ... from this gun ... in your head.'

Out of the corner of her eye, she caught the other driver's window beginning to roll down, a gun poking through the top.

Peter's eyes and pistol stayed locked on Tori. He didn't know that the other barrel was pointing at him.

20

TORI'S RELIEF STOPPED COLD WHEN THE second pistol swung toward her. *Who are these people? Why are they using me for target practice?* She wasn't going to buckle, not without a struggle, but first she needed to know her enemy. 'Hey, Peter, is this fair ... two men versus one woman?'

'*Four* men,' corrected her driver, proving at least one of the quartet was an idiot.

Her hand slowly pulled her satchel closer. 'Please, Peter, why are you doing this?'

'What is this, fuckin' Twenty Questions?'

She slid her hand over the case and, finding the patch on the flap, she silently peeled it off with a fingernail. 'Peter, can I at least know your name, your surname, I mean?' Careful not to move her arm, she worked her wrist back and forth threading out a long thin strand of fibreglass-reinforced plastic that had stayed coiled inside the flap, dormant until now and undetected by countless airport security systems.

'How about Peter With-A-Gun? Happy?'

She wasn't, especially when the roller doors behind them suddenly started rattling and jerking their way down, bringing more and more gloom into the warehouse. Ludicrously, the sound reminded her of the *ts-ts-tsss-tsss* of the hi-hat cymbal opening the sinister theme from the old TV show *Peter Gunn*.

Peter With-A-Gun's eyes briefly shifted away from her to the doors as they groaned their way down, cutting out the light from the street.

The warehouse was almost black, apart from the light above Peter's head and the slice of moonshine from the skylight shimmering off the SUV's doors.

Tori put her foot over one end of the cable and twisted the other end to lock it tight. 'Can you at least tell me what's going on?' she said, pushing a whine into her voice, wondering if it would be too much to force out a helpless tear or two.

Unseen, she moved her foot to the side then, in one fluid motion, she raised the cable's diamond-tipped point and jabbed it through the gap between the seats, zeroing in on where Peter's heart would be if he had one. His eyes bulged and a gurgle churned in his throat. She yanked the shiv back out, its reverse barbs flaring out and ripping at his organs like a harpoon being pulled out of a shark fighting for its life.

Before his pistol hand had time to drop, she unclicked her seatbelt and pounced, pulling his hand toward her. She locked her fingers around his, twisted his arm to her right and, gritting her teeth, rapid-fired eight bullets into the van, dodging the shards of shattering glass as best she could.

Her first shots shattered the driver's window then the back, two of them missing and spraying sparks off the car body. The cracks hammered her ears and her wrists strained from the unnatural angle she'd had to shoot in. She was ready to duck and dodge but not one of the three men in the other vehicle fired back.

She pried the gun from Peter's hand, watching for the slightest movement or glint from the SUV, but the only flicker came from behind and a moment later a whoosh of flame flared up. The sparks from her strays had ignited the leaking fuel.

Grabbing her coat to shield her face, she twisted round and fired the gun into the rear window six times, making a hexagon. Using her satchel to protect her hand, she punched through the glass and, after wriggling into her coat—for protection not warmth—she slithered through the hole, glass crunching around her.

Flames were already shooting up from between the two vehicles, smoke spewing all around her. A thin sheet of fire shot between her legs from under Peter's car, tearing along a drip line to the roller door. She jumped sideways but her foot splashed in a pool of liquid oozing from under the vehicle. She leapt out of the puddle just before it erupted with a roar and ran for the doors, her head swinging around looking for a fire extinguisher that didn't exist.

She shoved the gun in her pocket and tried to lift the roller door using the chain dangling by its side. It wouldn't budge. Remembering the door had been opening when they entered she realised her driver must have operated it remotely. She scanned the walls for a control knob and, finding one, hit it with her palm. Nothing. Flames leapt above the roof of Peter's car. The gasoline must have run under the SUV since that too was engulfed.

She turned from one side of the rollers to the other, looking for another exit, but the flanks were solid brick. The wall opposite had a door but it was unreachable, blocked by fire. The noise was deafening, with metal cracking and shrieking, glass shattering, a cacophony she hadn't heard since Afghanistan. The sound she was most fearful of—exploding gas tanks—was coming any second.

A red-hot hubcap spun through the smoke and past her head like a ninja star, thwacking into the door. The shutters were quaking ... not just from the hubcap ... someone outside was banging on them. Tori was struggling to breathe, and see. Her eyes were stinging from the smoke and gas fumes, her throat like an overcooked steak.

Two of the car's tyres exploded, spitting a ball of fire toward her along the ground, the flame stopping six inches short of the warehouse door, just close enough that she could see the outline of a hatch. She ran her hands around it until she found the bolt. She yanked at it, but it was stuck, rusted. She pulled, she pushed, tried twisting, but it wouldn't shift. More banging from outside, harder, louder, and someone shouting.

'I can't get out,' she choked, her eyes and throat burning. 'Fire! Fire in here!' she called, then coughed, dry retching as an explosion burst behind her, the noise smacking her eardrums. She turned her head to see the hood of the car rocket into the air, somersault and fall back to cleave itself into the SUV's windscreen, where she hoped the driver was slumped with one or two of her bullets in him.

She dripped with perspiration, both from fear and the intense heat, and realised she was still in her coat, synthetic, a fire hazard. She snatched the gun from the pocket, sloughed off the 'fur' and flung it as far away as she could. She was about to bash at the barrel bolt with the gun when she remembered it was loaded. Rather than release the clip and empty the cartridge, she stood to the side and fired two oblique shots at the latch plate in rapid succession, blowing it away. She yanked the hatch open just as the car's fuel tank exploded behind her, the shock wave buffeting her through the opening. Her arm banged against the rusted metal, ripping her sleeve and forcing her to drop the gun, just as an arm in a red and white sleeve hooked round her waist and carried her into the relative safety of a Manhattan street.

'I always liked that ski jacket,' she told Frank as she passed out in his arms.

21

THATCHER SHOOK HIMSELF AWAKE AND CLIMBED out of his armchair. Buttoning his tux he toddled back into his computing nerve centre, smiling when he saw the third screen from the left was finally flashing confirmation that Storm King was on the Caribanco job. The screen on his far right, however, was worryingly blank. It had been fourteen hours since he'd messaged Red Scorpion, and still nothing.

Red wasn't simply a rival, a competitor for clients, an adversary who he'd been forced to refer Axel to. When Red had beaten him in a phone auction for three bottles of 1955 Bin 95 Grange Hermitage, the pair learned they were neighbours. With few friends who'd appreciate a wine of such class, Red had invited Thatcher over to share a bottle and a meal. Once together, bemoaning the challenges of their 'profession' and the enemies they tended to pick up along the way, they'd downed not one bottle but two. By their fourth dinner, over a 2007 Château d'Esclans Cuvée Garrus Rosé that went perfectly with Thatcher's Wagyu steak tartare, they'd agreed on an elaborate mutual defence protocol: if either failed to respond to a message for more than twenty-four hours, the other could trigger a one-time remote access to their encrypted workplace CCTV and conduct a visual check.

Thatcher had ten hours before he could initiate the protocol. Ten hours for Red to message him with an invitation to dinner or send him a new recipe; anything to let him know everything was okay.

He wiped a finger around the bowl on his desk and sucked the garlic sauce from it. In his mouth, the buttery crust melted like bliss but did nothing to allay his unease.

22

THE NURSE PAUSED AT THE DOOR. 'Do you need anything, Mr Swyft?'

Frank lifted his eyes from Tori, still unconscious, and cracked a tired smile. 'A cup of tea. Is there somewhere I can make one, or buy one?' For almost the entire hour since Tori was admitted, he'd been cooped up with two of New York's finest. They'd given him water and questions and he'd offered the little he knew. A steaming cup of Earl Grey might clear his head, help extract a clue, something, anything that pointed to why Tori had been abducted and almost died.

Frank had shown the police Peter's text message and confessed that when the car sped past him with Tori banging on the window and the SUV ramming it, he'd thought the worst. Who wouldn't? With Peter dodging and swerving so valiantly and the pursuing SUV's lights out, Frank hadn't been able to see its registration plate or even if there was one. He'd run straight onto the road and flagged down a motor cyclist, politely commandeering his bike—'Yes, Officer, I agree that *politely* might be an overstatement'. Then, with no helmet or goggles, the wind slicing into his face and his eyes streaming, he fishtailed around the corners, chasing the two vehicles as best he could until he took one corner too tight. His back wheel had skidded into the kerb and he was thrown off into a stinking mess of garbage bags piled up in an alleyway behind an Italian restaurant. By the time he'd picked off the fish bones, slimy chunks of *vitello alla parmigiana* and a tangle of slimy pasta strips and remounted the bike, the two cars had vanished. He'd revved the engine and accelerated to the corner where they'd turned, but found the road empty. With no traffic around, he'd taken out his cell, pinged Tori's phone to get her location and called 911 before resuming the chase.

When asked, he tapped his phone screen and showed them the app the pair used to track each other's location, struggling to think of an answer if they asked why two professional advisers needed to monitor each other's movements. Fortunately, the cops didn't ask.

What they did ask was, 'Who would want to kidnap Dr Swyft?'

Or me, he added mentally, since he too would have been in the car if he hadn't been called back upstairs. He'd asked himself the same question more times than they'd asked him, and repeatedly he'd shaken his head. He had no idea. None.

Their interrogation was persistent and draining. Quite a few of his answers needed some crafty subtlety to avoid blowing the confidentiality of Project Chant but the fact that the men put up with his squirming showed they knew more about Wall

Street's need to keep secrets than he'd expected. They gave him leeway, neither pressing him for the names of the actual clients involved in the transaction nor what the deal was, apparently satisfied—at least for now—with his vague explanation that he and Tori were 'working on a deal between two big international companies'.

'Why did you separate from Dr Swyft just before the car ride?'

Frank's answer was as vague as he thought he could get away with, worried that if the cops knew they were supposed to be flying to China tomorrow they'd slap his and Tori's names on the No Fly List until they'd concluded their investigation. Ron Mada would kill him if he let that happen. Give their co-advisers at EuropaNational the chance to twist the fee knife and cut SIS right out of the deal? No way.

'A cup of tea?' said the nurse, tapping her cheek with one finger, her recently lipsticked mouth puckering slightly. Blonde and maybe an inch shorter than Frank, Sarah had been in to check on Tori seven or eight times, though after the third visit Frank started wondering who she was really coming in to see. 'There's a hot drinks vending machine in the waiting room,' she said. 'It does real *bad* coffee. Maybe it does tea? Do you want me to ...?' She let the sentence trail off and blinked her lashes at him.

'Er, no, but thanks for the offer. I'll check it out.'

'Well let me know if there's anything else I can help you with, Mr Swyft,' she said as she left the room. To the cops he'd been Chaudry—he had to be—but to the hospital staff he was Tori's next of kin, otherwise they wouldn't have let him stay in the room with her.

He gazed at her for several minutes, not something he would, or could do normally. Suddenly his mouth went dry.

Maybe he *did* need that cuppa, he laughed to himself a little nervously. He leant over to brush a strand of hair out of Tori's eyes and his finger lingered so close to her skin he almost felt the charge from her flesh.

Mercifully, his phone vibrated in his pocket. Mada. 'She awake?'

'No, but they say—'

'Do you hear me caring? Just make sure they fix whatever needs fixing so she's in good enough shape to fly to China tomorrow. Listen to me, Frank, if she's out of action the Golden Greek will flip us for EuropaNational, and our fee—and your bonus—go bye bye. And if she's feeling woozy, tell her she owes it to Axel which, by the way, she does. Lay it on as thick as you have to.'

Frank clenched his fist but held his tongue as Mada continued, 'One more thing ... I've got a bone to pick with you. The cops ... they just left my office and said you sent them. Did you forget Axel's rule about cops, Frank? Wonderful people, do important work, but never to cross our threshold?'

'Sorr—'

'Anyhow, they asked if we'd used that limo company before, which we hadn't. By the way, I got Lucille to phone them and tell them their Patrick or Paul or whatever you said his name was, got killed in that fire.'

'*Peter*,' said Frank, stressing the man's name, the least he could do to honour him. 'I hope she told them how brave he was, trying valiantly to outfox that SUV—'

Tori coughed, a dry hack, and one eye cracked open. She reached for Frank's hand. 'It was Peter who tried to kill me.'

23

AS THE TWO NYPD OFFICERS LEFT Tori's room, she took a straw from the nurse so she could drink from the glass without interfering with the tube up her nose. Her throat was parched and her head throbbed. 'When can I expect this headache to go away?' she asked.

'Soon,' Sarah said, leaning over to check the dressing on Tori's arm and glancing coquettishly at Frank. 'The doc says you'll be out of here by breakfast.' She pressed the gauze back down. 'Apart from this little cut, you're good to go back to work tomorrow if you want to. But meanwhile, it's rest. You too, Mr Swyft,' she added with a smile in her eyes, and pointed to the couch before letting herself out.

Between Sarah, the doctor and the two cops who'd rushed in to take Tori's statement, the hospital room had been a flurry

of activity from the moment she came to. This was only the
second time Tori had been alone with Frank. 'I hate hospitals,
the smell, the *this*,' she swung her uninjured arm around
taking in the drip, the tube, the bed, all of it. 'As for a hospital
breakfast, ugh! There, on the elbow of your jacket,' she said,
waving at Frank's ski jacket hanging on the back of his chair,
'is that pasta? If I'm not careful, they'll scrape it off and dish it
up for me. And, by the way, that thing I said about liking that
jacket? Wasn't me, never happened.'

'Ah, the old Tori is back.'

'And what's with the Mr Swyft thing? Are you Mr Swyft
my adorable husband or Mr Swyft my dutiful brother?'

Frank's eyes went a little glassy and he sucked on his lower
lip, apparently thinking more carefully about her light-hearted
question than she had intended. Seeing his expression, she
suspected she shouldn't have asked and rambled on, 'Judging
from those doey blue eyes the nurse keeps fluttering at you—
it's Sarah, right?—she thinks you're my hot brother, my hot
Pakistani brother by the way, which kind of freaks me out about
her medical observation skills.'

'Stepbrother?'

She shifted on the bed and sat back into her pillows. 'I don't
hate hospitals, I detest them.'

'That's clear.'

What wasn't clear was who Peter With-A-Gun was and why
he and his confederates had planned to kill Tori. She'd given
the cops as detailed a sketch of him as she could remember:
a mid-twenties Jersey boy, a redheaded left-hander, eyebrows
shaved, dark almost black eyes, a silver stud at the top of his
right ear and the cross-shaped tattoo.

There was one thing she'd held back … that she killed the
bastards before they managed to kill her. She told Frank the

truth as soon as she'd woken, and he agreed she should leave that bit out or she'd run the risk of a quadruple manslaughter charge. If the cops worked it out after forensics eventually made it into the warehouse, she could always claim shock-induced memory loss.

'Frank,' she said, patting his hand, 'if you hadn't gone back for the visas—'

'We'd probably be in adjoining hospital beds. Though given what happened, it does look like you were their target.'

'But why? And why the elaborate crash-bang scenario? Why not just—'

'To get you off guard? So you'd think your driver was a good guy until they had you secreted away.' He turned his hand over and held hers, tightly. 'Thank heavens I saw you banging like a nutter on that window.'

'Yet you still managed to find time for a plate of *pasta con crap*.' She laughed as she slipped her hand out of his and went to pinch her nose, forgetting there was a tube in it.

'The cops won't know for days who those men are … were. The steel rafters in the roof were already sagging when the ambulance and fire trucks arrived. It'll be daybreak before they can even start assessing the building to see if it's safe enough for forensics to go in. My guess,' he added, 'is there won't be much of those car wrecks left for them to sift through.'

'All they need is one tooth. And what about Zell?' said Tori. 'Why had he changed our account to this new car company? You don't think that's a little too coincidental?'

Dandong, China

WHEN TORI AND FRANK CHECKED INTO the hotel with the due diligence team and their pilots, the only room not ready was the one whose occupant had spent the previous day in hospital and almost the entire flight asleep. Frank, fussing over her, offered her his room.

'Enough, already. I'm fine,' said Tori. 'The doctors gave me the all clear and, if you didn't notice, I got seven straight hours' sleep on the *Batplane*, my only sedatives being your constant fretting and *their* partying.' She pointed to the huddle of people near the lifts. The beauty of Mada letting all seven of the team take Axel's Gulfstream G650 to Dandong was that it was non-stop from New York. That way, with the lawyers and accountants billing their client by the hour, even for travelling time, Skylakakis could hardly object to Mada charging him a fortune for the flight. The other fourteen who'd come to China had flown commercial to Beijing, eight heading from there to two assembly factories in Tianjin, and the rest to Harbin where Mingmai manufactured semiconductors.

'The only thing that almost *stopped* me flying here was Zell virtually ordering me to, the prick,' Tori said, scowling. 'I fixed him though. I told him I was coming for Axel and definitely not for …' She stopped when she saw Frank smiling. 'What's so funny?'

He shrugged, still smiling. 'Just glad to see you back in fighting form.'

She shook her head. 'I'm going to stretch my legs while I'm waiting for my room.' She pulled her coat around her and started for the doors. 'Come or don't come, it's up to you.'

With Frank constantly complaining about the cold, the walk only lasted ten minutes. His ski jacket had been plenty warm in Whistler and New York but, he griped aloud, the wind chill sweeping up off the icy Yalu River nearby felt like his skin was being stabbed by a thousand knives. 'I-It's easy f-for you to laugh in th-that fancy-shmancy new coat,' he said, his teeth chattering as he pushed back the door into the lobby.

She rubbed her cheek against the high collar of navy softness she'd bought after leaving the hospital. The blend of alpaca and silk with a quilted down lining had a lot going for it, especially with her other coat a shrivel of black plastic melted on the floor of a smouldering warehouse. She clutched at Frank's elbow. 'Come on,' she said, pushing him forward and trotting him across the pink marble lobby to the menswear store. 'I'm giving you three tasks: go in, try on, buy.' She shoved him through the entranceway. 'Something long. And no tweed,' she said with a shudder, thankful he'd left the old rag in Boston.

'That's five things.'

'And a solid colour,' she added. 'Dark. Black or navy. On second thoughts, not navy or people will think we're twins.'

'Do you think?'

'Well, your smitten nurse Sarah did. Anyhow, get yourself coated up and come model it for me.' She inclined her head to a cafe raised on a platform in the centre of the atrium. 'There'll be a reward awaiting you … steaming hot coffee and a warm body … *Yours*, I mean,' she added.

She turned to walk away but Frank tapped her shoulder and passed her a glasses case. 'It's FrensLens 2.0. Soti sent it care of our hotel in New York and I forgot I'd put it in my pocket. So while I buy, you spy.'

They'd trialled one of their client's FrensLens products before, the prototype. In essence, it was a camera, a web crawler and a brain all squeezed inside a pair of frames. Augmented as opposed to virtual reality, with some artificial intelligence thrown in. The camera was an eye-tracker and wherever she looked, whatever she saw, the inbuilt OFTOR app—for optical, facial, text and object recognition—would instantly scan the web to identify that person, building or object, sift out the key details and show them on the display. If she'd been wearing these babies when Peter With-A-Gun had greeted her outside his car, she thought, maybe she would have known not to get in.

She found a table at the cafe, slipped her coat over the back of her chair and sat down, wondering for the umpteenth time who Peter and his accomplices were, what they'd wanted and who'd employed them. If whoever it was had tried once, maybe they'd try again. The police theory was corporate espionage dressed up as a mugging; a gang aiming to steal a Wall Streeter's laptop so they could make a stock market killing with whatever insider information was hidden on its hard drive. The theory didn't gel with Tori since she knew more than the police, but whoever they'd been she was glad to get far away, and China was plenty far.

She flipped the FrensLens case open and the physical changes Skylakakis's team had worked into the new model jumped out at her. This time, the frames were clear plastic, less obtrusive, and so thin they looked almost flimsy. She weighed them in her hand then put them on, so light there was no way they'd keep slipping down her nose like the last pair.

A new feature was the earbud. She inserted it into her left ear and a 'Quick Tour' started up, the audio clear yet so soft that if someone started speaking to her it would be easy to tune it out. Another improvement was the text display. As she swung her head around, the words subtly changed colour so they were legible against any background. It came with a translator too, though she had to stifle a laugh when she glanced over to check on Frank and it named the menswear store *Ho's for Men*.

It wasn't yet lunchtime but with the air wafting the sweetness of dumplings and the grease of fried rice, she did feel peckish. Tori spoke Mandarin passably but couldn't read a word, so she hoped either FrensLens would do the trick or the menu would be tourist-friendly. She was close. It was a variety of English, labelling one dish *Spicy Cold Children* and another *God Swimming in Sweet and Sour Sauce*. As for drinks, she couldn't see herself asking for a large *Cock* or a *Cock Light*. Deciding food could wait until the welcome banquet tonight, she focused her FrensLens on some of the other customers in the cafe, noting the names of four government officials as well as a businesswoman from Shanghai. The internet didn't seem as useless here as she'd expected. Soti would be pleased.

At the next table, a portly man slouched over a large blue folder was the 'Party Secretary of Chaoyang Prefecture', and the woman reeling back from whatever he was snarling at her was

'Chairman of the People's Political Consultative Conference of Liaoning Province'. Tori pricked up her ears but either her Mandarin was rusty or he was speaking in a dialect, though when FrensLens kicked in she wished it hadn't. What he was saying would've steamed up a mirror in a brothel. As she turned her eyes away, the voice in her ear faded out.

25

New York City

WHEN THATCHER INITIATED THE PROTOCOL, THE sweat was pouring off him. He'd been checking Red's drop-box every ten minutes for the past hour. Nothing. Nothing. Nothing. Sitting at his terminal, he loosened his tie and removed his jacket, almost felonies for a man of such punctilious formality.

The procedure was multi-stage and elaborate, taking him a further thirty minutes to work through. Once he was in, his screen split itself into two windows, each slowly rotating through a cycle of six of the twelve cameras Red had installed inside and outside the rooftop apartment. Thatcher had visited four, no five times now and Red had shown him all the cameras, two hidden in cornices, two behind false cupboards, three behind artworks, one in the welcome lights at the front entrance, others on the roof deck and inside the elevator, one in the kitchen, and even one in the bathroom. As with Thatcher's own set-up, the cameras were all in real-time. In their world, recording their activities was not an option. If anyone hacked them and accessed recordings, say, of conversations with clients or subcontractors, the fortunes, even the freedom, of some very well-known individuals would be put at risk, let alone the trashing of their own reputations and businesses.

As Thatcher scanned the cameras, he prickled with discomfort, rubbing the back of his neck, undoing more shirt buttons, even taking his cufflinks out and rolling up his sleeves like his butcher father from Nottingham used to do at work. Room after room, all seemed normal, except for Red's absence.

With one camera to go, the one in Red's kitchen, Thatcher's fingers could barely hold his mouse without slipping. If something was wrong, this was where he'd find out. The sink was empty. No dishes piled up. He rubbed his hands on his pants, hesitating before he moved the cursor. Using the pan-tilt-zoom control, he pivoted the camera until it caught the edge of the countertop. Holding his breath, he panned along the bench and there it was ... a single can on the otherwise barren expanse of black granite, like a lighthouse on a rocky promontory. He zoomed in to read the label, praying it would say *escargots*, candied chestnuts, *foie gras*, caviar or truffle juice, anything except what it did say ... *confit de canard*, Red's hand-picked signal, a beacon of distress that only Thatcher would recognise.

At first, he couldn't admit it, busying himself by re-examining each screen, one by one, panning and zooming and tilting to explore every corner of every room as best he could, looking for a hint, any hint, that Red was okay. But he found nothing. He turned on the sound in case Red was locked in a closet and calling out, but all he could hear was the hum of air conditioning, no cries, no groans, no whimpers. He was about to call out through his mic but caught himself, astonished he could even think of doing something so dumb, potentially alerting the assailants—if there were any—to his electronic visitation rights, and giving them a reason to come for him too.

Thatcher wanted to scream, to bang on his walls, kick at his furniture, smash his chandeliers. *Who needs chandeliers anyway?* he rebuked himself. If he had any hair, he would've torn it out by the roots. He ripped off his shirt and pulled his T over his head, a shocking act for a man like him.

The reserve and poise he'd cultivated for years collapsed around him like a ruined soufflé, revealing the weak, insecure loner he'd always feared he was, finally forced to accept that while most people lived their lives wrapped inside the warm fabric of friendship, he had spun barely a thread.

He switched off the sound and wept for Red and at the harrowing epiphany that no one would run to comfort him and now, with Red gone, no one ever would.

Eventually he slipped a handkerchief from his pocket, antique white lace the dealer assured him had belonged to Queen Victoria. He unfolded it and dabbed at his eyes, straightening his back, like Her Majesty would have, and reminding himself that he didn't have friends because he had no need for them.

26

Dandong

TORI'S CELL PHONE RANG INSIDE HER coat pocket. Perplexed, she leant over to extract it. It was a burner phone, one of several she'd picked up when she'd bought her coat, and the only person who knew its number was currently sliding his arms into the sleeves of yet another coat just across the lobby.

'Tori … is that you?'

Her skin felt instantly warm and a smile curved her lips. She hadn't called Tex after the attack. She'd wanted to. She'd picked up the phone several times, at the hospital, on the plane, but each time she stopped. She didn't want to lie to him, to hold back the full story which, given his job, she knew she'd have to. *Hang on.* Her brow creased into a frown. 'How did you get this number?'

A hint of guilt stifled his attempt at a laugh. 'I heard about the attack on you and—'

First he had a phone number that had only just come into existence and now he knew about the attack. 'Tex, I'm thrilled to hear your voice, really,' and she meant it, 'but this is a new burner and I'm kind of uncomfortable that you—'

'That I know the number? Tori, I'm not stalking you.'

'Then how do you explain—'

'You worked at the Agency, so you know that with my level of security clearance I'm, er, obliged to, well, you know, log the names of anyone I'm … who I'm—'

'*Fucking*? Is that the word you're trying to avoid?' She quickly glanced around the cafe, but the only person whose mouth was open was busy stuffing it with a tangle of noodles.

'Please … I'm really sorry, but yes, I have to clear the names of any … of *the* woman I'm sincerely hoping to have a relationsh—Damn, even that sounds … Tori, look, the simple truth is … Come on, surely you understand.'

She did, but that didn't mean she had to like it. 'So some pimply-faced kid in an NSA basement gets to see my name on Narthex Carter's latest-piece-of-tail list and sets whatever dogs he has with him down there to track me down?'

'That's how the NYPD report got tagged to me, and when I read it I freaked and—'

'And this number?'

Like a shrug at the end of a long day, Tex's voice drooped. 'When your phone—your old cell—rang out, I called the hospital … They said you'd been discharged, so I re-read the police report, saw that the cell had been destroyed in the fire and I, well, yes, I admit to pulling a favour or two. Like I said, I'm sorry. Kind of.'

She looked over at Frank, shrugging out of yet another coat.

Frank! Of course. Tex would've found Frank's cell number in the police report, then Basement Boy would've geolocated it and searched for any other phone pinging the same cell towers at the same times.

It was a massive invasion of privacy, yet she was torn. Tex obviously cared enough about her to risk his job by misusing government resources. 'Hey,' she said, trying to squeeze a smile into her voice, 'I'm sorry too, for biting off your head. It's probably plane-drain,' she added, aware it could also be PTSD but hoping jet lag was more likely.

'I *thought* the echoes sounded like you were out of the country.'

'Didn't Basement Boy tell you I'm in China?' she asked, thinking he'd have a chuckle.

Instead he swore, and with unexpected gravity added, 'China? They told me you were in New York when they did the … you know, whatever it is they do.'

Immediately the problem hit her. She hadn't plugged the encryption device onto her phone—Frank had it with him—and she'd let Tex put his foot in it by mentioning not only his security clearance but her past with the CIA, and then she'd made it even worse jibing him about the NSA, both agencies that China's infamous spectrum sniffers would be trained to detect.

Tori shifted the conversation back to the incident in New York. Tex listened without interruption, so quiet that after a few minutes Tori had to ask if he was still there. Even when she finished he didn't speak, as if absorbing her account, agonising over how it had affected her or, worse, comparing it against what he'd read, perhaps speculating from her tone that she'd left crucial bits out of both accounts, which was true.

Tori's own experience with interrogation had taught her the value of silence, creating voids for a suspect's guilt to fill. She bit her lip and let the space hang until Tex was ready to end it himself.

When he did, he changed the topic to China's security crackdowns, suggesting that his concern was more than just their call being spied on. She told him that experts had assessed the trip at 'minimal risk' before she'd left New York, but that didn't satisfy him. His speech became guarded and cryptic, to make it difficult for any snoops listening in. 'The reaction's explicable in an Einsteinian way'—*in theory* was how she interpreted that—'though its span is too catholic'—*too undiscriminating?*—'and its tactics absent the Biblical character Ruth'—*ruthless*. That word weighed on her. Tortuously, he conveyed how non-Uyghur dissenters were also being swept up, including, he said, 'some of our Ross Gellers and Phoebe Buffays'—two characters she recalled from *Friends*, the old TV sitcom ... *US spies?*—and, more ominously adding that 'even Oscar winners should be careful'. Tori struggled with that until she realised he meant the Presidential Medal she'd received a few weeks earlier, that it might put a target on her own back. The second one in as many days.

Tori wasn't someone who let paranoia rule her life, but she knew ignoring such a direct heads up from someone like Tex— informed *and* well intentioned—would be high risk, despite what the experts had said. It wouldn't take much effort to be extra careful. With their client's counterparty a sophisticated telecoms company itself, she and Frank had already brought a collection of anti-spook devices with them, like the encryption device. Actually using them would be a good start, she thought, berating herself.

As Tex continued to circle the subjects of detentions and mass arrests, Tori zigzagged her eyes around the cafe then the lobby. The way Tex had heard it, there was havoc in the streets, although she'd seen no sign of it earlier. Inside the hotel, everything seemed equally normal, with people drinking and eating, chatting, perusing menus or business reports, porters tearing across the marble pushing trolleys laden with luggage, two lines of guests waiting at the reception desk to check in or out, guests sitting on the lounges, some tapping their feet waiting for latecomers, Frank over in the store *still* trying on coats.

She was about to tell Tex not to worry when, on her left, a shadow loomed up. Bracing her body but not wanting to appear startled, she turned her head slowly toward it. That face! Reflexively, her fists clenched under the table. Struggling to keep her expression deadpan, to bare no emotion, no alarm, this was shaping up as one of those moments of truth dreaded by every field operative. The moment when a quarry stumbled over an officer's true identity, blowing their cover, turning their life to shit.

It was worse if, like Tori, you'd left the game and had no extraction team, the only cavalry nearby being theirs.

It was the Iranian. A man she hadn't seen for years. A man she'd hoped she'd never see again. At the mere sight of his pitiless glower and the wiry shoe-brush under his nose, her pulse was breakneck.

According to FrensLens, Dr Masoud Mahdi Akhtar was 'once' the chief of Iran's atomic energy organisation, but his current role was 'unknown'.

'*You!*' he shouted at Tori, his finger stabbing the air as he closed in on her table, paying no heed to the chair in his way as he kicked it aside.

Tex was still talking but she'd stopped listening. Without saying a word, she hung up on him.

Her skin crawled. China was no place to be accused of spying in, least of all now.

27

Washington, DC

THE SECRETARY OF HOMELAND SECURITY PAUSED mid-drawl, and the Situation Room fell silent apart from the sound of bodies chafing against the high-backed leather seats which, by 11 pm, had ceased being remotely comfortable. Narthex blinked and looked up. Seeing President Diaz fixing him with a blunt glare and the entire committee gawking at him, he instantly blushed.

The secretary had been updating the National Security Council on the unfolding domestic crisis. In the last hour alone, a mosque in Tampa, Florida, had been bombed, a Muslim day-care centre in Little Rock, Arkansas, set alight and, in downtown Chicago, a clutch of Asian tourists were gunned down at a sidewalk Halal food cart, all seven of them 'Pope-slayin' A-rabs', as the deranged, racist shooter had shrieked.

Sitting opposite Narthex, the president's chief of staff lifted one of the empty cans of Diet Coke lined up in front of him and rapped it against the desk blotter three times.

'Dr Carter,' said President Diaz, 'perhaps you'd rather be somewhere else?'

Tori was who he wished was elsewhere. Despite the mayhem here at home, the riots across Europe and Latin America and the hundreds of deaths in Africa, his mind couldn't help cycling through the reports of the turmoil in China. He'd tried calling Tori back several times, but she'd either switched off the phone or thrown it away. Or worse.

28

Boston

LOLLING BACK INTO THE DEEP-BUTTONED LEATHER of his Chesterfield, Ron Mada wiggled his small feet on the coffee table like hand puppets in his silk socks, careful not to disturb the long column of ash teetering at the end of his cigar. Smouldering, it drooped closer and closer to the lilies on his necktie.

His spirits rose as if he suddenly wore wings. He closed his eyes and took a long, exquisite drag. The smoke, thick and hot and spicy, filled his lungs and for the first time in days he felt lighter, as if his burdens had lifted.

Exhaling, the smoke searing his eyes as they opened, he kicked the reality of the syringe off the table onto the floor.

Fuck Kong and fuck Swyft, he said to no one but himself. *And fuck me.*

29

Dandong

WHY WAS THE EX-HEAD OF IRAN'S nuclear agency here, *here* in a godforsaken Chinese city that until a few days ago Tori had never even heard of? And how did he recognise her after the doses of dazzle she'd given him that night in Tehran?

FrensLens gave her none of those answers but did tell her he'd lost his job in 2015, soon after the mullahs did their nuclear deal with President Obama. After that he'd become a ghost.

'You!' he repeated, even louder.

Her mind sped through her options. She no longer had the cable or the satchel. She rotated the ring on her pinkie, then thinking fast she picked up a chopstick from the table, winding her fingers around it, her thumb at the base, and twisting it upwards. But just as quickly she put it down. Killing him in public let alone in China was a very bad idea. Nervously, she glanced over at the clothing store to see if Frank had noticed but he was behind a mountain of coats.

'*You!*' Masoud screeched even louder. He was so close she thought she felt the spittle fly from his mouth. Her body coiled, primed.

Then he bypassed her table. Had he changed his mind at the last minute, deciding he was done with her, that she was filth, untouchable? Was he trying to disorient her, about to spin around and confront her?

Tense, she watched, and waited. His back to her, he raised his arm. She braced for him to swing around and swipe at her but, no, he was signalling to someone, getting help, maybe backup. Someone to arrest her?

She looked in the direction of his wave to where a lone man was striding across the lobby toward him, purposeful but not urgent. Hadn't she seen him before? The pulse in her temples was pounding.

Media photos? The in-flight magazine. Was this Jin Yu? The man approaching had the same thick black hair, narrow eyes, thin mouth and the wide shoulders that looked unusual for a Chinese.

It *was* Jin Yu. Thank you FrensLens.

Asif hadn't been shouting *You!* It was *Yu!* He was calling the famously inscrutable billionaire by his given name as if they were long-lost pals which, when Jin Yu reached the cafe, they appeared to be, with Asif slapping his back. Or were they? She detected a stiffness in Jin's response.

No one had mentioned Jin Yu was going to be in Dandong. He wasn't scheduled to be in any of their meetings or factory visits. He wasn't on the list for the banquet tonight. What was

Mingmai's founder and CEO doing in this shallow backwater of his surging empire?

As the Iranian guided Jin back toward his table, Tori buried her head in a menu, sneaking her eyes over the top, entranced by the scowl that rippled over Jin's lips as he sat.

She and FrensLens were too far away to hear the conversation, but the new model made a valiant attempt at reading their lips. 'My dear, Mas...d,' said Jin Yu. 'Kong sends y... his b... and I am personally gratef... you are h... to help g... our prog...'

Asif smiled through clenched teeth.

As Tori mulled over the feigned cordiality, pondering what *both* Jin Yu and Asif were doing here—surely Asif wasn't involved in Project Chant?—Frank came loping toward her across the lobby like a Great Dane returning a ball to its mistress, a calf-length black fur flapping behind him like a tail.

Another twenty feet and he'd draw attention to both himself and to her, giving the Iranian another opportunity to recognise her and tell Jin, a sure-fire way she'd end up on a spying charge even if, on this trip, she hadn't done any.

She swept up her things and quit the table, the menu fluttering to the floor. Frank was still prancing forward, as oblivious to the situation he was creating as the dead fox she was disgusted to see around his neck. Tori held out her palms trying to get him to chill, but he threw his coat wide open and was about to twirl around in his best imitation of a male supermodel when Tori yanked his arm and pulled him away.

'Hey, what about that promise of a warm body and steaming coffee?' he pouted, only half joking, and looking over his shoulder back into the cafe.

'What about your *not* steaming coat? How many animals got skinned alive to make that thing?'

'How could you even think …? It's mohair! They comb it out to look like fur. That coffee?'

'Like the body, not happening,' she said, moving her hand to the small of his back to steer him away from the cafe and toward reception to get her key.

'Tori, what's—'

'Walk. Don't look back. And no speaks.'

30

FRANK LIFTED THE MINIATURE JAMMER OFF the desk to show Tori. She nodded, seeing three of the four lights flashing green, then he dialled. The phone rang out three times before they got through. Tori expected a 'Bwandenburg' but instead all they heard was, 'Can't you people take no answer for an answer?'

Normally Thatcher's tone was petulant verging on hubristic, but this was a funk, a state Tori felt she had more of a monopoly on right now, having first escaped a bunch of thugs wanting to blow her brains out, and just now seeing a ghost who threatened to drag her past into her present. It was only 11.30 pm in New York so what was Thatcher's problem?

'It's me,' said Frank. 'I'm with Tori. We're finally in China and we need—'

'Is this line secure … Yes, good,' said Thatcher, meaning that the encryption pack Frank had set up was doing its job at both ends. He sucked in a breath. 'While you've been in the air, I've been sitting here … I can't keep this to myself any longer … Oh my God, Frank, Tori, something terrible has happened.'

Usually, Thatcher's histrionics were no more significant than another person's 'hello', but Tori could tell this was different, and serious. Never once had she heard Thatcher speak in the first person, and she knew from Frank that the last *I* or *me* or *my* he'd ever heard leave Thatcher's lips was on the day they left Eton.

'It's Red.'

'*Wed*?' Tori whispered to Frank, confused. 'He's freaking out because someone's getting married?'

Frank glanced at her and put a finger to his lips. 'What's red? You haven't developed another allergy, have you? It's not truffles, is it?' Frank looked horrified. 'You've not become—'

'Arrgh! Frank, no. Red Scorpion is missing,' Thatcher blubbered, 'and I don't know for how long.'

'What about the police?' said Tori. 'What do they—' A knock at the door cut her question short. She froze.

She hadn't called room service and wasn't expecting anyone else. Maybe Asif *had* recognised her. She imagined him outside the door, snickering behind his moustache and pushing a cadre of secret police forward, one of them yanking her by the hair into the corridor, Tori Swyft never to be seen again. She leant over the phone. 'Thatcher, someone's at the door. If it's who I think it might be, I'm in huge trouble.'

'Who would that be?' he said.

'His name is Akhtar, Dr Masoud Akhtar,' she said and spelled it out. 'He's an Iranian official, a *former* official, who I, er, came into contact with in Tehran a few years ago in, ah, well, compromising circumstances, for him I mean. I saw him downstairs just now, meeting with the CEO of Mingmai but I don't know if he saw me.'

'Thatcher will go on mute but will record everything, in case we need evidence.'

Tori ran to the bathroom where, in a matter of seconds, she ripped off her top, wet her hair under the tap, wrapped herself in one of the fluffy white robes hanging on the door hook and came back out. She signalled to Frank to hide in the bathroom. When he was out of sight, she looked through the peephole then swung open the door, pretending to rub her hair with a hand towel. 'Yes?' she barked like a typical hotel guest sick of housekeeping habitually checking minibars only after she'd just gone to the toilet, was taking a shower or a nap.

The woman from housekeeping stepped back, her hand quivering so much the card key she was holding could have doubled as a fan. A man stepped up beside her. 'Turndown?' he asked, his crooked smile revealing two missing teeth on his left side. His arms hung bowed, his biceps enlarged, and his hands, Tori noticed, had thick veins crisscrossing the backs while the palms were more calloused than those of someone who spent his days folding back top sheets and popping chocolates on pillows.

'*Bu yao, xiexie,*' Tori politely declined, slowly bowing. She lowered her head but not her eyes, giving the man an icy stare until he turned away. She closed the door, pressing it shut with her back, waiting for her heart rate to slow.

'What hotel does turndown before lunchtime?' she said, loud enough for Thatcher to hear, 'let alone sends two people, one scared to death and the other a Mr Muscles?'

Tori swung around and put an eye to the peephole, then reopened the door a crack and peered through. 'They're halfway to the elevators, not even pretending to offer service to other rooms. Frank,' she said closing the door again, 'you wanted proof I'm not being paranoid? That was it.'

'We'll get to that,' said Frank coming back into the room. 'But first ... the cops, Thatcher, what do they say about Red?'

'Nothing. They don't know yet. I've ... *Thatcher's* only just discovered this.' He explained what he'd found via CCTV and how he couldn't call the authorities until he'd first been to sanitise Red's computers.

Tori knew Frank was 'handling' Thatcher, which he did better than anyone, but given their own problems—her problems—this was taking too long. 'If you don't mind me changing the subject,' she said, now genuinely drying her hair with the hand towel.

Frank silenced her with a look and took over. 'Thatcher, we're so, so sorry to hear what you're going through, but we were actually calling you out of our own desperation.'

Thatcher's voice suddenly turned cold. 'If it's about this Akhtar chap, that's one thing, but if it's about Caribanco, that would be extremely disappointing.'

Frank had made plain to Tori many times that his friend saw himself as an artiste, utterly despising pressure and clients hassling him.

'You misjudge me,' said Frank, flapping his hand in the air as if he'd just pulled it from a fire and mouthing *I told you so.* 'As you witnessed, Tori's more than a little worried about Dr Akhtar but—' he paused to check the jammer was still working, '—with the internet restricted *and* state monitored, we can't check him out ourselves.'

Tori knew Frank's approach would pique Thatcher's interest but she didn't expect him to laugh.

'To be honest, that Tori finds herself in this pickle is rather wonderful ... Oh heavens, that does sound heartless. Apologies, dear lady. Thatcher is relieved to be of service, to get his mind off ... What you've asked won't take long, and it'll help Thatcher think straighter about Red. And about Cariban—' He was cut short by another very loud knock at the hotel door. 'Thatcher will record again.'

Tori crept up to the door and looked out the peephole. She turned and shrugged at Frank who had already slipped back into the bathroom, his head poking out. When she waved him back and he disappeared, she tightened the belt on her robe and opened the door.

This time it was a bellman with a billowing spray of mauve, white and blue flowers. 'For Dr Swyft, from Mr Jin Yu.' The porter bowed, bending so low his hair fell forward.

'Hydrangeas! How beautiful, and unexpected,' she said, genuinely touched. But as she reached to take the vase she suddenly faltered and the muscles in her stomach cramped. Where his hair had flopped away from his ear there was a tattoo ... a blue cross. 'Thank you,' she said, gritting her teeth, her hands shaking so much she almost dropped the vase when he handed it to her. She stepped back and closed the door with her foot, leaning against the doorjamb for support. 'Take these will you?' she said to Frank as he came out of the bathroom.

He picked up the jammer from the table and waved it at her. The fourth light was now flashing, a red one. They didn't know who was responsible for the first three sets of ears on them, but this one was clearly Mingmai. What wasn't clear was whether it was 'normal' corporate espionage or if Asif had spoken to Jin about her.

She nodded at Frank and pulled out the card sticking out of the flowers. 'What a dear, dear man Mr Jin is,' she said, forcing as much delight as the tightness in her throat allowed. 'And Frank, some great news. The note says he is here in Dandong.

Isn't that just a completely grand surprise?' she said wondering if either of the Old Etonians would think her stilted language the slightest bit odd. 'And even more exciting, he's joining us at tonight's welcome banquet.'

Eventually, the fourth light turned green. 'Bug's off,' said Tori for Thatcher's benefit. 'Gentlemen, we could be in really, *really* deep shit here.'

'You got that from a bug in a bouquet? Thatcher heard what you said about the Iranian and your Mr Mingmai but, Tori, you're in China. If no one is bugging you, it's because you're dead.'

'It's not the bug,' she said, trying to stop herself from shaking. 'It's the tattoo.'

31

THERE WAS NO PORTION, LIMB OR internal organ of a bird's miserable life that was off limits in Mingmai's evening banquet. The latest 'delicacy' Tori had been served slipped from her chopsticks. She'd pecked at local treats in many countries, but she was really struggling with the duck embryo boiled live and served in its eggshell.

She picked up the slimy morsel from the splattered white tablecloth as a waiter placed the next dish, a platter of gelatinous greenish-brown globs, in front of them ... 'thousand-year-old egg yolks' apparently. A second waiter was delivering a plate of 'phoenix talons', scrawny chicken feet that looked more like a street urchin had scooped up an armful of twigs, dumped them on a tray and poured a can of engine oil over them.

Jin Yu, who'd seated himself between Tori and Frank, reached across her, picked up one of the 'talons' with his fingers and dropped it on her plate. 'In my village we use these,' he said, wiggling his fingers then grabbing another foot. His mouth wide, he lowered the foot in whole, web, toes and claws. He chewed and sucked noisily at it then slid the foot out, bones intact but as devoid of meat as if they'd been dipped into a flesh-eating acid bath. He pointed the bone at her plate and smiled. 'Try them my way,' he said, winking, then he slurped one of the 'eggs' into his mouth.

Tori's stomach gurgled and pitched, a wave of nausea rising to her throat. She coughed into her fist and pushed back her chair. 'Thank you,' she said, only just managing to suppress her stomach's urge to contract violently, 'but the powder room calls.' She turned and almost ran from the room.

AS TORI HEADED back, the two waiters crossed her path, one rushing toward the kitchen with the barely-touched platters of eggs and feet raised aloft and the other flying in the opposite direction brandishing a roast baby pig impaled on a long steel skewer. Arriving at the table as the waiter presented the piglet's head to Jin, she watched the server slide it off the spike onto a platter on a side table, sharpen a knife from his scabbard and begin slicing. Tori almost expected to hear the animal squealing.

'Many Westerners,' said Jin, standing to pull out her seat for her, 'find our traditional fare a little exotic or perhaps … what is the word? … gross. So,' he pushed in her chair, 'it pleases me when a woman of the world like you is not only willing to try our dishes but, if I am not mistaken, enjoy them.'

She smiled, still a little green, and sat. Food aside, the evening was delightful. Jin was hospitable, solicitous, even funny at times, his every gesture thoughtful and attentive as he told her about his upbringing, his charity work and his pleasure in dealing with Skylakakis on the merger.

The fact his bouquet had been bugged was, as Thatcher had told her, normal for China. At least Jin had sent her flowers.

The one sour note in her mind was the lingering question of Asif's presence in Dandong, a topic she couldn't risk asking her host about, despite his charm.

Suddenly, Jin scraped his chair back on the tiled floor and stood, startling Tori. 'I'm so sorry, Dr Swyft,' he said, a calming hand on her shoulder. 'You're about to meet someone very special.'

Asif? She didn't feel calm. She felt ill again.

Without explaining, Jin swung to the right and dropped into a squat, his arms reaching out. 'Come to *baba*,' he said in Mandarin, his eyes aglow, shooting arrows of love to the cute little boy who had just entered the room.

Five, perhaps six years old and dressed in a neatly pressed blue and white sailor's suit, the boy released his nanny's hand and ran to Jin, wrapping his arms around him.

They hugged for a full minute, then Jin, his face beaming, pulled back. 'My son, please introduce yourself to Dr Swyft,' he said in English, glancing at Frank. 'She is your father's most honoured guest.' Tori felt flattered, but was intrigued why Jin singled her out when Frank and the other five who'd flown over were also at the table.

The boy wriggled out of his father's embrace and stood as straight and still as he could. 'Felicitations and a hale and hearty evening, Dr Swyft,' he said in an English even plummier than Frank's. The boy removed his sailor's hat with one hand and gave a slight bow. 'I wish to introduce myself. I am Jin Mingli,' he said, straightening up again. 'It is with great pleasure that I share my father's welcome. Perhaps if you visit Beijing, we can extend our family's hospitality to you there also. We have an indoor swimming pool ... and it has a slippery slide,' he said, glowing with a smile almost as wide as his eyes.

The father kissed his son and patted his behind. 'Now, off to bed,' he said. 'We will read in the morning, as usual.'

'Sir,' said the little sailor, refitting his hat and saluting Jin, 'may I have some pizza tonight, like in the Hollywood movies?' He licked his lips and glanced at his nanny as if she'd already told him he would be treading on risky ground.

'Sweet Mingli, you have already eaten, have you not?'

The boy dropped his head. 'It is true. But I have done all my homework. So please? Pretty please?'

The fact he could whinge in his second language was a feat that Tori saw had impressed Frank too, judging by his lifted eyebrow.

The boy's father held him at arms length and gazed into his eyes as if drinking in memories to keep for another time. 'Not tonight, my dearest. Go, have a good night's sleep. Tomorrow ... it's another day.'

Mingli kissed his father's cheek then turned and scooted back to his nanny.

As they sat down, Tori saw a tear welling in Jin's eye.

'He's a beautiful boy,' she said, thinking how lucky Mingli was to have this remarkably devoted father. Tori had never met a child as courteous and articulate, especially in a second language nor, frankly, a father comfortable enough to manifest such unconditional love for a child ... except perhaps her own.

'His mother, Dr Swyft, we were so in love. You know, she coloured her hair red, like yours.' His hand rose up, as if he wanted to touch her hair, but he stopped himself and looked away from her. 'I called her my *pen huo qi*, my flamethrower. She was an extraordinary, spirited woman, a handful if I'm truthful, not remotely the obedient Chinese wife.' Jin looked wistful. 'She died giving birth to our boy. He is all I have left of her.'

AT THEIR FLOOR, Frank got out of the elevator first, leaving Tori to say her goodbyes. He tapped his foot, waiting for her to exit, for the elevator to close and take Jin to the penthouse. The ride up had been awkward, the businessman fussing over Tori while she tossed her hair back as if revelling in his attention. And now, as he watched them, this final straw. Jin kissed her hand goodnight and, no, she wasn't going to … she did, she fluttered her eyelashes at him like a swooning schoolgirl.

Tori stepped out of the elevator and as the pair walked silently down the corridor to her room, Frank glanced at her. The Tori he knew didn't swoon, not at a man. At a reef or a wave, for sure, but at a man? Never. Maybe she'd got some dust in her eye. She knew as well as he did that flirting with the boss of the other side was a terrible idea; far, far worse than hooking up with a work colleague, a prospect he already knew was remote.

He pulled out the jammer as she opened her door. Four green lights. 'Let's find out what Thatcher's got for us,' Frank said, re-reading the text he'd received from Thatcher during dinner, asking them to call him.

Thatcher got straight to the point. 'About your Jin-san's money trail—'

'He's Chinese, not Japanese,' Frank snapped at him. He saw Tori's look of surprise since he usually treated Thatcher with kid gloves. But damn it, he was sick of Thatcher's blasé witlessness about anything non-British—apart from food, wine and music—especially tonight, with all the subtle signs Frank had picked up that pointed to Tori's Saint Jin Yu being a bigot ... how the man had wiped his hand on his napkin straight after shaking Frank's ... how he'd stopped taking food from a platter once Frank's hands or chopsticks had touched it ... and in the elevator, kissing Tori's hand and not even nodding goodbye to him.

The truth was Frank hadn't picked up on any of the signals until he'd seen Jin look at Tori with those aching, dreamy eyes of his, that hand that went to caress her hair ... an instant when Frank felt suddenly weak, empty, wounded. He knew he couldn't compete with a billionaire.

Thatcher went on, unperturbed. 'Frank, Thatcher can't care less what brand of oriental Mr Jin is. This call is simply to let you know you can expect the information on Caribanco by the time you're having breakfast ... at the latest by dinner tomorrow.'

'That's great, thank you,' said Tori, smiling as she pulled a petal off one of Jin's hydrangeas.

32

Sydney

WITH A SUMMER EXPLOSION OF WILD oranges, pinks and startling crimsons, last night's sunset had promised Sydney that this new day would be longer and warmer, the air lighter and clearer, the harbour an aquatic Arcadia.

Whenever Prime Minister Olivia Ryan was in residence at Kirribilli House, her pre-dawn security detail split itself over two inflatables, jet tenders that burbled away as the water lapped at the rocks below. She lowered herself into her kayak, its white gelcoat grey in the meagre light, and launched away from the steps.

This wasn't simply exercise for Olivia; she was genuinely thrilled at the spectacle of the Emerald City yawning and stretching awake. Nothing was more exhilarating than the swoosh of a paddle against the hush of dawn, the prickle of salt in her nostrils, the tickle of the splashes clinging to the hairs on her arms like silver sequins. This was her time; forty long, glorious minutes with no one to talk to, no reports to read, no phone calls to take, when she could clear her head to make room for whatever would confront her that day.

And today she'd be starting with her Cabinet's National Security Committee, hearing security agency ASIO's latest on the rapidly unfolding RUA crisis. Had her people done enough? Had the state governments done enough? She hoped so but 5.40 am wasn't the time to worry about that, not when she could see the sun's eye peeking over the headlands, its fingers uncoiling, ready to reach out and fire its first shower of light into the sky.

For the rest of the world, it was Sydney's New Year's Eve that was legendary, but for Olivia Ryan the city's sunrises, prosaic in their regularity, were transcendent.

With a few minutes to go before the sun would scatter its first specks of gold dust over the harbour, and ten minutes before the ferry rush started, the water was grey and serene. Overhead a drift of seagulls floated on the breeze. On the water, apart from the two security tenders ready to shadow her, were three pelicans, no four, she noted, as one loped through the air, wings outstretched, its ungainly feet splaying out to skid its heels across the surface for its watery touchdown.

What a morning, she thought, falling into a rhythm from the first pull of her paddle. The tenders kept far enough away on either side and slightly back so they gave her no wash and no noise. It was as if they weren't there.

Leaning into each stroke, she cut a path from Kirribilli Point straight across Neutral Bay toward Kurraba Point, heading directly into the first glimmers of the rising sun, tilting her head slightly so the brim of her cap would shield her eyes. With enough crow's-feet etched into her face already—*smile lines* her dear old dad called them—she wasn't going to squint any more than she had to.

HIGH ABOVE THE triangle of vessels, a small orb skulked unseen, its grey, meshed surface so matte it reflected not a spark of light nor attracted a single curious eye. Unnoticed, it rotated and twisted as the prime minister rowed, fine-tuning its aim to account for distance and momentum. Then, once in position, it shot out a single puff of spray that quickly dissolved into the dawn.

THE PRIME MINISTER loved the daybreak, crisp as lettuce, the tang of salt on her tongue. But today ... She sniffed at the air and strangely, it was more milky than salty, like yoghurt. She wondered if she'd spilled some of her Yakult and glanced down at what little of her T-shirt she could see under her life vest.

Her strokes slowed, though she couldn't fathom why. Her senses dulled. It felt like she was forcing her paddles through clotted cream. Her arms were seizing up, her eyes growing heavy, her head lolling on her neck. Her breath ...

As her paddle slipped silently from her hands, the last thing she heard was a kookaburra chuckling at her from the foreshore.

33

THE DRONE'S GPS MEASURED THE KILL as 5,388 miles away, a distance no projectile on the planet could cover with such pinpoint accuracy. The video feed coming back over SATCOM was as sharp as ever, letting the assassin enjoy the very moment when the life sputtered out of the prime minister's eyes.

Terror was art, to be practised, honed, refined. The traditional methods Islamist terrorists used—suicide belts, nail bombs, IEDs, Molotov cocktails, stabbings, kidnappings, beheadings, storming embassies, even hijacking planes—they fuelled terror, but they were messy and often needed tens if not hundreds of martyrs. And so much could go wrong. Yes, death by drone wasn't half as dramatic or exhilarating as pressing a button to blow yourself up, slicing a knife across an infidel woman's throat, or putting a pistol into a man's mouth, feeling the recoil and smelling the burning bones and flesh. But drones were efficient, they were clean and they could be operated by two people: the courier to deliver, assemble, arm and site it close but not too close to the target, and the artiste thousands of miles away, fingers poised and ready to drive the joystick. Drones didn't get cold feet at the last minute, destroying months of planning. They left no spent bullet casings for ballistics to test, no fingerprints to forget to wipe off, no footprints, no tyre tracks, no body parts or flecks of DNA for forensics to swab.

Most of all, RUA's drones offered the group not only an instant global recognition, but the prospect of a terrifying momentum as the assassinations started rolling out. After the pope and the prime minister, no world leader would feel safe anywhere, anytime. And they shouldn't.

Before Rome, no one knew of RUA's existence. Instantly, the world saw RUA as humanity's greatest scourge. They were wrong of course. By the time RUA's short wave of terror had finished, those who survived would understand, and they would be grateful.

The one downside of drones was that, without blood, the hits didn't feel like deaths. The assassin picked up the letter opener and pressed the point hard into the back of one hand, skin tingling, a satisfying drizzle oozing onto the tip. Licking the blade, the warm coppery redness tasted almost piquant against the cold titanium. *Allah is truly in the details.*

But there was one more task before breakfast. Even at this early hour, heads immediately started popping into the ten tiles on the computer screen, two whose shoulders often bore the insignia of China's highest ranked generals, one whose face was almost as recognisable as the giant portrait in Tiananmen

Square and several whose influence was more effective due to their faces not being known at all.

'It is done. *Fuxing!*' the assassin cried, the others immediately flinging their hands high to chant the full catchcry in unison: '*Fuxing Tao! Fuxing Tao!*'

34

Dandong

FRANK AND TORI REACHED THE END of their third and last factory visit, a chip fabrication facility on one of the Yalu River's hundreds of islands. The Mingmai reps stood in a line before the exit door, holding the due diligence team's coats out for them, one of them clutching a box with all the phones, tablets and other mobile devices they'd been precluded from taking with them into the sterile cleanrooms.

Jin Yu hadn't appeared at all that day, not at breakfast nor on any of the visits. For Frank, it was good riddance but Tori was apparently keen to thank him for being such a thoughtful host at dinner, despite the food. She checked with one of the Mingmai meeters and greeters, but he had no idea where Jin was. 'We ask, Dr Swyft, but this information not given to us. Very sorry.'

With Tori so obviously falling for Jin's charm, Frank had been biting his tongue about Jin's prejudice even though it had been weighing on him all day. He couldn't hold back any longer and took Tori aside. 'Does something seem odd about Jin to you?'

'What do you mean? Frank ... you're not jealous are you?'

She said it jokingly, but he turned his head away from her. 'Jin's worked you, Tori. Beguiled you. It's all in front of your face and you're not seeing it.' The instant the words were out of his mouth, he regretted them.

When she gripped his shoulder, he tried to stop himself shaking so she wouldn't know how worked up he was. 'Frank, yes, the man is charming, magnetic even, but I'm not about to ...'

'Tori, just ... be careful okay?' *And your Mr Wonderful is also a racist*, though he kept that thought to himself. He removed his hairnet, paper slippers and lab coat, swapping them for his overcoat and grabbing his cell phone and tablet from the box.

Maybe he'd gone too far, almost making a scene here, in public. It wasn't like him. Maybe Tori was right, maybe he was jealous of Jin.

Sensing he should change the subject, he dropped his devices into his coat pockets then pressed the fabric up against his face, brushing his skin against its satiny softness. 'Maybe my past love of tweed was ill-advised,' he said. 'Apart from the price. Did I tell you that this little number cost me as much as NASA spent to get a man to walk on the moon?'

Tori's frown relaxed into a smile as she took her own coat and phone. 'You don't actually believe that moon landing hogwash, do you? When I was a CIA trainee, they brought Neil Armstrong in to give us a tour of the film studio set. It's still there, in the basement at Langley.' Frank helped her slip her arms into the sleeves. 'Incredible, if you think about it,' she said. 'A few bulky uniforms and helmets, some scatterings of sand and rock glued onto a trampoline for him to bounce around on, and *boom*, Uncle Sam spooks the Soviets.'

'Come on, the ferry's waiting for us,' said Frank, not entirely sure she was joking. Through the exit door window, a feathery snowfall was being buffeted by a sprightly breeze and, beyond it, only a thin rim of sun hugged the horizon. 'Gloves,' he said to Tori as he pulled out his own.

The head Mingmai chaperone, also rugged up, pushed the door open and a smattering of snow blew in with the chill. 'It eleven below freezing. We walk quick to ferry then at mainland take minibus to hotel. You back hotel before dark.' She squinted outside then swept the white powder aside with her foot. 'Maybe after dark.'

The group had arrived at the plant via a different door. This one opened onto a vast, flat, empty space, almost as big as a stadium. Like a sports field, there were long white lines—snow in this case—which marked out large rectangles of black, wet asphalt.

A ten-foot cyclone wire fence topped with razor wire surrounded the entire area, the chain link dotted with fluoro yellow signs showing images of skulls, crossbones and lightning bolts. Many of the characters on the signs were rounded, more circular than Chinese. 'Is that Korean?' Frank asked their escort.

The woman nodded at the same time as Tori, adding, 'Island belong North Korea. Mingmai rent. Good deal. Jin *xiansheng* and Kong *xiansheng*, they very smart.' She fluttered her lashes at Frank, but her eyes were looking elsewhere.

'Bizarre,' he whispered to Tori as he fixed his cap to his head.

'That Mingmai rents this from the Norks?'

'The snow lines,' he pointed.

Their guide saw him and smiled, though he detected a tic under her eye. 'Water pipes under surface,' she said. 'For heating ... for factory.'

Tori and Frank stole a glance at each other. If there were hot pipes below, the scene would've been reversed. It would've been the large sweeps of asphalt that were covered in snow, not the 'pipes'.

'And why such a daunting fence—' Frank started.

'Check out the river,' Tori whispered, 'over there.'

He followed her eyes to where the jagged ice caked the water save for a lone, perfectly straight crack. The wide grey furrow scored directly across the river from the bluff below the outer edge of the electric fence to a low-slung structure on the North Korean side that looked like a jetty.

As they filed through the exit door, Frank heard a message beep from inside Tori's coat pocket. She stopped ahead of him and shoved her hand in to pull out her phone. They stepped back inside the door and she tugged off her glove with her teeth to read the message then passed it to Frank, her hand covering her mouth.

His first glance told him enough. It was from her 'friend' in Washington, the Tex she'd met in Hawaii. First Jin and now him. She'd mentioned this Tex fellow casually a couple of times, in retrospect too casually. Was Frank the only man on Tori's outer? He read Tex's message:

Australian PM died AM Sydney time. Initially believed heart attack but RUA video just claimed responsibility. VCS, take care. PLEASE.

VCS? Victoria Caitlin Swyft. If this Tex chap knew Tori's middle name, he definitely wasn't just a whirl on the waves.

Frank looked up to see Tori wiping a sleeve over her eyes. *Idiot*, he scolded himself. She wasn't upset about Tex, it was her prime minister. She'd raved about her over a midnight beer a couple of months ago. What had Tori said? *High above the trash tip of politics ... a beacon of cultural harmony.* Coming from the archly cynical Dr Swyft that was quite an endorsement.

Why, he wondered, would RUA kill an Australian prime minister let alone one like her? He could see the insane logic that led them to assassinate a pope ... an intractable fixation on the Crusades, a warped view that justice meant eternal payback for ancient wrongs real and perceived, a centuries-long contempt for Rome. But assassinating an Australian prime minister? It made no sense to him.

Nor did Tori being with this Tex fellow. Or Jin.

35

B Y THE TIME THEY'D LEFT THE ferry and were aboard the minibus back to the hotel, Dandong was already aglow: headlights, brake lights, lamplights, multi-storey buildings lit up as if a frenzied street artist had pencilled in hundreds of outlines with a lightsaber instead of a spray can. For Tori, it was a visual onslaught. Neons flashed, arrows pointed. If light made a noise, she thought, Dandong was ear-splitting, even louder when compared to the dead air across the river, in North Korea, where it looked to her like a mortician had zipped a black body bag over everything in sight.

She and Frank had been quietly debating RUA's motives when he managed to turn up a transcript of the latest kill video on his tablet.

'It was logical after all,' he said, 'assuming you have as warped a world view as they do. They picked her because Australia is—and I'm quoting—*part of the Crusader coalition with Rome, Russia, Europe and the Great Satan.*'

Hardly an original notion, thought Tori, wondering why it hadn't occurred to either of them earlier. 'Is that a list? A hit list?'

Another message bleeped, this time on Frank's phone. He pulled it up and started chuckling. Tori, keen for anything to lighten her mood, leant over and looked at the screen:

The awesome talent of Brandenburg's greatest aficionado impatiently awaits.

BACK IN HER room, after a fresh sweep for bugs—finding a new one in the light above her sofa—they encrypted then sat on the sofa and dialled. 'Is that Thatcher the Great?' said Frank.

'Finally, Chowders, an acknowledgement. But hold your standing ovation until you hear the performance which, like all good stories, is in three acts: Act One presents the Caribanco money trail, Act Two introduces Dr Masoud Akhtar and Act Three takes us around Akhtar's love nest.'

Tori put her hand over the phone. 'I hope he's not going to read the entire script to us.'

'To begin,' said Thatcher, and they heard him cracking his knuckles. 'Act One, where Thatcher raises the curtain on the Mingmai money after it left Caribanco.'

'At last,' Tori whispered to Frank.

'To cut a long trail so short that it belies the efforts Thatcher went to, almost all of it went to a bank in Pyongyang.'

Frank repeated the name of the North Korean capital slowly, as if he was chewing on the same implications that were filling Tori's head.

The amount Thatcher had traced there totalled just short of US$2 billion. 'You do know that sending funds into North Korea breaches international sanctions?'

This wasn't remotely what Tori had expected. She muted the phone and looked at Frank. 'If Kong has simply been window-dressing their financial accounts, that'd be one thing. For most clients, it'd kill the deal stone dead. But Soti Skylakakis ... I'm guessing he'd get us to confront Kong and force Mingmai to adjust the numbers in his favour. But this ... This is way different ... Funding the Norks ...' She started to get up but sat back down. She needed the full picture. Unmuting the phone, she said, 'Thatcher, give us Acts Two and Three.'

'The play's stakes rise as your Persian prince vacates his role—'

'I told *you* that,' Tori said.

'Well Thatcher confirmed it, but did you know that after he left his employ in Iran, his passport shows—'

'How did you access that?' she asked, impressed but not expecting an answer.

And Thatcher didn't give her one. 'Your Dr Akhtar swiftly became a fond and furtive frequent flyer ...' He paused, but getting no reaction to his alliterative flair, continued, 'spending considerable time in such tourist fleshpots as North Korea as well as Yemen and Syria, with periodic visits to China.'

'All places a nuclear expert might find his skills in demand,' said Frank.

'But he's also taken a shine to London,' said Thatcher, 'where he regularly recharges his batteries in a sumptuous suite overlooking the Tower ... Do you know that high-rise hotel at the Shard, Chowders? And do you remember Scrimpy ... from Eton? The blond blighter who couldn't keep his wandering hands off the young Lord You-Know-Who?'

Scwimpy? mouthed Tori. *You actually know someone called Scwimpy?*

'What about him?' said Frank, pulling on his shirt cuffs as if Thatcher was taking him back to places he would have preferred forgotten.

'Unlike present company, Frank, Scrimpy took our Eton cultivation to great heights, literally ... to the thirty-fifth floor of the Shard, where he is the hotel's night manager, a short-lived role if you ask Thatcher ... loose lips and all that.'

'Go on.'

'Dr Akhtar's room charges are always billed back to his employer. Would one of you fine folk like to take a stab at whom that might be?'

'Thatcher,' said Tori, exasperated. 'Can you just—' She was stopped by a knock at the door.

'At last,' said Thatcher, as if he'd been expecting the interruption.

'What now?' said Tori, getting up. 'Another bugged bouquet ... a turndown with TV cameras? Thatcher—'

'Yes, yes. Recording.'

Leaving Frank on the sofa, she pasted a smile on her face and swung the door wide open. 'Hello-o-o.' The fake sweetness dripped from her tongue like honey off a spoon on a hot afternoon. 'Champagne? How utterly delightful.' She waved the waiter in. 'Over there, on that table.' As soon as he'd popped the bottle, poured out two flutes, bowed and left, Tori started swirling her hand in the ice bucket. Frank got up to take his glass and sat back on the couch.

'Dear Tori, if you're doing what Thatcher thinks you're doing, don't bother. Those fine peaky bubbles are courtesy of yours truly, charged to your room of course, to toast the genius you are in the midst of rediscovering.'

'Thatcher!'

'Doesn't a bottle of Dom Pérignon buy a man some leeway?'

'Thatcher!'

His sigh through the phone sounded like a windstorm of disappointment but he quickly got over it. 'For the past two years Dr Akhtar's employer has been Mingmai and, hold the toast till you hear what comes next, his hotel bills are marked for the personal attention of a Mr Kong Feng, or should Thatcher say Kong *xiansheng*? You may now go ahead and toast.'

Instead, Tori dropped back into an armchair as she mulled over what she'd just heard. 'Kong,' she said, remembering how uncomfortable Jin seemed when the Iranian collared him in the cafe. 'Why has Kong got Mingmai embroiled with Iran's former top nuclear brain and bureaucrat?'

'Yours truly is putting the pieces together for you, but,' said Thatcher, 'with Mingmai's two billion dollars, those belligerent fruitcakes in Pyongyang could buy a lot of nukes, perhaps concealing them underground on a certain Mingmai island—'

Uncharacteristically, Frank swore.

'The F-word, Chowders? From you! Goodness. If you're contemplating any more, you might hold onto them until after you see Act Three.'

'Don't you mean *hear*?'

'Thatcher said *see*, old friend, but a mid-performance *hear, hear* would indeed be most welcome.'

Tori reached for the champagne. Suddenly, she needed a drink.

36

TIME-LAPSE SATELLITE IMAGES WERE A GREAT way to see how places changed over time. But, the remoter a location was, the skimpier the public archives, unless you were Thatcher and could redefine the word *public* at will. With access to virtually every geomap repository in existence, government, private or public, Thatcher had been checking out the visual histories of the three Dandong sites Frank and Tori had been inspecting.

Tori blanched. 'You've been tracking us?' she said, panicked that she'd unwittingly helped Thatcher violate the confidentiality of Project Chant. Telling him about Mingmai was one thing, but if the deal itself leaked out, Mada and their client, not to mention the securities regulators, would hang her.

'Thatcher remains your humble servant,' he said as if conducting surveillance on his friends was as objectionable as slightly overbrewing a pot of tea. 'Before you get overly excited at Thatcher's, er, diligence, perhaps allow yourselves to feast on a pictorial chronicle of the changes made over time to the last site you visited today.' He switched the phone call to video and as he started flipping them through a slide show of aerial shots that various satellites had taken of the island, Tori transferred the call to her tablet and placed the bigger screen face up on the desk. She and Frank huddled over it, watching what looked like a jerky silent movie of the island's last ten years. For the first six there were hardly any changes at all apart from the seasons, just a vast market garden scattered with indeterminate vegetation, chicken roosts and duck ponds.

'Wait,' she said at a frame date-stamped four years ago. 'Stop there and zoom in.' The garden had gone, indeed almost the entire surface of the island had gone, replaced by a huge open-cut excavation rimmed by a surface hardly wider than two of the six concrete trucks lined up around it.

'That hole is about 350 feet deep,' said Thatcher after telling them he'd set spatial recognition software onto the image. 'That's deep enough to bury a standing Statue of Liberty, including her torch. The perimeter spans around 300 feet by 300 feet which is roughly the size of the outfield at Yankee Stadium or, for you Chowders, all the tennis courts at Wimbledon jammed together.'

'This was ages before Mingmai leased the land,' said Tori, remembering what the lawyer travelling with them had told her. She'd asked him for the lease details after hearing the island was rented from North Korea.

'But it was after the money started flowing out of Caribanco,' said Thatcher.

Frank drummed his fingers on the desk. 'And then eventually, Mingmai builds a factory on top, a plant no one would normally bother visiting—'

'Unless,' said Thatcher, 'they were the finicky advisers tyre-kicking the assets for some giant transaction they won't even reveal to their humble confidant.'

Tori looked at Frank in horror. 'Thatcher, you've sniffed out what the deal we're working on is, haven't you?'

'The only question, dear Tori, is whether Thatcher would make a bigger killing by buying Ólympos shares or going short Mingmai, or both.'

Frank almost shouted, 'That's illeg—'

'Chowders, Chowders. Sip on some of those fine bubbles to calm yourself down. If Thatcher *was* going to insider trade, do you think he'd tell you?'

'Frank,' said Tori, hoping Thatcher had in truth been joking about trading, 'maybe the pit isn't Mingmai's at all. Maybe North Korea dug it out and covered it over before Mingmai leased the surface and they've been spying on Mingmai ever since.'

'If *someone* at Mingmai,' said Frank, 'has swung Pyongyang two billion dollars, why would the Norks want … *need* to steal the same company's intellectual property?'

'You're right, they wouldn't.'

'But if Mingmai is in cahoots with North Korea,' he said, 'and has been helping them fund and conceal a cache of intercontinental ballistic missiles—'

Tori didn't listen to the end of his sentence, seesawing her hands like something was in the balance. 'Whatever's going on here, we need to find out.'

'That won't be a cakewalk,' said Thatcher. 'For starters, laying your hands on visitors' permits for a cavern that no one knows exists will be—'

Tori looked at Frank, her eyes sombre. 'Did anything I said suggest we'll be seeking permission?'

37

Lake Otradnoye, Russia

NORMALLY, ROMAN IVAN RASKALOV WAS AS unaware of his skin, lips, fingers and toes as he was of his breathing or his pulse or his famously unkempt Einstein mop of hair. Not today. Each hair follicle was a nail hammering into his scalp, cold steel piercing every pore of his exposed upper torso, and other parts of his body were so frozen he feared they'd snap off, if they hadn't already.

Apart from pain, the intense, shuddering, brain-freezing pain, the single thought the man who Russians embraced as *Myslitel*—The Thinker—could repeat to himself was that he was utterly mad ... mad he'd surrendered his professorship at Lomonosov Moscow State University to accept the president's 'gift' of the prime ministership ... and madder still to accompany that even madder shirtless, horseback-riding bastard on what he'd casually portrayed as his latest outdoor *adventure*. In northwestern Russia. In fucking winter. The president's last infantile idiocy of the day had been to coax Raskalov into rat-tat-tatting the PP-2000 9mm submachine gun he'd handed him that morning into the ice sheet over Lake Otradnoye, daring him to perforate a circle and plunge through into the glacial water ... as if he were a penguin, or a crazy Finn. Raskalov was shivering so much he didn't know which was worse.

What His Macho-Excellency refused to accept about Russia, winters and normal human bodies was that they got cold, freezing, sub-fucking-freezing.

When Raskalov was offered the prime ministership, he'd not for a second counted on blowing his mornings—or his health—tromping around desolate parts of the country that probably hadn't seen a human, ever, and for good reason.

Back in his saddle on the shore, dripping, juddering, he pushed his glasses higher up his nose and looked around. Where was his maniac boss now anyway? Raskalov's eyes scoured the snow for hoof marks and the bushes for broken twigs.

Even if the prime minister looked up, he wouldn't have noticed the orb hovering high above his head. The matte gunmetal-grey mesh surface rendered it invisible against the towering canopy of leaves and branches, its hum so low the hiss of leaves in the breeze muffled it.

38

Washington, DC

NARTHEX STOOD ON THE CARPET OF the Oval Office, the Presidential Seal under his feet. 'Madam President, Prime Minister Raskalov's death ... I'm afraid it's—'

'Not RUA again?' She turned back from the window. 'Surely not.' Isabel Diaz slowly lifted her gaze to the plaster medallion of the Seal in the ceiling, took a deep breath and ran her fingers, both hands, through her hair.

It was a weird thing for Narthex to think, given the circumstances and where they were both standing, but he couldn't help wondering how much longer her hair would stay black. Remarkably, only a few greys had come through after almost a year in office. Seven, he'd counted when he started

161

here and it was still seven. He'd made it a game—a ridiculous one, he knew—watching out for them.

He stepped forward, presenting her with his tablet.

'Another video?' she said, her shoulders slumping. She dropped herself back into her chair and watched it.

'Roman.' She spoke the Russian's name slowly, reverently, before her mouth twisted as if she was biting back a sigh.

As far as Narthex knew, she'd only met Raskalov once, quite recently. It was after he'd flown to New York City to address the UN Security Council debate on Turkey, something she'd been certain he didn't have his heart in. Over their light supper at the White House—just the two of them—they must have connected, judging from the goodbyes Narthex wasn't supposed to have seen.

'How did those bastards … How was he killed?'

Narthex put his hand on the back of the visitor's chair beside her desk. He waited till Isabel nodded then sat with his tablet on his lap. 'Some kind of toxin, ma'am. But like with the two prior hits—the pope, Prime Minister Ryan—we can't work out how they deliver it, so everyone's speculating … calling it *death by drone*. That said, this hit was way out in the Russian wilderness—near the Arctic Circle—and the killer could've been hiding behind a crop of trees, some rocks, whatever.'

Isabel looked across the room to the portrait of George Washington. 'If that was the case, Narthex, there'd be tracks. Were there any tracks?'

'Er, no, ma'am. None the Russians are telling us about. General Vaddern's convinced RUA's using drones. If we knew what they looked like, we'd have a better chance of tracking them down. The challenge is that—'

'I know,' said the president. 'Whoever's editing the videos blurs or edits out any frame with a reflective surface ... in the pope's video, the windows, water glasses, mirrors.'

'Right, and in this one the ice sheets, and even Roman's ... Dr Raskalov's glasses were retouched. All they let us see is the victim, alive one minute then a toxin shoots out at them from off-camera and next minute they're dead.'

'Nothing from the toxicologists?'

He shook his head. 'The best hope had been the experts who the Vatican called in from the Mayo Clinic, but so far they've drawn a blank.'

Isabel swung her chair back round to the window. Was she hiding a tear? Narthex waited for one of her hands to rise to her face but they both remained on the arms of her chair, limp.

Was she looking outside ... for a drone ... wondering if she was next? It wouldn't surprise him. While the national capital had been a No Drone Zone for years, some had still got through—dumb tourists, and one even dumber reporter who quickly became a former journalist. After RUA burst onto the scene, the Secret Service had doubled human surveillance around the White House then doubled it again, trebled the security cameras and tightened the motion detectors.

'Narthex, my trip to Cuba—'

'In three days, ma'am.'

'I know that. Do you think we should defer it until—'

He nodded. Keeping a tight security perimeter around and *above* her was going to be hard enough in DC. Cuba would be a far riskier proposition.

'But if I don't go, then RUA wins, don't ...' She let the sentence trail off but swivelled back, this time her eyes fierce. 'What's the latest on the riots?'

He picked up his tablet, swiped the screen and opened up the flash notes his team had stayed up all night working on. 'The homeland first,' he said. The initial spate of hate riots, bombings and lootings had quietened down since the president had stood shoulder to shoulder between America's most popular Catholic leader—the man who could well be the next pope—and the head of the Center for Islamic Pluralism, the three of them united in binding the nation together, asking everyone to keep their guns holstered or, as the cardinal said, 'to turn our nation's anger to prayer'.

Narthex then covered Australia which, so far, had been surprisingly free from any serious violence, apart from what the media had described as a few 'nutters'. A key success factor, he told her, was the immediate solidarity of Muslim community leaders, their outrage at what they called RUA's 'monstrous atrocity'.

'And Russia?'

'The president is due to address the nation,' he looked at his watch, 'in an hour.' *Presumably not from horseback*, a thought Narthex wisely kept to himself.

His report also addressed Latin America, Europe and Africa but when he got to China, he was hoping to persuade Isabel to pick up the phone to Beijing, to ask her peer to moderate his crackdown.

The speed and canvas of civil liberty infractions were breathtaking, he told her. Being aware of a crime *before* it happened now carried the possibility of life imprisonment. Membership of unspecified 'international terrorist organisations' was a capital offence. Children as young as twelve could be charged as adults. Arrests had already mounted into the hundreds, four of them dissidents who the US knew better than China, people whose only perfidy was a passion for democracy.

And of course, as he also now knew, Tori was there, in Dandong. Though two thousand miles from the Uyghur epicentre in Xinjiang, the shockwaves from RUA were buffeting the entire country. Knowing Beijing was unlikely to heed even his boss's call to temper its clampdown, his best hope was that Tori's six years of CIA discipline and experience would keep her out of harm's way.

39

Dandong

THE FIRE EXIT SLAMMED SHUT BEHIND them sucking up every available lumen so what had briefly opened up as a laneway dissolved into blackness. The effluvium of ammonia and putrefaction was so scalding Tori stopped and squeezed her eyes shut. She heard Frank shuffle forward, knocking over a trashcan, a cat hissing and swiping its claws. Then an oomph and a wail as his foot hit the cat, kicking it further into the darkness, near what a scuttling suggested was a brood of rats. He stepped forward again.

Tori opened her eyes. 'What was that squelch under your foot?'

He groaned, and she saw his phone light up, its white beam moving around his feet until he found a newspaper and used it to wipe a viscous scum off his boots.

When he was done, she told him to switch his light off, to conserve his battery and give them a chance of remaining undetected. Guided by the splinter of moon sticking out from under a cloud, they inched forward.

When Tori's heel squished what felt like a soft slither of eels, she stopped and shuddered. 'Tonight's restaurant menu claimed they farmed their own produce. I think we're walking on it.'

'At least it's organic.'

Up ahead, about fifty feet away, a streetlamp gave off a faint yellow glow, its post kinked over like the hind leg of the mangy dog peeing on it. When they reached it, the mongrel shook off a cloud of fleas and scampered off down a wider street that led to the water's edge. They followed and eventually reached a ramp that led onto a long wharf, a muddle of fishing boats along it, all jammed up together as if keeping each other warm.

Tori and Frank went slowly, timing each step with the rise and fall of the creaking timbers, their hats pulled down over their faces, shoulders hunched as they tried to blend in. Most of the boats they passed were unattended. A few boatmen were asleep under furs and those playing cards or *mah-jongg* didn't bother to look up.

At the boat at very end of the wharf, Tori reached out over the stern and nudged a pile of thick pelts.

'Hmmphh?' the boatman mumbled, pulling one of the fleeces further over his face before rolling onto his side. She shook the old man again until he rubbed his eyes and blinked them open, then stared. '*Lao wai!*' He spat the words out as if to show them how unpleasant waking up to foreigners was.

She spoke back to him softly, in Mandarin, noticing Frank's jaw drop a little. The two or three occasions when she had translated so far, he'd obviously assumed it was FrensLens doing the work. When their hosts had been speaking among themselves, she'd feigned a typical Westerner's ignorance. If the Mingmai people had said anything of consequence it might've benefited their client's interests but Kong and Jin were too smart for that, and the rest had been too low in the pecking order to know anything useful. Even so, at dinner with Jin she'd still played naive, coyly fluttering her eyelashes just in case, except when she was trying to stop herself heaving from the 'delicacies'.

The boatman scratched his forehead under his woollen cap, clearly perplexed. 'You speak like a Beijing train station announcer,' he said in Mandarin. Tori was unsure whether to take that as a compliment or not.

Chen Fang, it turned out, wasn't a fisherman, rather a tour guide at the easternmost section of the Great Wall at Hushan. He was boat-sitting for his cousin who had taken his family to Harbin's annual Snow and Ice Show.

'Frank, our cruise director says we smell like shit.'

'How he can tell with that dead cow draped over his shoulders?'

Chen handed Frank an oily rag. 'Wipe shoes.' He said it in Chinese but his meaning was clear.

Manoeuvring through scuds of fog almost as thick as milk and pack ice—even though it was thinner than Tori expected— meant motoring to the island took an hour. After they clambered ashore onto an outcrop of rocks, Tori handed Chen one of their spare phones together with half of a torn American hundred-dollar note. They watched as he stuffed them in his pocket, waiting until he pulled the vessel back. When the hazy gloom enveloped him, they scampered to the electric fence, tramping around the perimeter to the rocks on the other side. A couple of times, the ground gave way under Tori's feet and she almost reached out to grab the wires but managed to rebalance without touching them.

'That could have been shocking,' said Frank, smirking.

'Not as much as your pun,' she said as they dropped down close to where they'd earlier seen the river's ice pack had been broken, amazed to find a jetty stretching long enough to berth a hundred-foot barge.

'Ah!' Frank cried as he walked into a lifting hook hanging off the boom of a massive jib crane. 'A jetty and a crane, I get,' he said, rubbing what was now the second scratch on his forehead, 'but the stuff we saw Mingmai fabricating up top doesn't need monsters like these.'

Tori pointed to a recess at the end of the short roadway. 'A tunnel,' she whispered. A few steps on, she stopped at a mound of discarded food cartons, scraps and cigarette butts that reeked like someone had stuffed sweaty gym socks with rancid cabbage and garlic and set fire to them. '*Kimchi* with a smoke chaser anyone?'

'Top grade security ... wards off the uninvited.'

'Unless they've got colds, which sadly we don't.' She slid a black box hardly bigger than a cigarette packet from her rucksack. It was a satphone signal repeater relay, another device Frank had got from Thatcher. Tori reached up and placed it near the top of the pile, between a broken jar and a puckered orange, giving it an unobstructed line to the sky. Without the relay, the satphone they'd brought to bypass the local cell networks would be useless as soon as they entered a building or, as looked likely, went underground.

They took a few moments to peer between the rocks, around the crane and near the mouth of the tunnel, looking for motion detectors and cameras which, given the gloom, they expected to be infra-red.

Not finding any, Tori stepped toward the chamber entrance. 'This is weird. Twenty feet high but only five across.' Except it wasn't. As she edged closer to one side, she saw that the 'rocks' flanking the entrance were a facade, fibreglass to the touch, hinged and on rollers ready to swing back, potentially extending the entryway's width to thirty feet.

They slowly advanced inside. About ten feet in Tori pulled at Frank's sleeve. Pointing two fingers at her eyes then into the passageway, she held him back while he squinted into the darkness. His eyes adjusted then widened as he saw what she'd seen: a faint red circle of dots ringing the passage like a necklace of tiny rubies. Hugging her coat to her body Tori tiptoed closer, careful not to cross them. She puffed out a deep breath, the cloud of vapour briefly revealing a crisscross of red laser beams.

Frank meanwhile, exploring the wall to their left, had found an alcove close to the tunnel entrance. He was checking out if it was a fork in the tunnel when a rumble of voices sounded from deeper inside the cavern. Tori looked over to him and he signalled for her to join him.

She darted over. 'They're not speaking Chinese,' she said. 'Puffier consonants ... not as tonal.' A moment later, FrensLens confirmed it was Korean.

'Who's there?' shouted one of the voices.

'If they've got weapons—' Frank started in a low voice.

'Assume they do, but don't worry, I've got this,' she whispered. Cupping her phone to smother the light from the screen, she spoke softly into it. Five seconds later an engine came revving from across the water and out of the fog. Another five seconds and an array of floodlights mounted on the outside rock face snapped on as Chen drew the boat close to the jetty. For the first time, Tori saw that the hull they'd trusted with their lives was little more than a flaking patchwork of rust.

A stampede of feet and shouts reverberated from inside the tunnel. Tori poked her head out of the alcove in time to see the laser dots vanish just before the tunnel lights fired up.

Frank drew Tori back into the niche as far as he could, now only partially in shadow, light reaching their alcove from both inside and outside the tunnel. 'Glad you told me to buy a dark coat,' he murmured, pulling his hat low like Tori's. 'The red one with the flashing lights on the collar that the salesman was pushing wouldn't have suited this situation so well.'

Hanging back for what seemed like several very tense minutes, but was probably seconds, Tori became aware of the heat coming from Frank's body as he pressed her against the wall, breathing heavily.

Then six men in khaki uniforms with pillbox military caps and rifles drawn ran past.

'Chinese NSG-85 sniper rifles,' whispered Frank.

'Impressive.'

'They certainly are, especially if—'

'I meant you knowing they're NSG-85s ... not 86s or 92s or whatevers. Damn impressive.' Tori knew guns herself well enough, but Chinese weaponry wasn't a strong suit.

'Some kids collected cricket cards, this kid studied artillery. Actually, he also collected cricket cards. But Chen? They'll—'

'He's fine. I offered him an extra hundred—'

'To risk his life?'

'To play super dumb, bow, scrape and apologise for his two stupid dogs that jumped ashore and ran in and out of the tunnel then off onto the island. It'll buy us time to take a look down there,' she said, her thumb pointing into the tunnel. 'Then he'll head back to our pickup point and wait.'

'If they don't shoot him.'

40

TORI BENT OVER TO REMOVE HER shoes then shoved them into her pack. Frank did likewise, grumbling, 'Trying not to make a racket would be a lot more comfortable if the concrete floor in here was heated.'

'Well, the air is, and you're wearing socks. Get over it,' she said, starting to run between the trolley tracks set into the floor, Frank following close behind. After 150 feet, the rails curved to the right and 100 feet further on, they came to a dangling curtain of black rubber straps. Peeking through them, she saw the tunnel open up into a transit area the size of a small concert hall. At the far end, near a massive set of elevator doors, sitting under banks of flickering fluorescent tubes was the trolley, more like a train. Scattered between the train and the curtain were twenty, perhaps twenty-five crates, in groups of threes and fours, each one large enough to fit a pickup truck. She scanned the space to see if there were any more guards but it seemed they'd all left to check out Chen.

Frank looked as sweaty as Tori felt, a combination of running in their coats, the central heating and, at least in her case, fear. Pushing through the curtain, she saw the line-up of crates to her right had their sides jimmied open, their contents gone. 'Let's park our coats in here,' she said, sloughing off her backpack, then her coat and tossing it inside a crate. Frank followed suit.

'Korean?' said Frank, pointing to the writing on the side of the box as they both slid their shoes and backpacks back on.

'I guess,' said Tori, tapping her FrensLens and shrugging. The device didn't seem to be working.

Frank indicated a water pump mounted on the wall behind them. He leant down to unplug it from the power outlet while Tori took an adaptor and transceiver out of her pack—more gear from Thatcher—and fitted them into the outlet. She replugged the pump then, from her pack's side pocket, took out a tablet. 'Fingers crossed,' she said, sitting cross-legged on the floor. She switched it on, networked it to the transceiver then drilled her way in to find any computer networks that operated from the same power circuit. 'And … bingo.'

As the screen image dissolved then reformed, she pressed *record*. Icons for five networks appeared and she opened the one for closed circuit TV, hoping to switch off any nearby cameras. Surprisingly, it wasn't password protected. 'Jesus!' she hissed. 'We missed the camera at the jetty … and two in the tunnel … and one just over there.'

'If they did see us, Chen's dead. They'll know he's lying.'

Tori pointed to the glassed-in guard station on their left. 'I don't think so.' Playing cards were strewn across the top of a table set up outside the post, with two of the six chairs overturned. The occupants had left in a hurry. 'We probably tripped an alarm and they grabbed their guns and ran.'

'For Chen's sake, I hope so.'

'And ours.' Tori scrolled through the camera control directory for each camera that had followed their path, deleting the last ten minutes' recordings, then switching those cameras off, as well as those in the transit area. That done, she skipped her screen from camera to camera, taking her and Frank on a tour of the underground spaces, a labyrinth of rooms with banks of computers, men and women in white coats hunched over them.

'Have you noticed all the rooms have a set of those on the wall?' Tori pointed to a duo of digital clocks, a green one with the current local time, and a red one, the numbers ticking down second by second: 11:15:45 ... 44 ... 43 ... 42 ...

'It's a countdown,' said Frank.

'You don't say! But what's it counting down to?'

41

TORI FLIPPED HER SCREEN THROUGH SEVERAL more rooms. 'The doorway, where that woman's walking. The wall must be six feet thick. What is this place, Frank, a bomb shelter?'

'There's your answer,' he murmured as the next room—a cavern—opened up.

She panned the camera upward from the floor, slowly sweeping it up a 100-foot metallic tube, from its fins and boosters, following the maintenance gantry past a flag and some text painted on the side until it reached the nose-cone.

'What does it cost,' said Frank, 'to build a rocket, let alone construct an underground complex to house it so that—'

'—no one has a clue you're doing it.'

'I venture it took a good chunk of the two billion that—'

'—went from Caribanco to Pyongyang.'

'Exactly.'

The massive chamber, judging by the ant farm of workers scurrying around on the floor and up and down the gantry, was easily 200 feet high, maybe more.

Tori took the camera higher above the nose-cone, zooming in on the rafters above it. Raking it across the roof from one cavern wall to the other, she saw they weren't mere roof supports; they were too sturdy and chunky for that.

'The roof's a slider,' said Frank. 'See the roller tracks?'

'Which explains the black patches and white "pipe" lines we saw above ground when we left the factory.'

Frank nodded. 'What's that text say … there, below the North Korean flag … something twelve?'

FrensLens kicked in and not only read it for Tori as *Unha* or *Galaxy 12* but automatically called up background on what it labelled North Korea's 'so-called weather satellite program'.

She read the text aloud for Frank. 'North Korea's early *Unha* rockets spun a series of *Kwangmyongsong* satellites—*Bright Stars*—into orbit, some successful, some unsuccessful, from their site at Sohae. They then launched the *Climate 1* satellite—*Gihu 1*—but that sputtered out six miles over Japan before crashing into the sea.'

She shifted to a camera trained on the rocket's other side and again panned up to the nose-cone, waiting for FrensLens to translate this new text. 'This rocket,' she told Frank, 'is sending the *Climate 2* satellite into orbit.'

'Sohae is only a ninety-minute drive from here,' said Frank, scratching his head.

'So?'

He coughed and pressed his lips together as if debating whether to disclose a state secret, which he then did. 'MI6 have been monitoring Sohae for years. It's a large-scale launch site, tried and tested. So why would Pyongyang duplicate all that infrastructure nearby, let alone go to the extra expense of doing it underground, and here of all places, smack up against the Chinese border?'

'Perhaps because you Brits, as well as the Americans, Japanese and South Koreans, you've all got eyes on Sohae so they decided to be a bit Marlene Dietrich.'

'If you mean they wanted to be alone, then it's Greta Garbo. But why go to all this secrecy and extra expense for a simple *weather* satellite?'

The activity in the rocket site was buzzing. She counted four, five, six ... seven clumps of people scattered at ground level either huddled around consoles or standing in circles and debating. Painters on a scaffold up at the nose-cone were dabbing on finishing touches as other workers climbed up the access arm and filed in and out of various sections of the rocket.

'If this is where Mingmai's two billion went,' Tori mused, 'the questions are why, and who authorised it?'

They sat in silence watching the people milling around inside the site.

'Look!' said Tori suddenly. She pointed to a tiny man standing near the foot of the rocket. He was jabbing his finger at another man's shoulder whose back was to the camera. She zoomed in and when his face came into focus she briefly closed her eyes. 'It's Akhtar. From the way this looks, he certainly didn't come to Dandong,' she said, forcing out a smile, 'just to savour the dumplings.'

Frank expelled a long breath. 'Those clocks. They're telling us that blast-off's in just over eleven hours, that's 10 am.'

'Two hours after we're supposed to be flying out, though if those guards find us here we might never make it back to the hotel.'

'We could request dumplings for our last meal?'

Tori made a face. 'So what's the scenario here? Iran working with North Korea?'

'The Iranians sacked him.'

'Possibly a ruse?' said Tori. 'Maybe so the Ayatollahs could disown him … as a blind … a cover for this? Plausible deniability's worked for our side, why not for theirs?'

What Tori felt increasingly sure of—and Frank agreed—was that the rocket or the satellite carried a nuclear payload. What wasn't clear was why. 'With the launch in eleven hours,' she said, 'we need to find out fast—'

'And then?'

'We stop it. Absolute worse case? We blow it up and …'

'Us with it?' Frank's eyes clouded over then he half-smiled. 'But my beautiful new coat! It cost me—'

'Yeah, yeah, NASA … man on moon, blah, blah.'

'Best case?'

'We assemble as much hard evidence as we can,' she said, 'shoot it across to DC—'

'To Tex?'

She nodded. 'So he can mobilise the right resources and we can scoot the hell out of China.'

At that moment a burst of shouting echoed down the tunnel and the quiet concern in Frank's eyes was doused with anxiety. 'Scooting out of this place has rather a more immediate attraction, don't you think?'

42

FRANK LEANT FORWARD AND CLICKED ON the CCTV camera watching the jetty. All six guards were screaming. Chen was standing at his bow, the boat bobbing about twenty feet out. 'We better move before we can't,' he said, stating what Tori thought was obvious.

She stopped the CCTV recording and cut their transceiver link but left the device in place. 'If the guards don't find this little dongle, it might come in handy later.' As they backed up to retrieve their coats, FrensLens began translating the text slapped on the sides of the crates. North Korea, North Korea, North Korea ... Maybe ten had been freighted in from Pyongyang. 'This one's from China, and that one,' Tori said before counting eight more Chinese crates.

'Is that Arabic?'

'Persian,' Tori replied. 'And there are … six of those. Hey, over there.' She tipped her head to the right where her eye had caught some paperwork poking out from under one of the crates.

Frank knelt down and as he eased it out the corner ripped on a splintered edge, and she saw a trefoil symbol come into view—the international warning sign for nuclear hazards. She stared at the page through FrensLens and a few seconds later a strange grin broke across her face.

Frank stared at her. 'We've just stumbled on what may be the world's worst nightmare, a nuke-equipped satellite—'

'Or rocket.'

'And it's North Korean, Iranian, Chinese, government or private, we don't know—yet you're smiling?'

'Take that booklet and I'll explain later. Let's head over there.' She indicated the guard station.

Frank stuffed the booklet into his backpack as they ran over. As soon as they entered the monitoring room, Tori slid into a chair in front of the computer screens. The middle monitor was paused on an image of a cartoonish car, a grey sedan stationary in the middle of an empty, soulless city street. As she minimised the window FrensLens explained it had been a scene from *Pyongyang Racer*, North Korea's first attempt at a video game, a local classic apparently.

She navigated to the server but it soon became clear that anything above a guard's pay grade demanded a more secure login and decryption.

Frank, looking over her shoulder as much as keeping watch, held out a credit card-sized flash drive. 'You'll find this handy.'

'MI6 wouldn't be too happy you stole their code cracker,' she said, inserting it into a slot on the side of the screen.

He touched his temple. 'If it stayed up here, is that stealing?'

She clicked on the flash drive's properties. 'Hmm, twenty-six megabytes of pure recollection jumping out of your brain onto this little drive, is that stealing? But heck, if it works … and we get out of here … I doubt they'll be complaining. They might even buy you a private box at Lords, assuming they have boxes at cricket … other than the ones the players wear over their privates.'

They waited.

'That's an impressive memory of yours,' she said when seconds later the network opened up to her. Starting from the top, she clicked sequentially on every directory, but as each one opened she closed it and moved on to the next. Any folder that didn't demand at least a second-step login wasn't worth wasting their time on. On her fifteenth attempt: 'Jackpot. Time to wave your magic drive again,' she said. Eight seconds later, when they were looking at a workbook of engineering drawings, the rocket schematics, she added, 'Damn! And there I was hoping for Jamie Oliver's secret recipe for dumplings with *kimchi.*'

'What is it with you and dumplings? Uh-oh,' said Frank, pointing to the jetty's CCTV, 'there's no time to check through the schematics now.' Chen was pulling the boat away and the guards were slapping each other's backs. 'Take a copy and we can look later.' He handed her another transceiver.

'How many of these did Thatcher give you?' she said as she inserted it into another slot. While the file was copying across to her tablet, she checked the CCTV again, and seeing there was still time, decrypted the password and opened another folder.

'Ugh,' she grunted as half the screen filled with an animation of the Earth rotating in space. 'Not another video game!' She was about to close it when the image began zeroing in on North Korea, then hurtled down toward the island, pulling up short to show the ground sliding open and revealing the tip of the rocket's nose-cone. 'Whoa. Is this what I think it is?' Two vertical slabs of the island's rock face drew back like curtains, exposing the craft's full height and its name, *Unha 12*. As a clock on the screen ticked in a mock countdown, the cartoon boosters ignited, belching a hellfire of flames and smoke ahead of lift-off.

Frank, she could see, was mesmerised as the simulated rocket started climbing, the thrust tailed off and the boosters jettisoned. Much higher, stage one fell away and higher still, stage two did the same. Finally the clamshell fairing at the nose-cone split apart exposing the payload, the *Gihu 2* satellite, and spinning it off into the upper atmosphere.

'If this is a true simulation,' Frank said, 'the rocket isn't nuclear—'

'With all bets on the satellite.' The control bar for the cartoon gave the clip another fifty minutes running time. 'I'll copy this too,' but as Tori spoke she saw that the wharf was now deserted. They'd missed the guards leaving. How close were they? Heart thumping, she clicked the CCTV across to the tunnel cameras, and saw they'd only just started meandering back.

The blue progress bar for her downloads was only sixty-eight per cent complete. Her fingers drummed on her knee, and Frank was opening and closing his fist.

He stepped over to where the guards' overcoats were hanging and unclipped a badge from an epaulette, then slipped it under the large red button in the centre of the desk. 'When they get back here, assuming you've finished by then and we're not dead, one of them will hit this reset button—'

'And the badge will stop it pressing down far enough to restart the security systems you're about to disable.'

'Right. We might get a few extra seconds before they notice it.' Smiling, he started flicking a few switches on the panel to Tori's left. 'And hopefully by then we'll be long gone. They'll never know we were here.'

'A brilliant plan.'

'If it works.'

Eighty-seven per cent. The voices from the tunnel were getting louder and more raucous. Ninety-four. Tori's fingers hovered over the transceiver. The instant the bar hit 100, she yanked out the devices, pulled *Pyongyang Racer* back up and they ran.

They'd just reached the first cluster of crates when something glinted at them from back in the tunnel, possibly the gold insignia on one of the guards' caps. They leapt inside a box facing away from the tunnel and waited. As Tori re-linked her tablet to the transceiver at the water pump, silently logging herself back into the power system, she was pressed so close to Frank she thought she could feel his pulse, or was it her own?

A minute later, the guards returned, laughing. As they passed the crate Tori and Frank were hiding in, one of the guards threw his cap into the air. Whooping, he pirouetted around to catch it, but caught them instead, his eyes widening in surprise. '*Suepai!*' he shouted, his cap hitting the ground as he unslung his weapon and levelled it at them. The others turned too, but Tori kept tapping at her screen, still trying to locate the power system, FrensLens dancing the word 'Spies!' before her eyes, as if she needed a translation.

Simultaneously, she blacked out the overhead lights and her tablet, grabbed Frank's arm and again they bolted.

The volley of gunfire was sudden … deafening. The thunder cracking off the concrete walls was a mixed blessing, strobing an escape route for them but also turning them into staccato silhouettes. The shots seemed to be flying everywhere, with concrete chips and splinters of wood pummelling them from all sides.

Frank tripped on a box lid and as Tori bent to help him up, a shell ricocheted off a wall and slammed into her left bicep. It was all she could do not to scream. The impact wrenched her upper body sideways almost knocking her over. Frank managed to block her fall. Her pain was excruciating, searing, like a spear tip twisting inside her arm. Tears streamed down her face even though she was squeezing her eyes, and her mouth, shut.

One of the guards must have caught her grunt, that first reflex she hadn't been able to suppress. 'I got one,' she heard him shout via FrensLens. 'One of that Chinese bastard's make-believe dogs.'

'Sounded like a girl.'

'A bitch then,' laughed the shooter.

'Same thing,' bellowed a third and they started firing again. By then, Frank had helped her round the curve and they were in the tunnel's main straight which, in the dark, seemed far longer than on their way in. As they tore toward the exit they heard the loud shuddering rumble of a roller door coming down ahead of them, even before they could see it.

'Maybe they'll slip on my blood,' panted Tori, giving a strangled laugh as wetness soaked down her sleeve. She stopped, feeling faint. The door up ahead was already two-thirds down and dropping fast. She took off the FrensLens and handed them to Frank. 'I'm getting woozy … if I don't—'

Not waiting for her to finish, Frank put on her FrensLens, wrapped an arm around her waist, lifted her off her feet and ran with her.

With five paces to the door, and the gap to the ground now only three feet and contracting, he put one foot forward and flung Tori low, head first as if she was a bowling ball, her body sliding along the shiny concrete into and through the gap.

Through a haze of pain, she heard one of the guards shouting and the door, now barely a slit behind her, pinging with shells. She closed her eyes. *Frank?* Then there was nothing.

43

Washington, DC

PRESIDENT DIAZ HAD HER BACK TO Narthex, her hands behind her head, elbows wide. To him, the light bouncing off the snow through the window glass gave her an aura, a halo behind her, like she was a crucifix.

'Madam President,' he said as she swung her chair around, 'it's China. Rumours of a split inside the Communist Party leadership. We've monitored two Politburo members saying that President Hou Tao is losing his—'

'—his grip. The German chancellor called me ten minutes ago with the same message. Hou's been a good friend to the West so I'm hoping the reports are wrong, but if not ...' She dropped her arms and leant forward onto the desk. What's our latest intel on the succession?'

As always, Narthex had his notes ready, but this time he didn't need them. His doctoral thesis, the paper the president had based hiring him on, analysed the instability and realpolitik stresses inherent in the Chinese power structure. It hadn't even been published when she'd called him ten months and two weeks ago, yet she'd still heard about it, seen it, read it, liked it. Everything he'd said in the paper had proved accurate as far as it went, but his more recent access to top-secret resources told him he'd barely scratched the surface.

'It's not good news, ma'am. President Hou's deputy, Zhao Guowei, is the most likely. Militarily, Zhao's a confrontational hawk. Economically, he despises how his Party has left millions of his countrymen starving while stuffing China's vast money pile into the US economy to feed *our* mouths.'

'Strictly inside this office, I'm not sure his point is outlandish.'

The aspects of his job Narthex liked most were Isabel's refreshing honesty and her willingness to see nuance where he did and, where she didn't, she was prepared to listen. 'For the past two years,' he said, 'Zhao's been China's top economic official. His anti-Westernism would have been a concern if President Hou hadn't kept him in check. But if Zhao takes charge, he'll not only gain control of foreign policy and the military, but he'll put his own man in charge of economic policy.'

'Which would mean ...?'

'He'll yank their money out of US Treasuries. He'll dump them. Ma'am, a Zhao-led China would force a sharp spike in interest rates ... global rates ... it'll slam business, cost American jobs and we'll be more exposed if ... *when* he threatens global security.'

'So we need Hou to stay on first.'

'What?'

'Not what. Hou.' She smiled.

'Ma'am?'

'Sorry, Narthex. It's an old Abbott and Costello routine, inappropriate and mispronounced I know but …'

She didn't crack jokes very often, so he knew he'd made his point.

Dandong

SHIVERING FROM SHOCK, HER LEFT ARM pounding, Tori was breathing quickly, too quickly. Her jaw trembled from blood loss, the cold and fifteen minutes of stumbling over rocks and frozen outcrops without gloves or a coat. If Frank hadn't come hurtling under the door just as it slammed shut, hadn't scooped her up and wrapped his arm around her for warmth and support, she doubted she'd have made it here.

After he'd lain her flat on her back, her feet up, arm on her chest, the blood flow staunched with a compress he'd put together from their two caps and some yarn he'd unravelled from her cardigan, he'd left her to look for Chen Fang. Tori tried peering through the mist and the night to the cove where she'd asked Chen to tuck the boat away but the scrub at the edge of the path was the limit of her visibility. What if Chen wasn't down there? Please be there, *please.*

She cast her gaze over the ridge to where erratic streaks of white light—spotlights—cut through the fog, sweeping across the river.

Suddenly, thirty or so feet below her, an orange spark flared up into a tiny flame. Then a long red glow of a cigarette lit up the boatman's nose and Frank's hand beneath it.

FRANK WRAPPED TORI in one of the fishy furs Chen had given them, the boatman standing near the rail, waving his half of the torn hundred-dollar note at her, babbling away. She watched a nub of ash drop off his smoke and fall over the side. She concentrated on breathing, limiting shock, getting warm as quickly as possible and keeping her limbs elevated. She lay back on a two-skin mattress Frank had prepared and pulled several more over the top of her.

She was ready to talk to the boatman, if her chattering teeth would let her. 'Chen, when you d-drop us off is when I'll g-give you the two hundred d-dollars we agreed on.' Several rounds of gunfire in the distance drowned out her last few words and Chen, either satisfied or scared, leapt for the controls, reversing the vessel into the river. After he'd steered around a bend where the fog gave them more cover, she repeated what she'd said, adding, 'I-i-if you get there f-fast and w-without us getting shot, you'll get a b-bonus … an *extra* t-two hundred.' She closed her eyes, hoping he'd understood her offer despite her stuttered Mandarin. When the boat turned and moved off again, the bow cracking through the ice, it seemed like he had.

WITH FRANK OUT IN THE MIDDLE of the road hoping to find a taxi, Tori propped herself up against a streetlamp. She crooked her bad arm over her head to reduce the haemorrhaging, her good one cupping the satphone to her ear. Wrapped in a musty pelt Chen had stiffed her an extra three hundred dollars for, she kept an eye on Frank, whose own fur cost them *five* hundred since it was a Chen family treasure, Mao Zedong having worn it on the Long March.

They were six or seven miles from where they'd initially 'hired' Chen. When three boat-mounted searchlights had started heading their way, Frank had directed him to drop them at the riverbank near this roadway.

Going to a hospital was out of the question. The hotel wasn't an option either. If the guards found their coats in the crate they'd have a pretty good clue as to who they were looking for, with both coats in size 'foreigner' and Frank's boasting a *Ho's for Men* label.

'It's Tori,' she said into the phone.

'Thank goodness,' said Tex. 'The number I had ... it's been off line for hours and I was—'

In different circumstances his relief would have been sweet. 'No time for that. Listen—'

'I've been worr—'

'And I've been shot.' She'd stunned him into silence. 'I need to give you some coordinates—'

'Are you oka—'

'Tex, thanks for your concern, but please. I'm not calling Tex my, er, friend, I'm calling Narthex Carter, adviser to the president—'

'Is this line—'

'It's a satphone so it's not using Chinese networks. I've plugged in an encryption module and I'm using a fake voice because I'm really a man and I'm standing on my head underwater which, as you can imagine is hard since, like I said, I've been *fucking shot*. So listen, pleas—'

'Where are you? Maybe I can get people—'

Her bicep spasmed and, as pain shot up her arm, she bent over as if trying to pour it out of her skull onto the pavement. She grit her teeth. 'Shut up and listen. I'm in Dandong. It's a city on the border of—'

'I know.'

Sure you do, she thought, but this wasn't the time. 'Whatever spy satellites you've got orbiting over here, get them to zoom in on ...' She started relaying the island's coordinates from the map on her tablet. She'd only managed to pass the latitude on to him when pain hacked into her shoulder like a tiger's claws, ripping into her muscle and slicing down to her fingers. She wanted to scream but somehow kept it in, sweat pouring off her forehead.

'You still there?' Tex asked, worry straining his voice.

She took three deep breaths and gave him the longitude. 'The satellites will see an island on the Yalu River. It's technically North Korean territory but part of it's leased to a Chinese company for a fabrication lab. Have you heard of Mingmai?'

'Everyone has, but not in the same sentence as North Korea.'

'Until now. Try throwing Iran into that sentence too.'

'What?'

'Mingmai's factory only takes up a fraction of the island but if your sats check out the southern riverfront, they'll see Nork military swarming all over—'

'Why is this an American concern? Ah, I don't mean, you know, that you being shot isn't ... but Norks running around on their own border, wouldn't it be for the Chinese to—'

'Tex, stop asking questions, okay? We're in deep shit over here, and if we don't do something ... if *you* don't do something, in nine,' she checked her watch, 'in just over nine and a half hours *everyone* is in deep shit. They're hiding an underground launch site there and at 10 am local time, they're blasting-off a rocket—*Galaxy 12*—and it'll send a nuclear-equipped satellite into orbit. Is that an American concern?'

'You know this for cert—'

'You don't belie—'

'Of course I do but I have to convince—'

'I was in there, Tex, I got shot there ... *after* I saw the rocket.'

'You've actually *seen* it?'

'Yes ... well, strictly no. I saw it via their CCTV, as plain as ... as that mole on your back. But I recorded a clip from the

CCTV to send you, as well as a copy of the rocket schematics ... and an animation of its flight plan—'

'You know what it's target is?'

She could see headlights coming down the road. Frank saw them too, and he pulled back behind a parked truck, making sure, she expected, that it was a cab and not a posse out searching for two foreigners. 'Tex, I'll have to end this call in a minute, but no, I don't know the target. I was kind of getting shot at the time so didn't hunker down with a box of popcorn to watch the flight path simulation. But I'll get it to you soon—all of it—okay?'

'How do you know the satellite's nuclear?'

Tori saw the yellow taxi sign on the car's roof at the same time as Frank stepped back into the road. 'Tex, I'll also be sending you a snap of some Iranian paperwork ... it's got the nuke trefoil plastered all over it. Plus a Dr Masoud Akhtar was there, in person, supervising the whole thing.'

'Doctor who?'

Frank was waving at her from the road, holding the cab door open. 'I gotta go. Google the guy.'

'Tori, this seems—'

'—far-fetched? Like the shell thrashing around in my arm? His name is Masoud Akhtar.' She spelled it. 'Like I said, bye.'

46

THE THIRD TIME CHEN FANG STEERED the boat round the rocky point toward the island's jetty he was trumpeting his horn, two of his fake gold teeth glinting in the spotlights. The glare meant he couldn't see the rifles pointed at him, but hearing the shouts of the men aiming them he spoke his piece quickly and loudly across the icy water. 'My name is Chen Fang. I have information, very valuable information. I am a friend.'

As his boat bobbed up and down, the old man raised his arms so high above his head his furs dropped to the floor. His taupe-coloured tourist department uniform billowed over his belt as if two sizes too big, in the harsh light making him appear scrawnier and more wizened than he really was.

The guards' first response wasn't encouraging, the clash of steel sliding against steel. Wondering if returning here was a mistake, Chen began to shake. 'I am a friend. I am here to tell you about the two foreigners you are searching for,' he shouted, his voice wobbly, less uncertain this time.

'Don't you mean your two fucking dogs?' came a man's voice.

Chen couldn't see him, nor any of them, but the voice was the one he'd heard before. 'I lied, sir, and for that I most humbly apologise.' He bowed so low his nose almost pecked his knees. 'But,' he said, raising himself back up and holding up his hands, 'they held a gun to my head and threatened to kill my family. One is a woman, a *lao wai* with hair like a firecracker. The man is dark skinned, a *yindu lao,* I think … both of them evil foreigners. Please, general sir, I return here by choice to assist you, to save my family.' He bowed again. *And to screw you for an even bigger reward than I got out of those filthy alien ingrates.*

ADDING BREAK AND ENTER TO THE litany of other charges facing them was trifling if it meant getting Tori antibiotics, dressings and painkillers. As the taxi rattled and squeaked past strip after strip of shops, most in darkness, Tori let Frank who was wearing the FrensLens keep watch of the signs. She was useless as lookout, her eyes frequently clamping shut as pain shot up and down her arm.

'There,' said Frank, pointing from the front seat. He turned to face her. 'That blue sign, the flickering one, FrensLens is translating it as *New Century Traditional Medicine and Western Sturgeon*. Hopefully it's *surgeon*, but if not, we can make caviar dumplings after we fix you up.'

If a battery of landmines wasn't exploding in her arm she might have laughed. Frank paid the driver, helped her out and, after waiting for the cab's tail-lights to disappear round a corner, he supported her across the street.

Apart from the barely strobing sign, the block was in shadows. As Frank shuffled her along, a man in a fur earflap hat, muttering incoherently through his beard and tapping a white stick, came toward them. He shouted as he drew closer, brandishing the cane, protecting himself from demons other than those Tori suspected were already in residence. Before reaching them, he turned into the doorway of a boarded up restaurant crammed with cardboard boxes and blankets.

'I'd got used to these furs. I'd forgotten how much they stink,' said Tori.

Frank looked quizzical until FrensLens must've translated the man's tirade for him. '*When fishermen move in,*' he quoted, '*property values plummet, so go away.* Really? The cafe he's squatting outside of is out of business and with the half-on, half-off neon up ahead, this area doesn't quite seem like the real estate's booming.'

When they got to the clinic doorway, Frank stood with his feet either side of a pool of urine and picked the three locks, one after the other.

Tori shifted to the left and glanced back at the vagrant. 'And pissing in other people's doorways doesn't impact property prices?' Something alive nestled up to her ankle just as the door clicked open. She jerked her leg back and it scurried off.

Tori stepped inside the blackness, sniffing the air as Frank closed the door behind them. 'Is that weed?'

'I think it's Moxa, what they burn for acupuncture, but if it is weed, a toke or two in your condition mightn't go astray.'

She couldn't see his face to tell if he was being flippant. 'If you're prescribing narcotics, my choice is Wagner's *Ring Cycle.*'

'For the rapture?'

'The tedium.'

Frank didn't bite despite being a true Ringnut, so much of a Wagner junkie that his usual ringtone was *Ride of the Valkyries*.

They lingered near the front door until their eyes adjusted to the feeble light slithering under it, waiting for any slow red beat of motion detectors. Satisfied the place was unalarmed, Frank lit up his phone and they entered the examination room which, with no windows and no external doors, had been in full darkness. He kicked the reception door closed behind them and switched on the fluorescents, lighting up a room crammed with treatment beds in three rows of four. 'Sticking needles into twelve naked strangers at once,' he said, 'is my idea of a jab well done.'

'Really? Another pun like that and it won't be this bullet *or* Wagner that kills me.'

He lifted her up onto the treatment table and put his backpack next to hers.

'They're not *actual* seahorses over there, are they?' she asked, woozy even before she saw the hurl of sickly dubious liquids on the shelves. Piss yellows, snot greens and sallow, anaemic pinks swirled around the insects, embryos and animal parts they were preserving.

Frank swung round to look. 'Just a moment ... I'm translating the labels ... do you mean that urine-coloured jar between the bottle of, er, *deer penises soaked in yak blood* and the flask of *flying squirrel faeces*?'

'You really do know how to impress a girl, don't yo—' She cried out, flinching, the pellet inside her arm suddenly attempting what felt like a triple somersault. 'Mmmph ... maybe we *should* do that Hollywood thing?' she said, despite both of them agreeing in the cab that gouging the bullet out, like in the movies, was a bad idea. Stopping further blood loss, cleansing the wound and treating her for shock were far better fixes than increasing the risk of infection by poking around in the wound.

'Lie back,' said Frank as he began opening cabinets and drawers.

Tori ignored him, sitting back up, taking the Iranian booklet out of Frank's backpack and snapping a shot of it with her tablet. Knowing the satphone wouldn't work indoors without an external relay or aerial, she took out one of the burners, plugged on the encryption module and, after linking it to her tablet, sent Thatcher a message asking him to give Tex the encryption specs.

Starting to type her message to Tex, she'd only written four lines when Frank rolled up with a table laden with packets and bottles and towels, an array of instruments and two bowls of clear liquid, one of them steaming.

'In what language does *lie back* mean *sit up*?'

She kept typing. 'Got to finish this first, it's to—'

'Tex.'

Had Frank snapped his name, like he was miffed? He wasn't jealous, was he? Not again. First Jin, now Tex? Hang on, she thought, why would she even think that? Disorientation from the shock or, she found herself wondering, wishful thinking? And this was before she'd taken any painkillers. 'Just give me a minute, okay?' She needed time to type, and to get herself together.

Adding to info I gave in my call:
i) the Persian is on SinoCorp payroll
ii) SinoCorp money trail to Norks
iii) left satphone relay outside tunnel entrance & transceiver inside, so your people can check what I told you

iv) attached is supporting evidence taken from location

v) remember, launch at 10 am local Sino time

TS

After sorting into one file the images of the Iranian booklet, the rocket schematics, the CCTV clip and the animation, she compressed it, encrypted it, attached it and hit *send*. 'Over to you, Marconi.' She lay down and turned her head to Frank, 'And to you, Florence Nightingale.'

'Francis Nightingale, if you don't mind. First, a broad-spectrum antibiotic,' he said, flicking a syringe and squirting a little liquid into the air. 'That's if you believe FrensLens.'

'Fingers crossed it's not crushed rhino horn or I'll be all over you.'

'Turn over and show me that butt of yours.'

'Sounds like you're the one who's taken the aphrodisiac,' she said, rolling over.

She felt him pull down the top of her pants, swab her skin and jab in the needle.

'Done.'

'Funnily enough, I knew that.'

He handed her a white cotton napkin he'd rolled into a sausage shape and she placed it between her teeth. Now lying on her side, her injured arm up, she bit down as she watched him remove the compress he'd improvised on the island. The gush had eased to a trickle, partly due to the cold thickening her blood and partly luck that the shot had missed both her brachial and deep brachial arteries. He uncapped a bottle of brown liquid, apparently the local equivalent of Betadine.

'No thyroid diseases, pregnancy or breastfeeding?'

'Get on with it ... please!'

'Sorry in advance,' he said and began flushing her wound.

Her teeth clamped down on the napkin like a dog with a chew-toy, and she writhed on the table, wondering if this was what being flayed felt like, a torturer cutting into her with a razor, slowly peeling off her skin, inch by excruciating inch.

When her tears had slowed, she opened one eye and watched him twist open another bottle.

'This stuff is Chinese magic,' he told her. '*Yunnan baiyao* ... myrrh, dragon's blood, ginseng ... more secret herbs and spices than KFC, but no calories.' He smiled, but she didn't, couldn't. He tipped a heap of the white powder into his palm and put the bottle back on the utility trolley. 'The Vietcong used to carry vials of this stuff around their necks to plug up gunshot wounds. Here goes ...'

With Tori's shrieks, neither of them heard the beep from Frank's phone.

48

Washington, DC

WHEN SATIRISTS TAGGED WASHINGTON, DC AS the Hollywood for ugly people, General P. P. Vaddern—a towering, meaty man—usually topped the A-list, with a likeness that wouldn't be out of place among the gargoyles at Notre Dame Cathedral. Yet on a first meeting, the chairman of the Joint Chiefs could be deceiving; his cologne like a homey, buttery corn on the cob and his genial, folksy accent like a friendly slap on your back. Until you realised the slap was holding in the knife he'd just stabbed you with.

Vaddern preferred to stand during meetings, to dominate them, even if they were emergency NSC sessions in the White House Situation Room, like this one. As he prattled on, President Diaz's day, her third in a row that had started at 4.30 am, was wearing her down.

Pointedly, she placed her hands on the table palms down, her scarlet nails and the pinpoints of her eyes challenging him until his dazzling mosaic of military decorations, and his mouth, stopped still. 'General,' she said, 'don't we have enough intel to justify me getting President Hou on the line?'

In stockinged feet, shoes left under the table, she stepped over to the nearest wall monitor. For the past ten minutes it had been showing them a series of live satellite feeds: an island at night lit up by lurching searchlights and a chaos of olive and tan dots where men in uniform swarmed on and off a jetty. 'Let's recap,' she said. 'First, GPS co-ords place this a micron inside the North Korean side of its border with China. Second, with so many uniforms, whatever they're guarding must be significant. Third, with the colour and cut of the cloth and those earmuff hats ... *ushankas* ... these are military personnel. North Korean, right General?'

Vaddern nodded and opened his mouth but she kept going. 'Fourth, despite all our eyes in the sky and ears on the ground,' she cast a prickly glance at the Director of National Intelligence Robert Hirsty, 'no one on this committee had any idea until an hour ago that the Norks were operating this site ... a base so damn close to China they could hop over to Dandong to buy their Starbucks and it'd still be steaming hot when they brought it back. Are we all on the same page so far?' Her eyes scanned the room.

Narthex, two seats away from where Vaddern was standing, coughed into his hand. 'What is it, Dr Carter?' she asked.

He spoke quietly, eyes down. 'Ma'am, er, I don't think Dandong has a Starbucks ...' He looked up and paused.

Her eyes were fixed on him as the room fell silent. All the paper rustling, the chair squeaks, the coffee slurps, they'd all stopped. Then she laughed. 'And that brings me to the additional intel your asset brought us, as yet unverified. Dr Carter, correct me if my summary omits anything. One, that factory on the island is leased by China's most well-connected company, Mingmai. Two, lurking under Mingmai's nose ... or built by them, we don't know ... is a massive silo with a rocket in situ. Three, blast-off is in,' she glanced at the clock, 'eight hours twenty. And four, with Iran's fingers in this—including those of a Dr Masoud Akhtar who I hadn't heard of before today—the rocket might well have a nuclea—'

'Ma'am, like you said, all o' that's unverified,' Vaddern piped up. He rubbed one of his huge hands over his Sahara of a scalp, as unblemished by hair as his temperament was by restraint. 'Buildin' an' launchin' a rocket from inside an underground silo ain't no—' He stopped, and Isabel followed his eyes to see DNI Robert Hirsty smoothing back the gelled black helmet that passed for his hair. 'Robby,' said Vaddern, 'I know that *you* know the Russkies been doin' the underground thing with their Dnepr rocket program outta Kazakhstan, but come on man ... the Norks?'

Almost a year in the job had trained Isabel to stop her eyes rolling at these boys' games. Today she'd had enough. 'Gentlemen,' she said, 'that this is happening underground suggests North Korea's trying to prevent us, or China, Japan, South Korea from getting advance knowle—'

'Unless China did some o' the buryin' for them.'

'Whoever it is—North Korea, China, one of them, even both of them—the launch would've gone off without us even having a chance to argue about it if Dr Swyft hadn't called this in.'

DNI Hirsty leapt up. 'Are you shitting me?' He banged his fist on the table, his bug eyes scuttling over the president. '*Swyft*? *That's* who Carter got this from? Don't you remember why she got booted out of the Agency?'

Narthex rose up in protest but the president, gripping the back of her chair, glared with what people called her Medusas at both men and kept glowering until they fell silent.

'I am aware the CIA and Dr Swyft parted ways in contentious circumsta—'

'There was nothing conte—'

'Director!'

'Yes, ma'am,' he said, sitting back down.

'You do recall it was only six weeks ago that I awarded her ...' she pointed a finger at her chest, '*I* awarded *her* a Presidential Medal of Freedom for her valour?'

'After I counselled you not to, ma'am,' he said, a defiant scowl kinking his upper lip.

Isabel's stomach tightened. 'Given we convened this afternoon solely because of the intel Dr Carter received from Dr Swyft, that earlier advice of yours isn't looking particularly astute.' Cutting off Hirsty's attempt to respond, she turned back to Narthex. 'You told me that Dr Swyft's been shot.'

'That's what she told me, ma'am.'

Isabel nodded so everyone present, especially DNI Hirsty, could absorb the weight of Tori's latest sacrifice. Yet for some reason he was smirking, like a seven-year-old bursting with a secret. 'General,' she said, one eye still on the DNI, 'please continue.'

Vaddern tipped his head at her. 'If what Swyft says is accurate, we can't exclude the Norks bein' in cahoots with China, which'd mean the site could really be China's.'

'Ma'am,' said DNI Hirsty, 'this council should know that Swyft,' he virtually spat out her name, 'has form with the Iranian ... three years back, in Tehran. I don't want to say too much except that she and he ... It was a honeypo—'

Snap. Narthex's pencil broke and Isabel noticed his mouth imitating a fish. 'Stop there, Director,' she said. 'I don't want to follow your unsavoury drift. Honeypot or not, was that sting Agency-directed?' She'd read Swyft's file before awarding her the medal, so she knew the answer and padded back to her seat to pour a glass of water, waiting for Hirsty to speak.

'Ma'am.' It was Vaddern. 'Mah opinion is that you don' pick up the phone to President Hou on the mere say-so of a girl who's likely hallucinatin' after bein' winged ... unless we can verify some o' what she's tellin' us.'

Isabel sighed and pointed her glass at the monitor. 'North Korean uniforms ... guns ... searchlights ... panic. More panic, General, than if you had a six-foot rattler creeping up one of those trouser legs of yours.' She placed the glass down. 'If we had a situation like this brewing right on our border— say Mexico's military was massing in Tijuana at a previously unknown missile site—and one of our allies knew about it, wouldn't you expect them to tell you about it before it shot off your ball—'

Narthex coughed again, and stood, close to the general but a head shorter. 'Madam President, if I may?'

She nodded.

'I agree with General Vaddern but only in part. Not the part, sir,' Narthex said, giving the general a black look, 'about our asset being delusional or some ... girl. Where I do agree, is that you, Madam President, should hold off calling President Hou. While I believe there's enough to warrant a call without verifying Dr Swyft's intel, calling him when we can't yet be certain that China has clean hands could jeopardise whatever needs to be done, as well as her safety. She's already taken one bullet for us—'

'Which is what assets are paid to do, sonny,' interrupted Vaddern.

Narthex put his hands in his pockets but Isabel could see he was pumping his fists. 'Assets? Swyft doesn't work for us any more, sir,' he said, barely concealing his contempt. 'She's a loyal citizen who stumbled over this and elected to do her patriotic duty ... at great personal risk.' He turned his back on the general and sat down. 'Ma'am,' he said from his seat, 'I've ... I've only had one phone conversation with her over this, a brief one. We've been trying for a second.'

The president turned to Hirsty, to find out what help she could offer Tori. 'Director, what other ... what assets do we have near Dandong?'

49

Dandong

MEDICATED, CLEANED UP AND SWATHED, TORI'S nausea and sweats were fading, the pain winding down to a dull throb. No longer wearing clothes caked with blood and dirt was itself a salve. The washcloth she'd left in the bathroom was almost as crimson as the clinic uniform Frank had found for her. She'd rejected it, and instead did up the last button on someone's powder-blue shirt, eased on their cardigan—a mauve knit—and black slacks. Sitting on the bed, she pulled a clean blanket around her. To give her space, Frank had gone to the bathroom. While waiting for him to return, she decided to roll through the rest of the launch animation she'd copied at the island. As she fast-forwarded toward the end, she suddenly froze, the little blood she had left turning to ice. 'Frank!' she shouted. 'Quick, get out here. The rocket. It's—'

'What?' He burst through the door, rushed over and slid onto the treatment bed beside her.

'Come on, come on,' she barked as the clip stalled on rewind, stabbing her finger repeatedly at the screen to get it going again. 'They're bringing on an American apocalypse.' The video skipped back to the frame where the nose-cone split and the payload fairing jettisoned. 'Here. We'll take it from here ... Satellite spinning off into orbit—nothing out of the ordinary—orbiting pole to pole at a circa 300-mile altitude, a complete revolution every ... see that number there ... every ninety-five minutes. With the Earth rotating beneath it, the satellite would eventually coil its way up and down over virtually every continent, but it's not going to do that.' She increased the playback speed to twenty times. They watched the satellite head south, traversing the South Pole, then proceeding up from Antarctica, on a north-northwest trajectory to cross the Indian Ocean, overflying Latin America and Central America, then passing over Louisiana.

Frank looked at Tori like he thought she was hallucinating from the drugs. 'This all seems pretty norm—'

She raised her hand. 'A bit longer.'

When it reached eastern Kansas, Frank jolted. 'Holy hellfire! No! They can't. No way. Tori, this isn't poss—'

'If someone doesn't stop them it's more than possible. *We* have to stop them.'

'Tex! You've got to call him. Now! Here, use this phone.' He took a new burner out of his backpack so fast he almost dropped it.

Tori switched it on and connected the encrypter. 'I've sent him the animation already.'

Frank pointed to the icon bouncing on her tablet. 'Actually, you haven't. The email's still sending. He needs a heads up. Now!'

She'd only dialled five digits when a text message came through:

URGENT re +. Call me but NOT to this number and NOT from that phone. TOSS that phone and leave clinic NOW. If I tracked you there, so can +. When you've left ... bowl into this with my T-match o's, b's & w's. Bottoms up twice, and long may you wind up your cuckoo clocks & freeze your balls off. From the Sultan of Swing.

'What the hell is this?' She showed it to Frank. 'Who knows this number?'

'Only Thatcher, but this isn't from him. We've got a different protocol for emergencies.'

'How are we supposed to call them back?' she said, packing her backpack and pulling the blanket over her shoulders. 'We don't have their—'

'—number? We do. It's there ... in the message.'

'It's gibberish, from someone who apparently likes Dire Straits.'

'Wrong. Dire Straits' album was *Sultans of Swing*, plural. Remember that cricket ball on my desk at work ... the one autographed by Wasim Akram?' His pitch dropped slightly, as if Tori should remember who Akram was.

'Your point?' she asked.

'Let's get out of here first,' he said, helping her down from the bed. He swept up the spare medications from the trolley, threw them in his bag and slung it over his shoulder, then grabbed hers and some blankets before leading the way to the door. 'Whoever crafted that message made it crackable only by devoted cricket nuts, in other words, very few people in China.'

'Including me.' She took the sheet of painkillers that Frank had missed from the trolley and slipped them into her shirt pocket.

'Sultan of Swing, singular, is a nickname for Wasim Akram.' He inched the door to the waiting room open and stuck his head out to check there was no welcoming party.

'I see,' said Tori stepping through. 'And all that stuff about *bowl into this with my T-match o's, b's and w's?*'

'It means the numbers of Akram's overs, balls and wickets in Test matches, *T-matches.*'

'Great. With Google kind of useless over here, how can we—'

Frank stopped at the front door and huffed. 'Tori, a chap born in Britain to Pakistani parents doesn't need Google to tell him a cricket score. When it comes to the gentlemen's game, I *am* Google. And,' he said, poking his head out the front door and looking around, 'when the text says *bottoms up* it's telling us to reverse the order, so we put wickets first, then balls, then overs. And because it says *bottoms up twice* we then have to reverse each of the sets of numerals. Take his wickets ... no, that's a bad example—'

'What's wrong with wickets?' said Tori, pulling the blanket closer around her and stepping outside.

'There were 414 of them.'

'Aha!' she said.

'And double-aha,' he said, 'since 41 is Switzerland's country code for which our faceless friend gives us a crosscheck, a place to *wind up your cuckoo clocks and freeze your balls off.*'

'Yours maybe.' She gave her best attempt at a laugh as Frank crushed the phone under his heel and kicked the pieces into the gutter.

The clouds hiding the moon had moved on, so the night was clearer than when they'd arrived, brighter. Tori looked up and down the street at the line of parked cars. 'So Robin, which one is the *Batmobile?*'

50

Washington, DC

DNI HIRSTY SHUFFLED THROUGH THE PAPERS in front of him searching for the answer to the president's question. Clearly unable to find it, he swung around to an assistant seated at the wall who Isabel noticed had been rifling through her own file. The woman drew out a sheet of paper and passed it to him. 'The closest assets we've got to Dandong,' he said, reading from the page, 'are 500 clicks away, in either Tianjin or Beijing. They'd take ten hours to drive, at best, and flying commercial, the next flight's not for ...' He turned to his assistant.

'Sixteen hours,' she said.

Isabel frowned. 'Can they charter?'

'Bad idea after Hou's declaration of a state of emergency. Anything out of the ordinary would stick out like the proverbial.'

'We've got no one closer?'

He shrugged. 'We had no reason to.'

Isabel's face dropped, incredulous. 'No reason ... with all this going on under your nose ... our noses?'

Hirsty was about to defend himself when the door opened. Isabel looked up expectantly, hoping either for lunch or a gun, but it was Gregory Samson, her chief of staff, an unwrapped muesli bar clamped in his mouth, a three-inch muddle of files wedged under an arm and his customary Diet Coke in hand. He shambled in, one of his highly-polished brogues closing the door. He splayed the files on the table at his usual seat and plonked down the Coke, a glug of the brown fizz slopping onto the paperwork. Taking the blue linen pocket square from his jacket breast pocket like a throwaway tissue, he mopped up the puddle. Then, taking the snack bar from between his teeth, he began ripping and crinkling the wrapper. 'Madam President, Mr Secretary, Mr Chairman, Directors of et cetera, et cetera,' he mumbled through a mouthful of muesli before dropping the packaging into DNI Hirsty's half-empty coffee cup. While Isabel thought the act unworthy she took more delight in it than was presidential.

Samson swallowed. 'We can verify some of the Swyft intel. In a moment the team's going to populate those screens with some historic satellite stills of that island.' His hand gestured toward the monitors and a sprinkle of honeyed nuts and grains scattered across the table. He licked a finger and dabbed them cluster by cluster, popping them into his mouth as he went. Isabel's stomach rumbled.

On one of the screens a new image appeared, *June 1988* in its bottom left corner. Samson continued. 'From the co-ords there, you can see it's the same island.' Isabel studied the image. 'But,' he added, 'there's no factory, no jetty, not yet.'

Not even a hut or a shed scarring the drab field of cocoa-coloured dirt, thought Isabel.

Like an old-school cartoon flip book, new images flashed onto the screen, the dates jerking forward, a market garden taking over the island with pockets of vegetation, two duck ponds and five chicken roosts. 'We're fast-forwarding the life of Island X,' said the chief of staff, 'a compilation in chronological order from 1988 to now. What you'll see next—'

'That's one hell of a pit,' said General Vaddern as the stills moved forward a couple of decades.

'True,' said Samson as the images continued to fly toward the present day, 'and the construction was decidedly quick for such a massive undertaking ... eighteen months, give or take, from paddock to pit to fireproof linings to concrete foundations to walls to sliding roof—'

'An' all that under China's nose.'

'And ours,' Isabel repeated, pleased to see the DNI had developed an urgent problem with the back seam of his tie, his eyes clearly avoiding hers.

General Vaddern glanced at Narthex and then at President Diaz. 'I grant you this here is damn solid, but what don' make sense to me, Mr Samson—'

'Hold that thought, General.'

Everyone watched as the images flipped through more and more seasons, barge after barge pulling up beside the island to unload crates from large to very large, all trolleyed unopened into the tunnel.

'Can we zoom in on the shipping labels?' asked the president.

'Our cameras are too high up for that kind of detail, ma'am.'

'Like I was goin' to say,' said the general, 'I git that they been buildin' in there. But an underground rocket launch site? It don' make a scrap o' sense to me, 'specially since the Norks have got their existin' launch station at Sohae an' it's only what, an hour's drive? Two hours' maybe? An' equal to that, where'd those Nork numbnuts get the dough to pay for all this?'

'According to Dr Swyft, possibly from Mingmai,' said Narthex.

'Ma'am,' the general paused, stretching an arm over the table for Samson's drink can, ignoring his filthy look as he picked it up. 'That's no chickenshit facility so I'm thinkin' that President Hou's gotta already know about it. Even if he didn't shell out the cash for it, it looks kinda like his proxy did. The CEO o' Mingmai's a government stooge, everyone knows that.' He downed a slurp of Samson's Diet Coke, wiped his mouth with the back of his hand and, as he swivelled back to face the screen, slid the can back across the table. 'Next time, Samson, bring us the real thing.'

This wasn't the first time Isabel had heard Vaddern make this 'joke'. Samson's eyes were simmering as he said, 'Hou *might* know, General, but there's still a fair chance he might not.'

'The Sinos *know*, young fella, take it from me.'

The door opened again. It was the vice-president, Spencer Prentice. Prentice and Isabel went way back, pre-politics, to when he'd been her trusted financial adviser.

Stepping inside, Prentice tossed her a bag of corn chips like he'd had a direct line to the grumblings in her stomach: jalapeño cheddar, her favourite. 'Ma'am, another mosque situation,' he said, standing near the door. 'An unexploded firebomb, inside this time.'

She caught the chip packet and ripped it open, briefly tipping her nose over the top to take in the tangy spice. 'Come in, Spencer, the committee's done for now.' She turned to the others. 'We'll reconvene in half an hour. Dr Carter, see if you can get Dr Swyft to join us by phone when we're back. And get some food sent in,' she said, shovelling a handful of chips into her mouth.

51

Island near Dandong

LYING IN HIS AFT COCKPIT, CHEN Fang was trussed as tightly as the live chickens at Harbin Zoo just before the handlers fed them to the tigers. Steel chains coiled around his body from his shoulders to his ankles, weighing him down. Two inches of murky water sploshed around him and when he twisted his head to get his mouth out of the slop, he saw the same six gun barrels still aimed at him.

Didn't they understand it had been a huge mistake, that all he'd wanted was a few extra yuan to stuff in his pockets along with the redhead's greenbacks? That whole wad was now in one of *their* pockets, their 'proof' he was an American spy, their justification for executing him here, now.

'Please, General sir, it's hard for me to breathe,' Chen shouted, burbling through a wash of water.

'And when I count three it will be impossible,' a Korean yelled back. 'One, two ...'

52

Dandong

IN AMONG THE THREE FORDS, TWO Buicks, a blue
Dongfeng, a white BYD and a red Chevy parked outside
the clinic, Tori selected an ancient Volkswagen, a car so old
it hailed from the era before VW even had emission controls to
cheat on and, more relevantly, before car alarms and computerised
ignitions. By the time she'd slid onto the cracked vinyl passenger
seat, Frank had already hot-wired the starter, and the ancient
engine was knocking and wheezing its emphysemic lungs out.

She coughed, pushing her door back open and shook the
ashtray choked with cigarette ends into the gutter. 'I said
Batmobile not *Buttmobile*.' After slamming the door shut, she
squinted out the windscreen, checking whether the desultory
glow coming off the rear bumper ahead of them was a reflection
of their lights or a streetlamp. 'Believe it or not, Frank, our

headlights are on. It'll be a miracle if you don't hit anything.' She wound her window down a crack and stuck the satphone extension aerial out. 'Now we're back out in the open, I'll be able to get that data to Tex faster.'

Frank crunched the car into gear and they rattled along Dandong's backstreets, not yet sure where they were headed. Tori switched on a new burner phone and punched in the numbers Frank started dictating to her. She put it on loudspeaker. 'Hello? ... Who's there? ... *Hello*?'

Static.

Frank spoke this time. 'Who *is* that?'

'Good, it's both of you.' The woman spoke with a clipped Asian-American accent. 'When you've encrypted that phone, call me again.'

'She hung u–u–U–P!' squealed Tori as Frank veered to avoid a scrawny dog nudging a bottle down the middle of the road. He missed, narrowly. 'She's more paranoid than fucking us, and we're the ones who've almost been killed ... twice!'

'If you must swear, it's fucking *we*,' said Frank, swerving back onto the road.

'Cricket king *and* grammar guru. How lucky am I?' she grumbled as she plugged the encryption pack on and pressed *redial*. 'It's ringing.'

Frank chuckled. 'And if she's paranoid you're deaf. I *can* hear it, you know, you've got it on loudspeaker.'

Tori tossed him a dirty look just as the woman picked up. 'Hey, Ms Sultan, can we stop playing gam—'

'It's no game when the people who almost killed your boss are trying to kill all three of us.'

'Axel?' Frank slammed his foot on the car's excuse for brakes, the balding tyres skidding into a slide. Tori lurched forward, the phone flying out of her hand and bouncing off the windscreen.

Frank managed to catch it at the same time as steer the car away from the postbox Tori was sure he was going to hit.

'How is Axel connected … Who the hell *are* you?' she said.

'Will Red Scorpion do?'

'You're a … a w-woman?' Frank stammered.

'Frank, is that a pick-up line they taught you at Legoland?' the woman said.

His lips pressed into a thin line as he rolled the car into a parking spot. Tori pondered what shook him the most, that Red Scorpion knew Tori had just been shot and precisely where they'd been holed up, that Axel's coma wasn't payback for a life of indulgence but a murder attempt, that Red Scorpion knew Frank had worked at MI6—Legoland being spook-speak for its HQ—or that Thatcher might not be the asexual or possibly gay man Frank had always suspected.

'Thatcher told you how to reach us, right?' Frank asked.

'You give me no credit. Thatcher has no idea about this, any of it.'

Frank scowled. 'But he's your friend.'

'A prudent rival is less dangerous than a foolish friend.'

53

THE LENGTH OF THE ALLEY WAS flanked with rear fences, gates and garage doors. This was apartment land, cookie-cutter blocks either side. Frank parked halfway up the alley where the buildings were low-rises so he could maintain the satphone's line of sight to keep it sending to Tex. He cut the engine and Red Scorpion continued.

'They intend to kill you before you find out who they are,' she said. 'They tried to kill Axel because he *did* know, which is why they're after me ... I was the one who told him. But before we get into the who and why, you need proof of my bona fides. Type this web address into your browser ...' The jumble of letters and numbers took Red a full minute to rattle through, Frank typing as she went. 'On that site, you'll find three video clips. Call me back once you've seen them, and be quick; the site is a oncer and will self-destruct in fifteen … no fourteen minut—'

'It's asking for a login and—'

'The login is Tori's father's birthday, six-digit format … month, day, year … and the password is Frank's mother's birthday … year, month, day. Bye.'

Tori turned to Frank, frowning. 'How does she know all—'

'She's Red Scorpion,' he said, amazed to find himself on the same side as a former nemesis.

Once they were logged in, three semi-transparent icons popped up, blue progress bars filling up beneath each of them. Frank began tapping at the icons.

'Let them loa—' Tori started, then leapt up in her seat when strobing amber flashes lit up their car's interior and the street. She flipped open the glove compartment and patted her hand around inside. 'Here,' she said, holding up a screwdriver.

'That's not going to stop a garbage truck,' Frank said, relieved that was all it was. He wound down his window to wave it through. When it stopped beside their bumper, unable to get past, he hot-wired the ignition again and drove further up the lane, still in a low-rise section but this time driving his wheels up onto the curb, leaving enough space for the truck to squeeze by once it finished banging and crashing the bins behind them.

'Put your window up. Jesus!' Tori said. 'It's freezing out there.' She placed the screwdriver on the seat beside her and pulled the clinic blanket over her knees. 'That truck's not exactly a Chanel No. 5 factory.'

Frank rolled up his window and turned the heater switch up a notch, the sputtering of the fan and the engine blocking out a little of the bin noise. By now, two of the icons had gone solid, a gold one labelled *Rome*, and a blue one, *Boston*. A red one was third, *Russia*. It was still loading. 'Twelve minutes until this site dies,' said Frank. He clicked the *Boston* icon and the clip started rolling. It began from a vantage point high up in a skeleton of grey tree branches, so spindly and weak he saw Tori holding her breath, waiting for them to snap and the camera operator to crash through, but he didn't and the shot panned slowly downward. 'Wait, is that …? It's Beacon Street.' Frank said, peering closer. Zooming left, the lens took them over the blacktop to the stately red brick facade they walked through regularly.

Below the shuttered bow windows and tangles of ivy winding through black wrought iron balconies, SIS's front door opened. 'Axel!' they both cried as their muffin of a boss poked his head out and put on his hat, a Gatsby flat cap in a beige herringbone. Frank gasped and pointed to the time and date watermarked in the clip's corner. 'This is around ten minutes before I got to him.'

Swaddled in a caramel cashmere coat with a fat cigar clamped in his mouth, Axel pulled his brim over his eyes and shuffled down the steps. Pausing at the last, he raised his eyes to the sky and took a long, deep puff of his smoke. As he exhaled, he nodded to an elderly woman passing by then stepped down onto the pavement and squeezed himself—no small feat—between the two cars parked out front: a black Mercedes SUV and an arctic silver BMW coupe. Frank was mentally noting all the details, since they wouldn't have access to the video long enough for a replay.

A puff of grey smoke wafted from Axel's mouth as he waited for a yellow school bus to rumble by. Frank took a screenshot to capture its licence plate.

The garbage truck growled up to, then past their VW, its orange flashes making Tori look like she'd lost even more blood. The light was so intense it washed out the screen so by the time they could see it again, Axel was halfway across Beacon Street, his shadow long and oddly thin behind him. He was walking slowly so as not to slip on any patches of ice, keeping an eye out for oncoming traffic. When Axel turned left at the pavement on the other side, Frank looked out the window and saw the truck take a right at the T-junction up ahead, its strobes fading away.

Axel strolled east, toward the entrance into Boston Common where Frank had found him. He ran his hand along the spear-finial fence like a child trying to make the bars tinkle, which maybe they would've if he hadn't been wearing gloves. He stopped at the steps directly beneath the camera and studied his cigar, rolling it around in his fingers like it was helping him visualise what to do about the information Red Scorpion had apparently just given him.

As Frank looked down on him, he imagined Axel's brow creasing beneath the cap brim, his head resting on his chins, his puffy eyes squeezed shut trying to work out who to tell, what to tell them, how to stay safe …

Frank shifted in his seat, staring at the screen. 'Remember I said there was a balloon? Maybe it wasn't from a kid's party. Maybe the balloon was hoisting the camera?'

'What's that?' said Tori, as a puff of grey mist, so pale, so diaphanous it was almost imperceptible, shot out from below the lens. The vapour trail settled over Axel's head and shoulders, hovering briefly until it wafted into nothingness.

Axel looked up, his eyes pinched in question. He seemed to spy the camera, his mouth opening but emitting no sound. His shoulders slumped, more than their usual droop, the cigar fell from his fingers and his knees buckled under him. He was halfway down when the video ended, sparing them the sight of him hitting the ground.

For a few seconds, all Frank could hear was the VW's engine pitting and the warm airflow hissing through the vents. 'It *was* a hit,' said Frank.

'The hospital performed every test under the sun but they missed the gas.'

'And why'd the killer record this? It doesn't make sense.'

'Everything makes sense, Frank. Apart from religion, politics and, of course, Wagner.'

Frank ignored her jibe about his musical preferences. 'We've only got only four minutes left.'

The second video opened on the hazy pre-dawn silhouette of St Peter's Basilica in Rome. After the first five seconds, the camera swivelled around to a wall, so close to the ancient bricks the cameraman could have licked them as he panned upwards, the motion fluid, as if the camera were floating. In one take, it rose past hundreds of rows of thin grey bricks, their edges ground away by centuries of weather, laid out as if all the Morse code tapped out in history had been layered on top of itself.

'In the Boston video, the camera's up a tree or under a balloon and here, it's on a scissor lift,' said Frank. The camera kept rising, scooting past one, two, three tiers of grimly shuttered windows, most of them peaked with triangular stone gables. Arriving at some shutters that were wide open, the camera shuddered to a halt and hovered. The left-side window casement had been pulled in like an invitation but at first they couldn't make out anything inside.

'I assume,' said Tori, picking up the screwdriver and tapping it against her leg, 'that this is the Vatican?'

As the video-burglar went in over the sill, the moon behind him cast a faint shadow against the glass, suggesting a rotund figure. 'See that water pitcher?' said Frank, pointing to the gold rim glinting in the moonlight. 'The intruder's shadow … it's about the same diameter as the pitcher is high. Is it a child?'

The video continued. 'What the …' Both of them went to hit *pause* but Frank got in first and scrolled the image back and forward a few times. 'There,' he pointed. 'It's not a person at all. And there's no scissor lift.'

They both stared at the reflection in the gilded mirror. A ball-shaped drone, a gyroscopic toxin-spraying, video-recording drone. Frank slapped the car's steering wheel. 'Damn! The Boston balloon … It was a drone, too. How did I miss—'

Tori pressed *play* and, piercing through the veil of darkness ahead of the lens, a needle of golden light whooshed into the room and located a man in bed, flat on his back. The needle began to draw circles around his face, faster and faster as a cloud of spray shot into the room. Then, in the long, solid cone of golden light, his face floated as if it was detached. His eyes were mesmerised, agape in a kind of raptured awe. Tori sucked in a breath. 'Are his irises—'

'Pink,' Frank murmured.

They were watching the uncut version of one of the world's most infamous video clips. The footage shot outside the walls or on entering the room had never been seen before. RUA had edited them out. The public version of the kill clip began with the Pope's head lit up, his eyes fluttering open, widening, then rolling back. The whole planet had seen it, been shocked by it. It had sparked riots, bombings, shootings, mass arrests.

Frank leant back in his seat and ran his fingers through his hair. '*Death by drone* …. this is the proof.'

Tori paused the video and turned to him. 'What's the link? I get how a bunch of extremist sickos might at a stretch go after a pope and two prime ministers to settle some crazy religious vendetta—'

'Fear ... global destabilisation ... the terror that unless China gives in to their demands their tentacles can touch anyone, anywhere and anytime.'

'Right, but Axel? Why would RUA want to kill Axel?'

'And if Red Scorpion is right—'

'Both of us ... and her.'

Up ahead at the T-junction, shadows shifting over the apartment blocks caught Frank's eye. 'Tori, if we stay here we may never find out. Look,' he pointed. 'High beams incoming from the right.' He whacked the gearshift into reverse.

54

A HUMMER ON STEROIDS SCREECHED TO a stop in the middle of the T up ahead. Its passenger doors swung open, a searchlight on the roof flaring and swivelling around into the alley. 'If those chaps are stopping by to borrow a cup of soy sauce, we'd better go find some,' Frank said. They both twisted their heads back as he reversed, then Tori saw the T behind them was also lighting up. 'Stop, stop!' she yelled.

Frank slammed on the brakes. 'Soy's in hot demand tonight. Time we get out and *run*!' He swung one hand over to the rear seat to get his backpack and opened his door with the other. Tori crammed all the devices as well as the screwdriver, into her own pack, snatched a blanket and shoved her door open.

By the time voices filled the air, boots hit the ground and the searchlights lit up their VW, Frank's shoulder had splintered a red doorway off its hinges and Tori was following him, tumbling into a courtyard. A sensor light snapped on, a weak, sickly yellow glow just bright enough for them to make out a stack of empty paint tins piled up against a wall beside a heap of carpet offcuts. What looked like a cairn of black river pebbles stood beside a trailer boat under a tatty canvas, a wooden ladder splayed on the ground in front of it.

Frank propped the door back up, snatched up one of the pebbles, kissed it and tossed it at the bulb. The advancing shouts drowned out the pop and the shattering glass as it hit the paving. 'Well bowled, Sultan!' Tori whispered. She jiggled the apartment building's back door. Hefty metal, it was bolted from the inside with a tight seal. 'No go.'

Moving quickly, they hoisted the ladder up, leant it against the right-hand fence and were about to clamber up it when they heard voices right outside. Tori held out her blanket. 'Use it as a distraction.' Frank tossed it onto the fence palings so it snagged, to make it look like they'd jumped over into next door. He then balled up another blanket he pulled from his backpack and threw it high and long into the adjoining yard as further 'proof'. The goons were close. 'The boat!' said Frank. They ran to it and Frank pried open the far corner of the tarpaulin, careful not to disturb either the grime or the icy water pooled on top. 'Get in,' he said, jutting his knee out for her to use as a step.

'The Boston Marathon bomber hid in a boat. Too obvious?' Tori said. But it was their only option so she gripped his shoulder with her right hand and stepped up onto his knee.

'People around here don't watch CNN,' he said.

'Does anyone?' She hooked her leg over the gunwale into the cockpit, then dipped her head and slipped under the cover. 'Stagnant *and* freezing. Perfect.' Her eyes stung and, trying not to breathe through her nose, she wriggled over to make room for Frank as he climbed in beside her, both of them shrouded in the blackness and stench. She heard him trying to lip the canvas back over the rails when the muster of incoming boots crashed into the courtyard.

Intense but fleeting bursts of light, like lasers, pierced through a rip in the cover as torches swung around searching for them. 'The ladder. Up, up, up,' shouted a voice in Mandarin. The jerky creaks of the ladder against the fence told Tori their distraction was working.

Huddled and shivering at the stern of the boat, a few inches of icy, rancid water pooling in the bow, they waited, Tori trying every technique not to breathe the putrid air and not to throw up.

'That way,' yelled a woman from above them, presumably the first up the ladder. A moment later she grunted, her boots thumping down on the other side, and what sounded like three others scuttled up the rungs to follow her over. 'I think I see them,' the woman shouted and Tori heard them clambering over what she guessed was the next fence.

Lying still, taking in as little air as possible, Tori strained her ears, trying to glean whether anyone was hanging back. Unless the fumes got to them first, it looked like they were going to make it. She squeezed Frank's hand, a cue to let the hush outside tick over a bit longer.

They waited.

Suddenly, her bag began vibrating beside her. It had to be the new burner. She had forgotten to switch it to silent. Her hand flew into her bag and she fumbled around, just managing to silence it before the ringer started. They waited. Nothing. They waited longer. Nothing.

To make light of her blunder, she whispered, 'Why did the Hobbit put his phone on silent?'

The answer came quick as a flash. 'He was bored of the rings.'

But it wasn't Frank. Tori's stomach clenched. Her hand still inside her backpack, she gripped the screwdriver feeling Frank coiling up beside her, ready to spring at the man who'd beaten him to the punchline.

The original voices and boots had faded into the distance. Yet mere inches away was a man so fluent in English he could crack literary puns, and who at 2.15 am was unlikely to be a stranger on his way home from book club.

Was he going to shoot at them anonymously, through the hull, so they'd die not knowing their killer? Or would he tear back the tarp, stare into their eyes and shoot them point blank?

Tap. Tap-tap. He was taunting them, a tease, prolonging their distress.

With the air stinging and her body shaking from fear and cold, Tori desperately wanted to shut her eyes but forced them to stay open, training them upwards, waiting, wired for the first sign of movement.

Tap. Tap-tap.

The canvas ripped back over their heads, the light blinding. 'Up!' he said in English.

Tori got to her knees, so numb that she rose with a demeaning wobble instead of the cocky defiance she'd intended. Frank followed but, with two good arms, managed it better than her.

Unable to see, a blaze of torches shining into her eyes, she held the screwdriver low, below what she hoped was their captor's sightline, tightening her grip when she heard the unmistakable click of a gun clip, and the rasping grind of the slide telling her that she, or Frank, was in its sights. To her left, one of the torches bobbed up and down as the man holding it racked his gun too.

One screwdriver versus at least two firearms, both at close range. Her mind raced. Based on what Red Scorpion had given them, these gunmen had to be connected to the island, to Axel's coma, the pope's death, the attempt on her life in New York. How had they tracked them down?

'Dr Swyft,' the man said smoothly, his voice coming from behind one of the torches and, she guessed, one of the guns. 'It's a rare delight to find anyone in this country who shares my passion for Middle-earth even if it is under such strange circumstances.'

The voice was so amiable it chilled her blood.

It was also familiar.

55

Washington, DC

NARTHEX FOLDED THE PAPER TOWEL INTO a neat square and patted his face dry. He leant toward the washroom mirror and blinked repeatedly hoping the eye drops would soothe at least some of the scratchiness from his three all-nighters.

He checked his watch. *Damn!* He'd dozed off in the cubicle for longer than he thought. Luckily, it was still three minutes before the NSC reconvened in the Sit Room. Unluckily, he was going in empty-handed. Nothing Tori said she was sending him had come through, and no one—not he, the NSA nor the CIA—had been able to contact her.

Frantic for her safety, and anxious he'd let down the president, he crumpled the towel in his fist and chucked it at the wastebasket where it bounced off the rim and onto the floor. He burst out of the washroom into the corridor, barging straight into one of his staff, Loucineh, reams of paper flying out of her hands, though she managed to hang onto her tablet.

'*Ooph* ... Glad I found you.' She pressed the tablet into his hands and bent down to the scatter of papers, whisking them back into a neat pile. 'It's what you were waiting for, from that Swyft woman.' She was crouching on the floor looking up at him through her eyelashes. BT, before Tori, he might have held her lingering gaze, but now he quickly diverted his eyes to the tablet screen, focused on the email. 'Have you viewed the attachments?' he asked, keeping his eyes on the screen and off Loucineh.

'When her documents came through, I couldn't find you,' she said, still gathering papers, 'so I took it all into the Watch Floor.' The Watch Floor was the Situation Room's 24/7 high-tech control, support and communications centre. She began to get up. 'I watched them run the clip through facial recognition and, yes, what Swyft told you about the Iranian guy being there is correct. I left them working on other faces so I could try find you, to give you a heads up.' She held the papers out to him. 'Printouts of the rocket schematics. Don Juan,' she said, using an office nickname Narthex didn't like for her co-worker Dong-won, 'says they're in Korean, and he's working on a translation.' She separated two pages out. 'And these are part of an instruction manual for some kind of nuclear device, though you don't need my Persian language skills to tell you that,' she said pointing to the hazard symbol. She loaded him up with the papers. 'There's also an animation of the rocket's flight path but I didn't get to see that.'

They both heard someone running and, looking down the corridor, Narthex saw it was Blue Coat from the Watch Room. 'Loucineh! Dr Carter!' the man called.

Narthex had sketched Blue Coat several times, a man in his mid-twenties, square jaw, floppy ginger hair, blue eyes and—strange for someone so young—longish ear lobes. Narthex had only ever seen him hunched over his computer screen, always in the same navy jacket, and never flustered no matter what demands were flying at him. Until now. Narthex knew his actual name, of course, but it was the perennial jacket that stuck in his mind.

'Dr Carter!' Blue Coat puffed. He skidded to a stop, his hair falling in his eyes and the security pass he had looped around his neck swinging ahead of him and almost stabbing Loucineh in the stomach. 'Before you go in, sir … the Swyft materials … they include a simulation of a rocket trajectory and satellite orb—'

'Loucineh told—'

'It's the whole thing, sir, launch, boost-phase, staging, burn, cut off and orbit. And sir, there's more.' Blue Coat paused as if afraid to go on, took a deep breath and then continued in a rush. 'If it's for real, sir, their plan is to set off a super-EMP over Kansas forty-five minutes after lift-off and what that means—'

'Arma-fucking-geddon.' Narthex whispered it, almost unable to get it out, feeling the colour sap out of him.

56

Dandong

JIN YU STEPPED FORWARD INTO THE light, the long barrel of what looked to Tori like a Ruger Mark III in his hand. 'The guards on the island tell me they shot one of you. Was it you, Dr Swyft?'

She nodded mutely, grappling that this was Jin. With a gun. Pointed at her.

'They have been severely reprimanded. Please accept my humble apologies.'

Maybe Jin *didn't* know what was going on beneath his plant, she hoped, though she was aware that she, or her meds, were clutching at straws.

'Yes, Dr Swyft, I am terribly sorry … sorry that they didn't kill you.' Jin's frosty laugh cut through her.

He shifted his torch beam over her cardigan sleeve, playing it over the spot where the dressing bulged. 'Mr Chaudry,' he said, 'I take it you acted as nurse to the good doctor?'

Frank didn't bite, but Tori could feel his anger, could feel his hand draw close to squeeze hers, but feeling the screwdriver he slowly took it back.

Jin moved closer. 'Mr Chaudry,' he said, 'don't let your gallantry go to your head, not with two guns trained on you.' He raised the muzzle of his own up to Tori's arm. Even before he stroked it against her she cringed. He rubbed it lightly, delicately, almost a caress. Then, without warning, he leant forward, driving his weight behind it, digging the metal tube into her dressing, screwing it in clockwise and anti-clockwise, probing for her wound. When he found it, Tori couldn't suppress her cry and Jin began gouging, pushing and twisting even more.

The pain shot white shards into her eyes, fuzzing her head as sweat poured off her and her knees weakened. She felt hot blood soaking into her sleeve, as Jin's breathing became heavy and fast, like he was deriving some sick sense of satisfaction.

Why hadn't she heeded Frank's warnings about Jin? The man she'd admired, the loving father, the charming host ... in truth he was a loathsome, repulsive, sadistic bastard.

Bent on denying Jin any more gratification she squeezed her eyes shut, forcing back the squirms and grunts and grimaces, to be as unyielding and buttoned up as possible. She focused all her attention on gripping the screwdriver tighter, steeling herself to jab the tip of the blade into his chest, throat, eye, or whichever part of him he was stupid enough to leave vulnerable for a crucial one or two seconds.

As if he'd read her thoughts he pulled the gun away and she heard him step back. She opened her eyes to see him wiping her blood from his pistol onto the sleeve of one of his lackeys. 'Dr Swyft, my Precious,' he said with a malignant smile. 'Do you recall the sage advice that the elf Gildor gave Frodo?'

Tori could barely stay upright let alone answer. Her arm was an excruciating mass of torn nerve endings, her head thick, eyes wet and blurred, her dressing soaked and blood running down her arm, dripping off her fingers into the boat. She knew she had a sheet of painkillers in her shirt pocket but dared not reach for them.

'Surely you know it?' said Jin. '... No? How about this ... *Do not meddle in the affairs of wizards, for they are subtle and quick to anger.*'

'Where was the subtlety in what you just did to Tori?' sneered Frank, Tori wishing he'd kept quiet.

Jin stepped forward and smacked his pistol across the bridge of Frank's nose with a sickening crunch of bone. A spatter of his blood hit Tori's cheek.

'Subtlety is relative,' Jin laughed, 'which you will both soon discover.'

57

TOSSING A ROLL OF BLACK TAPE to a henchman, Jin told him in Mandarin, 'Cover their mouths then bind her arm, tight. I don't want her to die, not yet.' Turning to Tori, he said in English, 'I apologise for not carrying fresh bandages, but duct tape is amazing. As they say, if it doesn't fix something, just use more,' he laughed. 'But before my, er, assistant gets close enough to bind your arm, I suggest you surrender that little weapon you're holding down there.'

She gripped it harder.

'No?' He swung his pistol to point at Frank. 'What if I blew Mr Chaudry's head off? Would that change your mind?'

She raised the screwdriver and held it out.

He trained the gun back on her. 'So many people, Dr Swyft, have commented on your good judgement. Your client Mr

Skylakakis. Your boss Mr Mada. So good to see how right they were.'

One of his guards took the screwdriver then reached inside the boat and lifted out their backpacks. Taking one from him, Jin jiggled the pack, weighing it. 'You won't be needing these any longer.' He handed it back to the guard.

Another of his men was climbing up the ladder and at the top he unsnagged the blanket Frank had thrown there and threw it down. Jin managed to catch it and hand it to Tori without moving his pistol off her. 'Here. I can't possibly have you bleeding *and* freezing to death, not when I'm planning a far more dramatic way for you to die.'

He spun on his heel and, as he headed out of the courtyard, issued his instructions in Chinese. 'Tape up her arm, tie them up, take them back to the island and extract what they know and who they've told. Once you've checked it against their devices, take them to the airfield and strap them in beside the chute door on *Tuoma*. I'll jettison them into the Yellow Sea as shark bait when I fly back to Beijing. Don't screw this up. Nothing must get in the way of *Fuxing Tao*.'

To Tori it sounded like he said *foo-shing dow*, but her Mandarin only went so far. Judging by Frank's raised eyebrow and the slight shake of his head, he wasn't getting any help from FrensLens either.

Whatever *Fuxing Tao* was, if it came out of Jin Yu's mouth, she knew it couldn't be good.

Suddenly, wrenching her mouth away from the strip of duct tape about to cover it, Tori shouted to him, 'Axel Schönberg … the RUA assassinations … the rocket … the nuke … you're behind it all, aren't you? What would little Mingli think of his devoted *baba* if he could see …'

Jin stopped at the gate, flipped his gun to one of his men, and turned. 'To you, I may look like a—'

'A fucking monst—' she started to scream, as the guard punched her in the stomach, a second man holding Frank back.

'—but what you *think* you know, Dr Swyft, is only *this* much,' Jin said with a smirk and bringing a thumb and index finger close together. 'Whereas the big picture,' he spread his arms wide, his coat fanning out behind him, 'it is *all* for my son … for China's children … for the world's children. For *your* children if you were to have any … which sadly you will not. When *Fuxing Tao* triumphs, history will revere Jin Yu and its other architects, even if you don't … can't.'

There was the *foo-shing dow* thing again, thought Tori. What the hell did it mean?

Jin took out a phone and smiled as he watched the tape being wrapped over her mouth and around her head. He waited until it was done, then dialled.

While Tori couldn't be sure, it sounded like he began his call with, 'My dear Mada … Ron … And how is ye olde towne of Boston today?'

A black panel van—longer and taller than an SUV—rolled up to the gate as Jin exited the yard, sauntering out of earshot and turning right, phone to his ear and gesticulating as if chatting to an old friend.

Mada? Why was Jin calling him? Tori fumed. The change of limo services in Manhattan … maybe it hadn't been coincidental at all.

Jin's flunky grabbed her arm and jerked the roll of tape round and round it with as much empathy as a plumber fixing a leaky pipe. He ignored her squirming, her muffled cries and her blood, covering every spurt or drip with a new loop of tape up and over her arm. As he brought his hand around, stretching out more and more of the tape, he brushed the back of it against her breast. Seething with pain, she tuned out his violations, denying him her victimhood and, finally, when the end of the tape tore off the cardboard ring, he yanked her arms backwards to zip-tie her wrists behind her. The tape over her mouth wasn't enough to stop her wails from shattering the night, yet not a single window lit up above them. The locals, it seemed, knew better than to rubberneck.

Frank tried to intervene, to help her, but a guard stepped in his way, pistol-whipping his already bloody face and high-kicking his stomach, winding him and sending him reeling backwards into the prow of the old boat. The guard pulled him up and grabbed his wrists, lassoing a zip-tie around them. He shoved him to the ground to bind his ankles, then lifted him by the back of his belt, dragging him over to the van, before hurling him into the back, leaving him groaning and writhing on the floor.

'Why did we bother cleaning out the cargo bay?' laughed Tori's guard as he continued to wrench her arms behind her, forcing her fists open. Like her, he knew the classic escape trick, that clenching your fists thickened your wrists, making it easier to slide them out of the zip-ties when your captors weren't looking.

He pulled the ties tight and before she could figure out a way to grab the knife from his belt and cut off his balls he moved round to face her. His mouth curled into a salacious twist only a few inches from her own, his breath hot and stinking of sour cabbage. Calmly he touched his gun to her kneecap, then pushed it between her legs, slithering it slowly upward, dwelling at her crotch before pressing it in. Tori grunted and went to jump backwards, and he snapped at her in English. 'Move and I shoot pussy.' He licked his lips and slid the barrel in and out of the thigh gap at the top of her legs. Tori clamped her jaw shut, wishing for the assault to end quickly when, over his shoulder she saw another guard approaching, snarling silently. Creeping closer, he eyed Tori and put a finger to his lips. Then holstering his gun, he reached around and tugged his colleague's pistol from his hand, whacking the grip into the man's kidney. From his waist up, her tormentor lurched forward, squealing, '*Cao ni zuzong shiba dai!*' which she translated as something like *Go fuck your ancestors to the eighteenth generation.*

Her defender shrugged the curse off. 'She is Jin's plaything, not yours,' he said, leaving the man hunched over, swearing and muttering in Mandarin, while he and another guard frogmarched Tori out the gate to the van. A grey mist was spewing up out of its exhausts, its side door was open and the interior lights on. She could see Frank inside, doubled over on the floor. Another two men were leaning back against the grille having a smoke and she could see Jin halfway to the T-junction, still on his phone, his long coat billowing as he walked back, one hand waving into the night. A guard heaved her and Frank's backpacks into the rear, laughing as one of the bags narrowly missed Frank's head.

'Ah,' said Jin, arriving back at the van. 'The good Mr Mada wanted to speak with you but I told him you were both, er, tied up writing your reports giving the green light to Project Chant. Hey,' he said turning to his men, 'are you idiots? Take those backpacks and put them in the front cabin. And bind her feet as well.' The guard who'd protected her reverted to type, ducking to lash a zip-tie around her ankles, pulling it so tight she could hardly stand, then flung her into the van feet first. While the interior light was still on, she scanned the hold for any sharp edges or corners or loose tools, anything to slice into her bindings. There was nothing.

'Mr Chaudry, you seem a little dazed,' Jin said, snatching a cigarette out of the startled mouth of one of his guards. He leant inside and stubbed it out on Frank's forehead, letting it sizzle against his skin as Frank thrashed like a freshly caught fish tossed onto the deck of a boat. 'I've always wondered if cigarette burns showed up on chocolate skin. Now I know.'

58

Boston

THE MELANCHOLY OF MADA'S BARELY USED private phone droned through his office. Previously he'd used the line exclusively to listen to his mother's senile babbling, but lately to filter updates from Axel's doctors and his own oncologist. Those calls were as unwelcome as his mother's. He stubbed out his cigarette and, after reaching into his drawer, steeled himself with three peppermints. Expecting the usual routine of no news or bad news, he was surprised to hear Jin Yu's genteel charm, odd since Mada had never given Jin's assistant this number.

With whooshes of wind breaking up Jin's words, Mada guessed the billionaire was out for a stroll or was phoning from a vehicle with an open window. But both seemed unlikely since Jin said he was calling from Dandong where, from the array of world clocks displayed on Mada's computer, he saw it was 2.40 am.

He appreciated the calls from Jin and Kong these last weeks. Yes, they were irregular, yes, in deal parlance they were the 'other side', but why the hell shouldn't he help them after they'd managed to shoehorn him into a highly sought-after cancer drug trial. So what if the favour meant trade-offs, like the snippets of information Jin and Kong would wheedle out of him about Project Chant. Some of it was confidential, okay *all* of it, but Mada rationalised that. He was keeping the deal on the even keel that Axel no longer could.

The wind coming down through the line subsided. 'Swyft and Chaudry like Dandong so much, I wouldn't be surprised if they decide to stay here,' said Jin, making unusual chitchat.

Mada laughed, actually thinking *good riddance*. He didn't have enough middle fingers to gesture his true opinion of a woman he detested more than his chemotherapy, a twice-weekly millstone which, courtesy of Mingmai, at least offered a skerrick of hope. All Swyft gave him was fatigue, fuss and frustration. If Jin had phoned to tell him she'd been killed in one of the riots springing up in China, or the secret police had arrested her on some spying charge dating back to her CIA days, he wouldn't have shed a tear. For Chaudry he would, but not for Swyft, not with Project Chant as good as done.

Swyft! Before she'd left for Dandong, did she or Chaudry even pause to consider asking Mada for any insights he might have about the place after his trips back there in the eighties? Sure, his local knowledge was stale and, sure, he hadn't mentioned it to them specifically but it was in the files if they'd bothered to look ...

After the call, he stood to stretch. At the windowsill he opened the lacquered box. *1983*, the card said. A year before

Mada's wife died. She'd loved their visits to eastern China. He fingered the card, hand-pressed, tactile paper stock, wondering what his then friend, Liaoning's governor, was doing today, whether he was still alive. Mada lifted the elongated white marble block out of the box and upended it. He *hurred* his breath on the engraved characters at its base, then pressed the stamp of his surname in Chinese against the back of his hand.

He held his hand out to look at it, pale hairs poking through the red calligraphy like trees in winter. He wondered about the two symbols, if they really said *Ma-Da* or if the governor had been having one of his little jokes with him. He put the block back and closed the lid, licked two fingers on his other hand and tried rubbing the ink off. It wouldn't even smudge. He closed his eyes, snickering as the memory of the gift presentation returned. He'd tried to rub the ink off then too and his host had smiled, saying, 'Chinese ink indelible. Strong and enduring. Like Chinese people.'

Like Mada was. Once.

59

Dandong

LIKE LOOSE SAUSAGES, TORI AND FRANK rolled around on the car floor, their legs and arms cuffed and mouths taped. They were tossed and flipped and pounded as the van lunged its way to the ferry jetty. The cargo hold was in darkness apart from the flashes that streetlamps sent jittering across the driver's compartment privacy screen.

As the vehicle hung another sharp left, Tori's feet smacked into something soft. She hoped it wasn't Frank's head. So far she'd crashed into some part of him seven times, the door three times with him following fast and rolling into her, the locker down the back twice when the maniac at the wheel put his pedal to the metal and, when he slammed on the brakes, into the partition at the front. Eventually, the van took a wide and long curve to the right, like it was heading into a looped overpass, flinging them into the left-hand door, Frank's shoulder caroming off her wounded arm for the third time. By now, it had been struck so many times, she was almost numb to the pain, her tears almost dried up. But this was the first time her hands could almost reach his and with a bit of shuffling they did. She grabbed hold, locking them together. He got the idea and did the same.

Once his fingers were firmly gripping her wrist, she let go and carefully slipped off her pinkie ring, the one that Tex— as if he had ESP—had sketched as a superhero's powerband. Given to her by a Russian FSB agent who she'd turned five years ago, the small silver ring had been waiting for its moment in the sun—or in this case, the dark—its spring-curled steel shim concealed inside a groove in the inner rim. Unfurling it, she felt around for the zip-tie ratchet mechanism that locked Frank's makeshift handcuff in place. She slid the metal in through the recess, pushing it between the locking bar and the teeth, separating them so she could unthread the long tongue of plastic and free his hands.

Knowing they would be thrown around again any second, she passed him the metal prong and he was quick to return the favour. Once he'd freed her hands and feet, he did his own feet. Tori worked two fingers under the duct tape, stretching it and loosening it over her mouth so they could talk yet appear as if they were still gagged. Frank did the same.

Holding the metal with one hand and loosening the tape with the other, he nodded toward the steel locker they'd been crashing into at the back. 'What do you think they're hiding in that thing?'

The next streetlight flash showed them how big the cabinet was. 'I wouldn't hold your breath,' said Tori, reaching into her shirt pocket for the sheet of painkillers. 'It's probably a supply of

Jin's thousand-year-old egg yolks. On second thoughts, do hold
your breath.'

If she could have read Chinese in the light let alone the
dark, she'd know that the recommended dose was two pills
every four hours, but she popped five from the blister pack and
swallowed them dry.

'*XING XING*,' THE voice started in a wakey-wakey singsong
as the van door swung open, but the words broke off when the
interior lights didn't snap on automatically. 'Stay back,' he told his
comrade, their eyes adjusting to the gloom with no captives in
sight. They snapped on their flashlights, slicing zigs and zags of
light into the cargo bay.

'Fuck, is he dead?' The torch was on Frank, curled up in the
front corner of the cargo bay. His mouth was taped, his hands
and feet stretched behind his back, his eyes closed.

'No, he's breathing. But the woman!' shouted the other
guard. 'Where is the woman?'

The second guard grabbed the side of the van and lifted a leg
up. 'I'm going in—'

'Don't be a fool,' said his accomplice, dragging him back with
one hand, his torch circling every surface inside, methodically,
one by one, even the roof like Tori might be a Spiderwoman, or
a ninja. His light dwelt on a mound of blankets. 'Is she under—'

Feeling a little higher on pain meds than someone exercising
her Second Amendment right to bear arms should be, Tori burst
out of the rear locker firing one of the Norinco QSZ-92 9mm
handguns she and Frank had found in there. Her first shot got
one guard—her abuser—in his gut, a little above where she'd
intended to hit him. Simultaneously, Frank rolled onto his

stomach, brought his gun forward and, just after Tori clipped the other man's right shoulder, shot him in his left, spinning him backwards.

She stood at the door, peering down at the men squirming and squealing on the ground below, only a little perturbed by the buzz she got from seeing the blood spouting from her assailant's stomach, his hands desperately trying to staunch the bleeding. 'Help me, help me,' he screamed.

In time, she thought. Possibly. Maybe. Perhaps after that manicure she'd been meaning to have, and after a few more of the awesome painkillers that were making her feel invincible. She patted her pocket to make sure they were still there, then poked her head out, squinting into the dark. There were no more men, not even at the ferry, berthed and lit by a solitary bulb at the end of Mingmai's private pier. The air was cold on her face, making her skin tingle quite pleasantly, another plus from the pills. If anyone else had been out there the gunfire and shrieking would've given them ample warning to arm themselves or hide, or both. Pricking up her ears, she waited, listening to a few more of the heartbeats pounding in them, then jumped down. Grabbing a torch from the ground, she flashed it around, into the trees, toward the jetty, but no one else was here.

Frank replaced her at the door, a pistol in each of his hands, their laser sights pinning red dots on the two guards' foreheads. 'Don't move, and don't get any ideas,' he told them in English.

Tori repeated it in Mandarin, embellishing it with a few expletives for emphasis. Nodding her thanks to Frank for the cover, she kicked both guards' guns under the van, removed their knives from their sheaths and slipped them into a side pocket on her newly acquired Kevlar vest. Then, sticking her gun into her belt, she stepped over to stand behind her assailant's head, listening to his moans and cries but not feeling like they meant anything.

Expecting her to put a boot into him, he flinched, begging her not to do whatever the grim blackness in her eyes betrayed. She silently glared for a while, letting him fret then suddenly crouched and slid a roll of duct tape she'd found in the locker off her wrist, ripped the tape off the roll and pressed it over his mouth, winding it around his head like they had done to her and Frank.

She rose up and positioned herself between his legs, kicking his left knee out, widening the gap. 'From up there, you piece of shit,' she said in her best Mandarin, tipping her head toward the van, 'I would've shot your balls off. Except,' she nosed her toe into his groin, 'they were too small a target. But from down here,' her upper lip curled into a menacing snarl, 'I can't miss them.'

As the blood continued to pump and spurt from his stomach, he writhed and groaned incomprehensibly. She ripped the tape off his mouth and he began pleading. 'No, Swyft *nü shi*, please, no. I sorry. Very sorry. I follow Jin order. Help me. Please help me.'

Tori chewed her lip, trying to decide. When she remembered that revenge was a dish best served cold, and it sure was freezing out here, she decided to plate it up.

This wasn't just for her, she decided, but for every woman this prick and all the other pricks like him had molested. That was her justification, her rationalisation, the excuse she kept telling herself as she wound her left foot back and slammed it into his balls. She welcomed his ululant throat gurgling and curdling, her eyes fixed on the reflex spray of blood as it rained over her boots, a black pair the Macy's shop assistant had promised were showerproof. Looking down on them, Tori recalled how long she'd taken to choose between the black and the red pair. Now she had both.

As he twisted and swore, her dad's old adage came back to her, that two wrongs didn't make a right, so she drew her foot back and made it three.

60

Washington, DC

ISABEL NOTED THAT GENERAL VADDERN HAD taken a chair, his body tilted forward. The beads of sweat on his scalp were like a score of tiny TVs, reflecting the wall screens that he, she and the rest of the NSC were watching. All of them were inhaling and exhaling like they shared a single set of lungs.

Narthex was whizzing them through the simulation, showing the rocket's post-launch phases at six times normal speed.

The data meters oscillating at the bottom left of the screen gave the satellite's orbit altitude at 510 kilometres, 317 miles. Its speed across the skies was 27,396 kmph, 17,023 mph, meaning each full orbit at that altitude would take 94 minutes 24 seconds.

After a mere forty-three minutes of flight time—just over seven on fast-forward—the satellite was threatening the Oklahoma/Kansas border.

Narthex dialled the clip's speed back. 'This is where it gets ugly.'

The room sucked in another communal breath. One of Vaddern's giant hands was pulling at his chin, the other squeezing the back of his head. The president gripped her armrests while others were loosening their collars or tightening their fists. All of them were on edge, tensed, wired, waiting for something they didn't want to see.

Despite this being a simulation, a cartoon, despite Narthex warning them what was coming, the instant the speakers cracked like a million whips and the intense whiteness of the blast bleached the colour out of everyone's faces, they leapt out of their seats.

Everyone except the president. She kept her cool. She stayed in her chair.

Given her calm determination, her resolve, the others looked anywhere but at her, fidgeting with their pens, taking a sip of whatever hot drink was now cold, tightening the ties they'd only just loosened or adjusting a bra strap, anything to hide the indignity of their frailty of character.

Unknown to them, Isabel hadn't been more composed, not the least bit commander-in-chief-like. One of the buttons on her cardigan had got caught in her armrest and she'd been stuck. She stared silently ahead.

The first time she'd heard about EMPs—electromagnetic pulses—was only a month into office when a congressman collared her, jabbering about 'the greatest threat America faces, apart from you ... unless you can protect us from it'.

Electricity blacked out, lights dead, heating and cooling systems *poof*, computers *phht*, electronic media and communications off-air, transportation networks immobile—cars, trucks, trains, shipping, air-traffic-control—ATMs out of order, banks frozen, fuel pumps empty, hospitals and emergency services disabled, command-and-control systems impotent, water taps dry, toilets overflowing with sewage, food spoilt, sickness and crime rampant.

Within a year, he'd said, 200 million Americans would be dead. The explosion itself, even the radiation poisoning, they'd be benign. The perpetrators—the killers—would be winter, disease, starvation and societal collapse.

The bizarre part, he'd told her, was how two congressional committees—*two*, he'd stressed, and both reporting before she'd entered politics—had rung ear-splitting alarm bells about EMPs. But Washington had never heeded them, despite the solutions being easy and cheap.

As she watched the people in the Sit Room slowly drop back into their seats, the white fireball bloomed into a stunning vermillion aurora. It wavered briefly then dispersed as ringed pulses of electromagnetic radiation, their thickness and strength petering out as they stretched across the Lower 48, even into Canada and Mexico. After this EMP, the only states left functioning would be Alaska and Hawaii.

Surprised Narthex was still standing, she noticed he was skimming a document Loucineh had briefly entered to hand him.

He began summarising it aloud. 'Madam President, this blast is set to go off high in the upper atmosphere, 300 miles up. What happens then—what those rings we saw represent—is it sends out three pulses, called E1, E2 and E3.

He told the Sit Room that virtually every unshielded piece of electronic kit in the E1's path, whether in the air or on the ground, was a suicidal antenna, ready and waiting to couple with the pulse and fry itself.

Isabel couldn't help remembering how the congressman had badgered her, harping on how 'easy and cheap' the solutions were. All it took, he'd said, to protect the nation's critical infrastructure, like power grid transformers, was to shield them inside metal skins, what scientists called Faraday cages. The skins would take the hit, not the devices. In the home or office—he'd said—simply wrapping kitchen-grade alu-foil around electronics ... even dumping them in metal trashcans and closing the lids ... would work. Easy. And cheap.

The committees had estimated the federal cost at two billion dollars. Today, Isabel guessed, even if that had grown to thirty or forty billion, it was trivial, less than what her Defense Department outlaid in a month.

Easy and cheap ... yet no president had taken the issue seriously. Not even her.

'Technically,' said Narthex, reading on, 'the blast radiates ionising gamma rays. Any atoms that block their way, like the oxygen or nitrogen in the air, get their electrons stripped off.' He looked up, and Isabel nodded for him to continue. 'Those liberated electrons start plummeting toward Earth at near light speed. But when they hit the planet's geomagnetic field, it flips them ninety degrees. The electrons fan out in every horizontal direction to blanket the country, surging up to 200,000 volts through every cable, wire and piece of operating equipment. In short, ma'am, frying the nation's power grid. Literally. Instantly. Even lightning protectors can't stop them. As well as knocking out the grid itself, ma'am, an E1 pulse would zap most motors, computers and communications devices. And everything I just said ... it happens in a nanosecond.' He dropped his broken pencil to the floor. 'A billion times faster than that.'

He paused for questions but all he got was open-mouthed silence. 'Okay, next come the E2 and E3 pulses,' he continued, running his finger down the script. 'The E1 that I just ran you through is bad, but the E3 is the worst, so I'll skip to that. Where the E1's super fast, the E3's a slow, deliberate pulse that can last from tens of seconds up to a thousand. An E3 works like a fireball, heaving aside the Earth's magnetic field as it expands, sucking hot ionised air from under it to shift across the geomagnetic field lines and force colossal currents into long power lines and electrical conductors.'

Isabel shifted in her seat. 'How far can they travel?'

'Hundreds of miles, ma'am, destroying unshielded transformers, everything, on the way.'

'Underground cables?' she asked, praying they at least were safe.

Narthex flipped over a page and scanned a couple of paragraphs. 'No good either, ma'am. The E3 is at such a low frequency it can penetrate the ground. And undersea cabling … that's at risk, too.'

As Isabel scanned the faces in the room, the iconic images of President Obama's NSC crowding around the same table flashed into her head. They'd been watching the kill raid on Osama bin Laden's Pakistan compound in 2011. They'd looked tense, stone-faced. Resolute. Determined. But unlike her, Obama wasn't confronting the suffocating possibility that in less than seven hours America might be blasted back to the pre-industrial age.

If she'd been stupid enough to let any White House photographers into the room, what they'd be recording right now, she observed, was thirteen dumbstruck men and women, unsure what to do, frantic that if what they knew leaked out it would escalate the anti-RUA rampages into a nation-wide torrent of panic, looting and shooting.

She unhooked her cardigan, bizarrely worrying she might pull a thread. Her mind raced, imagining the horrific things that mothers and fathers, sons and daughters, grandparents too, might be forced to do just to survive, taking self-preservation into their own hands, boarding up their homes and swarming the streets to prowl for food, supplies and weapons.

She reached back and unclipped the necklace Davey had crafted for her at school, to remind her about his school pageant this afternoon, the one Narthex had amazingly found time to help him with. Two strands of braided gold-coloured twine threaded with five tree leaves Davey had cut out of red plastic. The necklace wasn't hefty but with everything else weighing her down, planting it on top of the reports in front of her seemed appropriate.

'If we are to believe that simulation as well as Dr Swyft's other intel,' she said, getting to her feet and addressing the room, 'the rocket launches in six and a half hours. Forty minutes after that and America is history. We need options, people.'

61

Dandong

AN INVISIBILITY CLOAK WOULD'VE BEEN HANDY for their getaway but Tori had forgotten to pack one. 'Maybe these oafs stuffed one in their pockets.' She and Frank patted down their captors as they bled out in the icy sludge. They tossed the men's remaining weapons up onto the front seat of the van, likewise their comms so they could monitor Jin's other guards.

Frank had taken some of the painkillers too, not as many as Tori since FrensLens had told him the correct dosage, but he looked lightheaded enough that she knew he probably shouldn't drive. That said, he was in better shape than her.

'We better check for trackers, don't you think?' She stood beside the van, holding a blanket and pointing to the ground.

'*We?*'

'Okay, *you*. Remember,' she pointed to the duct tape wrapped around her wound, 'Tori ... bullet ... arm.' He pointed to his chest, his nose, still dripping a little blood onto his shirt, and the burn on his forehead, but she gave him no sympathy. 'As Sun Tzu say, *Gunshot in arm trumps gun grip to nose and cigarette to head.*'

Frank tried to laugh but winced, his hand flying to his ribs before he took the blanket from her.

As she made a phone call, she watched him flutter the blanket down like a picnic rug and drop himself on top of it, lying on his back. He pushed his feet out and slid both the rug and himself backwards across the spongy ice melting under the van. Two long and cold minutes later, and Tori's call complete, Frank slid back out and scrabbled to his feet holding a flashing red LED he'd pulled off the chassis. '*We* found it.'

He went to throw the device into the Yalu River. 'Hey, no!' Tori shouted. 'I get you fancy yourself as a Test cricketer but if that tracker goes dead Jin's other goons will suspect—'

'Got it,' and with a desultory underhand, like a dad teaching a kid to catch, he tossed the tracker onto the ground a couple of feet away.

BOUNCING THE VAN over the car park exit hump, they left the blood, gore and bodies behind in a steamy plume of exhaust.

Tori put her hand on Frank's, seeing him flinch as the van shuddered beneath them. 'About not calling an ambulance. We had no choice. Whoever was going to ferry us to the island will be here soon.'

'I hope not as soon,' he said, taking a right, 'as us strapping in on board Axel's plane. He removed his hand from hers and wiped the last drop of blood off his stubble. 'Are Simon and Marty set?'

Axel's long-time pilot and co-pilot had flown the team over from JFK and were staying at the same hotel. While Frank had been fossicking for the tracker, Tori had woken Simon, tasking him to get into their rooms, bribing a bellman if necessary, and bag up their things, including their passports, which in Tori's case meant four, a vestige of her old habits.

'Simon's a go,' she said, then paused. 'Did I actually say that? He's *a go*? Jesus, are we in a movie? He says we're all fuelled up since we were leaving at eight anyway, so prepping the plane for us won't take him long.'

'The due diligence team?' said Frank, adjusting in his seat. 'After we've left Chinese airspace, we'll need to let them know they'll have to fly home commercial.'

'If they still have homes to go to.'

Washington, DC

T
HE SECRETARY OF STATE CAUGHT THE
president's eye. 'Knowing what we know now, ma'am, it
might be time you made that call to President Hou Tao.'
'Really?' spluttered DNI Hirsty. He was half-standing,
struggling to slough off his jacket. He managed to pull his arms
out of the sleeves and sat again after he'd draped it over the back
of his chair. Isabel knew that Hirsty and Secretary Linden were
golfing buddies, so she wondered how far the DNI would go
in slamming his friend's judgement in front of her. 'Ma'am,'
Hirsty continued, 'Alex ... *Secretary Linden*'s unencumbered by
a detailed acquaintance with Swyft's history and the risks of
taking uncorroborated intel from her.' He ran a hand over his
hair. The slick of black goo he combed through it each morning
made Isabel wonder why the global demand for oil was still

in the doldrums. 'Even if you give Swyft the benefit of the doubt—*if*—' he stressed, 'then we still have to consider the risk that one or two of Hou's Politburo comrades might be behind this, with the Norks merely their pawns. Don't forget who's funding this operation ... one of China's largest companies whose own CEO is like *this* with the upper echelon,' he said, twisting one finger over the other and waving them at her.

Isabel rubbed one of Davey's red leaves between her fingers to help keep her tone calm and steady. 'Director Hirsty, I know your agencies have a problem with Dr Swyft. But you need to tell them to get over it. Even if they're unable to give her due credit for her work on the Nine Sisters, perhaps they might ask themselves who hunted down the simulation for us ... who extracted the rocket schematics ... who gave us the CCTV footage of the launch site, let alone who told us the place even existed? Was it Swyft, or was it your agencies? Who told us that the operation was being directed by the Iranian, Dr Akh ... Akh ...'

'Akhtar,' said Narthex.

'Him, yes. Who told us that it's Mingmai money behind this? If the answer to all those questions is the CIA or the NSA or Homeland Security, or some other agency you're keeping hidden from me, fine, but something's telling me it's Dr Swyft and her colleague Mr Chaudry, a *British* ex-intelligence officer. And I stress *ex* in both their cases. So am I right, Director?'

Hirsty sat on the edge of his chair, his eyes black, mouth grim and back straight, his entire body quivering with the self-control Isabel assumed was stopping him telling her where to stick his job, and hers.

Secretary Linden spoke again. 'Ma'am, if I may ... perhaps Director Hirsty was right to argue with me about making the call to President Hou Tao. I've been reconsidering my position since his, ah, interjection.'

Isabel nodded and he went on, 'Swyft says that Mingmai leases that island from North Korea. Arguably, that gives North Korea *and* China legal rights over the land. It means, ma'am, that you'd be threatening Hou that unless he takes the rocket out, we'll do it, which means we'd be launching an attack on Chinese territory, his territory.'

General Vaddern banged the table. 'Alex, you can't be serious?'

The secretary tightened the knot of his tie, a crimson that almost matched the colour that had come to Vaddern's cheeks. 'Dead serious, General. If Cuba forewarned us they were going to bomb our base at Guantánamo—land we lease from them—wouldn't you be telling Madam President that was an act of war? So if Hou Tao knows nothing about this, a unilateral act of aggression against North Korea—'

'In self-defence, a pre-emptive strike—'

'Sure, but Hou might also see it as an act of war against China.'

Everyone's eyes turned to the president. 'Go on,' she said, glad the secretary had cancelled his trip to Baghdad to be here.

'Thank you, ma'am. But if China *is* in fact behind this—and that's a possibility—calling Hou Tao severely limits our options for pre-emptive action.'

The secretary's argument had merit. 'You're saying we keep China out of it either way, hit the island first and talk later?'

'Ma'am, if we mobilise some of the Growlers and Super Hornets we got on board USS *Ronald Reagan* we could execute a surgical strike, intercept the rocket in boost-phase, when it's left ambiguous sovereignty.'

'Isn't the *Reagan* near the Philippines?'

'Yes, ma'am, which is some fifteen hundred nautical miles from the launch site—'

Hirsty raised a finger. 'Wouldn't we save time if we mobilised our F-16s at Kunsan?' Kunsan Air Base on South Korea's west coast was home to the US Air Force's 8th Fighter Wing.

'We *could* do that,' said Vaddern.

'You have a better suggestion?' asked Isabel, knowing he'd be sure to.

'Director Hirsty's right that we'd be faster if we mobilised outta Kunsan. We'd be even quicker if it was our 51st Fighter Wing outta Osan Base, but both Kunsan and Osan'd run the risk the o' Norks seein' us comin'. Plus, we'd have to do some damn fast 'xplainin' to our South K buddies.'

'That's true,' said Hirsty, 'but in the circ—'

'If I might continue, Director? If we don' wanna risk waitin' till blast-off, we can get those fighters on the *Reagan* to go full throttle at Mach 1.8, an' they'll be approachin' that island in an hour and a half, two hours tops. The Growlers'd jam all the electronics, the F/A-18s'd blow the rocket, the launch site, every damn thing on that island, to kingdom come and they'd be in and outta there so fast the Norks wouldn't know what hit 'em.'

'And China's reaction?' said Isabel.

'If Hou Tao claims we've breached his sovereignty, you express shock and dismay, ma'am, humbly apologisin' and heapin' the blame on Google Maps 'cause it didn't tell you China had a lease over the land.'

Isabel rolled her chair back. 'Like '99 in Belgrade?'

They all knew the awkward story when five American JDAM bombs mistook China's embassy for a Yugoslav arms cache.

'We were usin' old NATO maps that time, but NATO … Google … wrong maps, same idea.'

'China's got a long memory. One mishap is bad enough, but two …' She exhaled and started twisting a strand of her hair, wishing she had an elastic so she could pull it all back, to make her look more severe, more like the decisive commander-in-chief she needed to be.

Narthex coughed. 'Before we take the pre-emptive action the secretary and the general are proposing—'

'Carter, I'm not proposing. The president asked for options and I—'

'Of course, Mr Secretary, I apologise.'

The air crackled with tension as Vaddern raised himself up, pressing his bulbous knuckles on the table then flattening his palms in the middle as if it were territory he'd conquered long ago. 'Ma'am,' he said, glaring at her, 'no one likes war but if you gotta have one, you have one and I've told you we can do that if you so order. The question is, *Do we gotta have one?*'

63

Dandong

WITH THE HEADLIGHTS BEHIND HIM, JIN played shadow puppets. He toyed the silhouette of his long-barrelled pistol over the two men on the ground, like he was stroking each of their cheeks. The men were barely moving or breathing, the dark pool oozing around them in the muck and the ice making it obvious they'd lost a lot of blood. 'It's strange,' said Jin, lifting a tiny flashing device from the ground and putting it into a pocket, 'I see the van tracker but I don't see the van.'

He moved between them and stopped, watching as a puddle of blood rose to the crest of a piece of ice, then spilled over and ran toward his shoe. When it was a bootlace away, he lifted his foot and shook it above the two men's eyes so even in their daze they could see it. 'My two guests I entrusted to you. They don't seem to be here either. Do either of you have anything to tell me?'

He waited.

'No?'

He slammed his foot down onto one face, pivoting and crunching his heel into the man's nose until he detected the glorious sound of it cracking amid the pitiful shrieks. He swore at himself for forgetting to video it. The second man was now doing his best to crawl away.

Jin pulled back the bolt on his pistol, his current favourite, a Ruger Mark III Hunter .22LR with its elegant burnt sienna cocobolo grip and a single-minded 6.88 inch fluted bull barrel that hardly jumped in his hand when he took a shot. He leant down and yanked the man's shoulder back so he could stick the muzzle into one of his nostrils.

'Don't move,' he said, and the terrified man froze, unaware that behind him Jin's other hand was taking out a phone and activating its flash and video recorder. 'Should I call an ambulance?' He filmed the furious nods that slid the man's nose up and down over the muzzle. Then, capturing his own finger pulling the trigger and the artistry of the shell as it exited the top of the man's skull, with blood and chunky fragments of bone and brain whooshing into the night air.

He turned to the other man, now clutching his face. 'Is it too late for me to phone Emergency?' Jin asked, placing the burning hot muzzle in under the man's jaw. 'If you want your name in the credits, you'll need to say something. Rolling camera ... Action ...'

$$+$$

IN THE COMFORTABLE lounge at the back of *Xiaosan*, the customised six-tonne armoured truck that Jin took with him in his plane's purpose-built hold, he set up a conference call, using the randomised encryption his best engineer had perfected for the Ten Brothers.

No Brother ever complained about the hour of a call. Being a Brother was a twenty-four seven obligation, a duty that forbade meddling from clocks or weekends, vacations or families.

When Jin initiated a call, he liked to kick off with the good news if he had any, so he led with the night's successes: the mass arrests, riots spasmodically erupting, all of it fuelling the momentum, the need, for change at the top, for rebirth … for *Fuxing Tao*.

To ensure the Brothers were in the right mood for the bad news, he led the group's stirring call-and-response ritual not once but twice before coming to the real point of the call.

'Brothers, we need to bring forward the launch.'

64

Washington, DC

I F THE SIT ROOM DIRECTOR WAS sending in Blue Coat to do the update, Narthex knew the Watch Floor must be fighting through a shitstorm, tracking down, sifting, manipulating, checking and managing all the disparate pieces of data and intel the NSC needed.

Apart from Narthex's brief encounter with Blue Coat in the corridor earlier, he'd only ever seen him at his computer, eyes glued to the screen, fingers frenetic, tapping so fast he wondered how many keyboards the guy wore out each year. He'd drawn him once with five of them arrayed in front of his fast-moving fingertips.

Now that Blue Coat was inside the Sit Room for the first time, Narthex could see his red-rimmed eyes blinking furiously to keep the sweat from stinging them, his hands behind his back to hide their fidgeting.

On the screen behind him was a fuzzy still taken from Tori's CCTV clip at the launch pad. The image showed two men arguing at the base of the rocket, one of them confirmed earlier by Blue Coat's boss as the former Iranian official Tori had claimed him to be.

'What have you got for us now, Fred?' asked the president.

Narthex was impressed Isabel knew Blue Coat's name. Her recall for names of minor officials, members of the public she'd met only once before and for gardeners and waiters, it was astonishing. He was good with names, but he was better with faces. And character.

As Fred stepped forward and blinked some more, the image behind him began to clear. 'Er, sorry, Madam President. After we showed you the full CCTV clip, I've … er … we've … out there on the Watch Floor, we ran it through image enhancement and then put facial recognition over it. In addition to Dr Akhtar, we captured seventy-eight faces but, apart from him, we only got one match in our databases.' He turned to the screen, pointing a pen he'd been holding behind his back. 'That man there.'

As the faces became clearer, Narthex called out, 'It looks like Zhao Guowei,' then leapt from his chair so fast to get a closer look he knocked the pen out of Fred's hand.

Blue Coat, unsure whether to bend for it or leave it, clearly decided that speaking was the better course. 'Er, yes, sir, it is Premier Zhao Guowei, China's number two—'

'Ma'am, this is huge,' said Narthex. 'As you know, Zhao is the biggest hawk in the Politbu—'

'Dr Carter, I do know, and if you were about to say that if President Hou's number two is tangled up in—'

'—then China herself is clearly behind this and we're about to go to war,' said DNI Hirsty. He was smiling bizarrely as if getting in first made him the hero of the moment, the brilliant strategist whose insight changed history, a fact he'd make sure he'd humbly disclose in his inevitably bestselling autobiography.

'*Some* people,' said General Vaddern, not giving a stuff about challenging Hirsty's self-regard or his place in history, 'might say that's the obvious answer, ma'am, but if that is Zhao—and it sure looks like him—there's a greater chance he's gone rogue, that he's goin' behind Hou's back.'

'How so?' snapped Hirsty.

'Geez, Robert, think about it. If the true might of China's behind this, why'd they bother bringin' in some Nork nut jobs to escalate the risk of a screw up, of a leak, of blackmail, dammit? China might need some of Iran's technology to do this—though I do doubt that—but do you seriously reckon they need Pyongyang's help or even its land? Come on, man!'

'The Nork island's a perfect hiding—'

'Hirsty, China's got more hidey-holes than a zillion colonies o' squirrels, so I don' buy—'

'What's that?' said Isabel as the image crisped up even more. 'There, behind Zhao's ear ... A tattoo ... Is it a cross?'

'Well, he ain't no Christian, ma'am, if he's playin' at a game like this.'

'Adolf Hitler was a Christian but that didn't stop him.'

65

Dandong

TORI TRANSLATED THE NEWS COMING OUT of the car radio faster than the FrensLens Frank was still wearing. When they heard President Hou had declared a formal state of emergency, Frank immediately changed how he handled the hefty vehicle. He shifted from caution to a studied measure of arrogance, driving neither too fast nor too slow. Hopefully a warning to any local cops out on duty at 3.45 am that pulling over the self-confident, cold-blooded thugs they'd inevitably find behind the menacing windows wasn't worth making their already miserable night even worse, and risking them never seeing their families again.

Tori pressed the tip of the satphone's extension aerial out a gap in the top of the window and, tearing off a fresh strip of duct tape pressed it down to give the phone an uninterrupted signal. 'We still have to give Tex that heads up. And now we know Jin's at the centre of—'

'Whatever *foo-shing dow* is. He didn't *actually* admit to anything when you blurted it all out.'

'He didn't deny it,' said Tori, 'going on with all that self-serving shit about the big picture, history revering him, that whatever he's doing is for the world's fucking children.'

Frank shook his head. 'Talk about crazy brave. I couldn't believe you came out with all that when we had guns in our faces ... and that was before you OD'd on the painkillers.'

She began to dial Tex. 'And what about Mada ... did you hear Jin call him?'

'I did.'

'It sounded very chummy.'

'He was probably covering himsel—'

'You said you saw him rushing away from the office when ... Damn,' she said as the call dropped out.

66

Washington, DC

JUNIOR ANALYSTS WHO DID THE GRUNT work, the people who actually raked and sifted through precipitous haystacks of data to find the single, tiny, lethal needle, rarely won the right to deliver their findings personally to the inner sanctum of US national security. Now, Blue Coat was getting that chance a second time.

Narthex noted he'd changed into a crisp white shirt, ditching the pale blue that last time had distractingly got darker and darker. His flush wasn't so tomatoey either, this time a paler pink, more like a Fuji apple tinged with yellow and green.

The president stood for him. 'Mr Hayek,' she said as she shook his hand, 'your last visit was very helpful.'

'Er, thank you.' He stood to the side. 'That tattoo you saw last time, the one behind Mr Zhao Guowei's ear,' Hayek began, pointing the remote control over his shoulder to return the shot of Zhao to the screen. 'Our initial difficulty was the prevalence of this symbol across cultures: the Christian cross, the mathematical plus symbol, the crosshairs of a gun and the number ten in Chinese and a variety of other Asian languages.'

'And your best guess in this case?' said Narthex, pre-empting someone else getting nasty if Blue Coat didn't get to his point.

'We think it's a Chinese ten, a *shi* in Mandarin,' he said, clicking his remote and superimposing a + over Zhao's tattoo. The symbol covered the tattoo almost perfectly, apart from where the tattoo skewed over an angry vein bulging in the man's neck. 'Because it's also a plus and a crucifix, as well as a logo for multiple businesses, when we ran it through a series of pattern- and image-matching programs we found, as you'd expect, billions of hits. So we honed down our parameters, limiting our search to cases of a similar tattoo being linked to anyone turned up by Dr Swyft's intel … known actors if you will … like Premier Zhao up there … and one step of separation away, people those known actors are themselves directly connected with. So far we've turned up six, well five on top of Premier Zhao.' He clicked again and the new faces appeared. 'That one next to Zhao is Jin Yu, the CEO of—'

'We know who he—'

'Yes, of course you do.' He clicked on Jin's photo—a front-on view—and a clip rolled. 'This is from a security video shot three weeks ago in New Jersey, at Teterboro Airport after Mr Jin flew in on his jet and was walking into the terminal.' They watched silently as the billionaire strolled toward the camera and then past it, giving them a momentary side view of his head. 'There!' said Fred, freezing the clip on Jin's profile just as a gust of wind puffed up his hair to reveal the + tattoo.

Narthex was a self-taught cynic, an avid disciple of *anti-*conspiracy theory, that when the facts point equally to conspiracy and coincidence, you should normally run with coincidence. He'd been struggling over what to make of the Jin-Zhao connection ever since Blue Coat had picked Zhao out for them. He had tortured his brain searching for a reason that was less catastrophic than the 'obvious' one for why China's second-most powerful politician would be arguing with an Iranian nuclear expert hired by Mingmai, both men standing at the foot of a rocket they'd gone to great lengths to conceal but was on North Korean soil and guarded by North Korean soldiers. Did Jin and Zhao sharing the same tattoo clarify anything or confuse him further? His mind raced.

On the conspiracy-coincidence spectrum, could the two small scratches of blue ink on these men's necks be as innocuous, say, as an entry stamp for some ritzy club that the Beijing elite liked to frequent? Or even more inane, something like senior high schoolers vowing to be best friends forever? Guessing wasn't going to get him anywhere. 'Fred, the other photos?'

'This one here,' he said, indicating the bright but blurry image next to Jin, 'is General Xu Qiang—'

'Hellfire!' cried Vaddern. As the image started sharpening he stepped over to look more closely. 'Damn, it *is* him.' He turned to face the president. 'Madam President, General Xu Qiang's as much a hawk as Premier Zhao Guowei. As one of the Central Military Commission's two vice-chairmen, he's been pushin' Hou Tao to seriously up the ante over the South China Sea islands.'

So far, Narthex agreed.

'So, ma'am, if this number ten tattoo thingy's tellin' us that Jin Yu's conspirin' on this EMP satellite not only with Zhao Guowei, China's top economic official, but also with the military through Xu Qiang, this thing's gotta reach all the way to the top … right up to President Hou.'

Blue Coat, who'd been staring at the toe of his shoe as it scuffed the floor like he was trying to scrape some detritus off it, raised his head and eyebrows, holding them up as if readying himself to jump off a cliff, then he went for it. 'If I might continue for just one more minute … to complete the picture … or pictures?' He enlarged two more photos on the screens. 'These next two men, while they also wear the tattoo and only one is Chinese, as you can see, they're not high-ups—far from it—and they don't live in China. One migrated to the United States from Dandong, the place where the rocket … Sorry, you all know that. The other is a local thug. They're both operating out of Queens and are members of a triad which, straight after the Chinese man arrived, changed its name to *Sons of the Ten Brothers* and curiously got all its members to tattoo the Chinese character *shi*, the number ten, on their necks.'

'And …?' said Narthex, wondering where this was going.

'Our hypothesis is that these men are local hired help, muscle, however you'd like to put it, for our three VIPs—Jin Yu, Premier Zhao and General Xu—and with their US triad being called *Sons* of the Ten Brothers—'

Vaddern strode back to his seat. 'You're sayin' that Jin and the other supremoes in China are covert members of a group called—'

'The Ten Brothers. Yes.'

'You're not serious,' said the president, reflecting Narthex's own thinking. As tempting as Fred's theory was, Narthex saw it as a soap bubble, elegant, seductive yet so quiveringly flimsy that the merest pin of a discordant fact would rupture it. Everyone in the room knew of Tori Swyft's role in ending the Nine Sisters crisis and it seemed the Watch Floor was letting that anchor their thinking, seducing them into dreaming up this so-called Ten Brothers.

But as he thought about it, Narthex did see some similarities. The Nine Sisters had also been highly influential and trusted people. They were sleepers, people who'd spent a decade at least camouflaging their real goals, in their case to save the planet by choking the rapacious economic system that was devouring its resources.

Blue Coat ... Fred ... clearly understood the reaction he was getting to his attempt to squeeze China's paramount business, government and military pegs into the same round hole. 'Ma'am, I know what you're thinking, that the Nine Sisters and the Ten Brothers is too coincid—'

'Mr Hayek, beyond your suppositions, have we got any facts to support the existence of this group?' The president wasn't snapping at him but her fatigue was showing through.

'Ma'am, it may seem like no more than an educated guess—'

'Facts, Mr Hayek. Have we got any *facts*,' she turned to the room, 'anything at all on a Ten Brothers network operating out of China? Mr Hayek ... Director Hirsty ... Does the CIA have anything? How about the NSA? Or are we left with SFA?'

67

HAYEK LOOKED DEFLATED, HIS EYES LOWERED, shoulders fallen. 'We've run this through Interpol, Europol and the Five Eyes,' he said, referring to the US's intelligence alliance with Australia, Canada, New Zealand and the UK, 'and we've tracked down an ancient Chinese legend from the Ming Dynasty—'

'Myths are facts now?' asked the general, incredulous.

The white of Hayek's shirt collar was turning as grey as his face. 'It's about ten brothers with super powers,' he said, digging himself deeper.

Isabel stared at him. 'Mr Hayek, tell me someone's interrogating the two men from Queens.'

'Er, that's the thing, ma'am. They're dead ... most likely.'

Isabel's chief of staff Gregory Samson crushed one of the empty Diet Coke cans in front of him. 'Fred,' he said, pushing his glasses up his nose, 'two questions: what's the step of separation that led you to these two thugs and how'd they die ... *if* they died?'

Narthex nodded, scoring two lines across his yellow legal pad with the new pencil he'd taken from the canister on the table.

'NYPD believes they died in a Bowery warehouse explosion.'

Narthex's heart suddenly sank. He pressed the pencil into the page so hard the point broke off.

'Okay,' said Samson, tipping the final dregs from his crinkled drink can into his glass, 'but how did you link these two goons to Jin Yu and those other two up there on the screen?'

The tattoo? wondered Narthex. In Tori's police statement, she'd mentioned a tattoo. Was it a cross? He pressed his eyes closed, trying to remember.

These Ten Brothers—if they existed—did Tori stumble onto something in Manhattan, and was that why the goons had kidnapped her? And what the hell had she walked into over in China, on their home turf?

If only she'd come back with him after Hawaii, none of this would've happened. At least not to her. He should've insisted, he chided himself, or at least tried harder to persuade her. If he'd told her how he felt, really felt, maybe she would have ...

His eyes snapped open as Hayek began speaking. 'There's *no* link to Jin, or to those others, not at this stage, but we're—'

'Holy Jesus,' said Samson. 'The president's hardly slept for three days and you're asking her to draw bows so damn long ... Hayek, your educated guess, if that's what it is, could start a war with China, so we need more than a fuc—'

'Gregory!' the president interjected, looking at the wall clock. 'Mr Hayek, we don't have much time here. If there's a launch, it's in less than six hours, at 9 pm—'

'10 am, ma'am.'

'It's 10 am in China, Mr Hayek, but 9 pm here. And General, am I right that we've got until 7 pm—*our* time—to green-light the *Reagan*'s fighters and they'd get to the launch site before blast-off?'

'Correct, ma'am. Well before.'

Narthex again saw the president glancing at the clock on the wall. Of course! In a little over an hour, at 4.30 pm, Davey's school drama pageant would be starting. He'd been with her when she'd promised the boy she'd get there. Maybe, with Hayek struggling to make a case, she was angling to briefly step out, to leave the team to continue strategising while she played mother ... possibly the last time she'd be able to if they didn't get this under control. If 7 pm was truly the last possible deadline for mobilising the *Reagan*'s fighters, she did have the time.

Narthex knew what a big deal the pageant was for the boy, and so for his stepmother. Even before he'd gone on vacation, and three afternoons in a row since, he'd spied the young Marlon Brando through the Oval Office window, swaddled in a parka and hoodie out on the South Lawn, posing at times beneath a towering southern magnolia, a threadleaf Japanese maple, an American elm, a white oak, or an Atlas cedar. The boy had looked up, twisting and swaying with each of them, hugging their trunks, adjusting the scarf his mother or one of his nannies had tied around his neck, trying to sense the essence of this tree or that, this one's grace, that one's dignity or another's frailty, to decide which giant of nature he was going to impersonate. And only then did he try to perfect the bare melancholic temper of his favourite, the white oak. Narthex had gone out on many of these occasions, drawing on whatever he could remember from his college acting days that might give Davey some inspiration. He and the boy seemed to have formed a bond, a connection. Unspoken of course, which was hard for them both since Narthex's ASL was still hopelessly inadequate.

Yesterday, when he'd accompanied Isabel outside to bring Davey in, the boy, leaning up against the oak had asked, with Isabel translating, 'If you were a tree, how painful would it be to lose your leaves?' Narthex jumped in with a line from a Sylvia Plath poem he didn't know he'd stored away: 'The blown leaves make bat-shapes, web-winged and furious.'

Davey, a good lip-reader, scooped up some 'bats', tossed them in the air and scampered through his bat rain back to the Residence.

Hayek stopped biting his upper lip, inhaled and looked around at the faces staring at him, incredulous faces, dismissive faces, one face readying to be somewhere else. 'Like I said, ma'am, we don't have a link from Jin Yu or the other Chinese men to the two from Queens—not yet—but we've got a team trawling through their phone records, emails, texts, video chats, searching their apartments, and we're—'

Isabel fisted her hands and pressed them against her temples in exasperation. 'Please answer Mr Samson's first question. What drew you to those two men ... the step of separation? You said one came from Dandong, was that it?'

'It was a *who*, not a what or a where, ma'am. It was Dr Swyft.'

68

IF THEY WEREN'T ALREADY LOCATED IN a basement, Narthex's stomach would have fallen through the floor into one. To make matters worse, DNI Hirsty stepped in. 'How's Swyft linked to those goons?'

'Like I mentioned,' said Hayek, 'the NYPD were investigating an explosion that supposedly killed both—'

'*Supposedly*?' Narthex thumped the table, astonished to learn the cops weren't buying Tori's story.

'Forensics, NYPD, firefighters, bomb squad,' Hayek explained, 'no one's been able to confirm what or who is or isn't inside the affected building. The blast was so quick it melted the structural beams. The only way the investigators can get safe entry is to pry off the roof. A crane's onsite and the earliest we'll know anything is late tonight, maybe tomorrow.'

'Why does NYPD *think* these gangsters died in there?' the president asked.

'Like I said, Dr Swyf—'

'Ma'am, I've read the police reports too,' Narthex interrupted, trying to set Tori's record straight. 'The night before Tor—Dr Swyft flew to China she was abducted, possibly by these two men. The perpetrators, whoever they were, tried to kill her inside that building. A stray bullet ignited some leaking fuel. She escaped but the kidnappers didn't. Her sole connection to these men,' he said turning his head first to Hayek and then to Hirsty, 'if it *was* these men, is as their unwitting victim. And neither Swyft nor the NYPD knows why.'

Oddly, Hirsty winked at Narthex.

'Dr Carter's given a fair summary of the witness statements,' said Hayek, 'but since they were given, NYPD's tracked down some further evidence. One interpretation suggests that either Dr Swyft knew or was in league with these men.'

'You can't be serious,' cried Narthex.

'Entirely serious, Dr Carter. As you'll see.' Hayek waved his remote at the screen and a muddy, grainy video started running. The clip looked over bare counters in a store, through the glass front door and into the night. Flurries of snow fell on a wettish pavement. A passing headlight briefly caught the street signs locating it near Wall Street.

Hayek cleared his throat. 'This is a security video shot from inside a jewellery store in the financial district. To reconstruct the events leading up to the explosion, NYPD tracked Dr Swyft's movements back to here. In a second or two you'll see a sedan and a black SUV pull up … there! … and these same two men, the Queens thugs, emerge from the drivers' doors … there!'

Narthex watched as they huddled under a streetlight, buttoning up their coats, the sedan driver flipping open and offering a pack of Marlboro to the other, the red and white carton strangely luminous in the pool of light. After they'd both taken a cigarette, he gestured toward the store's doorway. A sensor light hit them as they approached. Looking out to the street, they lit their cigarettes and took long drags in silence, one exhaling through his nose, the other making smoke rings with his tongue, his head tilting as his eyes followed the white circles, lingering, stretching, rising in the air, until ... 'There!' Hayek said, freezing the frame on the back of the man's ear.

As the image sharpened, Narthex saw the now familiar cross-shaped tattoo come into focus. His head, his back, every part of him was aching. It wasn't the revelation of another tattoo that affected him; he knew the driver had one from reading Tori's police statement. What was troubling him was what else Hayek had on Tori.

'SUV guy takes a phone call ... there!' said Hayek, rolling the clip forward. 'Sedan guy types a text ... there! ... They stub out their cigarettes and hurry back inside their vehicles, and soon,' he fast-forwarded, 'a woman approaches—'

'Tori Swyft,' said the president, her mouth hanging.

'—and the sedan driver gets out, his arms wide like he's greeting an old friend, she smiles back, he opens the back door and she slides in—'

Narthex couldn't stop himself from leaping to his feet. 'Those men tried to kill her,' he spat. 'Madam President, like I said, I've seen the police reports. Dr Swyft was working late on some corporate deal—which we now know involves Mingmai—and she got into the car to go back to her hotel. If Blue ... If Mr Hayek runs that video further, you'll see the SUV driver ramming into the back of his so-called friend's car as if he's a hostile. Then Swyft's driver takes off, feigning a getaway with the SUV in hot pursuit so she thinks her driver's the good guy. Ma'am, she didn't conspire with these men to dupe us, this was an orchestrated snatch off the streets and she only escaped by a hair's breadth.' He sat back down with a sigh. 'Fred, play the rest of the video. That'll prove—'

'Dr Carter, there's no more video,' Blue Coat grimaced. 'A power outage a few hours earlier must've switched the camera to battery backup. It ran out of puff the moment Dr Swyft closed her door. We've got nothing to corroborate her story—'

'And no one can get into the warehouse yet?' Narthex felt his control over the situation—his ability to protect Tori—falling away like sand through his fingers.

'Correct.'

'Her work colleague, Frank Chaudry, what about him?' asked Narthex. 'He's ex-MI6 and his statement backs her up 100 per cent. He corroborates the whole thing.'

DNI Hirsty snapped back in his chair laughing, a loud, unrestrained burst that ricocheted off Narthex's wall of despair. 'Carter, like you said, he's Swyft's *colleague*. A colleague who is by her side in Dandong, a colleague who, as far as we know, could be in on this with her, helping her make a fool of us, a fool of the president, a fool of you. So what if Chaudry is ex-MI6 … so was Kim Philby. Madam President, can we put an end to this elaborate fabrication? Swyft is smart—devilish smart—so what we need to be doing, which we're not, is uncovering the motive here. What will she, or whoever she and Chaudry—'

'Tori is no mercen—'

'—gain if they con these United States to declare war on North Korea and, de facto, on China?'

There was nothing Narthex could say. He knew Tori, knew this wasn't her, couldn't be her, not even remotely. He also knew that judgement clouded by friendship … more than friendship … wouldn't cut it in this room, and he'd be betraying the president's trust if he tried.

The last thing he wanted was for history to write him off as the fleeting star who led his president to war—or against one—because of a delusion, a fantasy and worse, a romance. He trusted his instincts but, as he slumped in his chair, what petrified him most was that maybe he was trusting them too much.

'A couple more things, ma'am,' Hayek was saying. He clicked the remote, bringing up a side shot of an old man, wizened, hunched in a chair, a pink checked blanket covering his legs. The image began to rotate until they saw the man face-on.

His scalp was freckled with age and anger, his only visible hairs those straggling out of his chin and nostrils. Saliva bubbled in one corner of his mouth and tendrils of smoke curled up from the cigarette stuck in the other.

The president gasped first, hers and everyone else's eyes wide in alarmed recognition. As pathetic as the old fossil looked now, this was the twisted, evil mastermind behind the Nine Sisters' plot to destroy the global economic system. It seemed like his eyes were watching everyone in the room, his mouth having the last laugh.

69

'WHAT'S THAT SCUMBAG MELLOR GOT TO do with this?' cried Gregory Samson. 'Hayek, this is a pretty long bow of yours, that the brain behind the Nine Sisters also dreamed up these Ten Brothers as an afterthought.'

Hayek fidgeted with his shirt collar. 'As a forethought, actually. And it's not just my long bow, sir. The DGSI—'

'The who?'

'The French department of homeland security. They couldn't find anything on a Ten Brothers, but they did make a connection between Professor Mellor and Premier Zhao back in the 1980s when both were at the Sorbonne, Mellor teaching nuclear physics and Zhao studying economics.'

'So what if they were at the same university,' Samson scoffed. 'That means nothing.'

'The French say otherwise, sir. They sent us this next shot. It's from a 1988 environmental protest outside the Élysée Palace.'

A mob of scruffy university types crammed beneath a yellow banner rippling in a breeze that blustered down Rue du Faubourg Saint-Honoré. The slogan—the French for *Growth Is A False God!*—was a Mellor mantra this room had become familiar with only weeks ago. Hayek clicked the remote again and zoomed in on two of the protesters' heads. One was bearded, the other clean-shaven, the red glow of their cigarettes flickering in their mouths, their arms linked and legs apart. The photo was so sharp Narthex could almost smell the heady, almost illegal aroma of their Gauloises. He shuddered as he guessed where Blue Coat was going with this, linking Tori through the NY thugs who tried to kill her to the Ten Brothers as well as through Mellor to Zhao, and again to the Ten Brothers. Mellor, as everyone in the room already knew, had been Tori's PhD supervisor.

'The French might say that man with Mellor is Zhao, but are *we* sure?' asked Narthex, straining to cobble together any defence he could in advance of the allegation. 'Zhao, if it's him, is so young there, scrawny and—'

'The French are positive, and so are we,' said Hayek. 'Granted it seems like a long bow,' he looked at Samson, 'but this photo completes a circle of irrefutable links ... Mellor to Zhao, Zhao to Jin, Jin to Swyft and Swyft back to Mellor, her PhD supervisor. And when we add in the other ...'

Narthex stopped listening. He saw the president lean forward, her lips pursed and brow furrowed. His pulse, which had slowed to a fatalistic death march, suddenly started racing, a vice of panic squeezing his heart and lungs.

Zhao's connection to Tori's PhD supervisor, who became her adversary only last November, might be purely a fluke. But how many coincidences could he dismiss before his anti-conspiracy theory exploded ... before he had to admit at least a possibility that their spontaneous encounter on the beach, their romance, the sex ... that all along she'd been setting him, and therefore his president, up?

Hirsty, that greasy shit, had said she'd done honeypot missions before, so was Narthex another one? From their first moment, had she been drawing him in, trapping him in an elaborate lie, a ploy to push the United States into a war with China?

Cluelessness about why didn't stop it being true. And if *he* was thinking along those lines, the president's sudden demeanour—braced but reconciled—told him she was about to throw Tori to the wolves.

'Mr Hayek,' she said, 'there's an ancient Roman maxim, *salus populi suprema lex esto*—'

'That, ah, the safety of the people is ... the highest law?'

'Exactly,' she said, looking down the table at her council, 'and with our hands on our hearts, how does this administration fulfil that most solemn of duties in this case?' She didn't wait for an answer. 'First, we have to ask ourselves the common sense question: what possible reason is there for China to be a part of this, to orchestrate this? None. North Korea, sure, possibly even Iran might want to destroy the United States, the so-called Great Satan, but why would the pinnacle of China's leadership want to do that? They wouldn't. We buy more of their exports than anyone, we owe them more money than ...' Narthex imagined she was going to say *than all the tea in China*, but she didn't. She stopped, then said, 'Putting China at the root of this doesn't make sense, not with anything we know so far. So that makes me suspect someone is trying very hard to whip us into a Thucydides trap.'

Narthex knew what she meant and so did the general, judging by the deep wrinkles of concentration that creased his brow. Hirsty, however, looked flummoxed; clearly, an Athenian historian's theory of what drew Sparta into war with Athens didn't ring any bells with him. Samson obscured his own ignorance by popping open another can of Diet Coke and Secretary Linden found a sudden urge to flip through a pile of papers as if they held the answer somewhere between their lines.

Narthex mentally pieced the 'evidence' together, seeing how it fit Isabel's Thucydides theory. Today, China was Athens, the upstart, the rising new power. The US was the reigning but crumbling empire—the Sparta of old—hanging onto its supremacy by its fingernails, goaded—by Tori?—into suspecting the worst, and preparing for war, in turn provoking the Athenians to do the same.

With the room silently waiting for someone to explain, Narthex could see Isabel was getting impatient. Her tell, her right eyebrow, twitched only twice before she broke the lull. 'Let me simplify this. Is Swyft, deliberately or as someone's pawn, luring us into war with China, a World War III where history will brand us, *this* administration, *me*, everyone in *this* room ... let me be as blunt as I can ... as war criminals? Anyone?'

Clouds lifted off several faces, and theories—most of them fanciful—volleyed around the room. Isabel listened for five minutes then called a timeout. 'The North-Korea-as-China's-pawn scenario is seductive, but peel off the emotion and it makes no sense. Nor does Swyft lying to us, even if what Mr Hayek's given us strongly suggests she is. We need more intel, people. Until then, we've got two choices: we hold our trigger fingers until 7 pm hoping to learn more, or we take a massive, massive risk, and order our fighter jets to take off now, to pre-empt the launch and blast that island right off the face of the planet.'

'There's still the option of calling President Hou Tao?' It was Secretary Linden.

'If Zhao and Xu are indeed culpable, all that calling him will do is alert them to launch earlier, when we're even less prepared. If China's guiltless, telling Hou ... well, we went through all that before.'

No one countered, so she went back to her two choices. 'Doing nothing, hoping for more evidence, is still a huge gamble. If by seven we know nothing new but we don't act, and it turns out Swyft's intel is right, we'd be consigning our nation to instant oblivion.'

No one objected.

'At the other extreme, blasting this island to kingdom come right now or even later risks China reading it as a declaration of war. If Swyft's intel is wrong, if she's a traitor, we're the ones who'll go down in history as monsters. General?'

'Angels or devils, ma'am, if you act now or later, history'd see you as protectin' our people at home. And,' Vaddern added, 'with Swyft seemingly operatin' under the influence of Mellor or these Ten Brothers, and givin' us deliberately false—'

Narthex was fuming. After spending eight straight days with Tori, nights too, no way was she a spider luring him into a web of deceit, of treason. He felt ashamed he'd allowed himself to even think that was possible. 'Ma'am, Swyft's a proven hero. *You* acknowledged that only a few—'

'Dr Carter, the world has seen brilliant double agents before, we've even created our own fair share of ... No wait!' she held up her hand and he closed his mouth. 'Even if Swyft has no improper motive, if she's *not* a double agent, you can't deny the possibility she's been deceived.'

'Ma'am, I *know* Tori Swyft. She's smart, she's loya—'

DNI Hirsty leant back in his chair again and laughed, this time sharply, a knife across Narthex's throat. 'You *know* her, Dr Carter? You only *know* her? Why don't you fess up to the president about just *how* well you know her?'

Hirsty had waited for his moment, like a fox who'd jump a hen, its teeth bared and bloody. He waved a sheet of paper he shouldn't possess: Narthex's official register of interests. 'Swyft's your girlfriend. Am I right Carter? Maybe it's not just the president she's playing for a fool. Perhaps it *wasn't* fate when your eyes chanced on her radiance in that Hawaiian sunset?'

'Dr Carter,' said the president, her voice unnaturally quiet, her demeanour threateningly calm, 'if this is true and you didn't tell me ...' She let the sentence hang, and him with it.

70

I N NARTHEX'S EXPERIENCE, GETTING CALLED OUT of the Sit Room was rarely a good omen but after Hirsty managed to turn the president against Tori, and almost against him, he could have hugged Loucineh for it.

President Diaz, now so wary of Tori's evidence, had just quit the meeting to get ready to go to Davey's play. She'd be back in under two hours, she said, but would remain contactable, able to order the launch of the fighter planes at a moment's notice if she had to. Meanwhile, she'd charged the Watch Room and the agencies to drum up more evidence and, depending on what they came up with, left Narthex and the others on the NSC to thrash out their recommendation for the best or, more likely, the least bad course of action.

Outside the Sit Room, the corridor was lined with several floor-to-ceiling plastic tubes—soundproof phone booths. Loucineh pointed him to the nearest, where the upper wall phone—the black one reserved for unclassified calls—was flashing its red light.

Wrung out and strung out, he wondered if this mystery call was going to make or totally break his day. Before he could ask who it was Loucineh put a finger to her lips, nudged him inside the booth and swung the barrier closed. He stood for a moment, kinked his head to the right, then rotated it all the way around, the joints cracking as if he was limbering up for ... what? He didn't have a clue. He pressed the *loudspeaker* button. The line was hissing, scratchy with the slight echo of a long-distance call. 'Hello?'

'Tex, it's me.'

With one hand, he pulled his tie askew and undid the top button of his shirt while he ran the other through his hair. 'Your gunshot wound,' he asked uneasily, 'have you had someone—'

'Tex, that's not important. You've seen the simulation?'

'If it's true, it's—'

'It's true,' she said.

He knew he should be crafting his words carefully but there wasn't time for that so he let fly. 'Tori, listen to me. Please. I'm failing you here. Miserably. They're saying your story ... not story, sorry, the *evidence* you've risked your ... they're saying it's a sham, that either you've been duped or ... or you're in cahoots with some group they're calling the Ten Brothers.'

'But what do *you* say?'

He wanted to believe her, desperately, yearning to show her—and himself—that he trusted her, loved her even, and that he had the guts to trust his own judgement. But he was struggling.

If only the phone booth had a chair in it. His knees were flagging as much as his inner strength, a thousand eels slithering in his stomach, biting at each other, trying to wend their way up his oesophagus to his throat to gag him. He fought for air, his sense of duty wrestling with his intuition as he longed to believe her. He had to say it. 'Tori, I'm sorry, but we need … I … I need … to get something from you that independently verifies—'

She didn't explode as he'd expected. There was no shrill outrage, no contemptuous, *Don't you trust me?* Just a composed and poised, 'Frank Chaudry's beside me.' It was a good sign. So far. 'He'll tell you what—'

'It can't be Chaudry. I'm sorry. So sorry. We need a source completely independent … of … of you.' The bite in those words also cut into him, knowing she'd hear them as *we don't trust you—I don't trust you.*

Shuddering inside his haze of shame, he heard something press over the mouthpiece. Her hand? Was she speaking to Chaudry? Or did she press it against her heart? He turned up the volume on the speaker, thinking he could hear her pulse, but the heartbeat in his ears was his own.

A few seconds later she spoke. 'Dr Carter,' she started. Not Tex. Not Tex Carter, her friend, her confidant, her lover. Not even Narthex. But *Doctor* Carter. Distant, professional, and more than that, it was as bitter and cold as the winds outside. 'Dr Carter,' she repeated, 'Frank and I are running for our freaking lives, both of us literally bleeding for our adopted country—'

'It's not me,' he pleaded, knowing it was as much him as anyone.

'With my arm going septic, Frank's face smashed in and a shoot-to-kill militia hunting us down, forgive me if I don't believe you. But you, Dr Carter, you'd better believe *me.*'

'I do, really I do, but—'

'Jin Yu—the Mingmai CEO—he's a depraved, sadistic fucking monster who'll stop at nothing. Funding the Nork's rocket site and employing the Iranian to build a nuke for an EMP ... they're not his only covert gifts to humankind. Take RUA's drones ... the ones the media *supposes* they've been using for their assassinations. Well, they *are* drones and we believe they're Jin's, that he's not only working with North Korea but also with RUA.'

Tex had believed her about the rocket launch but even he found it hard to swallow her new claim that Jin, a man closer to Beijing than feathers on an unplucked Peking duck, was also funding and equipping extremists, separatists aiming to cleave their region away from his beloved China. 'Tori, working with RUA, that's—'

'Far-fetched. Like wiping America off the planet? Didn't you get your own eyes on the launch site via that transceiver I left behind?'

'No, er, not yet,' he added. Her transceiver was one way, possibly the only way, to independently verify her intel. He'd pressed that with the others, but the damn techs hadn't cracked a connection, concluding that either her transceiver didn't exist—*Another of her lies*, DNI Hirsty had muttered—or the Norks had discovered it and deactivated it.

'Then get your desk jockeys to check this out. Mingmai owns a drone-making company, it's called Pingyuan and—'

'*Making* drones doesn't make them assassins.'

'Tex, those RUA kill videos? Frank and I have seen some of the raw footage and—'

'What? How did—'

'The uncut material from the pope video ... it's got a drone entering his bedroom through an open window.'

If Tori knew what the drone looked like, if she had a photo of it, he could get it to Isabel's protection detail. After the drone speculation started, the Secret Service had brought in even more 'sky eyes', agents whose sole job was to stay back from the main presidential party and scour the air for anything looking remotely like a drone. 'Tori, you're certain?'

'Absolutely, though it was only a shadow.'

'Ah,' he grunted.

'But there's more … a clip they haven't made public, where they tried to kill my boss in Boston—'

'You're saying RUA's got people on American soil?'

'People? We don't know. But a drone? Yes. Frank was there, Tex. He stood over our boss's body, and he looked up and saw the drone—'

'He physically saw it?'

'In the branches of a tree. He thought it was a kid's balloon. Tex, that's the critical thing, the drone is spherical, the size of a soccer ball, with a kind of metallic mesh for its skin and no external rotors, no landing legs.'

'How does it fly?'

'Frank didn't see it moving but we're assuming it's gyroscopic.'

It seemed possible but something didn't gel. 'Your boss. What possible reason would RUA have for wanting to kill him? He's not a public figure, he's no—'

He heard the phone being muffled at Tori's end and after some mumbling in the background, she returned. 'I've got you on speaker with Frank. He's driving. Axel—that's our boss's name, Axel Schönberg—he latched onto something called *Shi Xiongdi*, which translates as—'

'Ten Brothers in Mandarin.'

'Right. He engaged a professional hacker—don't ask me who—to dig up dirt on them from the Dark Web and straight after that the drone gassed him. That was in Boston, and then the same people tried to kill the hacker, in New York. Now she's on the run, in hiding—'

'She?'

'The hacker. She was the one who showed us the raw RUA videos.'

'How'd she—'

'—get them? No idea, but the Ten Brothers, RUA, Jin Yu, the Norks, the rocket ... whatever their damn connection, whenever you get too close to finding out, they hunt you down. And, Tex, I don't know if this helps ... there's a tattoo.'

Despite his discomfort in doing so, he had to test her to see how much she was prepared to tell him, if it supported her innocence or her guilt. 'Tattoo?'

She paused. 'Shit, Tex. My painkillers haven't clouded my head so much I've forgotten you read my police statement.' She was almost shouting. 'You know that I—' She stopped again. 'Twice. I've seen it twice,' she said, her voice quieter, calmer. 'It's two lines, like a cross—Agh!' He heard her slap what he imagined was her forehead. 'Frank, Tex, I'm an idiot. It's a *shi*, the Mandarin character for the number ten, as in *Shi Xiongdi*. Ten Brothers. Why didn't I ... Tex, the first one I saw was on my driver, the guy who tried to kill me in New York. He had the tattoo, but you knew that.'

'The second one?' Had she seen it, he wondered, on Jin?

'It was on a bellman in our Dandong hotel. He brought up some flowers ... from Jin Yu.'

'Jin's got one too, Tori ... the *shi* tattoo. One of our analysts showed us a photograph.'

'What the hell is going on?'

'We're really not sure.'

'This Ten Brothers—'

'Tori, listen. Can you get the hacker to send those videos to me?' They'd go a long way to convincing the others that Tori was genuine, that the EMP threat was genuine.

'She's paranoid, understandably, so I don't know. I'll try. Ah, I'm getting another call. It might be her. Look, one last thing, and we don't know what it means but maybe your guys will. Jin said something weird last time we saw him. He was ranting, like one of *Macbeth*'s maniacal witches. Frank, what were his exact words?'

'Nothing must get in the way of *foo-shing dow*.'

'You hear that, Tex? He'll let nothing stop *foo-shing dow*.'

Why was this familiar? Tex pressed his eyebrows together to think, searching his memory, but nothing came. 'Who's Foo-shing?'

'You think it's a *person*?' said Tori. 'That didn't occur to ... Sorry, we gotta go.'

The phone went dead. He punched the speaker button again and again but there was nothing, not even static. He dialled the operator. 'That call. I need it back. It's urgent.'

'Sorry, sir. It came from a blocked line.'

'Fu-u-ck!' he yelled, a long, harrowing cry. 'Fuck, fuck, fuck!' His hands flew over his eyes, pressing down on them, his head shaking as he felt his brain bursting, not giving a shit if the booth's soundproofing wasn't strong enough to muffle him.

'Er, are you okay, Dr Carter?' The operator was still on the line.

He ended the call, standing there, trying to calm himself. There was a knock on the plastic door behind him. Turning, he saw it was Loucineh. He slid the door open.

'President Diaz is calling for you.'

He checked his watch, his face quizzical. 'But she's on her way to the pageant?'

'You're going with her apparently. Davey's request. You'd better run.'

71

Dandong

THE COTTON GAUZE FRANK HAD ORIGINALLY pilfered for Tori's dressings, now plugging up his own nostrils, was thick with blood. He could taste the latest drop on his top lip, the coppery tang warm on his tongue, but not in a good way. Left hand on the wheel, he tried to keep the vehicle straight while his other arm stretched back into the storage bay behind the front seats.

He rummaged for more gauze, fumbling blindly among the ammo magazines he'd stashed there, including some 7N31 armour piercers and some rubbery things, but they weren't the gas masks Tori had thrown in … something bigger, longer, which must have already been there. He yanked his hand away the moment he felt enough to suggest it was an inflatable sex doll. As his arm brushed against one of the 9mm PP-2000 submachine guns hanging from the hooks, his fingers touched the other backpack beneath them and he started unzipping it.

Tori picked up the incoming call. 'Hello? ... *Thatcher?*' She put him on loudspeaker.

'Tori, Frank, thank God I found you. Bless you, bless you.' Thatcher's words blurted out so fast he'd again taken his foot off the mental brakes that had been protecting the haughty persona he'd cultivated since Eton. 'What I've discovered about this Jin fellow ... My God, my God, my God. At first I thought Jekyll and Hyde ... but Caligula is closer ... His money moving ... it's only part of it. You're over there, with him, on his turf, and he's dangerous, exceedingly, perilously, brutally dangerous. I've been worried sick for your safety, trying this number and that ... I'm scared for you, Frank. You too, Tori. I'm really, really scared. If Jin Yu finds out you're crossing him, you'll be—'

'I'm afraid he has ... and we are.'

Thatcher was so distraught, he hadn't registered what Tori had said and kept babbling. 'I've tracked down information on a pharma lab he's got in Kinshasa, in Africa. The chief chemist there, a family man, a good man, an educated man ... but Jin ... you wouldn't believe ... he got his thugs to ... the poor man's eyes ... they gouged them out ... *Out, vile jelly*, Frank! Oh my Go—' He'd pulled the phone away but they heard him retching. 'Sorry,' he said, returning to the phone, 'even describing the horror makes me ... but I have to, so you'll understand what you're up against. And the man's tongue ... they cut that out too.' They heard him throw up again. 'It's like, *go thrust him out at gates, and let him smell his way to Dover.*'

In Frank's decades-long friendship with him, Thatcher never quoted Shakespeare. He had an aversion to it, entirely understandable considering how his school drama master had shamefully bullied the 'the Nottingham butcher's boy', continually throwing Bard quotes at him and demanding their precise citation.

'This Jin,' Thatcher continued, 'he's deranged, a charmer who sends flowers to your hotel room one day, Tori, and the next he'll be slicing up your liver with his finest silverware and sprinkling the petals over it as a garnish.'

'Why did he do that to the chemist?'

'The fellow had failed him. It was a message to others.'

'He couldn't use email?' said Frank, immediately regretting making light of the poor man's fate.

'Frank, Tori, you've got to get—'

'We know.'

They heard a screech at the other end of the line. 'You *know*? I'm too late? Oh my God, are you okay? What can I do? How can I …?'

To Frank, hearing Tori relating their night's events somehow made them seem routine and, compared to what Jin had put his chemist through, they were. So far. He couldn't get the chemist out of his mind. Tori kept talking and he kept driving, floating inside a kind of detached bubble until the throbbing in his face reminded him he was in a far-flung Chinese outpost at the wheel of a stolen mini-tank, the two of them running for their lives.

'… if we hadn't managed to overpower them and steal their truck,' Tori was saying, 'Jin would be chucking us out of his plane into the Yellow Sea as fish bait.'

'Dear, oh dear,' was all Thatcher could say between his sobs.

Frank extracted a soaked gauze plug from one nostril and tossed it over his shoulder. Then, using experience gained from rolling cigarettes and spliffs one-handed when he was younger and more foolish, he rolled a fresh wad and inserted it. 'There's more, Thatch.'

When Frank began to explain about RUA's assassinations, Jin's drones and the attempt on Axel's life, Thatcher interrupted. 'Frank, do you have a cold? It sounds like your head is full of cotton balls.'

'Tori got the brunt of the bashing. I copped a couple of jabs to my nose.' He didn't mention the kicks or the cigarette burn.

Thatcher took a noticeably deep breath and paused as if he was going to start blathering again, but then stuck to the business at hand. 'The videos. How did you get them?'

'Your friend, Red. She—'

'No! I mean, yes!' He was so exuberant that if he were the kind to punch the air or dance around the room he probably would have and, judging by the silence on the line, Frank suspected he might be doing just that. Thatcher came back on, slightly out of breath. 'Where is she? Why didn't she—'

'Thatch, the people chasing us—Jin, the Ten Brothers, all of them probably—they're hunting her too. It's why she disappeared. She thinks it's because of the job you referred to her with Axel. Which means that with all the stuff you got for us on the money flows, on Akhtar, and this intel from Kinshasa … you might be in danger too.'

'Maybe,' he said, sounding calmer now he knew all his friends were safe, at least for now. 'Before Thatcher goes all gaga again, there's more to tell you on Kinshasa.'

Frank shifted his eyes between the road ahead and the rear-view mirror. 'The chemist?'

'The chemist was working on a deadly gas designed to fool hospital bloodwork tests. Jin's been perfecting it for years, rendering it colourless and tasteless—invisible to the eye and imperceptible to the tongue. Its one flaw is a slight odour, a milky scent apparently. It's what the chemist promised to eliminate but—'

'—didn't.'

'Right.'

Frank instantly recalled the scent he'd picked up from Axel's body, even though he couldn't smell a thing now. 'We thought it was cappuccino on his breath. Thatch, how'd you get all this?'

'The chemist's son. He was outraged the police were doing nothing to avenge his father so he posted everything he knew on his social media page including the most gruesome photos— you never want to see them—then *he* went missing and the account got deleted, but through Thatcher it lives on.'

'Hell, Thatcher,' said Frank. 'Now you really *have* to leave your place.'

Thatcher was in full flight and ignored him. 'The toxic gas is called hebenon, which could be a clue or maybe it shows Jin's got a particularly black sense of humour. It's the poison that killed the ghost—'

'—of Hamlet's father,' said Tori. '*With juice of cursed hebenon in a vial, and in the porches of my ears did pour the leperous distilment*, blah, blah, blah,' her way, thought Frank, of showing the two Eton toffs that Aussie beach kids could learn the classics just as well as them. If the circumstances were different, he might have made a joke of it. 'Thatcher, what about an antidote?'

'Thatcher will pay a visit to the lab's servers and see what he can do.'

'Not from your place, please,' said Frank. 'Get somewhere safe first.'

'Yes,' agreed Tori, 'but before you leave, can you send what you've got to Tex in Washington?'

Frank understood her reasoning. What Thatcher had wasn't a level of proof that would turn the DC hardheads her way, but it might be enough to give Tex more confidence about her bona fides. Not that Frank was particularly keen for her to patch up that relationship.

'Doing it now,' Thatcher replied.

Frank glanced at Tori as she typed a heads-up message to Tex and pressed *send*. When he pointed out she hadn't blocked her outgoing number, she swore.

A second later, the phone was vibrating with a new call. 'Thatcher, I'm putting you on hold ... Frank, this might be Tex.'

72

FOR A REASON FRANK DIDN'T WANT to admit, he felt a mild sense of relief that the caller wasn't Tex. Tori joined the calls. 'Thatcher … Red, I've got you both on the line … Red, yes, I know you did,' she said after Red exploded, reminding Tori and Frank she'd wanted to keep Thatcher completely out of the picture to protect him. 'But it's too late,' Tori continued. 'With what he's already ferreted out—like the gas RUA probably used in those videos—he's already wading around in shit as deep as we are. We've been trying to tell him to—'

'Red,' said Thatcher, 'thank God you're okay. It was more than—'

'Shut the fuck up, Thatcher,' said Red. 'No time for gallantry. Do you have a safe house?'

'Thatcher's fortress is already a fortress.'

'So was mine, until it wasn't. You activated my CCTV. You saw those bastards got past every barrier I'd put in place. They knew where I lived, Thatcher ... me! No one has ever, ever, tracked down Red Scorpion. Not the NSA, not the FBI, not the CIA, not even your MI6, Frank.'

'That's not entirely true,' said Thatcher.

'Okay, *you* found me, but no one else did except these scum. And if they found me, they'll find you.'

'Red, you forget that—'

She talked over him. 'Engage your nuke protocol,' which Frank took to mean frying his on-site drives and cutting all links to his offsite backups, 'then get the hell out. Take nothing. Go downstairs, to your side door, and in ... hang on, in ... yes, in eight minutes you'll see a woman in a black jacket and a yellow helmet. She'll pull up on a red motorbike, a Ducati, at the entrance to the laneway opposite. Hop on pillion and she'll bring you to me. And it's freezing outside, so wear a coat and a beanie. Do you hear me?'

'Thatcher ... in public ... in a beani—'

Frank rolled back his eyes. What wasn't Thatcher getting about the word *run*? 'The cache from Kinshasa ... has it gone through to Tex? It's critical—'

'It's gone through,' Thatcher snapped, 'and Red, thank you for your offer of hospitality but the power here has just flipped to auxiliary, which means ... yes, someone has indeed cut the mains.'

'Get. Out. Of. There. If it's—'

'The CCTV's showing three rather burly chaps at the front door. Taking a screen shot ... sending it now ... Did you get it?'

'Got it,' said Red.

Tori's phone beeped and a photo popped up. 'Got it.'

She showed it to Frank who took his eyes off the road long enough to see the three men. None of them were familiar, not the one picking the lock nor the other two looking furtively back to the street.

'Red,' said Thatcher, 'tell your biker friend to stay away. These types won't give her a pleasant welcome. The two keeping watch are armed.'

'And they've got the tattoo!' said Frank.

'It's the motif,' said Red, 'for the—'

'Ten Brothers, *Shi Xiongdi*,' said Frank. 'We know that now.'

'That's who Axel asked me to hunt down,' said Red. 'Except *they* hunted *him* down, then *me*, now *all* of us.'

'No one hunts Thatcher. He is a chimera, a wraith, a puff of smoke.'

'Suddenly you're the Scarlet bloody Pimpernel?' Frank shouted as he powered the van into a right-hand turn.

Thatcher ignored him. 'By the time those fiends and, oh look, their support party at the side door, gain entry to Fortress Thatcher the elevator will be out of action, the stairwell door will lock behind them and a cool zephyr of nitrous oxide will brush their cheeks giving Thatcher more than enough time to vanish.'

'*Vanish?*'

'Thatcher's most recent renovations … a steel-lined space behind his dressing-room mirror. It's fireproof, water-cooled if need be and equipped with air scrubbers in case anyone tries to entice Thatcher away from a week's supply of food and champagne.' Frank suspected a Thatcherian week's stores would last most families for months.

'Power? Phone? Computing?' Red asked.

'All sorted, in ways neither these scoundrels nor the neighbours whose accounts Thatcher is piggybacking will ever notice.'

Frank heard fingers striking a keyboard, unsure which of the two hackers was responsible. 'Who's typing?'

'Creating a diversion,' said Thatcher with unruffled self-confidence. 'Composing the itinerary that Thatcher's travel agent would have sent him ahead of his urgent trip abroad this evening: Air France from JFK via Paris to, of all places, Kinshasa. That will spook them. Take-off is in two hours so when those chaps do manage to break in here they'll discover that as Thatcher rushed out the door, his itinerary fluttered to the kitchen floor behind him, as did his phone with his limo app open, showing—as it does—that a town car dropped him two minutes ago at Terminal Four.'

'Call the cops,' said Tori.

Frank covered the phone with one hand and shook his head. 'What would he tell them? That the notorious Fig Jam Thatcher, on virtually every government's Top Ten Most Wanted Hacker list, suggests they pop by his secret hideaway and save his despicable bacon ensuring he can go on stealing more of their secrets? I don't like Thatcher's solution either but hopefully it'll be enough. If not ...' His words trailed off as he lifted his hand.

'Okay, bad idea,' said Tori, 'but—'

'But hurry, Thatcher,' said Red, 'at least nuke—'

'Red, Red, Red, no need. Thatcher's premises have been a nuke-free zone for years. Like yours.'

'Meaning?' asked Tori.

'That Fig Jam Resort runs entirely off-piste. There is nothing here to nuke.'

'You're in the Cloud?'

Thatcher sucked in what sounded like a lungful of air.
'Artistes like Red and Thatcher would never trust their troves
to the very services they hack into every other day. Ah, good
news. Thatcher's guests have now made it into the stairway
to heaven. Nitrous oxide is now ... on. Fare you well, gentle
gentlemen ... and ladies.'

73

JIN YU STOOD THE FRESH GLASS of milk on the desk and waved away the nuisance on legs who'd brought it in. The North Korean woman stepped back, bowing from the waist, waiting. For what? His approval? His thanks she was still here, being paid to serve him in the middle of the night? Jin didn't know and he didn't care. 'You don't need to bow. I'm not Japanese,' he snapped at her in Korean, returning his attention to his laptop. 'Can't you see I'm busy?'

In Dandong, everywhere, Jin Yu was famously charming. Shocked by his discourtesy, one hand flew to her mouth, her other holding the second evidently substandard tumbler she'd brought in earlier. She turned and left the room.

'Shut the door,' he shouted after her needlessly. It was already closing.

74

Washington, DC

WHEN THE PRESIDENT, WITH NARTHEX TAGGING along, made a surprise visit backstage the ten child performers started jumping like human popcorn, all the more chaotic since they were dressed in tree costumes. Picking a handful of Davey's leaves up off the floor she speared them back onto the plastic green stalks she'd sown on his sleeves. Once satisfied with her handiwork, she wished them all good luck.

Davey's face fell. 'Wishing actors good luck is bad luck.' He signed the *bad luck* part slowly to emphasise the gravity of her error. 'What you're supposed to say,' he added, then cracked a big grin, 'is break a *limb*.'

This was the first time Isabel had laughed genuinely in days, snorting as she tried to explain Davey's joke to Narthex in between gasps for breath. Eventually, she stopped and looked serious, raising a finger and slashing it around like a *Star Wars* lightsaber. 'And may the forest be with you,' she signed back.

Davey got the hiccups.

As the hall's rear doors creaked wide, pushed open by two of her security detail, every head inside swung around. In a single motion, they all rose smiling and applauding even before the principal, waiting in the wings, could leap to the stage microphone and reel off the welcome he'd been practising for hours. 'Ladies and gentlemen, boys and girls, please give a hearty welcome to our most fervent school supporter ... Davey Loane's mother ... the President of the United States of America.'

She stood in the doorway looking for familiar faces, smiling and mentally applauding the school's thrift in recycling many of its Christmas decorations. Stepping in beneath the festoons of fake purple and pink bougainvillea chains, silver tinsel, golden streamers and metallic baubles and balloons, she charmed her way past the 207 pairs of eyes she'd been told would be beaming back at her.

A third of the way down the aisle, amid hugs and handshakes, she noticed a glimmer from above the stage and just for a moment, she couldn't stop a memory flooding back. A young John Travolta posing under the first mirror ball she'd ever seen, cocky in his *Saturday Night Fever* dance shoes and blinding white three-piece suit. At nine years old, a year younger than Davey was now, she'd loved the Bee Gees' song *More Than A Woman* that Travolta had danced to. With no record player in their trailer, young Isabel sang the song in her head every day, letting it transport her to a place she'd find her absent father's love and his wisdom.

She felt an agent's hand on her arm, gently pressing her forward. Travolta vanished and she took her seat beside Narthex in the centre of the front row.

She knew he'd be feeling awkward since he knew if it had been her choice, he wouldn't be here. Davey had begged her to bring his 'tree coach' and this was the boy's day not hers. Besides, Narthex and the rest of the NSC could do with a break from each other, at least until more evidence came through.

Narthex had shown gumption during the trip over in *Limo One*, she gave him that, using the time to brief her on the latest Swyft had sent him, claims that were getting stranger and stranger. Strange enough was the possibility of a gas-spraying drone that looked like a flying soccer ball. Even more bizarre was the claim that Jin Yu was somehow connected to RUA. Then there was the grotesque news from an African boy's now deleted social media account identifying the toxin itself, a gas last heard of in *Hamlet* and the horrific torture Jin Yu's people had inflicted on the boy's father, the chemist who'd mixed it up. Coming from Swyft, the 'evidence' might be genuine, it might not, but it was all with the Watch Room and the agencies, so she'd wait to see what they made of it.

What upset her most about Narthex was that he hadn't told her about his relationship with Swyft, opening himself up to being sideswiped by Hirsty. It wasn't that he'd hidden it from the government, he'd been scrupulous in declaring it, but he'd kept it from her. If he had confided in her … But enough, this was Davey's hour. An hour to clear her head while countless others tried to confirm and make sense of it all.

She took in the stage, the walls painted with greens and browns and greys, the floor strewn with leaves and a few tiny heads poking out from the wings to spy on her. A hand popped out and gave her a little wave, before the boy's head jerked back as he tried to control his hiccups.

The clock above the stage, high up in the centre of the proscenium arch, clicked over to the half-hour and the show began.

75

Dandong

'RED,' SAID TORI, 'WE NEED YOU to send those RUA videos to—'

'There are no RUA videos.'

'But you showed us—'

'They are *Shi Xiongdi*'s videos, the Ten Brothers' videos. With *their* targets ... *their* drones ... *their* gas. It's *their* conspiracy, with Jin Yu at its epicentre.'

'Do you have—'

'Proof? Plenty.'

Frank and Tori looked at each other, hopeful. 'Had you given the proof to Axel?' asked Tori, though she expected a no. If he'd known, he'd have gone straight to the authorities—he was no legal pariah—and he would've terminated Project Chant instantly.

'When I realised what I'd stumbled on,' said Red, 'I held it back from him until I'd covered my tracks. Or thought I had. Then I told him. Frank, that was around the time you were due to land in Boston on your way back from Whistler. It was my fault they got Axel,' she said, her voice breaking. 'I obviously missed something that led them back to me ... and then to him.'

'Yeah, what you fucking missed was warning *us*,' said Tori, shaking her head. 'You know, *before* I got kidnapped in New York, or *before* we flew over here,' her voice rose, 'into the fucking lion's den.'

Frank touched her hand and whispered, 'Tori, she knows she screwed up.'

Red continued, 'Frank, Tori's right to be angry. I'm angry with myself. When I heard they'd got Axel, I didn't know what to do. I panicked, I went on the run. I'm just a hacker, not a spy like you two were. And when I did contact you—it wasn't easy tracking down your damn burner phones, by the way— the reason I put you through all those hoops was so I didn't screw up a second time.'

Tori shifted in her seat, wincing as her arm brushed the armrest. 'Okay, truce. I get why they'd want to neutralise Axel and you ... and us ... but why would Jin, or these Ten Brothers of his, get into bed with an extremist movement aiming to secede from China ... why help them assassinate a pope and two prime ministers?'

'They didn't get into bed with RUA, they fabricated it.'

'What?'

'Where you have no enemy, invent one,' Red offered in explanation.

'But why?' asked Frank, still at a loss.

Tori whistled as it dawned on her. 'To create domestic anarchy, confusion, chaos all over China ... which justifies *you* taking the reins, you Jin and your glorious Ten Brothers.'

'Correct,' said Red, 'and with your make-believe scourge stretching its tentacles globally, assassinating foreign leaders to gain notoriety for its cause, the entire world would turn a blind eye if you took control of China and crushed them. If you go over the top and crush anyone else who opposes you, RUA or non-RUA, bad luck to them for being in the wrong place at the wrong time.'

'Universal relief that you've had the guts to purge a global enemy.'

Tori almost laughed. 'An enemy that doesn't exist.'

'Precisely,' said Red.

'If I said holy fuck?' said Frank.

Tori glanced at him. 'Not out of place, even for you.'

Frank steered into a left. 'Then why the rocket? You do know they're planning to—'

'—set off a nuclear EMP over America?' Clearly, she did.

'They're executing a coup to take control of China, mind-blowing, but I get that,' said Tori. 'But why kill hundreds of millions of Americans, obliterating China's most important trading partner, the biggest customer of her labour and resources, the country that fuelled China's growth and its modernisation. That makes no sense.'

'Actually, it does.'

76

Washington, DC

THE FIRST TREE ON STAGE BEGAN poetically, her branches unfurling as the wind rustled through her leaves. And Narthex's phone beeped.

'Sorry,' he whispered, responding to the president's dirty look. He switched his phone to silent, relieved that the tree was deaf so at least he wouldn't have distracted her. Then he gasped, mortified by his thoughts and grateful he hadn't whispered them to Isabel.

The message was from Tori's friend, containing the material about Jin and the poison. Her friend's pseudonym, on the other hand, meant trouble. How was he going to convince the woman sitting next to him, or the team back in the White House, to take anything seriously from someone who signed off as *Friend of Swyft, Friend of America*? Who was this moron?

Whoever they were, the file they'd sent through was so huge, Narthex still hadn't been able to view any of it by the time the second tree came on stage.

'Can you stop that?' the president hissed at him. 'Constantly checking won't make it download any faster.'

He put the phone on the seat beside him.

77

Dandong

'THEY SEE MAJESTY IN A GLOBAL apocalypse,' Red told them. 'Jin and the *Shi Xiongdi* are not your standard megalomaniacs. Their means are despicable, that is true, but they see their ends as noble.'

'So they're like Lex Luthor meets … Martin Luther?'

'I have no idea who either of those men are but, as I was saying, the Ten Brothers aim to reinstate China's glory, her traditions, her isolationism, her shunning of materialism. Not to the dire extremes of Mao Zedong collectivism, but to a China where the people again feel at one with the land, close to nature, where they have a simpler, slower life of moderation and harmony, a life where nothing is instant except a parent's smile.'

'That's an apocalypse?'

'Like I said, noble ends but evil means. It's why they want to change China's direction, to slay what they see has become the greedy pimp to the world's madam.'

'The madam being America,' said Frank quietly.

'Whose tempting tease of lifting people out of poverty, of untold riches is what ripped China away from her roots—from her *real* wealth—sweating them night and day in factory pens like caged chickens. They bleed themselves dry, whipping up delight after trivial delight to satisfy America's every whim, the waste from this so-called industry making cesspools of China's rivers, smog from her air, factories, roads and car parks from her fields. Did you know that in the last five years, China produced more cement than America used over the entire twentieth century?'

'Red, you sound like you agree with them.'

'I *am* an environmentalist, yes, but I'm no despot or mass murderer. Yet, if they do succeed, they will accomplish what Kyoto, Copenhagen, Paris and all the other climate change gabfests utterly failed to. With America wiped out, they'll not only free China of her ruinous madam, they'll rid the planet of our biggest polluter and squanderer of scarce resources. The genius of their plan is that by using North Korea's name, the rest of the world won't blame them.'

'Evil genius,' said Tori, as she replayed the simulation in her mind, visualising gamma rays radiating over North America, zapping every piece of unprotected electrical and electronic equipment in their path.

Frank clearly didn't notice the drops of blood he was splattering as he shook his head in disbelief. 'And they don't care if millions and millions of Americans freeze or starve to death, fall prey to disease, to vigilantes?'

'The more who die, the quicker they die, the faster *Fuxing Tao* will be achieved.'

'*Foo-shing* …? It's not a who?'

'If you pronounce it slightly differently, yes, *Fuxing* is a god of prosperity. But the Ten Brothers' *fuxing* means renewal, renaissance, rebirth. A new dawn. Their mantra, *Fuxing Tao* … revive Taoism … the ultimate purity … harmony with the universe, with nature … to go back to the Yin and the Yang … They want to take China and the planet back to the basics, the universal truths, with fewer people on the planet, fewer demands.'

As Red spoke, Tori tested the explanation in her mind, checking it off one by one against Axel, the drones, RUA, the assassinations, the tattoos, Mingmai's accounting deceptions to secretly fund North Korea, Jin employing Asif, the rocket, the nuke, the simulation.

Red's theory dovetailed with all of it, except for one thing: why would Mingmai bother pursuing Project Chant if *Fuxing Tao* was about to unfold? She went to ask, but paused. Despite the dire circumstances, she felt awkward breaching SIS's client confidentiality.

Frank had no such reluctance, or if he did he shook it off faster. 'I'm puzzled. We came over here to work on a—'

'Project Chant,' said Red. 'What, you think I don't know?'

Frank's eyes met Tori's and they exchanged a look of stunned amazement.

'You're struggling to see why Jin would put himself through all that trouble,' Red continued, 'if *Fuxing Tao* is truly about to succeed?'

'Exactly.'

Before Red could explain, a laugh cackled over the line, a man's laugh.

Tori reeled back in her seat. She wiggled the encryption module. It was definitely plugged in. The light was green. 'Who's there?'

No answer.

She snapped at Red, careful not to use names in case whoever it was had only just cut in. 'Those clips. Contact our mutual friend. He knows who to send them to.'

'So do I,' said Red.

Tori terminated the call, wound down her window a little and let the burner slip out of her hand onto the roadway. As she closed the window a glint of light hit her eye from her side mirror. Parking lights were creeping up on them from a hundred metres or so back. Slowly. Too slowly. Her whole body trembled as she shouted, 'Frank, *drive!*'

He planted his foot down, throwing her back into the seat until he swung the wheel hard to the left, squealing into a tight U-turn as Tori crashed into the door, her seatbelt cutting into her neck. 'What the fuck are you doing?' she shrieked, horrified, as she watched him barrel the car *toward* the oncoming vehicle.

78

T O LIMIT THE FALLOUT FROM SWYFT'S interference, Jin had managed to bring the launch forward by almost three and a half hours, to 6.40 am. So fuck her and fuck whoever he'd heard her speaking to, probably that traitorous bitch Red Scorpion. By blast-off time, in an hour, Swyft and Chaudry would certainly be dead, and hopefully the hacker too.

He leant back, his chair creaking. He enjoyed the sound and rocked back and forth, like a piccolo lightly skipping over the orchestra of rumbles coming through the bunker's thick concrete shell as the roof slid open hundreds of feet above him. The vibrations rippled the surface of his milk, the top of his glass a rather pleasing effigy of the pulse he would soon be radiating across America. The reverberations also provided the perfect bass line for *Winter in the Ozarks*, the first act in the school pageant.

The launch clock on his bunker wall was ticking down, now at T-55 minutes. With the school show scheduled to finish ten minutes before blast-off, regardless of when he chose to assassinate Diaz, he'd have plenty of time to watch the glory of the launch.

Still waiting for school kid number two, he toggled the joystick on his laptop, panning the camera across the audience, a glimmering sea of happy faces, Secret Service and TV cameramen.

A devoted father himself, he would let this bunch enjoy their smiles—their last—a while longer. Besides only one smile in the hall mattered. The one in front row centre, in perfect, unobstructed range.

His plan was to fire the moment her son—her stepson—came on stage when, exuberant parent first, dignified president second, she'd leap to her feet and, a second or two later, drop to the floor, dead.

He and his camera would lap it up and the world, watching through the other cameras in the room, would be in shock that RUA, having taken a pope and two prime ministers, had now removed the leader of the free world. A world, he laughed, that would be even freer, with no bloodsucking America to freeload off the rest of them, to feed her own extravagance and waste. *Fuxing Tao!*

He picked up his glass and saw his reflection, pure against the white milk. *Fuxing Tao!*

It was his brainwave to play into the world's paranoia about Islamism, so he had concocted RUA to kill President Diaz and the three others, each one crucial footsteps in the path to

Oneness, to enlightenment, to *Tao*. RUA was his murky Yin to the endgame's ethereal Yang.

Fuxing Tao would tear up the deluded path of China's past leaders. Like Deng Xiaoping, who didn't actually say *To be rich is glorious!* but might as well have, with his strident pro-market policies. And Xi Jinping, who'd picked up Deng's capitalist baton and ran even harder with it, bringing the world his policy of 'One Belt, One Road', except for the Ten Brothers it was the wrong road. And Hou Tao was no better. Even his name was a disgrace, an insult to *Tao*. The sooner Zhao replaced Hou, the better.

Jin banged his hand on his desk. All those leaders, one after the other, spoke of the benefits of trade, of industry, of development, but at what cost? Yes, shipping filthy raw materials into Chinese ports and crafting them into shiny trinkets and baubles for spoiled Americans and Europeans did create Chinese jobs. But to the Ten Brothers these workers were factory fodder, Western slaves on Chinese soil. And while a few pockets got tremendously enriched—like Jin Yu's own—this so-called 'progress' was sapping China's culture and bankrupting her soul.

Jin shivered in anger, like the reverberations across his milk. He took a sip but it didn't calm him. How could it when China was naively gorging herself on the world's coal, oil, gas and iron ore, shitting out pretty clothes, shiny computers and faster and faster cars, while ignoring how the West was cunningly forcing its own carbon, its own pollution, its own garbage down China's gullible throat ... poisoning Chinese air, Chinese wells and Chinese rivers, killing the country and killing the planet at the same time ... then having the audacity to blame China for it.

He put down his glass shouting, '*Fuxing Tao!*' He felt a little calmer. '*Fuxing Tao!*' Better.

Fuxing Tao would put an end to this very soon, and very abruptly. China would stand on her own feet again while America would fall to her knees, and momentarily President Diaz would be Jin's augury for that.

The other Brothers hadn't been as keen on his plan to execute Diaz, and Si, the Fourth Brother, had positively white-anted him over it. 'Three leaders are enough,' he'd said. 'Why do we care about this president when very soon she won't have a people to be president of?'

Si Xiongdi was a menace, a man without Jin's vision and, today, the others would see that.

Si had never been a proponent of Project Chant either. For Europe, he'd wanted a second EMP, but Si said enough was enough, and the others had agreed. So Jin presented the Plan B he'd been developing in the background. The audacious corporate merger would seat the Ten Brothers' money machine, Mingmai Inc, at the controls of a vast array of the world's IT networks, the forty per cent running with Ólympos inside and even more of them in Europe. Once the Ten Brothers controlled all those switches, it would be up to Jin when they turned them off.

Ah, the second tree was about to come out.

He poised his finger and listened for the child's name.

It wasn't Davey Loane.

79

FRANK LOWERED BOTH FRONT WINDOWS, THE outside chill lashing into the cabin. He could almost feel the sweat freezing on his forehead. He reached into the console between them and passed Tori one of the Norinco QSZ-92s. 'Rack the slide for me.'

'You're going to fire that thing left-handed *while* you're driving?' she shrieked.

'If I have to ... and so will you but right-handed and with the other gun.' He wiped a couple more drops of blood off his chin. 'Lights!' He flicked on the switches for all the exterior lights, high beams, fog lamps and roof-mounted search lights, using the joystick to swing them all at the oncoming vehicle, blinding and, with any luck, terrifying the other driver.

Tori loaded the pistol, placing it in the open palm he was holding out. Then, the icy wind hitting their faces like snowballs, she took up the second gun and racked it.

'Here goes,' said Frank, crossing the centre line and driving head-on toward the other vehicle.

'You're insane,' Tori howled, her body visibly shivering. She poked her arm out the open window, pointing her pistol at the car tearing toward them just as its parkers flicked onto high beam. 'Frank,' she yelled, turning to him, 'what if it's not Jin or his thugs, but ... I don't know ... some guy sneaking home after a night with his mistress?'

'Then lucky him. First, he'll learn a lesson about fidelity, then he'll freak, hang a right at that next street there, he'll watch us streak past in his rear-view mirror and hurl his guts over his dashboard. But if he keeps coming at us, welcome to a game of chicken.'

'If he wants the feet, he can have them.' She inhaled. 'Okay, let's do this.' As her fingers tightened over the gun's grip, one resting on the trigger, she looked so bitterly cold Frank started worrying she mightn't be able to shoot.

The oncoming car's lights blinded him into a white flash of oblivion and at the last second, believing he'd made the wrong choice, he braced himself for the impact, suddenly wondering if Tori had belted up. Then just as quickly, the street ahead of them was in darkness.

His heart pounding, two white headlights still searing into his vision, blood drizzling out of his nose, he pulled back onto the correct side of the road and switched off the ignition, stooping his forehead onto the steering wheel. 'The chicken's flown the coop,' he said, more breezily than he felt.

Tori slumped back and winked at him. 'I prefer dark meat anyway.'

Was that a come-on, or just a joke? Either way, Frank wasn't going to ask. The road behind and ahead of them was empty, apart from a mini whirlwind of leaves, plastic bags and paper that swirled along the blacktop, and a scattering of unfolded cartons that had Frisbeed out of the flat-top when the other driver swerved into the side street to escape the massive 4x4 that Frank was bearing down on him. Apart from the fading yap of the other vehicle bolting from the area, the whirr of the heater fan, and the groans and creaks of their engine cooling and their bodies collapsing, Frank felt a welcome stillness. He focused on lengthening his breaths, a rhythm of silvery smoke signals so weak they lacked even the puff to carry a fog to the windscreen.

As he pressed the button to raise the windows, Tori reached for his phone on the floor. 'That driver will be onto the cops any minute, which given Jin's influence, probably means whoever was listening into our conversation with Red will get to know exactly where we are, if they don't already.' She took the two-way radio they'd got from Jin's hoons out of the console and turned it on, a hiss of static filling the cabin.

Until now, they'd left it switched off to deny Jin a way to geolocate them, but since he was probably doing it already they needed to hear more than to hide.

'We've got to get to the plane,' Tori said.

The game of chicken had extracted a toll on Frank. He lifted his head and, even in the weak ambient light, the mirror revealed how washed out he was, how drawn his eyes were, his forehead starting to blister and a thin line of dark ooze snaking down from his nose. Tori passed him some more gauze and he wiped away as much of it as he could. 'Here goes,' he said, planting his foot on the accelerator again. 'But even if they are monitoring our phones, we need to call Mada, to tell him—'

'Zell? What if he's in Jin's pocket? What if he helped Jin with Axel?'

'And what if he's not and what if he didn't?'

She thought for a moment. 'I'll use the satphone.'

80

Boston

MADA LISTENED IN UTTER DISBELIEF. IF what Tori had said about Mingmai and Jin was true, it would yank his world out from beneath him.

Calm down, he told himself. *Think.* Yes, Swyft was an arrogant, conniving shit who'd totally conned Axel, but why would she cook up such an extraordinary lie? And Chaudry too, he was backing her up. At the same time, how could this be true? For starters, *his* Jin was the polar opposite of the ogre they were talking about. *His* Jin had got him into a cancer trial, no questions asked. The man's generosity, his contacts, his money, they were saving Mada's life, not that he would ever confess that to Swyft.

He felt a twinge of guilt taking favours from Jin and Kong but surely, after devoting his working life to Axel and his father before him, it hadn't been wrong to at least consider a future without Axel, a firm without Axel?

How could he have avoided discussing Project Chant with Jin or Kong when the men called so often to ask after his cancer, to hear how the trial was going, to ask if they could do any more for him? It was fairly natural, wasn't it, for the conversations to turn to deal matters?

But if Swyft was right … He dropped his head into his hands. *Think, Mada, think.*

He jabbed at the orange button on his phone. 'Lucille, please come in.'

He stood as she entered and extended a hand. 'Take a seat.' She looked wary, and he realised it was because he'd never been civil to her before. Her sweater, a peony pink one, made her face look sallow. As he waited for her to sit he noticed for the first time how slight she was. He felt as drained as she looked, though in his case it was the debilitation that followed each bout of treatment, the loss of fees from Project Chant, the dread that his life was about to fall apart.

They both sat.

'Ron, what is it? You're worrying me.' She leant forward and placed a hand on his. Suddenly he couldn't keep himself together and began sobbing.

'I'm sorry,' he said, taking a tissue from a drawer to wipe his eyes. She pulled herself back and though she sat steeply erect, her skin was softer than before, her colour pinker. Her eyes were open, welcoming like his Margaret's, though Lucille's were blue, cerulean blue, where his wife's had been that puppy dog brown he'd liked to tease her about. 'It's a lot to take in,' he said, 'but Swyft says Axel's coma … that it's because of Mr Jin … though I'm sure it must be his people, it couldn't possibly be him … She says they poisoned him … Axel.' He shook his head.

Saying it aloud had made it more real, even harder to absorb than hearing it from Swyft.

Lucille hunched over, her eyes shrank and her body trembled. Mada was sure he was imagining it but her hair, usually silver, was turning to ash. 'Surely not,' her voice quivered. 'Mr Jin's so ... so decent.' She knew about the drug trial of course. Mada had told her, partly to show he trusted her but also to avoid her being suspicious about his regular absences from the office.

Mada heard Lucille's phone ringing outside his office, the call light flashing in front of them on his. He glanced at his phone. This was a number he knew well: their client's yacht. If anyone was entitled to know that his second once-in-a-lifetime deal was about to crater, it was Skylakakis, but first they had to call Axel's doctor.

'Let it go to voicemail,' said Mada.

81

Dandong

AFTER ENDING HER CALL WITH MADA, Tori felt like punching something, but instead popped two more painkillers.

'Come on,' said Frank, 'speaking to him wasn't that bad, and if you take any more of those pills you'll be high as a—'

'Drone?' According to the SUV's GPS they were fifteen minutes from the airport. She reached to the dash for the two-way comms and clicked it on, but there was no chatter. 'If Jin's ordered radio silence over this channel it's not a good—'

'Hello again, dear friends,' Jin drawled through the box. 'You seem to have deserted my phone network, but I trust you're still enjoying your test drive? Chinese sweat and Western brains ... a marvellous arrangement, yes? It's been my country's story, but not for much longer.'

She went to press the *talk* button, but Frank stopped her. 'Don't give him the satisfaction.'

'I know you're there. I even know where there is. Oh, take the next right if you're heading to your hotel, not that you'll ever make it.' He waited. 'Still not talking? No matter. Do you like how my van handles? So much better in your custody than those two morons you left behind. That was impressive, by the way, your bullet of sweet vengeance to that cretin's lower parts. What I'd have given to video it for my collection.'

'He records his kills?' said Frank, his face aghast. 'Not just the RUA ones.'

'He probably catalogues them under *Jin's Greatest Hits*.'

'Hello-o?' said Jin. 'Still no speaks? Those men you left back there to die? Well, they did. They had a sudden urge to take a dive off that jetty and now they're sleeping with the fishes … Is that too Don Corleone for you? … No? Still nothing? You know, some movie critics thought Coppola made *The Godfather* a bit too long, especially *The Godfather Part III*. But not me, not for such a powerful documentary. Oh, you *didn't* take that right turn. Chinese street signs are such a bitch. Hey, if you pull over and wait, my men won't be—'

'Enough!' cried Frank, snatching the two-way from her. He turned it off then executed a left, away from both the hotel and the airport.

'Houston, we have a problem.' Tori pointed through Frank's window where a drone, like the one Frank said he'd seen in Boston, was tracking beside them.

'Pass over one of the PP-2000s,' said Frank, slowing the vehicle.

She picked up one of the submachine guns at her feet, checked the clip and handed it to him. 'You get one shot free, but every bullet after that you'll have to swallow one of those thousand-year-old eggs. Unless you'd like me to do it since I am the better shot.'

'You? Shoot that thing with one arm? I don't think so. Besides,' he said, bringing the vehicle to a stop, 'a man's drone is his castle.' He cracked open his door as the orb loomed closer, like a predator creeping up to sniff its kill.

'Wait,' said Tori, handing him one of the two gas masks she'd found in the glove compartment. 'In case it's loaded with hebenon.' They both slipped the masks on and Frank unclipped his seatbelt, placed one foot on the running board, then swivelled, aimed and fired. 'Phm! Omm shrt, nnm exx.' He slid back in and closed his door.

She pushed her mask up to her forehead. 'Translation?'

He lifted the rim of his mask off his mouth. 'Phew! One shot, no eggs.'

'Let's go get the bloody thing.' She opened her door and was about to put her mask back on when Frank lifted his again. 'Are we planning to take it home?'

'If we get that far. At the very least I'll send Tex a photo of it. Those bastards he works with will have to believe us now.' *And he will too.*

✝

BY THE FOURTH tree's performance, Narthex had skimmed most of what Friend of Swyft, Friend of America had sent through. He was now calculating which NSC members would pay it heed and which would scoff, even if he deleted the sender's preposterous alias before he sent it on. He drafted up a message forwarding it to the Watch Room and handed the phone to Isabel.

He saw the president's shoulders rise then fall as she huffed out a breath. She stared ahead, not at the stage and not at the players, higher, at the disco ball, like it was hypnotising her or giving her answers to questions he could only guess at.

82

Dandong

NOT KNOWING HOW FAR AWAY JIN'S men were, Tori watched nervously as Frank—mask still on—disabled the drone and lugged it into the back of the van as fast as he could. Once he was back at the wheel, their lights out and three quick street turns later, she pointed ahead and to the left. 'Over there, an open garage.'

As they got closer, she peered into the darkness. 'Looks empty,' she said, suddenly shivering as she remembered the last garage she'd been driven into.

Frank backed inside and killed the engine. He also disabled the interior lights so he could safely open his door without being seen from the street, then jumped out trailing the satphone aerial behind him.

Tori stayed in the vehicle to call their pilot. It wasn't five seconds later that she was calling out, 'Frank, how about some quiet?' She shook her head as the roller shutter rattled two-thirds of the way down.

The garage smelled fresh and clean, grassy, like a park just mowed, and she suddenly had one of her 'madeleine moments', like the narrator in Proust who dipped his little cake in his tea, the aroma, the taste recapturing memories of his childhood village. She was sitting on the swing, her tiny hands gripping the chains, her dad launching her into the sky. The image dissolved when their pilot answered his phone. 'Simon, keep this call tight. What's your status?'

'Pre-checks done, chocks pulled, ready to taxi.'

'Our stuff?'

'All done.'

'Marty?' she asked, referring to their co-pilot.

'In the crew quarters. Still sick from the street food.'

'Any other trouble?'

'Amazingly none, even with all this hoo-ha about a national emergenc—'

'Guards?'

'Only two. No craft are due for hours, in or out, so tower's unmanned. We're free to leave when we like.'

'Won't the guards—'

'Busy gettin' smashed on the *baijiu* I brought 'em.'

Ugh! *Baijiu*. To her, the drink tasted like her fifteen-year-old cousin's bedroom smelled, of two-day-old mac and cheese, bodily fluids and butane. The only time she'd tried it had been like liquid razor blades going down her throat.

'I gave 'em the two bottles I bought for my brother's fiftieth. The store guy said they're infused with velvet deer antlers, a big aphrodisiac over here. When I left the guards, they were sloggin' 'em back shot after shot … lots of *ganbeis*. That means—'

'*Cheers*, I know. And cheers from me.' She put the phone on the seat and was about to tell Frank the news when the garage started vibrating like they were in a subway station. A few seconds later, the road outside was scritching like God was ripping two giant strips of Velcro off the blacktop, one after the other.

Tori squinted into the gap below the shutter to see two vehicles flash by.

'Similar models to this one,' said Frank, ramming the shutter back up. 'Jin's men.'

She updated him on Simon as he leapt back into his seat and started the engine. Lights still off, they rolled slowly out of the garage, waiting at the verge. 'Head right,' she said, checking the GPS. 'It's one-way the wrong way but with your chicken skills we'll do fine. Whoa! Stop!' She pointed to the sky ahead of them and passed him the PP-2000 again.

'Do you think it saw us?' he said.

'We'll find out soon enough but either way, let's see if you can keep your record.'

He opened his door. 'Those eggs,' he said, aiming, 'still on offer?' He fired.

'You obviously hate them as much as I do. Another perfect shot. A girl could get egg-cited.'

'Not while I'm driving,' he said, passing the gun back to her. He floored the pedal, swinging the steering wheel hard right and bouncing the van over the gutter, back wheels fishtailing into the freshly grounded drone, knocking it flying across to the other side of the street.

83

SIMON HURTLED DOWN THE GULFSTREAM'S AIRSTAIRS even before they pulled up.

Frank braked wide of the wingtip, far enough away that the jet blasts on take-off wouldn't blitz the SUV. Before leaping out, he snapped on all the spots, fogs and high beams, training them down the runway as Simon had suggested in their last call. The airport was non–towered tonight and while the G650's infrared-enhanced vision system meant they could get away without runway lights altogether, he'd said he preferred at least some.

While the men were lifting the drone between them, Tori fiddled around in the back of the SUV. 'Marty any better?' she called out.

Simon looked up. 'Stopper-uppers and a couple hours' sleep should do the trick.'

After the two men lugged the drone up the airstairs and secured it in a cargo bin at the rear, they ran back down to collect the backpacks and see if Tori had finished.

She poked her head out of the SUV. 'All done.'

Simon went to offer her a hand and looked inside. 'I knew negotiating big corporate deals was tough, but do you really need an arsenal?'

'Boy Scouts taught me to be prepared for all eventualities. It's why I wear two pairs of socks to bed.'

'She's joking, isn't she?' he whispered to Frank, but loud enough for her to hear.

'Frank has no idea, even if he'd like to,' she said, a glint in her eye that she immediately shut down, not least because it felt disloyal to Tex. Strangely, she liked how being disloyal felt wrong. When this was over, she thought, maybe there was a future for them, assuming he forgave her for doubting him.

Simon helped her down from the back. 'Hey,' he said, pointing to a six-foot long, thin box inside, 'no way we can leave a MANPAD here.' The acronym stood for man-portable air defence systems, or more simply, shoulder-mounted surface-to-air missile launchers. He looked around. 'I wouldn't want someone turning up and using it against us.' He pulled it out, hoisted it over his shoulder and carried it up the airstairs. 'We'll dump it when we're safely over the Pacific.'

AFTER SIMON LATCHED the cabin door, he handed them some bottled water and told them to strap in. They'd all agreed there was no time for pre-flight bathroom breaks. A clean escape had more going for it than clean faces and fresh dressings. Belted up and facing Frank across the table, Tori sent Tex a message attaching the drone photo, then double-checked she'd deleted the smiley-face emoticon she blamed on the painkillers. Even so, she popped another analgesic, swallowing it down with a gulp of water, the soothing of her arm more urgent than worrying about bladder discomfort. She screwed the lid back on the water bottle and rested it on her lap, closing her eyes. 'Wake me up when we're out of Chinese airspace. This is forty-wink time,' she told Frank, snuggling into one of the blankets Simon had thrown over the seats to protect Axel's golf-ball white leather.

Her eyes closed as the plane pulled forward, pressing her head back even further into the padding.

'Did you see that movie *Argo*?' Frank asked, ignoring her shut-eye request. 'You know, the one where the CIA rescues the US hostages from Iran?'

'Me ... sleep,' she said, her eyes closed.

'Remember the climax at Tehran airport, with the Iranians chasing the 747 down the runway?'

'Hollywood crap,' she said, opening her eyes and unscrewing her bottle cap again. 'We got a presentation on it at Langley, believe it or not.' She took a sip.

'On the fake moon-landing movie set?'

'Funny fellow. Here's the first fact. In the real deal there was no chase at all. So that scene was total Hollywood bull. Second, a Boeing 747's take-off speed back then was,' she scratched her memory for the number, 'I think it was 150 knots—'

'Around ... 170 miles per hour.'

'Yeah, and since you're intent on stopping me sleeping, I calculate that as ... 275 kilometres per hour,' she said. 'But whatever, let's just say the plane was going so freaking fast there wasn't a cop car or military truck in existence in 1979 that could've reached even two thirds of that speed without blowing their engines first.'

'Cars've come a long way since then.'

'What's the booklet you're reading?'

'The plane specs. They were in the seat pocket. They say take-off fully tanked takes 6,000 feet of runway. Do you think we could outrun a couple of Jin's SUVs over a mile and a bit?' He pushed a button in the armrest. 'Because it looks like we might have to.'

A 360-degree camera display appeared on the touchscreen table between them, and Tori saw two vans flying through the airport gates. 'Simon. You there? Simon?' Frank called into the intercom.

'Yeah, incomings at eleven o'clock. Been keepin' my eye on their lights racin' up the entry road. We're balls to the wall already at, like, 100 knots and headin' north o' that so I'm hopin' to have us airborne before those bastards get anywhere near the runway.'

Tori shot a dark look across the table. 'I don't think we need to worry about those guys outrunning us. If *we* were carrying MANPADS—'

'So might they,' said Frank. 'Simon, push her harder, they're probably armed with—'

'I know and I am.'

Tori swiped the screen, splitting the image into two windows. On one, she simultaneously touched one of the attack vehicles and the *fix* icon so the camera's motion sensor would stay locked on it. Then on the other window, she rotated her thumb and forefinger, shifting the view off 360 and with three fingers, sideswiped the view from nose camera to wing camera to undercarriage, and several more until she reached the tail camera. She tapped *fix* again even though they could see nothing but a blaze of white from the array of lights they'd left shining on the SUV.

Back on the other screen, one van was closing in while the other slowed. She zoomed in. 'The guy riding shotgun ... he's preparing to use the launcher.'

The plane's nose started to lift and Tori unclipped the phone handset from the wall. 'Time for our entertainment. Agreed?' She felt the back wheels leave the ground. Frank nodded furiously and she dialled.

As the plane climbed, Simon started banking to the right harder than Frank would've thought safe, pulling quite a G-force on his two passengers. As they angled into the turn, the white glare showing on the tail screen slipped sideways and was replaced by a flash so penetrating that it took three seconds before they could see anything on the screen again. The remote-controlled detonator Tori had rigged up in the back of the SUV had worked.

'Don't you love a good diversion?' said Frank.

She might have punched the air with her good arm, if it didn't suddenly weigh so much. With her head crooked to the side, she watched the lightshow on the touchscreen table until Simon's bank got to sixty degrees and Frank called to her to watch it through the window across the cabin. There were rat-tat-tats of bursting, blazing and torching from the assorted weaponry in the back of the SUV, then the dual fuel tanks went, the lot finally spewing forth a dazzling Vesuvius of flames and violent sparks of reds, oranges and yellows into the night sky like New Years' fireworks.

'Go shrapnel!' cried Tori. 'If none of it manages to hit those creeps, hopefully the shock wave and flying debris will distract them long enough for Simon to get us out of range, which I calculate at ... at this speed ... circa fifty seconds.'

'If this works, then we'll have a movie night and watch *Argo* when we get back.'

Suddenly, the flash they were hoping *not* to see left one of the SUVs, a missile rocketing toward them.

'Maybe hold off on the movie night.'

'Hang tight, folks,' Simon said over the intercom, 'and grab your sick bags.'

'I like his optimism,' said Tori.

84

SEVEN TREES JIN HAD WATCHED SO far, and not one of them the president's stepson. With the eighth about to come out he again poised his finger over the trigger icon on his touchscreen, waiting for the kid's name. A message beeped both on his phone and his laptop. He ignored it. If the next kid was hers, he wasn't going to mess up the hit to read another report from his men about how they'd fucked up chasing the redhead and her brown boyfriend.

Damn! This eighth kid was Catherine somebody. How many simulated bits of vegetation did he have to put up with before he could kill the woman in the front row?

He read the message:

Cao! Fuck! He threw the phone down on his desk so hard some of his precious yak milk spattered out of the glass. His people had failed him again. Not only had they let the two foreigners steal the van, there'd clearly been a botched assault at the airport and, worse, he was hearing about it not from his incompetent goons but from San Xiongdi, his Third fucking Brother.

Breathe, he told himself. He wouldn't dwell on Swyft and Chaudry any longer. Not now that San Xiongdi—the PLA's Air Force commander General Chang Yang—had ordered a squadron of his fighters, his *birds of prey*, to blow them out of the air. They were as good as gone.

Picking up his glass, the fourth that idiot woman had now brought in, he licked the drip off the side and held it high, looking through it at the ceiling light. This one had the perfect opacity, a solid arctic white. Satisfied, he drank it down in one gulp.

85

THE BARK MAKE-UP CAKED ON THE weeping willow's face cracked each time she grinned at the stomping coming from the 200-odd pairs of delighted feet in the auditorium. Her melancholic, heartbreaking performance a triumph, she trailed her branches gracefully stage left, dragging her roots behind her.

Once Jin discovered C-SPAN was streaming the event live he'd been able to watch her on split screen. What an irony that her tree was a native of China, a symbol of immortality and rebirth. Perhaps he'd get Zhao, as one of his first acts as Hou Tao's successor, to declare it the national tree of *Fuxing Tao*.

The woman had brought him in more milk. He took another sip, a habit he'd started when hebenon first became viable. He rolled it round in his mouth, coating the top of his tongue and importantly the frenulum fold beneath. Satisfied with his routine—you could never be too careful—he put down the glass.

The camera had moved off the president and now aimed at two women five seats to her right. They kissed, the blonde one cuddling the baby girl they'd been playing musical laps with for the whole show, and then the brunette shoved a bottle into the little gurgler's mouth.

He adjusted the lens back to the president. Her posture and demeanour were still perfect, to be expected from the most televised woman in the world. Diaz had stayed surprisingly straight through every tree so far, not a single slump. Her smiles and applause were just right, too. Not too much, not too little, her feet tapping the floor after each act with enough vertical movement that she'd come across as engaged and not aloof should one of the cameras at the side of the hall be filming her. Her hair was in its usual bob, her blouse a crisp white, low collared with a double string of pearls—not so long as to be extravagant and short enough they almost concealed the fabled scar from her childhood attack. Her suit was grey, elegant yet boringly understated. If only she was one of those women who wore reds or yellows or other shouty colours. It would look so much more dramatic when he killed her.

The blond man seated beside her suddenly sat forward, a bit like an expectant puppy but without the lolling tongue. Good. Her stepson had to be up next. The real show was about to begin.

Jin steepled his hands together and interlaced his fingers, turning his palms outwards to crack his knuckles like a pianist about to perform his finest concerto. With barely enough time to return his fingertips to the joystick he heard the auditorium speakers crackle. 'Ladies and gentlemen, please welcome Davey Loane to the stage.'

The man beside the president put his hands on his seat and tensed. He was clearly fixing to jump to his feet but Diaz, without looking at him, pressed a hand to his leg and shook her head. He smiled weakly as if he'd been reprimanded, sat back and took a moment to look at his phone. His face clouded over.

He looked up, virtually into Jin's eyes. He looked down at the phone. And up again.

Jin knew something was wrong.

86

Washington, DC

THE MESSAGE THIS TIME WAS FROM Tori: *On plane, ready for take-off.* She'd got to a plane. She was getting out. Thank God, after what he'd read—and a couple of times seen—about this Jin Yu ... a savage, not a man. He read on:

Here's proof for your doubters re Jin's drones: photo of one we shot down before it got us. That's my hand on it to show size. Bringing it home to you, for your experts to analyse toxin, mechanism etc. Hope you have strings you can pull to get us through Customs! Looking forward to seeing you
TS

He almost smiled as the image of her hand, a little blurry as it downloaded, stared back at him. It made it real that she was on a plane. That she was safe. But she hadn't been safe, not if they'd had to shoot the drone down *before it got us*. He felt nauseous.

He shuddered as the photo came through, the black ball below her hand stark against her skin, pale except for a flake of dried blood, its edges curling. *Fuck you, Jin.*

He remembered kissing that hand, pressing each beautiful finger one by one against his lips, her hand caressing his neck, fingers stroking his eyelids.

Focus, he reminded himself. The drone ... 'Spherical,' she'd said, 'the size of a soccer ball, with a kind of metallic mesh for its skin'. He looked up. He looked back down. He tried to swallow but his mouth was dry. This drone ... and the one in Boston ... they were the same size, the same shape as the disco ball above the stage.

He couldn't afford to jump to conclusions, to frighten the crowd unnecessarily, create a panic. Tori's drone was black and matte and the ball up there ... he suddenly didn't want to look at it, but he forced himself to ... it was twinkling and joyful, winking pretty rainbows all over the stage. Like every other disco ball he'd ever seen.

But what if some bastard with a cross-shaped tattoo had stuck that mosaic of tiny mirrors all over a drone and smuggled it in here days ago, hanging it from the ceiling at the back of the stage like it had been there for years, missed by the president's protection detail.

A drone. Hiding in plain sight.

Narthex's body wanted to crap his pants, to vomit. He wasn't trained for this. He was an adviser, an egghead, not some Tom-Cruise-bullet-blasting hero. He could spout on and on about weapons policy but put him anywhere close to an actual weapon and he went to water.

If he made a fuss about this and he was wrong, he'd send the whole place into chaos, pandemonium, bedlam. He'd have Secret Service agents shooting, kids screaming, parents panicking, cameras rolling, the whole sorry mess for everyone to see on national TV, international TV and forever on the internet.

If he was wrong, he'd paint himself a fool on the biggest canvas conceivable. Losing his job would be the least of it, and he was only hanging onto that by a thread, thanks more to Davey than his own skill.

He could go back to academia, if they'd risk hiring damaged goods. Or, grasping at the only other straw he could think of, maybe he could surf. He'd always wanted to surf competitively. His thoughts whirled, feeling a powerful rip dragging him way, way out of his depth …

WHAT HAD THE man beside the president seen on his phone? Obviously her assistant, he'd been slumped over the damn phone almost the entire time after escorting her in, reading and typing out messages and passing them to her. But this time it was different. Jin's risk antenna rarely failed him and the tension in this man's body, the way he was gripping the device, the sweat forming on his upper lip … Jin knew his moment of glory needed to happen now. Already recording, he poised his index finger in the air, holding it steady.

✝

WHAT IF HE *wasn't* wrong? Narthex felt spiders crawling over him, up his arms, under his clothes, over his back, tingling on his scalp, creeping into his ears. They left sticky trails of silk everywhere, over his eyes trying to blind him, slithering over his lips, their tiny threads stopping him from opening his mouth and calling out.

He looked up. That ball up there … It *was* the same … shiny, glitzier, but the same. Fuck it. He didn't have a choice, he had to do what was right not what was safe for him. He squeezed his eyes shut, not to pray but to fill his body with energy, with courage.

He felt his teeth unclenching, the spider silk stretching as the blood rushed into his muscles, engorging them, breaking the bonds as his eyes opened and his body drove him to his feet. His mouth screamed the first thing that came into his head: 'Rosa under attack! Rosa under attack!' Rosa was the Secret Service codename for the president.

He shouted at the top of his voice, so loud he wondered if he'd have any voice left. 'Davey,' he yelled, amazed he could and, like a wild man, swiped his hands sideways to the left, to the right and back to the left again, screeching, 'Kids … Trees … Get … Off … The … Stage … Left … Right … Run!' He prayed they'd lip-read him, follow his frenzied gestures and get themselves safe. They understood. The kids who'd come to the sides to be Davey's chorus were tearing back into the wings, but Davey did a running leap from the stage into Isabel's arms, hugging her tightly, a flurry of shiny greenish-white leaves almost suspended in his wake.

'That disco ball,' Narthex pointed. 'Up there!' His voice was a shriek, his throat spasming, his words trembling like a mad street-corner Bible-basher. '*Shoot it down. Shoot it down,*' Narthex bellowed. 'The disco ball. NOW, for fuck's sake, NOW!' His body was shaking so much he had no idea his phone was vibrating again.

87

The island

JIN WATCHED AS THE KIDS CLEARED the stage and four of Diaz's agents unholstered their guns, aiming, it appeared, straight at him. Two more charged in from each side of the front row toward President Diaz like Pamplona bulls, pushing, shoving, tossing, headbutting and freaking out everyone who'd thought until a moment ago it was an honour to be seated so close to the president, now desperate to get themselves as far away from the target as they possibly could.

Her stepson's dive off-stage ... Wow! Electrifying and poignant at the same time, Jin couldn't have scripted it better himself. In his mind he was already editing the video, making the leap Jackie Chan style, pausing Davey mid-air when his toes had just left the stage, his body outstretched, then flying slow-mo into his mother's arms. And those leaves fluttering behind him! What a touch.

The tears, the anger this would spawn. The revulsion. The terror that a pope and two prime ministers weren't enough for RUA, they also had to take down the leader of the fucking free world. If they could get her, no one anywhere was safe. Who'd be next?

China would have to take fierce, drastic, authoritarian action—more than Hou Tao had already—and no one would say boo.

With two TV networks filming in the hall, the world would see the whole thing live, but only Jin would give them the kill shot. He'd release it five minutes before the EMP struck.

He'd have to be quick, but the video of this mother and son would be his masterpiece. His *Pietà*. And he, the modern Michelangelo.

88

Washington, DC

BULLETS WHIZZED OVER NARTHEX'S HEAD. HE should've been relieved yet his heartbeats were fast, his breaths short, his body fighting off this fearful intruder under his skin, the clinging, frightened man who felt unprotected and vulnerable, *his* neck and shoulders tense, *his* stomach clenched. Isabel might've been speaking—shouting—at him, he didn't know. He concentrated, transmitting all his might, his *and* this stranger's energy, into the rounds flying through the air, willing them to obliterate the threat and make the stranger in him feel safe. His eyes were faster than the bullets, marking out the path, leading them to the disco ball and when they hit it was glorious. Hundreds of squares of mirrored silver paper erupted from the shattering globe like a massive confetti bomb. But he didn't clap, he didn't crack a smile, he squinted, listening for the telltale pop of gas, looking for the explosion of a canister, a flicker of flame, but all he could see was a micro-galaxy of tiny falling stars twinkling their way down to the floor.

The stranger was gone leaving him empty and drained, his skin prickling, sheer slow-moving nothingness draped over the dispirited, slouching frame of a man waiting to hear if he was the president's saviour or her fool.

He braced himself and turned toward her, but something moved at the top of his vision, not from where the disco ball had been but closer and higher. He turned his face up to the proscenium arch, wondering why a speaker would emit steam, even a short, wispy puff like that, no longer than a child's pinkie. Smoke? Perhaps a stray bullet had hit it? He tried to blink it away but the tiny cloud spun itself into a gossamer cone, drawing itself out, elongating and angling down.

The Secret Service agents ... where the fuck were they? He looked left, right. The closest was the female brick to his far left, ten feet away, trying to push through the scrum of panicked people on her way to the president.

Shoulder first, he pitched his body left, knocking Isabel sideways and jolting Davey from her arms. The boy's head narrowly missed the lip of the stage as he disappeared under it. Isabel managed to stop herself falling by grabbing hold of a man's arm. Narthex went to help her but his feet froze to the floor, his face at first hard and cold, like a block of dry ice.

His eyes misted over and his mind suffused with a kind of rapture. It slowed him down. It was refreshing, reassuring. Everything was okay. He inhaled deeply through his nose, detecting the faintest whiff of something he couldn't pinpoint ... Heaven perhaps ... Tori maybe.

All the cameras saw was his eyelids drop, his legs buckle and, as he fell, his head hit the edge of a chair, a spray of blood splattering Isabel's blouse just as an agent stopped her reaching for him. The agent gathered her up in his arms and sprinted in the opposite direction shouting, 'Rosa coming through! Rosa coming through!'

89

DAVEY SCRAMBLED OUT FROM UNDER THE stage, sobbing, confused, trying to make sense of the turmoil. Isabel was gone and other people were trying to flee, kicking over chairs, tripping over shopping bags, rucksacks, coats and scarves, their faces contorted, in tears, mouths gaping open in cries that read like 'Help!' or 'What's happening?' or 'Get me out of here!' The two nice ladies he'd seen from the stage feeding their baby had dropped their bottle behind them where it had rolled under one of the chairs. Narthex lay at his feet, quiet, motionless, a red, oozy gash across his forehead. His eyes were closed, and although he wasn't moving, he was crying, his face wet with tears. Davey bent down and, with a finger painted like a twig, prodded Narthex's chest. He shook his shoulders. Then he did what people in the movies do, putting an ear to his mouth, but he felt no breaths, just the wet of the tears and the cold of Narthex's lips against his skin. Davey leant back and wiped his friend's face, realising Narthex hadn't been crying. The tears were Davey's.

His friend was dead.

Dead because of him. Isabel hadn't wanted Narthex to come but Davey had nagged her, thrown a tantrum, and she'd given in. He bit his lip to stop himself bawling but it didn't work. He wiped his eyes, wishing he were more like the man everyone told him he was supposed to be.

He'd wanted Narthex here to see how he'd worked in the poetry he'd quoted to him. And now there was no poem and no Narthex. Because of Davey.

Through a veil of tears, he squeezed the words into the front of his mind, wiped his hands on his brown, tree-trunk pants and signed to his friend, *The blown leaves make bat-shapes, web-winged and furious.* He knelt down on the floor, brushed some of the silver squares into a little pile, scooped them up and tossed them back into the air, a big toss, while he prayed to God they'd carry Narthex's soul up to Him.

It didn't work, the little mirrors fluttering back down, all of them. As one landed on Narthex's phone, the screen lit up making the little silver square appear black. Davey leant down and blew it off the phone, worried it was a Devil's sign, and saw that a message had come through. Was it from the Devil, or was it God saying sorry because he hadn't caught any of the mirrors?

The boy knew that reading other people's messages was naughty, but God wasn't people so he picked up the phone. It wasn't God but Davey was still glad since with a name like

Friend of Swyft, Friend of America the sender had to be another kind of superhero. He opened the message:

Antidote for hebenon: fresh yak milk. Administer under tongue within 60 seconds of apparent decease.

90

Dandong

'*CAO NI MA DE BI!*' JIN shouted the shocking profanity, flinging his arms, swiping the phone off his desk and knocking over his glass so it shattered in the corner, a tenuous thread of white liquid trailing back to his desk along the concrete floor.

He'd failed. *He* had failed, not Kong Feng, not his goons, *him*. This was entirely down to him.

Si Xiongdi, the Fourth Brother, would use this against him, crowing how Jin had overreached, how he had warned against it, that this latest example of Jin's 'high-handed vanity' proved he was a threat to *Fuxing Tao!*

It was a setback, but that was all it was. Jin would show Si Xiongdi. He flicked to another screen, the rocket. After blast-off, no one would care he'd screwed up the Diaz assassination, a blip in the glorious march to *Fuxing Tao!* Name any general who hadn't suffered one blip, one loss. Si wouldn't have an answer to that!

T-20 and counting. Twenty minutes to blast-off.

He peered at the launch site. The roof was fully open, the access arm completely retracted, the area clear of personnel. Perfect. Beautiful. He tapped his screen and searchlights blazed into the sky, announcing the new dawn twenty minutes before the winter sun could start creeping out itself.

He twisted his head side to side, cracking his neck, like a prizefighter about to get up from the canvas and deliver his knockout punch.

91

'SIMON TOLD US TO GET OUT the sick bags but no, you said, instead deciding to pray that you wouldn't puke.' Tori grimaced as some of it slopped off the table onto the blanket on her lap.

'You might want to take that shower now,' Frank said, a little gingerly, tugging at his collar.

She unclipped her belt and folded the blanket to wrap the mess, dropping it to the floor as she stood. 'That was some flying! I'm going up to the cockpit to give Simon the pat on the back he deserves. If you find God's back, feel free to pat His too.'

'Guys.' It was Simon over the speaker. 'Check out the cameras. Way up ahead, there's this, like, massive column of white light goin' up into the sky, like a beam-me-up-Scotty thing. It just switched on. Looks like it's comin' from your island.'

Tori picked up the blanket she'd been sitting on and wiped the touchscreen. It was still a little smeary. 'Your vomit, your table,' she said, dropping that blanket onto the other and leaving Frank to navigate the screen as she clipped back into her seat.

'It *is* your island,' said Simon, 'co-ords confirmed.'

'That's one hell of a beam,' said Frank. 'Simon, can you get us closer?'

Tori picked up the armrest phone and dialled Tex. 'It's got to be the roof,' she said as the phone began ringing. 'Frank, they've opened it to go early. Jin knows that we know so he's launching now. Jesus. If Tex can't get someone to stop this, forty-five minutes after lift-off we'll be telling Simon to take us to London and asking your folks to put us up.'

'Hope you like curry.'

'You do, obviously,' she said, indicating the table. 'Come on, come on,' she said into the phone. 'Tex isn't answering. Damn, it's gone to voicemail ... Blah, blah,' she said as his recorded greeting played. 'Tex, it's Tori. We think Jin's shifted the countdown forward. We're going to fly near the launch site, the island, to check and ...' Frank had split the screen again, the 360-degree live images on one half and on the other an image of their plane superimposed over a terrain map, showing Simon following the Yalu River toward the island. The 360 screen started strobing.

'We're taking stills and videoing as we go,' said Simon. 'That'll get you something solid to send back to your buddy in DC.'

'Tex,' said Tori into the phone, 'call me when you get this ... it looks like they're getting ready to launch any time now ... We'll send some shots through to your office.' She turned her head away from Frank and whispered into the mouthpiece. 'When I get back, when this is over, we need ...' She paused. 'Tex, when I get back, we need ... *I* need ... to see you ... to make things good between us. Like in Hawaii. Tex ... I think ... I think I'm falling in love with you. There, I said it.' She hung up.

'It's terrifying yet beautiful.'

'*What?*' said Tori, wondering if Frank had heard her.

'The light column,' he said. 'See, there, the roof's wide open and there, is that the tip of the nose-cone? If Simon gets good shots of this, no one'll doubt us.'

'Frank,' said Tori, unclipping and standing, 'in case Tex doesn't get my voicemail in time, send him a text message saying countdown's happening any minute now and we're sending through images to prove it.' She moved across the aisle to the seat opposite.

'And you ... you're doing?'

'Visualise me as Jeff Goldblum in *Independence Day* hacking into the island's network.' She sat. 'I'm aiming to neuter the nuke before it leaves the ground—'

'That's not quite what Goldblum—'

'Has Mr Cricket and Mr Grammar graduated to Mr Movies now ... first *Argo* and now this?' she said, typing on the virtual keyboard on the other touchscreen table, but not looking up. 'Anyhow, you remember in the tunnel when we left that transceiver plugged in and the satphone relay outside?' Her fingers were flying across the keyboard. 'And I smiled and you groaned and I said I'd tell you later? Well,' *type, type, type,* 'now is later and, ordinarily, if I told you what I'm about to tell you I'd have to kill you,' she kept typing, 'but given what you've been through, vomiting your little tummy out, getting your nose punched in, the cigarette burn, getting bound and gagged, and playing the good doctor to me,' *tap, tap,* 'you deserve to live, so ... just a second ... good ... You remember Masoud Akhtar? How could you forget, right? ... It was three years ago ... Tehran ... when I first, well, *met* him ... I was there to compromise the Iranian nuke systems—'

'The Stuxnet update ... that was you?'

'No comment on that but if this nuke's using Iranian software, there's a good chance a little backdoor I planted back then is waiting for my key to open it.' More typing.

'You think you can stop this?'

More typing. 'That was my plan then and it's the plan now.'

'So we won't get to stay with my parents?'

'I'm sure they're wonderful people.' *Type, type, type.*

'Probably a good thing. If I turned up at the door with a white girl, they might get the wrong idea.'

Actually, she thought, *it might've been the right idea once ... before Tex.*

'Right,' she said. 'Here we go ... give me a few more seconds ... and ... yes, we are ... Damn! I can't get in. *Damn. Fuck. Damn.* They must've killed the transceiver ... or the relay battery died ... or who the fuck knows. Damn!'

She looked up at him, her face as grey and forlorn as the London weather she feared the two of them might soon be living under.

92

Washington, DC

PARENTS, TEACHERS, KIDS, FAMILY MEMBERS, FRIENDS, the media, they'd all been pushed back behind a cordon and were now rubbernecking at *Limo One* and the sharpshooters surrounding the car as it idled in the school's driveway.

Isabel was in the backseat, patched into the Sit Room speakerphone, a paramedic from the motorcade ambulance fussing over her, checking her eyes, blood pressure, vitals. 'Hang on,' she said into the phone and put a palm over the mouthpiece. 'Like I said,' she told the medic, 'the blood on my blouse is *not* mine. I'm fine, perfectly fine. Go look after my ...' her voice caught, 'my friend, Narthex Carter. He's the one who needs care.' The initial reports were that he was dead, but she'd been praying they were wrong. Davey, she knew, was safe and on the way.

Leaning slightly, she touched a button on her armrest and the eight inches of armour plating that masqueraded as the car door opened. 'Go. Now,' she told the medic. 'And thank you.'

Isabel felt the vehicle jerk. 'Nigel,' she told her driver as the door closed, 'if you just shoved this vehicle into gear, you can shove it right back into park. We're not budging until Davey is here beside me.' She patted the seat. 'That is a direct order.'

'Yes, ma'am.'

She went back to the phone call. Vaddern had just been telling her that Swyft's intel, previously dismissed as hogwash, had now been confirmed 'and more' by mysterious sources who, at her request, had been dumping the most extraordinary material on the NSC via Narthex Carter's office. 'General, what's the *and more*?'

Vaddern was so rapid-fire it felt like a train was running over her. 'So there *is* a Ten Brothers—'

'And you say we've got them speaking on an actual video call?'

'All o' the Ten Brothers, ma'am, yes.'

'Do we know *anything* about the sources who sent the material to us?'

'Usin' aliases—two o' them—and so far we can't backtrack to find 'em.'

She opened a bottle of water and drank from it, not because she was thirsty but to help her take all this in. 'So Narthex ... Dr Narthex Prometheus Carter,' she used his full name, to honour and respect him, 'the man who gave his life ... to save mine ... He was right to trust Swyft, when the rest of you ... and me, too ...' She stopped mid-sentence, wiping her eyes and biting her lip to suppress her shame. She had to pull herself together. 'General, this evidence, I want to believe it, I do. I want to believe Dr Carter's sacrifice was not in vain, but how can we be certain what we're getting from these unknowns isn't cooked up?'

'We're pullin' out all stops to verify it's legit, ma'am, but frankly, when you give all this to President Hou, he won't be applyin' no beyond reasonable doubt test, he'll be concentratin' all his efforts on stayin' in power in Beijing beyond breakfast time. Ma'am, what the NSC is recommendin' for your consideration ...'

There were multiple strands, some to operate in parallel, some in sequence. First, mobilising the Growlers and Super Hornets on board USS *Ronald Reagan*, getting them airborne immediately for the ninety-minute trip to Dandong. Simultaneously, sending President Hou a package of the key evidence so that in ten minutes—at 6.25 am Beijing time— when Isabel was back at the White House, she'd get Hou out of bed and walk him through it. Then, she'd request him to order a squadron of Chinese fighters to bomb the island so hopefully, she could turn back the US fighter planes and avert a war.

'If he won't, or can't, given one of the Brothers is Xu Qiang?' Isabel asked. Xu was vice-chairman of China's highest military command authority, the Central Military Commission.

'In that case, you'd seek Hou's permission for our planes to enter Chinese airspace so we can bomb the island ourselves.'

'If he won't give it?'

She heard the general inhale, imagining him looming over the phone, his medals dangling. 'You'd tell him that if he won't, you'd have no choice but to order our planes to do it, in America's self-defence. If that doesn't change his mind, ma'am, it might give him an out, so he'd be free to express outrage later, to haul in our ambassador for a dressin' down and that'd be that.'

'He wouldn't declare it an act of war?'

'I doubt he'd go that far.'

'I'm not a big fan of doubts if it comes to prodding China to declare war on us, General, but do continue.'

The longer he spoke and the more the evidence sunk in, the more she knew Vaddern was right. The greater likelihood was that Hou would be moved to act so quickly in crushing the Ten Brothers' plot that his people might have to restrain him from piloting the bombers himself.

'Is that it, General?'

'Not quite, ma'am. We've briefed your speechwriters to work up a script for you to give an address to the nation at 8.30 pm, from your desk.' In just over two hours. Vaddern gave her the key messages. She'd tie the attempt to assassinate her and the prior RUA killings to the Ten Brothers, outline the EMP threat, play a video clip of the island being bombed, ideally by Hou's fighters, confirm that RUA wasn't just 'no more' but it had never been—with the Uyghurs entirely innocent—and she'd give the nation comfort that the administration had been well prepared for the attack, ready to roll out FEMA's—the Federal Emergency Management Agency's—EMP alert and action program if it had been necessary.

'If we actually need FEMA's roll-out, how ready are we?'

There was a ruckus at the other end of the line just as her door opened and Davey jumped in, crawling over to her lap, kissing and cuddling her before she had a chance to put the phone on mute.

'Drive!' she told Nigel, dropping the phone on her lap and hugging the boy so tight she was crushing his remaining leaves.

'Ma'am,' she eventually heard Vaddern shouting from underneath Davey. She pressed her hands against the boy's cheeks and, smiling tearfully, held his face a few inches away then kissed him again. She put a hand to the side of her head, her fingers spread like she was talking on a phone. He nodded and slipped off her lap, handing her the phone and belting himself up.

'Swyft and Chaudry are near the island, ma'am, in a jet and they've sent us some shots and, ma'am, it's … ma'am, it's not good. Their latest is that the Ten Brothers have brought the launch forward … it looks like it's happening soon … possibly any minute … no time for us or Hou to stop it … and forty-five minutes after that it's …'

Good night, and good luck, she thought, channelling George Clooney's Ed Murrow, but what she said was, 'I want Hou Tao on the line, now.'

93

Dandong

FRANK COULDN'T SEE SIMON'S FACE, BUT his whistle over the cockpit intercom made it clear their pilot thought Tori's question was her weirdest this trip. 'Can our bird jettison fuel into the launch site?' he repeated.

She was dabbing a tissue on the shine of dark red oozing from her arm which, under other circumstances, would've prompted a change of dressings.

Realising what Tori was asking, Frank felt his mouth fall open. 'Tori, you can't be serious?' He stared at her, his hands clammy as he opened and closed his fists, but saw no slack in her face, not a shred of fear nor doubt, just out-and-out resolve. She was deadly serious. 'Jesus, if we *can* do that—'

'We save the world. Jesus exactly.'

94

Washington, DC

GETTING CHINA'S LEADER OUT OF BED wasn't necessary. He told Isabel he'd been at his desk ever since he declared the state of emergency at midnight. 'Mr President,' she said, 'if there's any background noise on this call, I apologise. I'm in a vehicle and—'

'*A ya*, Madam President, your motorcade is on my TV. I have seen the whole appalling thing. I was waiting for you to return to the White House to call you, so now we are talking let me express my relief that the vile filth who did this failed—'

'Not entirely.'

'The courageous Dr Carter? Yes, he made a strong impression when you brought him to Beijing. My sincere and deep condolences. Madam President, we have RUA in our sights as you know, and will not rest until we slice off its head, cut out its heart and eviscerate—'

'Please excuse me for interrupting but time is short. Are you alone on this call? I, er, I need to talk to you about ...' she paused, picking her phrasing carefully in case anyone with him was aligned with the Ten Brothers, '... a personal matter, an extremely personal—'

'Madam, my two advisers here are entirely trustwor—'

'I promise it won't take long, and you can bring them back after ... if you think it may be helpful to my problem.'

'*Gan kuai zou!*' he snapped. Isabel heard footsteps then a door slamming. 'You may now speak freely, Madam President.'

'Two logistical things before that. Is this your most secure phone?'

She heard a faint dial tone. 'No,' he said, with a shortness of tone she'd heard before, frustration at what he'd once called *the charming paranoia of American presidents*. 'I'm calling your office on it now and they can reconnect us.' He hung up.

Isabel placed the car's handset back into its rest and, waiting, she watched Davey. He was still, his eyes on the smartphone he was holding on his lap, his fingers—still painted like twigs—tightly wrapped around it like it was a talisman. She guessed a Secret Service agent had lent it to him, perhaps to play a game on it as a reward for his bravery or a bribe to keep him settled. But Davey wasn't playing. He just stared at it.

Her own phone lit up and she picked up before the first ring. 'Yes.'

'Madam President, you had *two* logistical items. What is the second?'

Before asking him for a *his eyes only* email address to send the evidence through, she told him she wasn't alone on the call, which he probably knew, with Vaddern, as well as the rest of her NSC listening in from the Sit Room.

'General, give my best wishes to Elly.'

'And mine to Xiaoqing.'

Isabel knew that Vaddern and Hou shared history but had no inkling they were so chummy and was surprised—impressed— the general hadn't thrown it at her as an *I know him better than you* thing during their tennis match over whether to phone him or not.

'Mr President, we're sending you solid evidence that Premier Zhao Guowei and other people close to you are plotting to do to you what they just tried to do to—'

'Your media says that was RUA. To suggest Zhao is involved is preposter—'

'I couldn't believe it either, but Narthex Carter did … thankfully and …' she hesitated, still struggling to process what he'd done for her, 'it's only because he did that I'm alive, able to forewarn you. What we're sending through proves that you too are a target. We have little time. *Very* little.'

He let Isabel sketch out the nightmare, Vaddern adding brief clarifications since she hadn't actually seen the new material herself. When Hou confirmed the documents had come through, Vaddern skipped him through them and when he got to the photo of Premier Zhao Guowei with Professor Mellor in Paris in the eighties, Hou exploded. After what the Nine Sisters had done, Mellor was despised in China. The final toll of the fast train pile-ups Mellor's acolyte had orchestrated, Hou reminded them, was 12,603. 'I have trusted Zhao with my life. Until now.'

95

Dandong

'TORI,' SAID SIMON, 'G650S CAN'T DUMP fuel.'

'Shit!'

'The F-18s I used to fly could do it, and some big passenger jets can, but most small planes are engineered these days so they don't need to.'

'Shit, shit, shit.'

'If there's no other way to stop this thing ... if it truly is Armageddon and all, like you say ... we could, you know ... well, we could do a kinda ... how do I say this? ... A bye bye birdie, if you get my drift.'

'You mean *kamikazes*, suicide bombers? Fly ourselves into the launch site?'

'We die, the people down there die, but we save—'

'We definitely can't dump fuel?'

'I wish we could.'

'We need a few minutes to think … to find another way.' Tori grabbed her backpack and took out her laptop, searching through her music. Finding what she needed, she connected to the plane's sound system via Wi-Fi. 'Simon, Frank, you can accuse me of sick humour, but if this doesn't help one of us, I don't know what will.'

She turned the sound up to max and hit *play*. The plane's speakers erupted with the cracking sound that mimicked a surfboard breaking and the legendary manic laugh that started the Surfaris' *Wipe Out*. Tori closed her eyes, the cymbals crashed, the drums pounded, and at fourteen seconds the twangy riff reverberated through her body, pushing everything but the problem at hand out of her head.

'Tori, are you totally nuts?' shouted Frank from across the aisle.

'Shh!' She held a finger to her lips. 'Thinking.'

TWO REPEATS LATER, Tori cut the music yelling, 'The MANPAD!' She spoke into the intercom. 'Simon, can we open the door mid-flight and fire the MANPAD into the launch site?'

'Heck, why didn't I …? Let me think. Where's that music … Just joking. Give me a sec … The first answer's a no … our main exit opens outwards … the airstairs remember? And the windshear'd probably rip it off and smash it into the starboard wing and engine so—'

'Emergency exits?'

'Sure! The aft windows over the wings … they're inwards openers, so if I drop the cabin pressure you two can safely open one of them.'

'We won't be sucked out?'

'If there's no part of you hanging out, you'll be good.'

'And the missile?'

'That's the tricky part ... MANPADS are surface-to-air and—'

'We'll be air-to-surface, so how do—'

'We're moving, which'll confuse the gyro, and they're infra-red heat-seekers, fire-and-forget, so we can't shoot until we've got some heat to hit, like the rocket's engines firing up. Until then—'

'We'll have to circle, be a target for the very people who know we're up here?'

'Right, and if the launch tube on that MANPAD's sealed at the back we're good, but if it's open ... and I know we're not gonna be worrying about damage to the cabin interior ... but if it's an open-ender, it might blow back a flame, so whoever's not doin' the shootin' better not be standin' directly behind it and they better have a fire extinguisher at the ready.'

FRANK HAD PLACED the missile launcher on the cabin floor, the missile loaded and the BCU—battery coolant unit—lying next to the gripstock, ready to be inserted at firing time. Even though this one had a back-sealed launch tube, Frank had propped two fire extinguishers on one of the seats, in case something went awry. Simon was watching him from the cockpit via the cabin CCTV, explaining how to remove the cover from one of the emergency exits.

The mood was grim. Tori was silent, pondering the probabilities, all of them bad. What if the MANPAD failed to operate properly? What if they got shot down before they had a chance to fire it?

Tex still hadn't called her back. If this was it … the end … did she really want him to hear her profession of … of love … in a voicemail?

'Holy …' said Simon. 'Stop doin' what you're doin' and look at the touchscreen.' He sent through a direct feed of his dash vision system. 'See at the top there, those three orange-coloured icons?' Plane-shaped, they were skipping across the screen from the northwest. The risks they were facing had jumped from extreme to stratospheric.

'They must be hostiles if there's three of them, right?' asked Tori, hoping she was wrong.

'At that speed. See those numbers beside the icons? … That's speed, altitude, direction. They're at Mach 1.6 and they're suppressin' their IDs, so they gotta be PLAAF, Chinese air force. My guess is they're Chengdus out of Shenyang military base, J-10s maybe, and birds like that'll be carryin' air-to-air missiles, which if they're BVRs … meaning they'll target beyond visual range … we're in super-deep sh—'

'Drawing a line on their trajectory, it looks like they're headed to the island, not to us.'

'They musta worked out we're gonna get damn close to the launch site, so with them comin' down from the northwest and us comin' in from the east, that's their quickest intercept point.'

Tori blinked. This couldn't be happening. 'Will we get there before they do?'

'My calc is that from our circlin' point here, it's five minutes thirty for us to reach air zero. For them at that speed … nope they're up at Mach 1.7 now … I'm thinkin' seven minutes tops.'

'Which means,' said Frank through his headset mic, 'they'll be firing those missiles at us, and pretty soon.'

'And the thing is,' said Simon, 'a G650 don't come with a MAWS, sorry, missile approach warning system, so we won't know the missiles are comin' till my night viz sees the reds of their eyes.'

'Tex ... why hasn't he called us?' said Tori, her body weak. 'He'd have got those photos by now.' She started dialling. 'If I have to interrupt him giving the president her manicure, so be it,' she laughed weakly. 'Simon,' she said through the intercom, 'can you feed this call I'm making through the plane's comms so you and Frank can hear as well?' *Wait,* she thought thinking it through. *Can I give Tex a proper farewell with Frank and Simon listening? Fuck it, if we're all going to die up here, what do I care if they hear me?*

96

Washington, DC

LIMO ONE WAS GETTING CLOSER TO 1600 Pennsylvania Avenue, Isabel talking to her Chinese counterpart and Davey still staring into space. When she had a chance to think about it, while Vaddern was leading Hou through a couple of the clips, she realised Davey must be in shock. He had been very close to Narthex, especially since Narthex had taken to the boy and had been giving him acting lessons. Davey was in shock; he had to be. It would come for her too, she knew that, but now wasn't the time.

She wanted to lean over and cuddle the boy, as much for him as for herself, but it was her turn to speak, to ask the leader of the world's second-largest economy to save hers, the most sensitive, crucial question she'd ever delivered.

Davey, ignoring that she had started speaking again, swung his legs up onto to the seat, twisted around to kneel and tugged at her sleeve. She yanked her arm away and shook her head at him, her eyes narrowed in an unmistakable frown making it as clear as she could that he should sit quietly. He continued tugging at her sleeve again and again, then began flapping the phone he'd been holding so close to her face she could see that a call was coming through.

Hell, this was Narthex's phone. The protective cover, with blue waves swirling on its sides … she'd seen it repeatedly as he passed it to her during the pageant so she could read the Sit Room summaries. The dial code on the screen told her the call was coming from a satellite phone.

'President Hou, my apologies but I need a moment.' She swiped her finger across the screen to answer but before she could speak, a torrent of words gushed out at her.

'Tex, we're totally fucked over here. I need you to get a message to the president that—'

'Dr Swyft? Is that you?'

'Who the fuck is that?' she screamed. 'Where's Tex Carter?'

If Tori didn't know, thought Isabel, this wasn't the time to tell her, and even if it had been, Isabel wasn't sure she could get the right words out of her mouth. 'Tori—'

'Who the *fuck* am I talking to?'

'The president.'

'Oh, shi—I thought this was Tex's number. Sorry. Sorry, ma'am. Look, the island, the rocket, the EMP, how much do you kno—'

'Enough that I've got President Hou on *my* phone a half-sentence away from asking him to order an immediate bomber strike to take out the rocket before blast-off if it's possible.'

'It's too late, the—'

Isabel felt the colour drain from her face. 'It's launched already?'

'No, ma'am, but we've only got a handful of minutes here, so—'

'I'm putting you on loudspeaker so President Hou can hear as well.'

She held Narthex's phone close to the mouthpiece of her own, noticing Davey was smiling at her like he knew he'd done a good job. 'Mr President, I have Dr Victoria Swyft on the line. She's perilously close to the island. Tori, speak to us.'

'President Hou, President Diaz, I'm with Frank Chaudry in a Gulfstream G650, call sign ... Simon what's the call sign? ... S7-AXL ... piloted by Simon de Vere. We're in the air, five minutes from the launch site. We're preparing to fire a MANPAD—a rocket launcher—at it, which may or may not work. If it doesn't our only alternative is ... is to fly our plane into it.'

'My God!'

'Time's exceedingly tight, ma'am, but we've got three unidentified jets approaching us from the northwest and their speed, Mach one-point-something, no it's Mach 2 now, they're PLAAF fighters, maybe Chengdus presumably armed with air-to-air missiles. If they take us out *before* we fire our missile, or before we get to the island, the rocket will launch and the satellite will reach the United States in three-quarters of an hour. President Hou ... we need you to get those fighters to support us not,' her voice trembled, 'not to kill us.'

'Wait,' said Hou. It sounded to Isabel like he'd put his phone on mute.

'President Hou, please ...'

Silence.

'Please!' Tori shrieked. 'It's four minutes twenty, but less if they let those missiles go.'

'Mr President! cried Isabel.

HOU TAO WAS sick to his stomach with the enormity of the betrayal and the stark, unpalatable consequences if he didn't act. He turned to the painting of the Great Wall hanging behind him, but this time its depth, its brown, almost sepia tinge wasn't taking off his edge, wasn't calming him like it usually did. His eyes settled on the flag draped beside the artwork, drifting from the brass finial at the top to the fly end at the floor, letting the lustrous bright red of China's destiny draw away his panic. The Americans didn't know all of the Brothers' names, not yet anyway, but every face on that video they'd sent him was a man he'd worked with, drunk with, dined with. He knew their wives and their wives knew the other wives. China spread a massive population over a vast land, but its circle of power and influence was tiny.

How could those bastards do this ... and to him?

Now that he knew who he could trust, he buzzed his two advisers back into his office. As they bustled in, he was already scratching out a note at his desk to withdraw the commissions of three of the Brothers, Premier Zhao Guowei, Vice-Chairman Xu Qiang and one face the Americans wouldn't take long to identify, General Chang Yang. Chang had only recently become commander of the PLAAF so it must have been him who'd ordered the fighters to take out the Swyft woman's jet.

He took the fountain pen Jin Yu had given him—it was appropriate—looked at his watch, then signed, timed and dated the page very precisely. He looked up to see the two men standing opposite him with their mouths agog as they listened to two raving shrews—one, the president of the United States, the other unknown to them—both screeching out of his red phone.

He handed the page to the older man, took up another sheet and put his head down to write on it. 'Take that first page to Bo Yi, he will know what to do with it.' He glanced up at the other man—his son. 'And you will take this one to Deng Mo and tell him that by this paper I order the immediate arrests of every one of these names. There are,' he finished the last two, taking extra care with Jin Yu's name, 'ten of them.' He passed it over his desk. 'Tell Bo and Deng that our beloved country's security depends on taking this action in minutes not hours. I will explain later, now go!'

As the men scurried to the door, his son turned his head. 'What are the charges?'

'Treason. It's written on the sheet.'

As they closed the door behind them, Hou unmuted his red phone and spoke over the women's hysteria. 'I am here. I need a few more moments.' He pressed *mute* again, picked up his black phone and speed-dialled Chang Yang. 'Chang, it's over. I have withdrawn your commission and—'

'What have I done to warrant—'

'Shut up and listen. If you don't want your wife, your mistresses, your three sons and your ... five grandchildren arrested, tried and executed as co-conspirators, you will do precisely as I say, and without delay. You have ordered three fighters into the air near Dandong to shoot down the Swyft woman's aircraft.'

'How did you—'

'That is a yes?'

'It is.'

Swyft was now screaming 'two minutes, two minutes'. He didn't have a second to spare. He had to act. 'Chang, patch me through to the squadron leader. And know this: if our fighters shoot her plane down, your sons will be executed within the hour and I will force you to watch ... Why am I still waiting?'

'It may be too late.'

'It *will* be too late for your sons if you don't patch me through now.'

FRANK WATCHED THE three fighters streaking across the touchscreen table at Mach 2.5, the gap narrowing to thirty-five nautical miles. Tori was screaming into her phone, still getting no response from Hou. Simon appeared to be ignoring the ruckus, pumping himself up for the craziest thing he'd ever attempted in his life. Frank had already pulled out the escape hatch and snapped the BCU into the MANPAD's gripstock to ready it for firing. He was sitting at the table, focusing on numbers. The J-10s, at their current speed, would reach air zero themselves in ... seventy seconds, meaning Simon only had a ten-second window, not even that if the fighters launched their missiles anytime soon, which Frank was sure they would. According to Simon, China had missiles that could travel at up to Mach 4 which, if they were let loose now, would vaporise the G650 in ... But what was the point of doing more calcs? However short it was, they'd be hit before Simon could get in close enough. They'd be dead and the rocket would be free to launch.

'No!' An unfamiliar voice came over the phone. He identified himself to Tori and the others as General P. P. Vaddern, chairman of the Joint Chiefs. 'President Hou ... if you're there ... we're looking at a satellite feed and your fighters have just fired on the plane, an American civilian plane. Please, sir, order an abort or a redirect. For Christ's sake, do something … say some—'

Isabel spoke over him. 'General, get Hou's office on another line and—'

'We've been tryin', ma'am. They won't interrupt him.'

Frank now knew it was no longer a question of *if* they'd die. Weirdly, he wasn't thinking about death but about Tori, about him and Tori, how she could've been the one.

Now, there was this.

He stood up, looked across the aisle at her, then lifted the MANPAD off the floor, raised it over his shoulder and went to the open hatch.

WHEN CHANG HAD called Jin five minutes ago, confident his J-10s would take out the interlopers long before they did any damage, Jin hadn't wanted to take any chances and sent a squad of his guards out to the jetty, armed to the teeth, as a fail-safe. He now had an additional screen on his desk and was watching the four icons verging toward the island, three from the northwest and one from the east. With blast-off at only T-40 seconds what were the fucking J-10s waiting for?

There was no going back.

This was it, what he'd worked decades for.

He focused on the CCTV, the launch site cleared, the bells ringing and now, yes, the sound suppression water system activating to start flooding the cavern ahead of ignition.

'DECISION TIME, FOLKS,' said Simon. 'To get there before the missiles get us I need to speed up, and that'll reduce our MANPAD's chances. So we got two options ... Option one is as soon as we fire our gun, prayin' it hits the target, we fly the hell out of here with me tryin' to duck an' dodge those missiles, or option two is—'

'—we *kamikaze* into the launch pad,' said Tori, 'and take the rocket out ourselves. We have to be unanimous on this. If just one of us says *run*, Frank you fire that thing on your shoulder and Simon you go hell for leather out of here ... if the missiles don't get us first. What's it to be? Simon, you first.'

'*Kamikaze.*'

'Frank?'

He was standing by the hatch, the MANPAD on his shoulder pointing ahead, toward the island. 'Same.'

'We're all agreed then. In forty seconds we find out if God exists.'

'I'd prefer we had longer,' said Simon. 'But here goes ...'

97

I F JIN YU BELIEVED IN ANY kind of heaven, this was it. *His* moment. *His* page in China's history, world history. At T-6 seconds the sight was transcendent, the main boosters igniting with vivid oranges and fiery reds as they roared to life. He turned up the speakers, his bunker crackling like twisting, writhing metal sheets echoing off the thick concrete walls. At T-0 his floor, walls and ceiling rumbled as he watched the solid boosters ignite and the explosive bolts ping and snap as they released the ship from the pad.

It was perfection. In forty-five minutes the United States of fucking *Meiguo* would begin its inexorable decay and he, Jin Yu would have delivered on his promise. He, Jin Yu was the Tenth Brother but as he saw it, he was the father of *Fuxing Tao!*

Only two duties were left: his Last Supper of phoenix talons which his 'good friend' Hou Tao would choke on later this week, and a toast, to himself and to *Fuxing Tao!*

VADDERN CAME BACK on the line, his voice urgent. 'Tao, listen to me … The boosters are firing. The rocket's in launch … *Hou Tao!*' he screamed, '*talk to me!*'

'MISSILES REDIRECTED.' HOU spoke fast, packing the most information into the smallest package. 'S7-AXL,' he said, giving the G650's call sign, 'bank hard south, bank hard south.'

'If they still can,' said Vaddern quietly.

98

AS JINYU REACHED FOR HIS glass, the milk began to shake, the bunker floor began to growl and the tumbler began moving across his desk toward his hand as if fate had willed it so.

The walls thundered, the noise deafening, so loud it was excruciating. His stomach was churning, his throat gagging, his head bursting. He flicked off the volume and couldn't comprehend how, but it got worse.

Disoriented, bewildered, he grabbed the glass before it slid off the desk and raised it to his mouth, the liquid splashing his eyes. The lights were flickering ... the room now pitch black apart from the tiny farewell flashes of his screens ... he felt the desk shifting under his hand ... the bunker crunching ... his knees buckling ... the walls cracking and crumbling around him.

$$+$$

OPEN-MOUTHED, STUNNED, IMPOTENT, the NSC sat in the Sit Room watching satellite images of the island exploding in real-time. Vaddern slumped on the table. 'Ma'am, the rocket's been taken out.'

Isabel's voice was quiet. 'Was it the missiles or Swyft's pla—'

'*Fuckin'* hell, Hou,' came Simon's shriek through the phone, 'couldn't you've made that any fuckin' tighter? ... Sorry, sir, no disrespect.' Then he screamed, '*F-u-u-u-u-ck.*'

So did Tori.

99

TWENTY SECONDS LATER, WHEN SIMON STARTED to level out, Tori realised he'd flown them into North Korean airspace. 'Simon, President Hou, we've gone into North—'

Simon began a fresh bank as Hou answered immediately. 'Dr Swyft, you are quick indeed. I was waiting for you to be clear of the island before I invited you to fly here to Beijing so I could thank you and your colleagues in person.'

'But, sir, the North Koreans will—'

'When the Middle Kingdom tells the Hermit Kingdom— how do you say it in your idiom?—*not to fuck with us on this one*, as I just have, you will be fine. President Diaz and I must leave this call with you now to discuss matters of state so let me thank you for your service to my people.' Diaz signed off too, adding that she'd call Tori later.

Despite busting to go to the toilet and being desperate for a shower, painkillers and new dressings, Tori wasn't budging from her seat until Simon got them safely north of the border at the Yalu River.

As he turned to the north, the inferno far to their right was like a golden sun rising short of the horizon, the land around it speckled with tiny lights, houses woken by the explosion, not enough time yet for the smoke to cast a pall.

100

TORI AND FRANK WERE SEATED ACROSS the aisle from one another, to give each of them maximum sleep space. She had finally taken her shower, he had redressed her wound and Simon was flying them back to Boston, not Beijing. By another unanimous vote, the trio had decided to get as far away from China as possible. 'Remember those forty winks? They're calling me more than ever,' she told Frank. 'Wake me up when we're landing. If the president calls while I'm asleep, ask her to thank Hou for—'

'I know, for his gracious offer and ask for a raincheck.'

'Right, he's got more than enough on his hands anyway. But if Tex calls—'

'Wake you up. I know.'

She pulled a fresh blanket over herself, retracted her table, snuggled into her seat and reclined it all the way back. 'Hey,' she said to Frank, her eyes closed, 'now you've fixed me up, what about *your* shower? I feel like a new woman.'

'I'm getting there,' he said, 'but I'm just checking something.'

She heard his fingers drumming on his touchscreen, loudly.

'Tori,' he called to her, 'I'm confused. There's a news report about President Diaz, but we were only speaking twenty-odd minutes ago.'

'If you want to deconfuse, go have a shower and get some sleep … like me, mmm.' She pretended not to hear his belt unclip and she rolled onto her right side. A second later she felt a pat on her leg, and when she sneaked a peek, he was in the seat across from her, his feet astride hers. She heard him bring her table back out and felt it resting on her knees. She ignored it.

'Tori, put your seat up. You need to look at this.'

She scowled at him, raised her backrest, lowered her legs and watched her touchscreen flicker on. 'No sound?'

'Something's up with the satellite feed … good images, no commentary.' He oriented the screen sideways so they both could see the feed. It was shot in an auditorium.

'What the …?' Tori watched as a stampede of people of all ages were trying to stuff themselves through the hall's exit doors, leaving chairs, clothes, bags, balloons and other paraphernalia strewn all over the floor behind them. The news ticker scrolled across the foot of the screen:

WASHINGTON, DC, LIVE:
… President Diaz survives assassination attempt …
… "RUA responsible" say WHITE HOUSE SOURCES …
… Brave official dead, Name WITHHELD …
… MARKET ROUT, S&P 500 FUTURES DOWN 8% …

'It's got to be Jin. How …? But that's *not* live, Frank. That's why you're confused. See that 5.10 pm EST at the bottom right? This was shot *before* we got her on the phone. Hell, one minute she survives a hit and the next she takes our call, cool as. What a woman.' She picked up the armrest phone and started dialling. 'Tex better have his phone back. If I get put through to her again, I'll have to kill him,' she smiled.

The replay cut to a dark-suited man tossing a boy over his shoulder, the news bar identifying him as the president's stepson. 'Secret Service,' said Frank. 'What's with the leaves all over the kid?'

'Get the commentary and we'll both know,' she replied with the phone pressed to her ear.

They watched the camera pan back to two beefy women, also in dark suits, who were hovering over a man on the floor. He, too, was in a suit, blue, his body skewed oddly, his face turned away from the lens. The agent at his head turned him onto his back, her body blocking his upper torso from view. She bent down and hooked her arms under his shoulders at the same time as the phone gave Tori a busy signal. She pressed *redial*. The agent at the victim's feet mouthed *One, Two, Three*, and the pair hoisted him up. Running sideways like two balletic crabs clasping the body between them, they crisscrossed the hall this way and that, dodging chairs and castoffs to avoid bumping him.

As Tori hit *redial* a second time, she noticed Frank looking at her, an odd expression on his face. He reached out a hand. 'Tori …'

'Come on, Tex,' she muttered. 'Why isn't he … *No!*' Her voice was detached, a whisper. She was suddenly shaking, her hand over her mouth, her eyes closed. She felt the phone being taken from her other hand.

Was that really Tex's face she had seen as the agents twisted their way to the doors? It looked like his face, yet it didn't. This one was pasty, ashen. Lifeless. A gash on his forehead dripped blood down his cheeks, into his mouth and over his eyes, those penetrating, insightful, beautiful eyes …

Closed.

Tears streamed down her face but she was silent, her whole body trembling and limp at the same time, exhausted, drained from what she and Frank and Simon had been through. And now … this.

Not a word passed between her and Frank, but when he leant across and held and kissed her hand, she felt his tears too, and she let out a quiet sob.

She tried to breathe, to slow everything down, her heart, her lungs, to squeeze the image of Tex's lifeless face from her mind, to make it unhappen.

But there was nothing she could do.

He was gone.

101

Boston

THEY CAME IN STRAIGHT FROM THE airport and, garbed in blue hospital gowns, gloves, paper slippers and hairnets, Tori and Frank joined Mada, all three of them standing near the wall by Axel's bed. The patient's eyes *were* fluttering, just like Mada had said when he'd phoned them on the plane. 'It's a miracle,' he'd said.

'At least we got one,' Tori replied, wishing it had been two.

'One that Saint Thatcher won't ever let us forget,' Frank told her. If he was trying to lift her spirits, he was utterly failing.

Axel was looking so much better but Mada so much worse. He looked so weak that even his shadows had stopped running away from him. Maybe it was because he'd been keeping vigil over Axel for fifteen hours straight, maybe it was his own health, maybe it was the blue from the gown washing out his skin, Tori didn't know, but he seemed markedly thinner than when they'd last seen him, which was saying something. Regardless, she still nudged Frank to stand between them, a cordon between Mada's spleen and her spite.

The doctors, three of them, and two nurses were delicately easing tube after tube out of Axel's body and placing them on the trolleys semi-circling his bed. As they extracted the last, from his nose, a few dribbles of white liquid spilled onto his lips, the lower of which beginning to quiver, three of his chins following in sympathy.

'Praise the Lord!' Mada exclaimed.

Praise Thatcher, thought Tori, *for finding the antidote.*

The male nurse cranked the back of the bed up a little and, when Axel's head had risen high enough for him to see above his stomach, he opened one eye then the other, lifting his eyebrows several times to stretch them, both together then one by one. For as long as the three employees had known him—in Tori's case only months, decades in Mada's— eyebrow raises were his sole form of workout except for the effort involved in drinking and eating and spinning his gold *begleri* beads around his fat fingers. Looking straight ahead, Axel hadn't yet seen the trio of smiles waiting for him along the wall.

The other nurse dipped a cotton bud into a glass of milk and dabbed some under his tongue.

'*Ptooi.*' He spat it out. 'Haven't you people seen where that stuff comes from?' His eyes rolled to the side, and then his head. 'Ah, my three musketeers.' He rubbed his paunch. 'Strangely, I have a sudden craving to eat some Chinese.'

'And what about food?' joked Ron Mada, Tori shocked to learn a sense of humour had been lurking beneath the man's venom.

As a nurse left to fetch a menu, Tori felt Frank glancing sideways at her. She'd been a snivelling wreck on the flight back but he'd cried with her, held her hand, comforted her, hugged her, everything she'd normally prefer a guy in need of a shower wouldn't do but was glad he did. She'd told him things, private things, stories about her she'd never told a soul—apart from Tex—and it felt good, better than she'd expected.

FRANK FELT CLOSER to Tori than ever. She'd opened herself up to him. He'd listened, he'd comforted her. From that moment on the plane when he thought they were going to die, he knew that he … they … It was too soon, and he wasn't sure he could even think what he wanted to think. Her body was so close, mere inches away. He could feel her warmth. He could smell her fragrance, lemony, woody. Her hair sparkled under the lights, with reds and oranges so intense it was like her strangled spirit was trying to breathe life back into her. He stole a look at her eyes, to see if the wild, passionate shimmer of the ocean she loved so much was flowing back into them, but they were still cold, frosty.

He wanted to touch her, to let her know he was here for her. He edged his arm toward her, his fingers stretching out to hers. But no, it was too soon. He closed his hand so tight it was like he was punishing his fingers for even thinking it.

Axel coughed and his face suddenly clouded over. Frank's face flushed with guilt, fearing Axel had seen his hand, but his boss's eyes weren't on him, nor on Tori. He was looking at Mada.

Axel shifted on his pillows. 'Ron, there's a couple of things I've been meaning to tell you, but first, pass me my *begleri*.'

Mada stepped forward and handed the chain with the two gold beads to Axel.

'Excellent,' Axel said. He started swinging the beads one way so they twirled around his finger, then the other way to unwrap them, and kept repeating it until Frank started to feel a little dizzy.

'Ron, look at me not the beads. Okay, here goes … Stop being such a shit. Also, you don't have cancer.'

'What?' Mada's face went as white as his beard. He was only still on his feet because Frank had grabbed him and was propping him up.

'The oncology trial. Yes, I know about it. I found out a few minutes before I collapsed. Ron, the trial's a fake, a hoax, a sham. The clinic was a front. Jin Yu was poisoning you so you'd think you were sick. Stop the treatment, stop the cancer. And like I said, stop being a shit, especially to Tori.'

EPILOGUE

THE MAN WHO, COURTESY OF TORI Swyft, remained General Secretary of the Communist Party, president of the People's Republic of China, chairman of the Central Military Commission, what the Americans call the commander-in-chief, unlocked his desk drawer. He pulled it open leaving the key in the lock. With a mixed sense of relief and frustration, he pushed back his chair, the high-back that a billion Chinese and hundreds of millions of others would see in his TV broadcast once he buzzed in the usual scrum of technicians, fiddlers and fakers.

Hou Tao's desk was startlingly bare for a man with such responsibilities, the expanse of polished redwood free of files and books, not even a computer. Just his four phones—two red, one grey plus a newish black one—his old-fashioned paper flip calendar displaying today's historic date, a canister of pencils and pens and a glass of yak milk on a golden star-shaped coaster that, set against the red of his desk, evoked his country's glorious flag. He brought the liquid to his lips, his eyebrow quizzical as he sniffed it and swirled a little in his mouth, its fragrant sweetness pleasing for the first time.

He looked down at the photograph in his drawer and raised it from its cushion, pressing it briefly to his heart. He held it before him, the portrait facing him like a mirror of the man he'd liked to have been, the man he'd like to become.

Resting on the strong wide neck was that renowned face of serene, almost cherubic perfection, the full lips whose words meant so much to so many even today, and in their shadow the mole, a beauty spot not a blemish. The long fine nose, a pioneer's nose, led up between the gentle yet penetrating eyes to the sweeping forehead that flew halfway up his head, parting Mao Zedong's hair wide, like the proverbial Red Sea.

'Our people's great liberator,' he whispered.

After taking another sip he placed the glass on its coaster, wiped his hand on his jacket then flourished a finger down the side of the photo as if he was scrawling his own signature over Mao's. After one last press of the frame to his heart he placed it back on the cushion and locked the drawer.

In a few minutes, Hou Tao would tell the nation about Jin Yu, about the Brothers, about their deception, their treachery, their framing of the Uyghurs, the theft of billions of yuan.

He wouldn't mention how the Americans had alerted him, and Diaz wouldn't take credit for it when she spoke; that was agreed. He wouldn't speak of his part in saving America. She would do that and he would humbly tip his head, letting her praise wash over him.

Suddenly his face pinched under the crush of pretence, and he slammed his hand on his desk. Jin fucking Yu! Evil. Proud. And unforgivably, an abject incompetent. What hubris, fancying himself as the brains in a group as audaciously brilliant as the Ten Brothers.

Since when do pawns have brains?

He laughed and wet his lips. If Jin *had* been so smart, why didn't he grasp it was Hou Tao's bidding he was doing all along?

You, a Brother ... Me, the Father.

Jin Yu had been a late convert to *Fuxing Tao!* whereas Hou's entire life had been a preparation for it. He'd realised it at an early age. His own name a cue, a portent.

Fuxing Tao! would now take longer, but he knew that a year or two, five even, was not long to wait to tie the final knot in the golden thread that had been delicately weaving China through its five millennia. For Americans, even a month was an eternity, but what else do you expect from barbarians with no history, no culture, no sense of time? Where China had a thread, the Americans had tiny, greasy strands of transient floss rubbed together and sugar-coated for them by populist charlatans and con artists.

Diaz and that meddlesome Swyft, they fancied that they'd saved him ... saved his country. He would let them enjoy their delusion.

Life was so beautiful.

He held the glass high. '*Fuxing Tao!*'

He wiped his lips, patted his hair to the sides trying to widen his part, and called in the TV crew.

If you enjoyed

THE
TAO
DECEPTION

then look out for the next book
featuring Tori Swyft.

For more information, please visit:
www.PanteraPress.com

AUTHOR'S NOTE

Electromagnetic pulses (EMPs) are no fantasy. I first became aware of them as an emerging threat while chairing the risk committee of a global insurance company. The effects of EMPs were first noted in 1859 with what's been called the 'Carrington event', a natural solar flare so strong that not only could people read a newspaper at night but the newly laid transatlantic cable was disrupted and telegraph machines caught fire. A century later, it was man's turn. In 1962, the US's Operation Starfish included a nuclear test above a Pacific Ocean atoll 900 miles from Hawaii. The EMP was so powerful Hawaii suffered power outages and telephone and radio blackouts.

Carrington and Starfish occurred long before a world that, today, is so vitally connected and reliant on electronics. Add to this the threats from the rocket, satellite, missile and nuclear programs of rogue nations like North Korea, and nuclear EMPs are a serious global threat.

If you want to see the potential for the threat, read the 2004 and 2008 reports of the US Congressional Commissions to Assess the Threat to the United States from Electromagnetic Pulse Attack, and the 2015 hearings of the House Committee on Homeland Security. From the UK, read the 2012 House of Commons Defence Committee Report, 'Developing Threats: Electro-Magnetic Pulses'. And from the global insurance industry, see thoughtful papers from Lloyds of London and Swiss Re.

And my thanks: for advice on Tori's and Axel's medical treatment, Dr Mark J. Sagarin and Dr Francis Matthey FRCP FRCPath; on missiles, fighter jets and Gulfstream G650s, RAAF Flight-Lieutenant MS; on Mandarin idiom, Wang Xiao Bin; for Tori insights, Craig Kirchner, Abbey's; on papal matters,

Chris Geraghty and former Australian Ambassador to The Holy See, John McCarthy KCSG QC. (Where I've got anything wrong, it's my bad.) And unending thanks to my wonderful editor Lucy Bell, Susan Hando (for PR), Katy McEwen (for rights), Alison Green and Luke Causey (for design), Martin Green (music), Desanka Vukelich (proofreading), and the great teams at Pantera Press, Bloomsbury and Allen & Unwin.

PRAISE FOR JOHN M. GREEN'S NOVELS

'With the sophistication of John le Carré and the pace of Jeffrey Archer ... a 21st century story of treason and betrayal'
– ABC RADIO

'... as good as John Grisham, Robert Ludlum, Lee Child or Jonathan Kellerman ... knife-edge plot, sophisticated themes and empathetic characters put Green in the front rank of Australian thriller writers' – THE AUSTRALIAN

'One of the most surprising thrillers this year'
– THE CANBERRA TIMES

'With such a breakneck pace and charismatic lead character, it's easy to see this turned into a Hollywood blockbuster'
– THE SUN-HERALD

'... moves at a cracking pace and is impossible to put down ... a compelling writer of master thrillers'
– THE AUSTRALIAN FINANCIAL REVIEW

'Unputdownable' – THE WEST AUSTRALIAN

'... one of those *pick it up and can't put it down* reads'
– THE SYDNEY MORNING HERALD

'A cracking thriller ... Green's meticulously researched novel draws readers in from the outset ... the action is relentless as the fast-paced plot heats up ... It all makes for a tense series of chapters leading up to a terrific climax'
– THE DAILY TELEGRAPH

'An atmospheric thriller' – THE AGE

'WARNING: Fasten your seatbelts & please remain seated for the duration of this thrilling ride' – THE READING ROOM

ABOUT JOHN M. GREEN

Author of *The Trusted*, *Born to Run* and *Nowhere Man*, John's latest thriller, *The Tao Deception* is his second novel featuring fiery, smart surfer and ex-spy Dr Tori Swyft and his third with the inspiring US President Isabel Diaz, the first woman to 'actually' win the White House.

In his professional careers, first as a lawyer and then as an investment banker, he acted for Buckingham Palace, Rupert Murdoch, Kerry Packer, Alan Bond, and prisoners in Long Bay jail (none of those mentioned above) as well as companies in a range of industries. Two years before the global financial crisis, he left his day job as a banker so no one could suspect him of creating the whole mess.

As well as writing novels, John has straddled the worlds of story and business having twice been on the board of a book publisher, and in 2008 co-founded Pantera Press, home to some of Australia's finest new (and prize-winning) writing talents.

John now also sits on the boards of the National Library of Australia, Centre for Independent Studies, and two listed companies.